RENDER HARMLESS

A Josh Haman Novel

RENDER HARMLESS

A Josh Haman Novel

by

Marc Liebman

ISBN-13:978-1-946409-32-4: Paperback
ISBN   978-1-946409-33-1: Ebook

BISAC Subject Headings:
FIC014000FICTION / Historical
FIC032000FICTION / War & Military
FIC0012000FICTION / Action

Cover Work: Christine Horner

Address all correspondence to:

Penmore Press LLC
920 N Javalina PL
Tucson, AZ 85748. USA
www.penmorepress.com

Marc Liebman

TABLE OF CONTENTS

Chapter	Title	Page
BACKSROP		vii
PROLOGUE		xi
Chapter 1	OVER THE IRISH SEA	1
Chapter 2	THE BOOK OF REBEKAH	11
Chapter 3	GREETING CARDS	19
Chapter 4	REVELATIONS	27
Chapter 5	THE LADY AND THE SABRA	33
Chapter 6	MERCENARY REDUX	41
Chapter 7	ONCE ENEMIES, NOW FRIENDS	53
Chapter 8	MANIFESTO	89
Chapter 9	WHO'S IN THE ZOO	91
Chapter 10	STEWART HOUSE	127
Chapter 11	HAPPY NEW YEAR	169
Chapter 12	BASTARDS IN THE SERVICE OF THE KING	179
Chapter 13	OUT OF CONTROL DOTS	191
Chapter 14	FIND AND NEUTRALIZE	229
Chapter 15	ODESSA STILL LIVES	239
Chapter 16	FLAG BRIEFING	271
Chapter 17	CONNECT THE DOTS	281
Chapter 18	TRAINING GROUND	305

Render Harmless

Chapter	Title	Page
Chapter 19	ARRIVALS	329
Chapter 20	DUELING CONTROLS	379
Chapter 21	LOST BUT PRESUMED FOUND	413
Chapter 22	ROUND UP	443
Chapter 23	ICING ON THE CAKE	449
Chapter 24	STICK TIME	457
Chapter 25	WTFO	477
Chapter 26	BLOWBACK	485
Chapter 27	CONVERSION	495
	Postscript	509

Marc Liebman

Acknowledgments

Writing a novel, if you have never done it, it, is a very lonely activity. There's no one but you, your mind, and the keyboard. However, when it comes to getting a book to market, writing it is really only the beginning of the process.

So I would like to thank Chris Paige, who acted as combination of book editor and proofer, and challenged me on numerous occasions to improve the manuscript.

I would also like to thank Michael James, Fireship's publisher for his patience with a writer who is still learning, and will continue to learn, his trade. Then, there are all those who have passed through my life and some in small and some in large part, had an influence on this story. Last, but certainly not least, there is Betty, my wife of four-plus decades, who has allowed me the time to follow my dream and become a novelist.

Marc Liebman
December, 2013

Backdrop

The Cold War was at its height in 1976 and 1977, and spy vs. spy between the free world, led by the U.S. and the Soviet Union and its allies, was a series of battles that few knew about. Little of what was known ever made it into the newspapers.

The U.S. was still assessing the impact of the North Korean seizure of the U.S.S. *Pueblo* in 1968. The Central Intelligence Agency (CIA) and National Security Agency (NSA) suspected the Soviets had succeeded in building working units of the cryptographic equipment on the ship, but did not know that they were decoding messages by means of the code keys provided by the traitors John Walker and Jerry Whitworth, both of whom were in the U.S. Navy.

Nor did these agencies know that the CIA's Aldrich Ames and the FBI's Robert Hanssen were providing critical information about U.S. agents inside the Soviet Union that resulted in agents being arrested, tortured, and killed. Those unexplained losses contributed to William Colby's paranoia, and, as the head of the agency, he instigated a witch-hunt for traitors within the CIA and elsewhere that sapped morale within the intelligence community.

Across the Atlantic, the U.K.'s intelligence community was still reeling from the revelations and defections of the 1950s and 1960s that damaged its credibility and revealed that the county was well penetrated by the Soviet Union. In 1976, MI5 and MI6 still did not know about Melita Norwood, Ray Fletcher, John Symonds, and other traitors.

Information gathered from defectors who made it to the U.S. and the U.K. confirmed there were leaks, but the paranoia was so strong that agencies thought the defectors were plants providing disinformation. When KGB archivist Major Vasili Mitrokin tried to defect in 1992, he was turned down by the CIA, so he went to the British. His treasure trove of information on the KGB proved to be astoundingly invaluable in its revelations and led to many arrests.

This novel takes place in 1976, when Gerald Ford was the President of the United States and his CIA director, George H.W. Bush, was trying to restore the morale and prestige of an agency damaged by revelations of domestic spying. In the U.K., Prime

Minister James Callaghan was running a country that was going broke and dealing with labor unrest that was on the verge of turning violent.

In Moscow, Leonid Brezhnev was leading a country that was struggling to meet an increasing demand for more and higher quality consumer goods, while at the same time maintaining parity with the U.S. in new technologies and nuclear weapons. Its successful funding and equipping of North Vietnam in its war against the U.S. and the takeover of Cambodia and Laos hardened Nixon's and Ford's view of the Soviet Union. This led to Kissinger's strategy that culminated in Nixon's well-publicized trip to the People's Republic of China.

In the mid 70's, the Soviet Union had another pressing problem besides a deteriorating relationship with the U.S. and an inefficient economy. It was trying to repair its alliance with the People's Republic of China after a series of clashes along the Amur River, which forms the border between Soviet Siberia and northern China. These skirmishes led both countries to change their policies toward each other, and towards the United States.

In Europe, terrorist groups appeared, adding their names to the list that included the Provos in Ireland and ETA—the Basque separatists—in Spain. Italians were trying to come to grips with the kidnappings and assassinations by the Red Brigades, or Brigate Rosse. Despite the arrest of Brigate Rosse's two founders in 1974, the organization continued operating into the 1980s, and there is evidence that the group was active as late as 2007.

At the time this novel takes place, Germany was divided. East Germany, whose official name was the Deutsche Demokratische Republik, a.k.a. the DDR, was created in 1949 from the zone allocated to the Soviet Union at the end of World War II. Other nations often referred to it as the German Democratic Republic, or G.D.R. In the same year, West Germany, or the Bundesrepublik, was created by combining the British, French, and American occupation zones. Both countries soon had their own armies, navies and air forces. The Volksarmee, or People's Army, served the East German Government and was one of the larger military formations in the Warsaw Pact, which was an alliance formed by the Soviets to counter NATO. East Germany's Ministry for State Security, or Stasi, was the intelligence-gathering secret service of the Socialist Unity Party of Germany. The West German military, known as the Bundeswehr (German for Federal Defense), had the Luftwaffe, the Heer, and the Kriegsmarine—the Air Force, the

Army, and the Navy respectively—and were fully integrated into NATO.

The East Germans started building "the Wall" in 1961 around West Berlin; this infamous barrier along the heavily fortified border between East and West Germany was designed to prevent East Germans from escaping to West Germany. Reunification was a pipe dream, no matter which side of the wall one lived.

West Germans, and to a lesser extent East Germans, were still dealing with the aftermath of the Munich Massacre during the 1972 Olympics, when eleven of Israel's athletes were kidnapped and killed. In 1976, the Israelis were four years into Operation Bayonet, hunting down and killing of the leaders of Black September responsible for the Munich Massacre.

The Baader-Meinhof gang had morphed into the Red Army Faction and the lesser known but more violent and anti-Semitic Revolutionary Cells, which conducted 296 bombings between 1973 and 1995 that made German law enforcement and intelligence agency officials shudder. Even though most of the Red Army Faction founders and leaders were either dead or in jail, their message, that the individuals running the government were the same ones who were in charge during the Third Reich and should be removed from power, had won support among some segments of the German population.

It is against this backdrop of terrorist groups using Europe as their battleground, traitors and intelligence leaks in Western intelligence agencies, and on-going proxy wars in Africa and the Middle East that RENDER HARMLESS takes place.

Marc Liebman
December, 2013

Marc Liebman

Prologue

Saturday, August 11th, 1973, 0221 local time, San Diego

The lock on the back door of the modest home in Point Loma surrendered with a soft click. The pick went back into a soft pouch, and a man, clad in black pants, turtleneck, and balaclava, eased the door open and slipped inside the small three-bedroom house. Satisfied that no one heard him enter, he drew his weapon and screwed the suppressor onto the barrel. He knew that the lightly oiled threads would not make a sound.

He'd bought and then tested the ankle-top boots he was wearing to be sure that their soft soles would not squeak as he worked his way to the three bedrooms. Inside the master bedroom, he stood at the end of the bed for a few seconds to make sure the mounds were breathing and to identify the heads. He fired once into each head, and the up and down movements of the light blanket stopped.

Satisfied, he went into the next bedroom, which he identified as a girl's room. His orders were to kill everyone in the house, so another round went into the head of the sleeping form. The third bedroom was empty, so he went back to the other two, picked up the empty brass cartridges, and laid them on the kitchen table, along with the Makarov pistol, the suppressor, and a card, confident that none bore his fingerprints, nor could the Soviet-made weapon and special sub-sonic ammunition be traceable to him. The San Diego police, the FBI, and the CIA would have no doubt as to who had hired the killer when they saw the card, which had his agency's logo on one side and the words *Death to traitors and deserters* on the other. This was not his first mission in the U.S., nor, he suspected, would it be his last.

Chapter 1
Over the Irish Sea

Thursday, April 22nd, 1976, 1512 local time

Rain splattered against the flat windscreen so hard that it could be heard over the whine of the rotors and turbine engines and created a film that distorted the pilots' view of the opaque grayness of the clouds. The wipers couldn't keep it clear for more than a few seconds. Not that it mattered, because the pilots of the twin engine helicopter with the side number GC 827 were flying on instruments.

Lieutenant Josh Haman was scanning his flight instruments as he maintained a steady one hundred and ten knots, three thousand feet, heading southeast over the Irish Sea toward Royal Navy Air Station Yeovilton. Every few minutes he would steal a glance through the side windows at the charcoal colored cloud bases, which were as dark as the sea below. Instrument flying was second nature to the U.S. naval aviator, who was on an exchange tour of duty with the Royal Navy. He'd interrupted his scan of the flight instruments to check the engine gauges when the radio crackled in his helmet's headset.

"Fleet Air Arm Golf Charlie Eight Two Seven, this is Prestwick. Contact London Center on one-one-nine point three. Good day."

"Roger, Prestwick, London on one-one-nine point three. Thank you and good day." Fleet Air Arm Lieutenant John Osborne, co-pilot, wrote the new frequency on his kneeboard before changing channels and pressing the floor microphone button with his foot. "Good afternoon, London Center, Fleet Air Arm Golf Charlie Eight Two Seven is with you, level three thousand."

"This is London Center, roger, radar contact. Maintain three thousand. Please contact RAF Rescue at one-two-zero point three over."

Haman looked at his co-pilot, who shrugged.

Josh keyed the intercom. "What do you think they want?" He was less than a year into a two year exchange tour with the Fleet Air Arm, and a couple of months out of the conversion course to the HC.4 Commando, which was a Westland modified version of the U.S. Navy's H-3 Sea King.

"Don't know. But our air force friends wouldn't ask London Center to call unless they have something better for us to do than droning through this muck." Osborne was an experienced HC.4 aircraft commander and Haman's Fleet Air Arm sponsor, tasked with helping Haman and his family adjust to life in the U.K. and the Fleet Air Arm.

One of the Fleet Air Arm of the Royal Navy's missions was the same as the U.S. Navy's: fly a helicopter to a specific location to insert a small team, then come back a week or so later and pick them up from a different landing zone, without the bad guys knowing you did it, or at least making it difficult for them to shoot you down. In response to a Royal Navy request for a helicopter pilot to share lessons learned flying in Southeast Asia, Josh had been selected because during his second tour in Vietnam he'd created and taught a syllabus on combat search and rescue and special operations tactics.

"RAF Rescue, this is Golf Charlie Eight Two Seven. What can we do for you?"

"We have an SOS from a small freighter by the name of *White Star,* which is floundering about seventy-five nautical miles southwest of you, and the crew believes the ship may not survive the storm. Could you go take a look? We've got a ship on the way to help them, but they are still six to eight hours away. Over."

Josh was already nodding in the affirmative, figuring this was the understated British way of asking them to go rescue the ship's crew, if they could. He gave John a thumbs-up before disengaging the autopilot.

"Roger. We will take a look and report back."

"Squawk three-two-one-zero and steer two-four-zero for fifty-five nautical. Descend at your discretion. Reported base of the clouds is one thousand feet, sea state is five, repeat *five,* and winds are reported to be two-four-zero at twenty-five gusting to thirty-five miles per hour. Stand-by for last reported position of the merchant ship *White Star*."

Osborne took down the last known position of the merchant ship, a five thousand ton Liberian registered freighter, with general cargo from Lisbon on the way to Belfast. RAF Rescue gave him the frequency M.S. *White Star* was monitoring, and said they would notify the ship that they were on the way.

"John, I'm going to stay at three thousand until we get to about twenty-five miles from the ship and then descend to five hundred. It will make it easier to maintain contact with the rescue center until we go down to find the ship."

"Good idea."

Using the five by seven inch kneeboard card that had their flight and fuel plan as a ruler, Osborne plotted the latitude and longitude of the ship before keying the intercom. "The *White Star* is right smack in the middle of the Irish Sea, about ninety-five miles from the nearest land, east or west."

Josh wanted to run by a plan with his co-pilot, who had more time in the HC.4 than he did, although in terms of total helicopter and flight time Josh had many more hours. "Here's what I'm thinking. My guess is that some of the sailors are injured. So we'll fly around the ship to figure out the best way to pick them up. We should have about an hour of fuel once we find the *White Star* before we have to head east and find a place to land."

"That should work. But once we find the bugger, we won't have much time to play around, because you and I both know from experience that very few ships are where they say they are. Just a reminder, the Irish Sea can get nasty in a hurry. We've got a major front coming in behind us from the Arctic. It is already bringing lots of wind and rain. Then there is the little problem of figuring out how to pluck sailors off a ship that wasn't designed to handle helicopters."

"Yup, we'll have to figure it out when we get there." Josh looked at the stop watch. "About ten minutes before we start down."

The radio crackled. "We show you ten miles from *White Star*'s last reported position, over."

"They want to learn what our intentions are without asking." Josh's mind was racing ahead. "Tell RAF Rescue we're leaving angels three for cherubs five and will report when we find the ship." Naval aviators use *angels* to differentiate altitudes above one thousand feet from *cherubs,* which are those below one thousand.

"That's ugly." The words came out of Josh's mouth as soon as he leveled the helicopter at five hundred feet and had his first close look at the boiling dark gray waters of the Irish Sea. He stared out the rain-streaked side windows for a few seconds, trying to gauge the wind speed and direction.

John studied the clouds and the choppy waters beneath them. "Let's go ten miles past their last reported position and begin a ladder search. I'm going to use thirty knots for the wind speed. In this muck, we won't be able to see much more than about five miles."

"Sirs, I see a ship, four o'clock!" The strong Scottish accent of Petty Officer Stan Clark, the leading air crewman, was clear over the intercom. Except for two ten-man rafts, Clark and two crewmen, the helicopter's cabin, which was designed to carry nineteen to twenty-three fully equipped troops, was empty.

"Clark, I've got a tally on the ship. Josh, turn right to about zero-one-zero," Osborne advised his aircraft commander. "With this wind, we'll be drifting sideways as much as we are going forward. We can adjust the heading once we get pointed in the right direction."

Josh clicked the mike two times to acknowledge and rolled the helicopter to the new heading. At five hundred feet they were flying in and out of the clouds, so he went down to two hundred feet and slowed to seventy knots indicated airspeed.

"I see a freighter and am going to come around from the stern to see if we can read the name," he said.

"I'm pretty sure that's the *White Star*. It looks like she is listing and a bit down at the stern." John switched from the intercom to the radio. "*White Star, White Star*, this is Royal Navy helicopter Golf Charlie Eight Two Seven, do you copy?" John clicked the mike twice and then repeated his call.

A man came out on deck, pointed to his ears and shook his head.

"They either don't have a working radio, or they're on another frequency. Josh, creep by the bridge as close as you dare. I'm going to show them this." John held up his kneeboard, on which he had written the radio frequency in big numbers.

Josh slowed to fifty knots true airspeed; he guessed their speed over the choppy water was less than ten knots. He estimated the tips of the rotor blades were less than thirty feet from the side of the ship.

"Just got a thumbs-up!" John called over the noise of rotating blades and scudding rain. A moment later, the radio crackled to life.

"Navy helicopter, this is *White Star*. We are without engine power and taking on water. Don't know how long we can stay afloat with manual pumps. We have limited battery power because we can't keep the emergency generator working for any length of time. Over!" The transmission which was scratchy and hard to understand.

"How many souls on board, and how many are injured?"

"We have twenty-three, that is two-three souls on board. Four have broken bones from being tossed around. We have them splinted. Over."

"We've got room for them all, just barely," Josh keyed the intercom. "If it takes an hour to pull them all off, we'll be down to about eleven hundred pounds of fuel at best. That means about an hour of flying, just enough fuel to get to land at ninety knots."

"So we take them all on board?"

"It's either we pick them up, or they'll be in lifeboats when the boat sinks in a couple of hours. It'll be their choice. Ask them!"

"Sir, this is Petty Officer Clark. I have a suggestion."

"What's your idea?"

"Sir, we have the two door gunner body harnesses, plus the horse collar. Jeffries will run the hoist and I'll go down to the ship and strap them in; that way we can hoist them three at a time, and it'll only take eight trips up and down."

"Good idea, Clark. Get everything ready."

John keyed the radio. "*White Star*, are you ready to abandon ship? If so, we are ready to pick everyone up. Please advise?"

"They've got to make a decision." Josh was thinking out loud. "Until we showed up, they were going to try to keep the ship afloat because they had no other choice. Give them two minutes, then tell them that we don't have enough fuel to wait around while they check with their owner."

"I won't be that direct." John smiled as he looked at Josh. There was a difference between the direct, American way of speaking and the more understated British approach.

"Royal Navy helicopter, we are ready to abandon the ship. Any instructions?"

"Everybody, here's the plan," Josh announced over the intercom. "I'm going to hover over the forward cargo hatch at about ninety feet. That should keep us above any whip antennas on top of the mast. Have them come out in groups of three, already in the harnesses and with some way to stay lashed to the ship until you hook them up to the hoist, Clark. I don't want you or any member of the ship's crew to go over the side into the water, so you need to figure out how to prevent that as soon as you get on board. After you are on the *White Star*, I am going to fly around until you wave us back. Once I get into position I will stay there and pick everyone up. If we are lucky, we won't need a litter. I don't plan to fly around and then re-approach for each pick-up. We should be high enough so there won't be too much rotor wash. Understood?"

"Aye, sir." Clark's brogue was clear.

"John, we're not going up into that goo to call the RAF Rescue Center. It is a waste of gas and we might have trouble finding the ship again. We'll tell them what we've done when we're on the way back in."

Josh knew that maintaining a steady hover in the HC.4 was going to be a bitch. The good news was that the gusty thirty to thirty-five knot winds would keep the helicopter in translational lift which, if nothing else, would reduce the power and fuel burn needed to hover ninety feet over the water. In order to keep the hoist centered over the ship's forward hatch, the nose of the fifty-five foot, ten inch long helicopter would need to be well out over the water, which meant that he would have to look back over his right shoulder to see his reference points on the ship. "John, give me full throttle on both engines and call my power and rotor RPM."

"Done. I've dialed in one hundred and four percent on both engines. That's as much as you're going to get without using the emergency throttles."

"I expect the RPM to drop as we take on the survivors and get heavier. Let me know if it drops below one hundred percent."

"Will do. Don't muck this up. Remember, we're not wearing survival suits, and we'll have just minutes to get into a raft, *if* we get out of the helicopter before the cold water incapacitates us!"

Josh nodded. Both men knew that the odds of surviving in water temperatures below fifty degrees Fahrenheit were not good.

The slow creep into position gave Josh time to confirm the reference points he needed to maintain a constant position over the pitching and rolling freighter, sighting on the crane twenty feet below and the corner of the bridge.

Out of the corner of his eye Josh saw the radar altimeter oscillate between eighty and ninety feet as the deck of the *White Star* pitched and rolled. Each gust changed the airflow over the rotor blades and transitioned the helicopter in and out of translational lift. This forced Josh to use subtle but constant movements of the collective, the cyclic, and the rudder pedals to adjust the power drawn from the two Rolls Royce Gnome 1,400 horsepower turbo shaft engines to keep the helicopter in a stable hover.

Josh could feel the strain in his neck and shoulder muscles from the tension as he kept the helicopter in a constant position relative to the *White Star*. He was more worried about the hoist jamming or the engines failing than he was about keeping the big helicopter over the small freighter.

From his co-pilot's seat, the future sixteenth Duke of Leeds saw Josh flex his fingers every few minutes and noted that even when he did, the helicopter, despite the gusty winds, stayed in position over the *White Star*. He knew from flying with him on many occasions that it was Josh's way of keeping his hands relaxed enough to maintain a gentle touch on the controls. John kept quiet, other than reporting every couple of minutes; "Gauges are green, rotor rpm 101%." He made hash marks on the side window with a black grease pencil to keep a count of the number of survivors hoisted on board.

"Got a number one generator caution light. Resetting. Power is still good, " John reported. About thirty seconds later, "Caution light is back on. I am recycling the generator." The light remained on. "Am assuming the generator has failed and am going through the check list to turn everything off that we don't need."

"Just make sure I don't lose the stabilization equipment and the hoist controls. We're not going anyplace until we get the guys off the *White Star*. We can fly without one or even both generators if we have too." *Oh fuck, is this an isolated failure or the start of more serious problems?*

"Check." There was a slight pause. "Maybe it's cooled down. I'm going to recycle the generator now." Another pause. "Number 1 generator caution light is still on, so I am going to turn it off again and pull the circuit breaker." John's hand went up and down the console. "Everything is off except the automatic stabilization equipment, radio, and the controls to the hoist. We should have plenty of electrical power. As soon as we leave the hover, I'll turn the transponder and the lights back on."

"Good." Josh kept his eyes on the bobbing freighter, wondering how much longer he was going to have to maintain a hover. The bolts of pain his neck and shoulder muscles were sending to his brain were becoming more insistent. *How much longer?* Sweat ran down his forehead into his eyes, blurring his vision, stinging like tears. Josh kept blinking to minimize the blurring of his reference points on the ship.

Thirty minutes later, both pilots heard Clark report, "Sirs, I'm back on the helicopter and we have all twenty-three on board!"

John counted his reckoning on the side window. "I've got twenty-three as well. Let's go home."

Josh eased the cyclic forward to lower the nose as he added power with the collective to keep the HC.4 level as it accelerated. Reaching seventy knots, he began a slow climb to five hundred feet.

"John, I need a break. You've got it. Keep it at five hundred feet so we don't waste fuel climbing, and I'll call the RAF." Josh held his hands in the air as John Osborne took control of the helicopter.

"I'm going to head zero-nine-zero at ninety knots. We should have a twenty to thirty knot tailwind. We're not going to make it back to Yeovilton with the gas we have left. Our best option is Newquay St. Mawgam, about an hour away. The RAF has its survival training school there; 7 Squadron flies Canberras from the base."

Josh found the base on the IFR chart and made a few quick mental calculations. "Got it. I'll dial up their non-directional radio beacon when we get closer, and we should be able to follow that in. Right now we're way too low to pick up any navigational aids. The fuel warning lights should come on about ten minutes before we're out of fuel, which will give us just enough gas to land and taxi in."

"Sounds dicey," John observed, "but doable." After a moment of concentrating on flying, he continued. "St. Mawgan used to be home to the RAF's 22 Squadron, which flew Sea Kings for rescue missions in the Irish Sea. Now 22 is up in Northern Wales. I heard that they've been filming scenes for *The Eagle Has Landed* on the base. It created quite a stir, with stars like Michael Caine, Donald Sutherland, and Anthony Quayle meandering about."

"Let's hope we don't make a dramatic entry worth filming!" Josh thought for a few seconds. "I didn't mean to be pushy back there, but we didn't have much choice. The crew needed help.

They'd have been in the water long before the nearest ship got there. I wouldn't want to depend on a lifeboat in this weather!" *No more lives lost. I've already lost too much already. Way too much.* Josh felt his eyes sting again, and blinked hard.

"I agree. By the way, that was a tidy bit of flying. Well done."

"Thank you." Josh looked down at the chart, embarrassed by the compliment. "We couldn't have done it without Clark's idea of getting three up each time, and the guys in the back doing all the hard work. I don't think I could have kept in a stable hover much longer."

Riiiiight. Typical, thought John Osborne. *Always giving credit to someone else. No wonder everyone who's worked with him, including me, would follow him into the jaws of hell.*

Chapter 2
The Book of Rebekah

1922 local time, RAF Newquay St. Mawgam

The Officers' Club was in a red brick building that had been built in 1936, then expanded during World War II by the U.S. Army Air Force, when, owing to its location near the east shore of the Irish Sea, the base was used by the Air Transport Command. A staff car dropped them off; spending the night and flying the helicopter back in the daytime seemed a good idea, now that the injured crewmen had been transferred to a local hospital and the rest put on a train to London.

John waited until the second mug of beer was slid over the polished English oak to their corner spot at the bar. "Josh, Rebekah told my Gwen that your first wife was murdered, and that you had a pretty rough time of it. I was sorry to hear about that. Do you mind telling me what happened? If I am prying, tell me—I'll understand."

"No, you're not prying. I just don't talk about it much." Josh took a deep drink of the dark, foaming Guinness before he spoke again.

"Here's what happened. Between my first and second tours in Vietnam, I fell in love with a girl named Natalie Vishinski. She was wonderful. Right after I got back from my second tour, we were married. That was in June, 1973. Then in August, I was out on a mini-cruise to Hawaii and she decided to spend the weekend with her parents, because we were doing an upgrade to the kitchen of our house and the place was a mess. Her mother was a concentration camp survivor and was having another minor breakdown, and I am sure she went over to help her dad, who was having a rough time dealing with it."

Their dinner arrived, and Josh took a sip from his beer while he debated how much to tell. Then he decided, *Why not?* It was part of his life, and if he and John were going to be friends and crew members, the guy ought to know.

"What happened is pretty simple, it's what happened afterwards that got ugly."

"What do you mean?"

"Well, an assassin picked the lock to their house and shot each one of them in the head. Three rounds, three dead people. The bastard left the gun and the three empty brass casings on the kitchen table on top of a card that had the KGB logo on one side and the phrase "Death to deserters and traitors" on the other."

"They were killed by the KGB? Why?"

"According to our FBI, that's our Federal Bureau of Investigation, which is the equivalent of a combination of your Scotland Yard and MI5, the KGB has targeted former officers who deserted the Red Army after World War II, or who defected. My father-in-law was a major, commanding a machine-gun battalion, when he walked away from the Red Army in 1945. He had been drafted in early 1939 and survived six years of war, going first into Poland and then back to into the southern Caucasus before ending the war in Austria. He'd been given a battlefield commission and awarded the Hero of the Soviet Union twice—that's their equivalent of your Victoria Cross and our Medal of Honor—along with other medals for bravery. The FBI agent in charge of the investigation and I think he was assassinated because having a recognized war hero defect was an embarrassment, and the KGB wanted to make an example of him."

Josh thought for a second. "Artur was not a fan of Josef Stalin or the communists. He was from an area on the Romanian border, and his small village was frequently... *visited* by the Cossacks. Pogroms happened even more often under Stalin than they had under the Tsars. He saw women raped, livestock killed or stolen, and houses torched. He often told me that he'd resolved that if he survived the war, he would find a way to leave. He had two brothers. If they are still alive, they are living in the Soviet Union. He was always so happy when he got a letter, and he saved them all. Anyway, to make a long story short, he was very active in helping get Jews out of the Soviet Union, contributing time and lots of money, and the FBI thinks that is another reason he became a target."

"Oh my God! You read about these things in John le Carré novels, but you don't think they really happen."

"Well they do. And, they never found the bastard who did it. After about a year, the FBI special agent in charge of the investigation gave me the card and the casings as souvenirs, after they'd gotten whatever evidence they could from them. I laminated the card and drilled holes through the tops of the casings so I could string them together with a piece of safety wire. He also showed me a report generated by the CIA which indicates that within the First Directorate of the KGB is a section that does nothing but track Soviet émigrés and determine which ones they want assassinated. Every once in a while, I look at that card and realize who is sitting across the iron curtain."

"*That's* the simple? What's the ugly afterwards?"

"Are you sure you want to hear this? It is pretty bad."

John put his hand on his friend's arm. "If you are willing to talk about it."

"O.K." Josh paused. A vision of Natalie flashed before his eyes, and memories rose from the recesses of his mind. "I went into an abyss and damned near didn't come out. In many ways, I was like an alcoholic who hit bottom, but with the help of some close friends, I managed to surface. As the years have gone by it has gotten easier, but every once in awhile I think of Natalie and what could have been. It is not that I don't love Rebekah, because I do with all my heart, but it is different. She knows it, and I know it."

"Ouch..." John tipped his mug.

"Yeah. Ouch is putting it mildly." Josh took a long swallow, then gave some attention to the chips and sandwich before him. "The first bad thing that happened was that they didn't discover the bodies until Monday morning, when Artur didn't show up for work. Second, the police didn't know who to call. Eventually someone thought to contact the synagogues in San Diego, and when they talked to our rabbi he quickly arranged to have them buried, because Jews bury their dead within twenty-four hours. The rabbi who'd married us recognized Natalie and contacted the Navy; by the time I got back they were already in the ground. I stood at the cemetery there with our rabbi for more than an hour, I am told, looking at three mounds, at first stunned, and then sobbing."

John didn't say a word; he could see tears forming in his squadron mate's eyes.

"I called and told my parents and went back to the house. It was so empty, and I just stared at the walls. I didn't eat much, didn't shave or bathe for days, and wore what I had on from the visit to the gravesite. I sank into a funk and didn't care if I lived or I died. I lost about twenty pounds, and if you ask me what I did, I can't tell you. It's not a blur, it's just gone. My two best friends—guys I knew from my tours in Vietnam, Marty Cabot and Jack D'Onofrio—came by every day and tried to cheer me up. They'd force me to bathe, but after they'd leave, back into the hole I'd go. The only thing I did was go to synagogue every day to say Kaddish, which is the Jewish prayer for the dead. Jack filed leave papers for me so I didn't have to go to work for thirty days, but then I had to go back to my job as an instructor. It was all I could do to drag myself to the squadron and do my job. After about two weeks, the commanding officer took me aside and told me that there was no way he was going to let me fly, and that if this continued, he'd be forced to recommend a psychiatric evaluation, which would likely result removal from flight status and separation from the Navy. That Friday morning, he gave me two weeks to get my shit together. He was telling me that I was about to lose everything I had worked for, but I didn't care if I lived or died."

"Was that the bottom?"

"No, the bottom was when I read the medical examiner's report on Natalie and found out that she was two months pregnant. I believe she was going to tell me when I got back."

"That's bloody awful!" John rubbed his head. "I would have gone bonkers. Knowing how hard Gwen and I have tried to have a baby, now that she is pregnant, I'd have gone over the edge if I found out something like that from the medical examiner. Good God, man." John took a steadying draught of beer.

"I showed up for services that night and the rabbi pulls me into his office saying, "There is someone I want you to meet because I believe she can help you." I told him that I wasn't interested in dating, and he said she was old enough to be my mother, but, more importantly, she was a psychiatrist who had been through a similar tragedy. I don't remember the conversation that well, but from what I understand, he begged me to talk to her in his office that evening."

"Did you?"

"I did. Something inside me said, 'Dummy, what you are doing is not working and you need to try something else or else you will soon be living in a gutter.' So, that evening, Leah Gutman—that was the shrink, I mean psychiatrist—and I talked for almost three hours. I found out that her first husband had been a paratrooper in the Israeli army and was killed in '56 in the war at Mitla Pass. She went through the same deep depression, and as a psychiatrist, she should have known how to deal with it. For her it was worse; she had a daughter who was ten at the time and adored her father, so she had to help her deal with the loss too. It was too much, and Leah's parents had to take the girl away for several months because Leah wasn't fit to take care of herself, much less a ten year old."

Josh drew little circles in the water that had pooled on the bar. "So, we had another session on Sunday, and then three days a week for the next six months. I never told my skipper what I was doing. The sessions were in the evening, and I forced myself to do my job during the day. At the end of the two weeks he gave me some encouragement and said, 'Keep going, you'll make it, and there'll be no board or psychiatric evaluation.'"

"Good-oh." John waved to the bar tender to refill both their mugs.

"Yeah, that was good news. About three months later, I climbed into the cockpit for the first time since Natalie was murdered and realized—*remembered*—how much I enjoyed flying. I flew with the skipper and we did the basics for four hours. We flew around San Diego and the coast, and I hovered a bit and did a couple of take-offs and landings. We did what I wanted to do, and everyone on board but me knew that that was his plan. It was a godsend, and from that point on it was a matter of learning how to grieve and get on with my life. That took another three or four months."

"So then what happened? How did you meet Rebekah?"

"Oh, I forgot.... That's actually the most important part. Sorry, I was reliving a nightmare." Josh took a deep breath, thankful that the memories were back in the compartment, walled off from his daily life, knowing that every so often they would resurface. "One day Leah says to me, 'I would like you to come to my house for dinner and meet someone I think you will like.' I said, 'I don't think I'm ready,' and she said, "Yes, you are, and I will almost guarantee you will like this young woman.'"

"The yenta strikes." John laughed, if for nothing else than to lighten the mood. "Did I use the word correctly?"

"You did! Anyway, I show up and I am introduced to this stunningly beautiful woman who is a year younger than I am: Rebekah Shahaf, who is Leah's daughter."

"Oh, that is wizard—I mean, very interesting."

"Yeah. One of the things that Leah did when she got over her depression was to come to the U.S. In San Diego she met Stan Gutman, who is her second husband. When we had dinner, Rebekah was in her last year at U.S.C. It turns out she was bored with all the nice Jewish boys she was meeting and wanted a partner whose life would be a bit of an adventure. She thought being married to a doctor or a lawyer would be very dull!"

"So *then* what happened?"

"Well, we went out for dinner a couple of times and started seeing each other. Her mother had told her a lot about me, and they spent hours talking about me and what I went through. We had a lot in common; all three of us lost ones we love. Anyway, to make a long story short, a little over a year after we met, Rebekah and I got married. We are friends, soul mates who have lost loved ones."

"So there is a happy ending?"

"Yeah. Rebekah could have had any man on the U.S.C. campus, or hung around L.A. and snared a rich guy…. But no, she picked me, a poor young naval aviator, so I am very lucky. And now I'm in the U.K., flying with the Fleet Air Arm and drinking with a future duke. That's pretty cool."

"I'll drink to that." John waved to the bartender, who was away from them at the other end of the bar, and tapped the table to signal another round.

Chapter 3
Greeting Cards

**Friday, April 23rd, 1976, 0810 local time,
Frankfurt, West Germany**

The black Mercedes 600 screamed wealth and power. When it stopped at the gate of the five-star luxury Schlosshotel Kronburg, the blond-haired young man in the BMW parked on the street outside was ready.

Through the rolled up window and his Zeiss binoculars, Dieter Stiglitz saw a well-groomed female carrying a Nikon camera equipped with a big zoom lens stepped out of the car. Standing in high-heeled shoes on the loose gravel , she snapped pictures of the gate house and hotel that was, before World War II, the Hollenzollerns' summer palace. History classes had taught Dieter Stiglitz that before 1870, when the Kronburgs bowed to Bismarck's pressure to join a unified Germany and the Kaiser's inner circle, the Hollenzollerern family had ruled Hesse as an independent country.

Dieter studied the burly man with close-cropped hair and a dark suit standing behind the front passenger door and surveying the area around the car in noticeable, well defined sectors. The man's actions screamed "bodyguard." He waited until the attractive woman in a black pants suit and a stylish, short haircut finished taking pictures, then he held the back door open for her before resuming his position next to the driver.

Once away from the palace, the big Mercedes turned left on Hain Strasse and headed south toward Frankfurt. Dieter gave the limo a hundred meter headstart before slipping his idling BMW 1800ti into first gear.

Once he sure that the black Mercedes was following the same route through the city that it had taken the past four days, Stiglitz turned left and passed the sedan, known as "der Grosser Mercedes," taking a shortcut to an empty parking place on Berliner Strasse that had been blocked off with cones. A dark-skinned man of average height with a close-cropped beard of jet-black loaded the orange cones into the BMW's trunk before slipping into the passenger seat, while Dieter jogged a hundred meters down the street to where he could see a parked VW Beetle with faded green paint.

When the Mercedes passed a telephone pole just behind the VW, Dieter pushed a button on the small aluminum box in his hand, setting off five kilos of plastic explosive pressed onto the steel plate inside the VW's door. A four thousand degree Fahrenheit jet of flame and molten metal shot through the Mercedes' one inch thick armor plates in the door and incinerated everyone inside. The steel frame of the 600 shrieked as the shock wave shoved it about a meter to the left, while hundreds of ball bearings perforated its doors, fenders and glass at the same time they shredded nearby cars.

Satisfied that the burning VW was unrecognizable and happy that other cars besides the Mercedes were pulverized and on fire, Dieter headed back to his BMW where, once inside, he shook the other man's hand. By the time the first emergency vehicles arrived, Dieter was driving in the opposite direction, a quarter of the way to Mainz and the apartment of the man beside him.

To a casual observer the man going up the stairs ahead of Dieter, Mohammed al Jahani, was a Turkish gastarbeiter or guest worker. The door to the apartment clicked shut with a noticeable, precise metallic sound like a door closing on a vault.

"Coffee?"

"Thank you." Dieter sat in one of the four chairs at the kitchen table and looked around the apartment. It was sparsely furnished with what he guessed was second-hand furniture.

"What's next?"

"We wait. I have a car sitting in a parking lot in Wiesbaden. After I re-connect its battery, which will take all of two minutes, you'll follow me until I find a spot for it in downtown Wiesbaden. Then we will drive out to Rhein-Main Airport, where I have a third car parked. On the way to the airport, I can drop you off at the train station so you can get back to your apartment."

"Do you not need help with the third car?"

"No. The target on this last one is special. You will enjoy reading about it the papers tomorrow. After I set it off, I'll take the train back to the airport, drive into Wiesbaden to set the timer on the second car, and go home to Geissen. It will be a long day, but worth it."

It was after five when Dieter unlocked the third car, whose paint had seen better days, and got in. Spider cracks on the right side of the front window made driving difficult and the car illegal to drive on the street, yet no policeman stopped him. Traffic going back into the city was moderate, and thirty minutes later he was double-parked in one of the few neighborhoods of Frankfurt that hadn't been leveled by B-17s.

He was looking at a plain gray concrete building whose unrepaired façade had holes gouged by shrapnel from bombs exploding nearby and a sooty black stain from a major fire. Even though the fire had occurred in 1936, the owners hadn't tried to clean the blackened concrete, and no government official had any intention of forcing a repair.

Dieter waited until he could slide the car into a parking spot on the opposite side of the street. He locked the car and went looking for a place to eat. When he returned, he counted twenty-six people standing on the steps in the warm summer night as he extended the antenna on a small aluminum box. With the small two-position toggle switch in the on position, the green light confirmed that the transmitter had established a link to a receiver. His watch read 7:46.

Smiling and thinking that his father, if he knew what he was doing, would approve, Dieter brushed his blond hair out of his eyes and pushed the red button that set off five kilos of plastic explosive packed against a bent piece of steel which directed the blast at the building. Twelve kilos of ball bearings embedded in the explosive made mincemeat of the people on the steps and turned the heavy oaken door into a loosely connected collection of matchsticks hanging on its steel hinges. The small brass plaque, identifying the building as Temple Beth Hamidrash on 27 Altkanig Strasse, buckled from a direct hit by a one centimeter diameter ball bearing. The concrete behind it, pulverized into powder, floated down to mix with the pool of blood on the steps.

Dieter was drinking a beer at a gasthaus on the outskirts of Wiesbaden when the one-hour kitchen timers wired in series in the second VW touched zero. At the sound of the sirens, he dropped a five Deutschmark bill on the counter and walked out.

As in the others, Dieter had used bent steel plates on the inside of the passenger's side to direct the blast that sent ball bearings tearing through the unoccupied first floor of Hertie's, Wiesbaden's largest department store. The explosion, at just before ten in the evening in a city not considered worth bombing during World War II, shattered windows throughout the business district of the small city known for its spas and casino.

With the two fireballs he'd seen as pleasant memories, Dieter dropped an envelope in the Deutsche Post mail box. Three bombs in two cities in one day! *That should get the attention of the autorities.* He figured it would take two days for the letter, which didn't have any traceable finger prints, to get to the popular national magazine *Stern,* and another day or so for the magazine's editors to debate whether or not to share it with the police.

Saturday, April 24th, 1976, 1426 local time, Schloss Theissen, West Germany

On one wall of the second story room were floor to ceiling windows; they provided an unobstructed view of the Harz Mountains fifty kilometers southwest of Bonn. The spring afternoon sun was moving down toward the horizon in a sky dotted with puffy white clouds. The passage of a front that had dropped a cold rain which left the bricks and gray granite on the patio between the building's wings glistening.

While it was referred to as a schloss, which translates to castle in English, the building wasn't a fortress. Instead it was a west-facing U-shaped three story building that had been completed in 1897, built with stone from a local quarry.

Besides the resident, Herr Baron Albert von Theissen, whose family's wealth was measured in billions of safe Swiss Francs, there were seven other men at one end of a table that could seat thirty, but which was still lost in the middle of the immense second floor dining room. The seven had arrived in time for dinner on the Friday night before a two day working session.

As they waited for dessert to be served, Albert von Theissen decided to change the direction of the conversation.

"Sehr gut, it is very good that we're now registered as a party; we've filed the petitions and we're on the ballot to contest twenty seats in the Bundestag. Also, we have a party platform and a strategy. Now, I ask, how much is it going to take for us to win? What do we need? How much money to hire staff for local organizations? How much for a party headquarters staff? How much for advertising? How much for whatever I have left out?"

"What do you mean, Herr Baron?"

In his late sixties, Oskar Zimmer was the oldest man in the room by about ten years. He was invited because he had been Theissen's first flight instructor. Business was not his strong suit, but the former Stuka pilot and Templehof Airport manager knew how to lead men and knew how to get things done. He looked every bit the military pilot, and if asked, he would tell you that he was ready to climb back into the cockpit to fight for his Führer and his country.

"How much money will it take to win five seats? How much more will it take to win seven, or even ten?" Theissen looked at each of the other six men at the table.

Helmut Stiglitz looked at the numbers he had scribbled on the pad in front of him. "We'll need at least ten million marks per seat, maybe more, just for advertising. No one knows our party or our platform. Two million marks should cover the costs of a staff to run the campaign, and another million for expenses. Figure fifteen million per seat to be safe. If you think of this as a military campaign, the fighting is done with the ads and speeches, the rest is logistics."

"Helmut is right." Viktor Horst owned a dozen jewelry stores in Bavaria that catered to the middle class. After losing a hand and a leg fighting the British at Dunkirk as a member of the 1st SS Leibstandarte Adolf Hitler Division, he had been sent to Dachau, where he'd supervised the melting down of gold fillings into bricks and the evaluation of jewelry taken from those arriving in the camp. Horst spent four years in prison while investigators tried to find enough evidence to try him for war crimes. They couldn't, because in the chaos of the spring of 1945 he'd made sure that anyone who knew what he did was dead. Within a year of his release, he opened up his first jewelry shop.

"I agree with Viktor and Helmut. Their estimates seem reasonable," Graf Ernst von Spee said. His cousin had been a naval officer under the Kaiser, and a ship had been named after him. As the last surviving male in the line, by default he'd inherited the title. "It may be off, but not by much. I think it is a good working number." Von Spee had followed the family's naval tradition. With the surface ships of the German Navy bottled up in harbors along the German and Norwegian coasts, von Spee had spent the last two years of the war as Goebbel's trusted courier between Berlin and the banks in Zurich. Now he was a merchant ship captain.

Von Spee paused for a few seconds and rubbed the jagged scar on his cheek. To this day, he could still feel the burning sensation from the shrapnel of a British five inch rocket that had slammed into the bridge of his destroyer. "Alois?" It was almost a command for the most un-Germanic looking man in the room to speak.

Alois Brunner was short and fat, with dark skin and jet black hair that everyone in the room assumed he dyed to cover his gray hair. His friends kidded him by saying that he didn't walk, he waddled. Brunner usually remained quiet during meetings, but when he spoke everyone in the room paid attention to the man who had been the brains behind the smuggling of huge amounts of cash out of Nazi Germany in non-German denominations and gold. Not only did he know where it went, but in what amounts—and how much more it was worth today. It was all in his head, and in a ledger that everyone involved knew existed, but not where it was.

When the war started, Brunner was a currency trader in the Reichsbank. He kept himself out of the army by making his superiors rich with his shrewd trades, buying Swiss Francs with the devaluing Reichmark. By doubling the fees the Swiss banks charged and keeping half, he created a nest egg worth over ten million dollars that remained hidden from investigators in the very banks with whom he did business. In 1944, his superiors, who knew the war was lost, tasked Brunner with converting Reichmarks, which would be useless after the war, into Swiss Francs, British pounds, and U.S. dollars, and putting the money in numbered accounts which he controlled in banks in Zurich and Geneva. The party members and SS officers didn't question the amounts when they were given the account numbers after the war so they could live comfortably. He also deposited money into accounts that would fund organizations that would be used to finance the smuggling of Nazis out of Europe.

When Nazis needed money after the war to flee investigators or restart their lives in Germany or abroad, Alois provided it—for a fee, of course! As part of each transaction, Brunner took a healthy cut and kept detailed ledgers that no one ever saw, documenting who provided the money, where it went, and how much it would be worth.

Alois had already done the math in his head before von Spee finished speaking. "One hundred and fifty million marks for ten seats, or three hundred million for twenty, is not a problem. We have plenty of money." He tapped the table with a pudgy finger. "But we cannot just transfer those large sums into a new party bank account. Too many questions will be asked. It has to come via donations which have to be reported and are monitored by the government. Our names and some of our friends' names have to be protected. So I suggest that our wealthy members set up offshore accounts at banks I recommend. Then they can make donations, and I can make up the difference between their contribution and what we need and make the transfers happen. Not all at once, but in such a way that we will not run out of cash. I will also make sure there is a proper accounting and that it will all look legal." Another tap for emphasis on the first word of the next sentence. "*My* accounting firm will make all the arrangements."

"Can my business help?" It was Horst. He always wanted to be involved if he thought he could get a piece, however small, of the action.

"Yes, those of us who have businesses or well recognized names will all become sponsors of The New German Party. We have to be quiet, but efficient leaders. Others will make donations. Some of our early supporters will be very generous."

Von Theissen looked around the table. "So fear not; our campaign will be well funded. My question to you is, can we win? And if so, how many seats?"

"Herr Baron," Horst spoke before anyone else could answer. The hook that functioned as his left hand clunked against the edge of the table. "The question is not how many can we win. The question is how ruthless do we want to be to *ensure* we win."

Chapter 4
Revelations

Josh took his seat across from John at a table where place settings of Sterling silver utensils with the emblem of the Royal Navy on their handles rested on a linen tablecloth. John nodded a greeting, then spoke.

"Just before we left for lunch, the maintenance officer told me they found the relay that caused the number one generator to go off line."

"So it wasn't the generator?" Josh leaned back to allow the waiter to put down a plate of fine china with a blue and gold band that held his grilled cheese sandwich and chips. The waiter set the plate in front of Josh so that the Royal Navy crest centered on the rim farthest away, dropped two ice cubes taken from a sterling silver ice chest on a nearby cart into his glass, then poured a bottle of Coca Cola over the ice.

"No it wasn't. When the relay burned out, the surge took out the transformer rectifier, so nothing we could have done in the cockpit would have brought it back on line." John Osborne spread his napkin on his lap.

"That relay is right under the floor of the cockpit in the avionics compartment. I'm surprised we didn't smell it. "

"I am too." John used a set of silver tongs to drop two squares of sugar into his tea, which he was stirring in a figure eight pattern as he gathered his thoughts. The break also allowed for a natural change of topic. "Josh, I want to ask you a question that's a wee bit sensitive."

"Go for it." Josh had taken an immediate liking to John when they first met, and his wife Rebekah got on well with John's wife Gwen, so the two couples had become close friends. He sensed in the Yorkshire-raised future duke a fellow warrior, one who was both proud of and somewhat embarrassed by his title.

"You never talk much about your experiences in Vietnam."

"It's in the past, and I don't want to bore all of you about a war that was on the other side of the world." Josh took a test bite of his sandwich to make sure the cheese wasn't like lava.

"Part of your role here is to teach us the lessons that you learned there, so we do want you to talk about them."

"But I don't..." As soon as the words came out of his mouth, he realized they were defensive and unnecessary and stopped before completing the sentence. "The covert penetration syllabus is built on my experience; it's what I taught when I was an instructor in our H-3 RAG. I've adapted it to what the Fleet Air Arm does." The term RAG stood for Replacement Air Group, which was a hold-over from World War II when naval aviators transitioning to a new airplane were trained in special squadrons.

"No, that's not what I mean. All of the blokes in the squadron enjoy flying with you, and you've taught us mission planning techniques and tactics which are now part of our doctrine." John stopped to take a sip of his tea. "Look, this is a bit embarrassing, but I know, as do all the other pilots, what those ribbons under your wings are, and we'd like to know more about the events themselves. It is not too often we have in our midst one who has been awarded two Navy Crosses and three Silver Stars."

"I was very, very stupid on more than one occasion and lived to tell about it."

John chuckled at his friend's self-depreciating humor. "Josh, you and I both know there is more to it than that."

"Look, the missions happened. We did what we were supposed to do and were very lucky in that we lost only two guys. The lessons learned from those and other missions are baked into the syllabus we're using." Josh didn't want to sound guarded, but realized he did.

"We'd like to hear what really happened on the missions."

"Is that coming from John, or from the pilots in the squadron?" Josh now realized why the two of them were alone at the table.

"Both. It is also coming from the Commodore, and I was elected to ask the question." Josh could see his friend was embarrassed.

"So it is a formal request?"

"I guess so. He didn't make it one, just asked me to ask you."

"When a commodore asks you to do something, it is difficult to refuse." Josh was sympathetic for how uncomfortable his friend was.

"In this case, you can refuse; and we, including the commodore, will understand."

"It's a fair question. What I can do, assuming I can get permission to talk about them, and you can classify the briefings as Most Secret, is to go through the actual events and details of a few of the missions."

"Superb." Osborne's relief was visible in his face.

"I'll need some charts of South East Asia, and then I'll put the briefings together with titles that will make it fun and informative."

"What do you mean?"

"I'll give them titles like *Preventing U.S. Marines from Re-enacting Custer's Last Stand*. Another will be *Making Headlines Around the World*. I think I'll call a third *In Combat Search and Rescue, Persistence Pays*."

"Great! I'll schedule them in the training plan a week apart. When can you have the first one ready?"

"Give me a day or two after I get the charts and the blessing from Washington." Josh tapped the table with an unused spoon. "Then we can create the slides."

"Splendid! Can you give me a preview?"

"Sure. The one about Custer's Last Stand started when we were asked to pick up a Marine recon team that was cornered in the demilitarized zone between North and South Vietnam. All the Marine H-46s were down due to a combining gearbox problem, and the landing zone wasn't big enough to get two Hueys in at the same time to get everyone out in one lift. We'd just finished changing an intermediate gear box and were in a test hover when the tower called and asked if we would go get the eighteen survivors and two bodies."

Josh paused as he remembered that on every March 29th, the anniversary date of the rescue, he received a card and a bottle of expensive scotch from the Marine officer, who had just been promoted to major. The last one had reached him in England, and when it showed up Josh had wondered how the major knew where to send it.

"We learned on the way up that the recon team had been on the run for three days and the North Vietnamese Army had trapped them in a clearing on top of a ridge. Close air support was keeping the bad guys off their backs, but it was just a matter of time before they were overrun.

"To get them out, we plopped our H-3 down in the midst of a small clearing on the top of a hill, and we got the shit shot out of us. We took off with everyone aboard, including the two bodies, but we started losing the number one hydraulic system about ten minutes after we were airborne. When the second started to go, I put the H-3 in a rice paddy. When we airlifted the helo back to Phu Bai, it had well over one hundred and fifty holes in it from seven point six two and twelve point seven millimeter rounds."

Josh let the steward put two more ice cubes into his glass before pouring in the last of the bottle of Coke. "A twelve point seven millimeter armor piercing round had gone through the armor around the hydraulic actuators and smacked into the back of my armor plated seat. I looked down, thinking the last thing I'd see on this earth would be my guts sprayed all over the instrument panel, but the round had spent itself on the armor. Another one hit the overhead circuit breaker panel and blew the throttles out of my co-pilot's hand but didn't even scratch him!"

The memories started flooding back. "The second one was a rescue in Haiphong which made newspaper headlines. On the way in we killed about a dozen Russians who fired on us from two Soviet freighters anchored in the harbor. We used the grenade launcher and the mini-gun to take out the twelve point seven millimeter heavy machine guns mounted behind sandbags on the ship superstructure. The next day there were headlines in *Isvestia*, *Pravda*, and the *New York Times* about how an American helicopter attacked neutral Russian ships. We got in a lot of hot water over that one, but after a week or so, cooler heads prevailed."

Josh munched on a cracker with a small piece of Stilton cheese. "*Persistence Pays* will be about spending twenty of twenty-four hours in the air trying to pick up an injured A-7 pilot who went down in the mountains west of Vinh. We put a guy on the ground in a first attempt, then it took three more trips before we got both of them out. There was lots of triple A in the valley, and everyone who went in got shot up pretty badly. And the weather was shitty--rain and low clouds, although that made it just as difficult for the North Vietnamese as it did for us. I was more worried about *finding* our guys than getting them out."

"Wizard! I can't wait to hear more."

"I'll also put together a fourth one: two planned, deep penetration missions, and focus on how the routes and landing zones were picked. Don't know what I'll call it, and there are limits on what I can say about what the SEALs did."

"Well," John said with a grin, "no one will doze off during these presentations!"

Chapter 5
The Lady and the Sabra

Wednesday, April 28ᵗʰ, 1976, 1522 local time, London

"You and Sasha stay here, I'll go get us a snack and something to drink." Gwen took the folded stroller from Rebecca and put it, along with the bags of new maternity clothes for both women, in the netting above the seats. By the time Gwen got back to their first-class compartment on the train from London's Waterloo Station to Yeovil Junction, the eleven-month-old Sasha was stretched out, fast asleep.

Gwen handed Rebekah a cool, but definitely not cold, bottle of apple juice from the small cardboard tray she was carrying. She smiled down at the sleeping boy. "Worn out, is he?"

"He was overdue for a nap, so we'll have a bit of quiet." Rebekah continued stroking the back of her son's head as she stretched her legs and shifted to make herself more comfortable. Sasha didn't move. "When are you going to tell John you're pregnant?"

"Tonight's the night. John and I have been trying to start a family for some time, and we've had several false alarms, so I wanted to make sure before I told him. The doctor called just before we left this morning and told me that I'm three months pregnant. He thinks the baby will be due in late November or early December. I'm going to see him again next Wednesday."

"Congratulations! The first six or seven months are wonderful as you feel the baby grow inside of you, but the last month or two, all you want is for it to be over."

"That's what I've heard." Gwen held up her bottle of apple juice. "The one thing he did say was watch my intake of alcohol. None would be best, but a glass or two of wine a week is O.K.—but no more." She took a long swallow. "What do you do to keep from putting on weight?"

"I watch what I eat and exercise as much as I can. After Sasha was born, I went back into the dojo and worked like a demon to get the excess weight off."

"Dojo? What's that?" Gwen tilted her head. It was the first time she'd heard the word.

"Oh, a dojo is a Japanese word for a place to work out. In the U.S., it is a generic term for a place to practice martial arts. I am a student of karate, which is a Japanese form of martial arts that originated on the island of Okinawa. It is very similar to taekwondo, which is Korean. Once I knew I was pregnant, I switched to studying tai chi, which has many forms or movements that aren't as violent and are much more suitable for a pregnant woman."

"How long have you been ..." Gwen searched for a word.

"Practicing?"

"Yes."

"Since I was thirteen. I didn't like ballet, didn't want to be a cheerleader, and didn't want to be on a drill team. Drill teams in American high schools do line dance routines at American football games. It is a big thing in California."

"Oh, I see. The outfits are a bit scanty, aren't they?"

"Yes, they are. If you're lucky, the skirt is mid-thigh." Rebekah giggled for a few seconds and became more pensive as she spoke. "Growing up in Israel, we didn't have soccer—what you call football leagues—for girls, so when I came to America I didn't know how to play, and it was way too late to catch up, so I chose karate. It was different. My step-father went nuts when I told him, which I think was probably another reason I chose it. Anyway, it's good for you because it is a discipline that trains the mind and the muscles. It is also quite a work out."

"Remind me not to get into a fight with you!" Gwen said laughing.

"Don't worry. Much of the training is about how to avoid a fight. But it also gives you confidence that if you are attacked, you know how to defend yourself. I think that appealed to me as an Israeli because, as a nation, we're always fighting for survival."

"Did you practice fighting in matches?"

"I did, and I enjoyed the competition. Stan, that's my step-dad, hated them and found excuses not to go. My mother was fascinated with the psychology of the matches, which were very structured and tough to win. You scored points by landing punches in certain areas of the body. Punches to the head were forbidden. I liked doing kata, which are the stylized forms, and did quite well demonstrating them in competitions. Back home, I have a whole roomful of trophies!"

"Where do you practice now?"

"I do tai chi in the back yard, except when is it is really cold and rainy. I try to set aside an hour every day, usually when Sasha is napping. Now that the weather is nice, he plays in the yard while I exercise."

Rebekah finished the bottle of apple juice. "When we moved to the States I was almost twelve, and my mother married Stan Gutman when I was thirteen. Stan, who was really good to me growing up, asked me if I wanted to change my name, and I said no, I wanted to keep my father's last name, Shahaf, in his memory. In Hebrew, depending on the context, it can translate to someone who is a dreamer, or to one who wants to be free." Rebekah mused for a moment, thinking that it was an appropriate name for her.

"How long had your family lived in Israel?"

"For generations. My mother's side came from Germany, and she has a prayer book with her family tree that goes back into the late eighteen hundreds. My real father's family lived in Palestine. Both my grandfathers were members of the Palestinian Brigade that fought with the British during World War II, and then fought in the Israeli war of independence in 1948."

"So you are a true Sabra?"

"I am—born in Israel; and like the plant, prickly on the outside to protect what's inside."

"That explains karate instead of cheerleading or drill team or ballet."

"Yes, is does, and to some extent, it also explains why I married Josh."

"How so? It had to be more than Stan not liking him..."

"Oh, it is." Rebekah thought for a moment. This was the first time she'd told this story to anyone other than her mother. "First, the Jewish boys I met in high school and college were, well... dull to be around. I spent my junior year in Granada, Spain studying archeology and digging in Moorish ruins. I speak English, Spanish, Hebrew, and enough Arabic to make myself understood. Most of the guys I met had never been out of the U.S. for more than a week or two, they only spoke English and just enough Hebrew to get through their Bar Mitzvah, and all wanted to go to either medical school, law school, or business school, get a job, settle down, blah, blah, blah... All I could think of when they talked about what they were going to do with their lives was, ***BORING***! There was no adventure. All they wanted to do was make money--and lots of it! The oppositional side of me liked meeting someone who was not in the Nice Jewish Boy mold."

Rebekah laughed as Gwen giggled and pulled off her shoes to flex her feet and wiggle her toes.

"Stan kept telling me while I was growing up that you can fall in love with a rich man just as easily as you can with a poor one, so only date rich guys. I tried that, but none of the guys interested me. Josh was very different. He is intense, focused, and he grew up here in Europe. When we met, he was a ***man,*** if you knew what I mean. He'd survived two tours in Vietnam and the horrific experience of the murder of his first wife. Josh said that one of the joys of the Navy is that it gives him a chance to see the world while he serves his country. When we were dating, he said he was going push for an exchange pilot tour, which meant living in a foreign country for several years—and here we are. He was different and exciting. We'd never be wealthy, but life with him would be an *adventure!*"

Gwen started to speak, stopped, and then thought, *Why not?* Rebekah's candor and openness was one of the reasons she liked the woman. In many ways, she was like the sister she never had. "Did he tell you about his first wife?"

"Oh yes, he did. We talked many times into the wee hours of the morning. Before we were introduced I heard about what he went through from my mother. She said, *he has to tell you the story.* I wouldn't have married him if he didn't."

The conductor opened the compartment door. "Afternoon. Tickets please." Gwen took Rebekah's and handed them to the conductor. "Thank you. Ladies, we have about an hour to Yeovil Junction."

After the conductor closed the door to their compartment, Gwen fished around in her mind for the right words. "How does..."

"How do his memories of Natalie affect our relationship?"

Gwen didn't mind Rebekah finishing her sentence, because it often went the other way. "Yes. I apologize for being so direct, so if you don't want to talk about it, that's all right with me. From what

John has told me, her death was bloody awful. No one should have to go through that."

"I can't change what happened, but I can help him deal with it. Josh loves me; I know that, he knows that. There are times that he can't help but think of her, and there is nothing in the world that I can do to prevent that. Sometimes I even know when it happens; other times I don't. My mother told me that over time, the flashbacks will become less and less, but it has been only three years and the wound, so to speak, is still pretty raw. It would be a lot easier to get over if it was just a senseless crime, but knowing that a KGB assassin killed your wife in cold blood is chilling. To Josh, it is very personal and makes the Soviet Union much more than some merely political enemy. He hates with a capital H the KGB and everything they stand for."

"How do you help him?" The words just came out of Gwen's mouth, and then she was sorry she asked.

"Mostly by being there as someone he can talk too.."

Gwen didn't know what to say so she just sat there with her hands on her lap.

"So, my confession is over.... What was it like to grow up in a famous family?"

"Oh, it is not the fairy tale that most people imagine. Really, there is not much to tell..." Gwen stopped with a deprecating wave of her hand.

"I can't believe that. Josh said you are a distant relative of Prince Phillip."

"Very distant!" Another pause. "My great-great grandfather was Danish and a member of the House of Schleswig-Holstein-Sonderburg-Glücksburg, to use the correct full name. There is no way I can describe the family tree without a diagram, but suffice it say that the family name was made up over the past couple of hundred years from many inter-marriages between German princes to Hessian, Greek, and Danish royal families. Anyway, along the way, some of my family members became part of the House of Battenberg which became, during World War I, the Mountbattens. My father, may he rest in peace, was Danish, which explains my blond hair and fair complexion. Anyway, he came to England in 1940, after Denmark was occupied by the Germans, and met my mother. At the time, he was a reserve officer in the Danish Navy. He made several trips back to Denmark, and stayed for more than a year as a member of the resistance. When the war ended, he and my mother commuted back and forth between

England and Denmark. While I was growing up we had homes in both countries, but most of the time we lived in England."

"How'd you meet John?"

"We were formally introduced. My mother was having a reception to raise money for one of her many causes to provide medical care for children in war torn nations, and I agreed to come along to help. I suppose part of the reason I went was that sense of duty that they drill into you as a child. John was in uniform, standing off by himself, drink in hand, looking very lost. He was there because his mum wanted him to come, and they were going out to dinner afterwards. I asked my mother, "Who is that chap?" She said, "I don't know, but he is certainly handsome; I'll find out." Less than a minute later, Kate Osborne was walking towards me with John in tow."

"That's it?"

"Yep, the four of us went out to dinner and we started, as you Yanks say, dating. John was acceptable to my very traditional mother, who thought that it was O.K. for *other* royals to marry commoners, but not for members of *her* family."

"What happened to your father?"

"He died in 1956 of a heart attack. He left my mother, my brother and sister and me quite well off. My brother runs the family business, which imports wines and beers from all over the world. My sister is married to a barrister."

"There has to be more to the story of Lady Gwen! We're way too much alike." Rebekah's eyes were smiling as she poked Gwen's shin with her bare toe.

"You're right, there is. I had a couple of choices when I got out of university. One, I could go to work for my brother. I love him, but could never work for him. I wanted to study art, but my mother insisted that I learn a proper profession, so I became a nurse, thinking that it would be useful when I became a mother, plus I could always get a job. Then, after I finished, I went off to Florence for a year—to study art. Initially, my mum thought it was a splendid idea until she came to visit me. When she saw the small flat, she looked around and said, *'This won't do!'* She insisted I get a larger one and buy a bigger car! She couldn't understand how I could be happy in a one room, three hundred foot apartment and drive a Fiat Topolino!"

"So what happened?" Rebekah sat back smiling, thinking of the arguments that she and her step-father used to have.

"I listened to her, then said that I was twenty-two, with a nursing degree and a trust fund that gave me a nice income; and as long as I stayed within my means, she couldn't say or do anything, because in the eyes of British law, I had become an adult at the age of eighteen. It was all about control; I was the youngest and had left the nest. We had a huge fight, and she left in a huff. Looking back, I think my mum was afraid I would run off with someone who would whisper nice things in my ear with an idea of sponging off me for the rest of my life."

"Did you and your mother make up?"

"My mum and I didn't talk for a month, so I called her and we had a conversation that was barely civil. The next one was better. She eventually came back to Florence a couple of times and even liked the men I was seeing. In the beginning she didn't trust her baby, but I demonstrated that I had a brain and some bloody common sense. I did what I wanted to and got an advanced degree in art, learned Italian and how to cook like a native. After two years, I sold the Fiat, packed up, got on the train and came home. I had been working in a hospital for about two months when I was introduced to John. We'd been married about two years when he was asked to help Josh and you out. It isn't as exciting as your life, but it has had its moments."

The two women smiled at each other in enjoyment of their shared lives.

Chapter 6
Mercenary Redux

Saturday, May 1ˢᵗ, 1976, 1325 local time, Schloss Theissen

Klaus von Ritter walked up the steps to the manor house as if he owned it. Driving through the woods had been a painful reminder of his family home in Prussia near the Polish border, built about the same time and in the same style as this manor, albeit smaller. At the end of the war, he'd been in Italy with the remains of the 1ˢᵗ Parachute Regiment, who'd surrendered to the Americans. The thought of living in East Germany under the thumb of the Russians was something he could not stomach; with his family dead and the house destroyed, he had been stateless and broke when he was released from the POW camp in late June, 1945.

The only skills von Ritter had were those of a professional soldier, and in the wake of six years of global war, there were plenty of opportunities for a man with his skills. The money was very good, but the risks were high; you never knew when your employer would turn on you or be put out of power.

In 1955, just back from Africa and out of work, he had learned that the newly created Bundeswehr was forming a parachute unit and was looking for men with experience. Trim, fit, and hungry, and wanting steady, less risky work at age thirty-six, he applied, thinking that the worst the new army could do would be to turn him down.

In the space on the application for previous jobs, he wrote, "Self-employed; provided contract military assistance abroad." Under relevant experience, he typed:

- Unit—1st Parachute Regiment, 1938—1945
- Rank at time of surrender—Oberst

- Three airborne assaults—Holland, Norway, Crete
- Continuous combat—1939–1945
- Decorations: Knight's Cross with Oak Leaves; Iron Cross, First and Second Class; and others.
- Will provide details and references in an interview.

A week after he mailed the application, his phone rang. It was a captain asking him if he would come in for an interview. Now, twenty-one years later, while not wealthy, between his savings in Swiss banks and a government pension as a retired Oberst, the former first commander of the Bundeswehr's parachute unit, he had more than enough to live on. The question was, what would he do next in his life? After all, he was only fifty-seven and wasn't ready to retire.

Von Theissen waited on top of the steps and held out his hand. "Oberst von Ritter, it is so good to meet you. You come with very high recommendations. I read about your war record in your dossier. Very impressive!"

"Thank you, Herr Barron. Schloss Theissen looks like it is a magical place." He paused, then decided to go on; wealth aside, he and Von Theissen were peers. "It looks very much like my family's home that was destroyed by the Russians. Now, with their East German puppets in place, there is no chance to rebuild it. I have not been back since my last leave in the fall of 1944."

"It is unfortunate that you lost your land; but I understand and am not a fan of the Russians either. I spent a couple of years flying fighters, first against the British and French, and then on the Eastern front. In the beginning the Russians weren't very good pilots; but they were fast learners, and by the end of the war they had planes that were as good as ours, and better trained pilots. I know; I flew some of the Russian planes."

Von Ritter gave him a puzzled look. All he had been able to find out from his sources was that von Theissen was a fighter pilot with a respectable fifty-three kills who had disappeared into Luftwaffe bureaucracy in 1943. Some thought his family had pulled strings to get him out of the cockpit and into a safe job in headquarters so that he would survive the war to keep the family line intact. Von Theissen answered the unspoken question.

"It is no longer a secret what I did, Klaus. My job was to go around the Reich and occupied countries looking for Allied aircraft that had belly-landed to see if we could get them back in the air.

The American planes were the easiest to make from parts. We could attach a wing from one onto a fuselage from another. The British airplanes took much more fiddling and tinkering to get everything to fit. Then, once we had it all together, we would start them up, and once we were convinced they were not going to explode or fall apart, we flew them. So, yes, I have flight time in Mustangs, Thunderbolts, Spitfires, Hurricanes, and even the Russian Yak-9, which was a very good plane. I also flew in a B-17 once, but most of my time was spent flying fighters."

The use of his first name suggested to von Ritter that he had crossed a threshold. He was sure that von Theissen had access to his Wehrmacht record, and maybe his Bundeswehr one. The caller had been very circumspect and only said that he would be able to use all—and the caller had emphasized the word *all*—of his experience in an assignment that would be lucrative. Was he interested?

"Let us go outside and have a drink. Do you have a preference?"

"Some of your wine, Herr Baron, would be very nice."

"Good choice, I like you already." Von Theissen turned to his man, Sturmer. "Leave us the bottle on some ice out on the patio, and I'll call you if I need you."

"Yes, Herr Baron." Sturmer bowed and headed inside.

Von Theissen didn't bother to sample the opened bottle, just poured two full glasses of wine into traditional German wine glasses with the wide green stems called roemers. He knew that Sturmer had tasted it to make sure that it had not gone bad. "To our fallen comrades."

"Fallen comrades." Von Ritter enjoyed the fruity scent of a quality Rhine wine and took a swallow, then followed his host's lead in sitting down.

"To Germany."

Von Ritter responded. "Germany."

"First, some ground rules for our meeting. This conversation never took place. If we hire you, we will never again meet, talk on the telephone, exchange correspondence or acknowledge that we know each other. Second, you will get very specific tasking, and, as needed, additional funding. If you run afoul of the law, you are on your own. Your contact may recommend lawyers to help you, but that is your choice. Am I clear so far?"

"Yes, very clear, Herr Baron."

"Good. You will also never meet your contact. He will instruct you on the means of communication. Before each operation, you and your contact will agree on what we will call expense money. You will provide enough details on how it was spent to satisfy us that you are not just adding to your personal savings account. If you need more people, we can, if you wish, make recommendations, but whomever you add to your team will be your decision, and you will be responsible for their actions. Understand?"

"Yes, Herr Baron, I do. What you want me to do is set up a direct action team that will conduct covert actions on behalf of someone or some organization, neither of which I will know. How and who is selected for the team is up to me."

"Yes, Herr Oberst, that is correct. You will be told what the desired results should be. If you figure out who has hired you, keep it to yourself. Failure to do so would be unpleasant for you and your team."

You mean if one of us talks, we will be killed, or tortured and then killed, or turned over to the police. "Understood. Herr Baron, can you tell me our theater of operations?"

"Germany, but your operations may take you to other countries."

"How many men will I need?"

"It is up to you. I would suggest three on retainer to start. And by retainer we mean they have no other job, no freelancing. They work for just for you and, by definition, the people who give you your missions."

"Herr Baron, do you have a retainer in mind?" Von Ritter knew this was going to come down to money. If there was enough, it would not be hard to recruit some of his former comrades. If there wasn't, he wasn't interested.

"We think that twenty thousand deutschmarks per month per man is a fair amount. Your retainer would be thirty."

Von Ritter tried not to react, but he knew that he'd drawn a breath. The salaries were well above market. In the past, he'd been paid in U.S. dollars; at the current exchange rate of about two point five deutschmarks to the U.S. dollar, these numbers translated to about eight thousand dollars a month for team members and twelve thousand a month for him, plus whatever unspent expense money they would share. "Sign on bonuses?"

"We hadn't thought of that. What were you thinking?"

Ah, Von Theissen and his group, or whomever they were working for, had never hired mercenaries. "In most contracts, there is a signing bonus of one or two months salary paid when they sign to their contract, depending on how hazardous the work will be; and then there are mission completion bonuses of a half a month's salary or more."

"I can approve the sign on bonuses. For the rest, I will have to consult with some others before they are approved. If there are contracts, they will only be with you."

The men I will hire will not need contracts; they will be loyal to me. "If you can agree in principal to the mission bonuses, we can discuss the amounts later." Von Ritter swirled the wine in his glass and took a sip before asking his next question. "Do you have sources for weapons and other material?"

"We would prefer if you do not rely on us for anything, but if needed, we can provide trusted sources. We'll reimburse you for any weapons and other equipment you purchase."

So we are going to be well paid and free to operate; but if anything goes wrong, hung out to dry. "What kind of missions do you plan on asking us to perform?" Von Ritter instantly regretted using the word "us" because it implied he had accepted the contract and had men in mind.

"The Soviets refer to it as wet work. I and my colleagues prefer to call it furthering a cause. Others would call it mischief and mayhem."

Ahhh, so this is political in nature. "Why me? There are others who do this kind of work. What about Skorzeny and his bunch?"

"Skorzeny is too well known. We are looking for similar experience but someone who has not come to the attention of the authorities. We think that is you."

Von Ritter spent a few seconds digesting this. "Will the team be given a reasonable time to accomplish the mission and survive?"

"These should not be suicide missions. We hope to give you enough time to plan. Your survival is out of our hands."

"Can missions be turned down or the timeline negotiated?"

"No to the first, and if needed, yes to the second. You are free to hire a reasonable number of men to accomplish a mission, but turn one down, no. You are either in or you are out."

So if we decide to walk away, then we become a loose end—to be eliminated. But there are plenty of places I can live quietly with identities from my prior work. Thank God I have kept the passports current.

Von Theissen, seeing that von Ritter's glass was almost empty, refilled it.

"Thank you, Herr Baron." Von Ritter took a long swallow. "How soon do you want this unit operational?"

"As soon as possible. We have a timeline in mind, but we will not have tasking for another month or so. We know it will take time to find, equip, and if needed, train the men; nevertheless we would want you, or whomever we hire, to start as soon as possible."

"I will be able to find men in a month. How long do you think you will need this unit to be operational?"

"Are you asking how long do I think it will be needed?"

"Yes, Herr Baron."

"Not long; a year, two at most."

Von Ritter took another long swallow. *I can do this for a year and then fade away. Whoever is funding this is taking a huge risk if their involvement ever comes to light. You can't keep these things hidden forever. When I quit, I will need, as the Americans say, a 'get out of jail free' card. If I get killed in the process, then it doesn't matter. But there will also be my men to consider.* "When do you need an answer from me?"

"I was hoping today." Von Theissen wanted an answer before he left the schloss. Von Ritter wondered how long he would remain alive if he declined. No matter. Von Theissen had chosen well.

He held up his glass as if to toast. "Herr Baron, if you agree in principal to the mission bonuses, I'm your man. Twenty thousand marks per man per month, and thirty for me plus expenses is good enough. One month sign on bonus for all of us, and we'll have another conversation about bonuses for mission accomplishment."

The two men clinked their glasses.

"Excellent."

Both men sat back and looked over the mountains and the green trees.

Monday, May 10ᵗʰ, 1976, 1330 local time, Washington, D.C.

The last slide from the hour-long briefing in the White House's situation room in the basement was still on the screen at one end of the room. Eight men were eyeing it.

"So let me summarize." The speaker was one of six civilians in the room. Two other men were wearing the uniform of their respective services: the Chairman of the Joint Chiefs in the Navy's summer white longs, and his Deputy Chief of Staff for Intelligence, who was in the Army's light green summer uniform shirt and dark green pants. On the government organization chart, five of the civilians would be listed as Director, Central Intelligence Agency; National Security Advisor; Attorney General; the heads of the FBI and the Bureau of Alcohol, Tobacco, and Firearms. The man sitting at the head of the table and speaking was the president's Chief of Staff. "First, the pressure on the local police forces has to be immense. If this goes on, there's going to be panic on the streets. In two weeks, Red Hand has killed or wounded three hundred and sixty-six people in Germany and the U.K.

"Whoever these bastards are, they are not shy. *Stern Magazine* got a typewritten note, no fingerprints, from the Commander of Red Hand that said the bombings will continue. No manifesto, no reason. Analysis says the syntax suggests the writer was well educated. If you don't know, *Stern* is a bi-weekly news magazine founded in 1948 that is widely read. It has a history of taking on causes and printing exposés.

"As you see, the preferred method of killing is a car bomb, sometimes with a shaped charge. Each vehicle was packed with ball bearings to maximize the casualties. Semtex is the explosive of choice, which is manufactured by most Warsaw Pact nations, some Soviet client states in the Middle East, the People's Republic of China, and North Korea. Based on the residue, the consensus is that the Semtex was made in Czechoslovakia."

Red Hand Bombings

Date	Location	Target	Method	Dead	Injured
4/23/76	Frankfurt	CEO, CitiBank, US	Shaped Charge hidden in a car	12	35
4/23/76	Wiesbaden	Herties Department Store	Shaped charge hidden in a car aimed at the store	0	0
4/23/76	Frankfurt	Synagogue	Shaped charge hidden in a car	48	62
4/29/76	Nurenburg	Herties Department Store	Car bomb	12	22
4/30/76	Cologne	CEO, DuPont Europe	Shaped charge	8	18
5/2/76	Innsbruck	Head Ski Factory	Car bomb	14	15
5/10/76	London	CEO Cadbury Chocolates	Shaped charged hidden in a car	12	26
5/12/76	London	CEO Citigroup UK	Car bomb	10	17
5/13/76	Frankfurt	CEO, GM Tech Center	Shaped charge hidden in a parked car	18	37
				134	232

"None of the vehicles can be traced, because the cars were built from parts and none of the part numbers match the original chassis number. This suggests that perpetrators have access to a shop and know how to fix cars as well as make bombs."

The president's Chief of Staff paused and looked up from his notes. "The FBI and ATF have forensic teams in Europe getting briefed by the Germans and Brits. Who's got the lead on figuring out who's behind this?"

"I do, sir." The speaker was the head of the CIA "We're gathering intelligence and giving it to the FBI to pass to the German and British law enforcement agencies. The CIA is also working with MI5 and MI6, but they, like us, have issues with leaks and defectors. We are being careful with what we pass on to our British counterparts."

The chief of staff of staff looked around the room at the other men. He knew that there was no love lost between the CIA and the FBI, but as long as the events were outside the U.S., the CIA had a role. "The president wants to treat this as a law enforcement issue. Therefore the FBI and ATF will work with the British and German law enforcement agencies, and the intelligence community will feed them whatever, and I repeat, *whatever* they turn up. The CIA will not take any direct action without the authorization of the president. The president asked me to make it clear that any interagency shenanigans will not be tolerated and if there are any such, those involved will be looking for new jobs. Are the president's wishes clear?"

The speaker looked around the table at each individual as they nodded yes, before he took a sip of the glass of water sitting next to his blue folder bearing the seal of the President of the United States. "I just want to remind you that he has a personal interest in this matter. Two of his biggest supporters and fund raisers died in that Mercedes, and the president is not going to stand on the sidelines while Americans are murdered in Europe, or anywhere else."

The Same Day, 2200 local time, Zehlendorf

Across the Atlantic and seven time zones ahead, Dieter Stiglitz fiddled with a 'rabbit ears' antenna to minimize the interference created by the East German government as he watched a Berlin TV station's latest update on the search for the mysterious Red Hand. The newscaster's last comment was, "The Bundeskriminalamt admitted that at this time they have no leads on Red Hand or their members. If you have information please call the number listed on the screen." Underneath the talking head, a subtitle listed a phone number.

He finished his bratwurst and potatoes and popped open his second beer of the evening before walking into the workshop in the barn. The former owner, who had built the concrete walled-in compound, was imprisoned for anti-government activities and no longer needed a home of his own. Dieter placed his half empty beer bottle on the shiny steel plate of the drill press and had just picked up a Volkswagen fender when the phone rang. He knew who was returning his call.

"Allo, Colonel."

"You have been very active."

"Yes, Herr Colonel Grünewald, I have." Dieter wasn't sure if that was the man's real name. He had spent a day scrolling through microfilm in the Bundesarchiv in Freiburg and found a picture of a young Grünewald, his decorations prominently displayed, with a notation that he had been promoted to captain.

"And your future plans are?"

"Wait a week or so and then go back. I already have half a dozen cars prepared, so it is just a matter of driving them to a location and setting the timers. And I have some more to build."

"You don't think you need to lie low for a few weeks?"

"No. I am convinced the Bundeskriminalamt doesn't know who I am or anything about Red Hand. After a few more bombings, I will have their full attention and will then tell them what I want. Right now, all they know is that Americans, Englishmen, and the Jewish bankers and businessmen who control them are dying. It is unfortunate that a few innocent Germans must die as well."

At the other end of the line Colonel Gunter Grünewald continued smoking his cigarette. Daily he promised himself that he would quit, but then he rationalized that when you work for the secret police, you are living on borrowed time, so why worry about living to a ripe old age? "Now three hundred and sixty-plus people have been killed or maimed, I think you have the authorities' full attention. You are killing a lot of your fellow Germans, which may turn them against you."

"How else can the Bundesrepublik's government and its citizens be taught a lesson for letting the Americans and British control them? It can't be helped."

More than ever, Dieter was convinced that socialism had failed to change Western democracies, and it was time for violent revolution. He saw inequalities in the capitalist system everywhere. Worse, the generation that led Germany into World War II was still in charge of the economy and the government. Other students he knew shared his opinion that there had to be a better way. The difference was that they were still talking; he was taking action.

"There are other ways to get your message out," Grünewald pushed back. "To start a revolution, you need an organization and a message, and you need followers."

"People will join us when we show that the government is powerless to stop us. The actions of Red Hand will serve as an alarm clock to wake up the German people. I know some who will join the movement when they are invited. Others will follow, and we will force the implementation of a new order."

Grünewald had heard this mantra many times. He opined that the frustrated young man liked to kill people. Ideology was just wrapping paper. "Let me know what you need."

"Thank you, I will."

With a click, the conversation was over. Grünewald surveyed the magazines and newspapers tacked to the walls of his office. After lighting another cigarette and filling his lungs with smoke, he opened the latest edition of *The Times* from a new stack of British newspapers.

Chapter 7
Once Enemies, Now Friends

Tuesday, May 11th, 1976, 1000 local time, East Berlin

A razor blade was slicing through the International Edition of the *Herald Tribune* to separate an article covering the death of the CitiGroup CEO when the phone in his windowless office rang. "Grünewald."

"Good morning, Colonel."

Grünewald recognized the voice of Oleg Krasnovsky, a Russian colonel who was a member of Section 11 of the KGB's First Directorate based in East Berlin, which was responsible for foreign intelligence and covert operations outside the Soviet Union. Section 11 had officers in each country where the KGB had working relationships; Krasnovsky was responsible for interface with the Stasi's covert operations in West Germany. "Good morning Colonel Krasnovsky, what can I do for you?"

"I would like to enjoy the fresh spring air today. Would you take a walk with me before lunch?"

Grünewald knew refusing was not in his best interests. "Let's meet by the fountain at Kaiser Platz in about thirty minutes." He also knew the walk kept them away from places where the conversation could be recorded.

"Excellent."

The rumbling on the cobblestone street of a wheeled tank transporter with a T-72 tank chained to the trailer caused Grünewald to look at the steel beast. It brought back memories of how shells from the seventy-five millimeter high velocity gun on his Panther tank went right through the sloping front armor of Soviet T-34s, setting off an explosion that blew the turret off. In thirty years, nothing had changed; he'd seen the intelligence reports on how, during the recent Yom Kippur war, the armor piercing rounds from the American-built M-60 tanks used by the Israelis had the same effect on the Egyptian T-72s.

Krasnovsky, an ex-tank officer, turned to his East German comrade. "You know, the war was good for both the Soviet Union and for Germany."

"How can that be? Millions died on both sides and we're still rebuilding." Grünewald had known Krasnovsky for more than a year, and knew the man had ideas that he expressed only in private, away from the prying ears of the tape recorders.

"I'll give you three reasons why it was good for my country. First, if you get past the millions of dead, both from the war and the purges in the 1930s, Stalin achieved what no Russian Czar could: he created a buffer zone between the traditional powers of Europe and the Soviet Union on the west, and defensible borders in the east. Now we have ice-free ports on the Baltic and the Pacific. Second, the Soviet Union is now one of the world's two super powers. Before any country does anything in the world, they have to answer the question: what will the Soviet Union do? And three, your country, which invaded us twice and France three times in the past hundred years, is now divided and a military pygmy."

Grünewald didn't say anything, just listened, wondering what the KGB officer was going to say next.

"And it was good for Germany. Hitler ruled Germany for twelve years. Can you imagine what Europe would be like if that madman had been in power for, let's say twenty years? So, the war, bloody and long as it was, ended Hitler's regime. That is good for Germany, even though the nation is now weak militarily. West Germany is strong economically, and, for a socialist country, so is the DDR."

"That is a one way of looking at the results of the war." Grünewald turned toward his Russian companion. "Is that the KGB's official position or yours?"

"It is my very unofficial analysis, which I would appreciate if you do not share with your fellow Stasi officers. I'm not afraid of what my superiors in the KGB will say, because when I was going through the school for staff officers I wrote a paper that expounded this theory." Krasnovsky let about twenty seconds of silence act as a natural break before he changed the subject to get to the real purpose of the walk. "Are you OK with the carnage Stiglitz is causing?"

"Yes, as long as the finger doesn't point back at us." Keeping the DDR's support for Red Hand secret was his job.

"That would be very bad."

"Agreed. We have a plan in place to shut him down if that seems about to happen." Grünewald looked straight ahead as he talked.

"And you are confident that your plan for Stiglitz and his attempt at creating a revolution will work?"

"Yes. It won't cause a revolution, but it will give the West German government a major headache, and undermine the American and the British influence as well."

"Good. We want him to discredit the West German government, but not start a revolution. It is, as you know, hard to predict the outcome of a revolution." Krasnovksy shrugged his shoulders for emphasis.

"Yes. Sometimes they go in a direction you can't control."

"We understand each other. I will inform Moscow." With that, Krasnovsky waved to the car that had been following them at a distance, leaving Grünewald to walk back to his office, immersed in his own thoughts.

Wednesday, May 12ᵗʰ, 1976, 0900 local time, RNAS Yeovilton

For the umpteenth time, Josh rearranged the pile of slides in front of him. The projector was in position; all he had to do was turn it on and the first image would be displayed. "You know, this show and tell is a two way street," he said to John Osborne, by way of encouraging him to continue describing a mission to capture a Provo munitions cache.

"The whole raid was a cock-up from the start." John toyed with the pointer. "We flew out to a farm near Cookstown, about sixty kilometers west of Belfast, with only twenty paratroopers. We wanted a larger force but were told "no." The Provos were waiting for us and we started taking fire from the moment we landed. When it was all over, we found thousands of rounds of ammo, more than two hundred one-kilo bricks of Semtex, grenades, mortars, RPGs, and a couple hundred or so AK-47s and Dragunov sniper rifles in the barn. I'm sure there were a lot of people up late at night trying to figure out how that many weapons got into Northern Ireland. The good news is that no one from our side died and we put a big dent in the Provos ability to fight for a while."

Josh looked around. "This is a bigger room than we used before. Why?"

"Most of the top operational planners from the Special Air Service, Special Boat Squadron and 2nd Parachute Regiment are coming. Your reputation precedes you! Getting them clearance to come was the reason we delayed the briefing. Should be fun."

"Great. Just what I wanted. More publicity!"

"You deserve it. The prior presentations were big hits, and the commodore was well pleased. So much more informative than reading reports! There's nothing like getting the story right from the horse's mouth. Without that, it is too easy for the planners to forget that things never go according to plan."

Josh took a deep breath to steady himself before his audience arrived.

Saturday, May 15th, 1976, 1410 local time, Buenos Aires, Argentina

The warm, fresh, moist air coming off the River Platte filled the cabin when the doors of the Lufthansa Boeing 707 were opened on the concrete ramp of the Argentine capital's Ministro Pistarini International Airport. Friedrich Starkeholz stopped for a few seconds at the top of the stairs as he inhaled and enjoyed the unfamiliar smells.

The walk to the terminal felt good to the fifty-seven year old after spending fourteen cramped hours on the jet. The refueling stop in the Azores had given passengers a chance to walk around the terminal, but he felt much better now that the flights were over.

He walked over to a man holding up a hand written sign with his name on it, and one other. "Guten tag. Ich bin Herr Starkeholz." He didn't know what else to say. He had been told that he would be met as he exited the international arrivals area, just not how.

The well-dressed man bowed at the waist, clicked his heels, and replied in perfect German. "Good afternoon, Standartenführer Starkeholz. I am Peter Kreutz and am your driver. I will be taking both you and Obersturmbahnführer Stiglitz to the estancia."

Sunday, May 16th, 1976, 1930 local time, Yeovil

It was after dinner, and Rebekah was wiping the face of the fidgeting toddler beside her.

With a smile, Rebekah addressed their guest. "So, Marty, How's Ma'i?"

Marty folded his dinner napkin and placed it beside his empty plate.

"She's fine, but the truth is, we're headed for a divorce. Ma'i hoped I would get out of the Navy after Vietnam, but three years later I'm still playing SEAL, and she's pissed. She keeps telling me that I've more than repaid the Navy for my education and it is time to do something else. She wants her hubby home every night, not traveling all over the world, risking life and limb for God and country, and just can't accept that I love what I am doing."

"Oh, Marty, I'm sorry! When Josh told me you were separating I hoped you'd be able to work things out. I know what she is going through, though. I worry about Josh all the time, even when he is, as he says, just going flying. A few weeks ago, he rescued twenty-three crewmen from a sinking freighter in the middle of a storm. He's the only one who didn't think it was dicey!"

"Well, at least he can tell you what he does; there's lots I can't tell Ma'i, so it is difficult to talk about what I do. She assumes that it is always dangerous, and sometimes it is."

Marty turned to his friend. "Jack said to say hello, and he gave me some papers to give to you about your two houses in San Diego. He said to tell you both are rented, and now is a good time to sell if you want to get rid of them. The papers allow Jack to list the properties. There's a power of attorney in there to sell them as well. All you have to do is put in the minimum price. But we both know that he'll sell them for above the market."

Jack had gotten out of the Navy after his tour in Vietnam. He'd used his GI Bill money to pay for a master's degree in hospital administration and had become a medical administrator. On the side he dabbled in real estate, buying duplexes that he then rented out, as well as selling houses.

"Selling's a good idea. I can't—we can't—live in either one. Too many damn memories. So I'll tell him to put them both on the market."

"So, when are you due?" Marty changed the painful subject and looked at Rebekah. "Josh didn't tell me you were pregnant again."

"Sometime in the end of August," Rebekah answered, shifting to accommodate the movement of the child within her body.

"Well, a belated congratulations. If I'd known, I'd have brought something."

"Not necessary. The fact you are here is enough. We haven't seen you in almost a year." Rebekah paused. "I gather the two of you have to talk."

"We do, but you can listen."

"Then I'll be back in a few minutes after I tuck Sasha in bed." With that, she rose awkwardly and headed toward the stairs, holding Sasha in her arms.

"So what's the real reason you came to Yeovilton? It wasn't just to see me." Josh refilled their glasses with wine.

"Tomorrow I'm going over to talk to members of the Royal Marines and the Special Air Service."

"Why?"

"Short answer, I'm doing a little research, and I may need a number two."

"That's ominous. What's going on?"

"You remember Admiral Hastings?"

Josh nodded. During their second tours in Vietnam, Admiral Hastings was the Commander-in-Chief Pacific's (CINCPAC) Chief of Staff for Operations. After a successful raid on a secret North Vietnamese missile base, the admiral had pinned the Navy Cross on both men in a ceremony in Hawaii attended by their wives.

"Well, now he is on JCS staff as the deputy for operations and plans. But before I go on, a little background is in order." Marty paused to sip his wine. "The Brits and the Germans tell us they don't have a clue as to who Red Hand is. They don't know who trained them, who supports them, or even what they want. To be blunt, other than a lot of dead bodies and forensics that tie the bombs to the same maker, they have nothing."

"What about the FBI, Interpol, Scotland Yard and the German police? Finding these guys is their job, not ours."

"They're leading the investigation."

Josh's interest was piqued, but he wasn't sure where this was going. "So why are you telling me this?"

Marty tapped his glass. "Because Admiral Hastings thinks either the CIA or JCS will get a presidential directive to locate and either take out the bastards or help the locals do it. Hastings wants to get started now, and wants me to lead a team that does its own research and comes up with a plan. He wants you on it."

"Is that an order from him?"

"No, Josh, it is not. It is a request, and he'll understand if you say no when I tell him Rebekah is pregnant and is due in August." Marty leaned back in his chair.

"Why should that matter?" Both men turned around to see Rebekah standing at the end of the table. "Let me make this clear. It is Josh's decision, and I won't second guess him. If he thinks something is worth doing, I'm OK with it, especially if the two of you are working together. At least I trust who's involved."

Josh stood up and held the chair for his wife. She sat down with one hand on the back of the chair and the other holding her swollen belly.

"Who else is involved?" Josh reached for Rebekah's hand as if to say, *we're in this together*.

"If you say yes, to start with it'll be the two of us, and I hope Senior Chief Gary Jenkins—you remember him—gathering data. I've asked Admiral Hastings to get him assigned to this project on temporary additional duty orders, but it hasn't happened yet. Then the three of us will hand pick the other members of our team."

"What about my assignment here? 846 Squadron is scheduled to leave on a month-long cruise on August 23rd to do some special ops training in northern Norway. I'm the ops officer and don't want to leave them in the lurch."

"That's what I have been told. But, if you say yes, the Brits will go along with your reassignment. They'll find a Fleet Air Arm replacement, or we'll send them another H-3 driver. This is going to be a joint team with the Brits. I was directed to get the Special Air Service involved."

"So this is a recruiting trip."

"Yup."

"When do you get the go ahead to stand up the team?"

"Honest answer is: I don't know. Right now, all I am doing is researching Red Hand and planning so that we're ready to go if—correction--when we're asked to go operational. Here's the good news. I want to work out of Yeovilton, if the Royal Navy can give us some space, because it is far enough off the beaten NATO path to be out of sight and mind of curious NATO heavies, and yet close enough to make it easy for us to get to the continent."

"What else can you tell me?"

"There's not much else that I can tell you here. I'll stop by 846 Squadron tomorrow after lunch and we can talk some more.

General Cruz and Hastings both asked me to give you their regards, which I'm sure, if they knew, would include best wishes for a healthy new baby."

Rebekah looked at her husband, whose eyes were far away. She could guess that he was thinking about how much he would love to work with Marty again.

Marty looked at his watch. "I've got to go. Again, thanks for a wonderful dinner."

Rebekah got up and gave Marty a hug. "I don't get to hug one of my favorite friends often enough," she said.

"Thanks. I needed that." Marty turned to his friend. "I'll see you tomorrow around lunch."

Rebekah gathered up the plates and waited until Josh came into the kitchen after seeing his friend out the door.

"I'll sit over here and dry while you wash the pots and pans," she offered.

He started washing the dishes, which were piled on the counter next to the sink.

"You're going to tell Marty yes, aren't you?"

Josh felt a momentary flash of discomfort, knowing that his wife had read his mind. "If Marty thinks this is important, then that's good enough for me. The fact that General Cruz and Admiral Hastings are involved tells me that this is not some fly-by-night operation. My guess is that someone very high up doesn't have a lot of faith in the law enforcement guys finding and taking out Red Hand."

"But why you? You're a pilot, not a detective. And, you're not a SEAL or a Green Beret who has trained for this type of operation."

"Good question. My guess is they want people with a variety of skills, one of which is the ability to fly airplanes and helicopters."

"You left out the fact that you also speak Russian, German and French."

"That too."

Rebekah took a pot out of her husband's hands and replaced it with her own hands. "Promise me that you won't do anything stupid."

"You know Marty and me better than that. Neither one of us is suicidal!"

"And if this team is going to be based here, then I will stay in England. If not, I'll go back to San Diego to be with my parents." It was her way of saying, "You're not a bachelor anymore; you have a son and will soon be a father of two."

Monday, May 17th, 1976, 1125 local time, Wiesbaden

Friedrich Starkeholz, head of ST Division, the unit in the Bundeskriminalamt assigned to combat politically motivated crimes, placed his green uniform cap on the hook behind his office door and made sure it was straight before he deposited his battered leather briefcase on one of the chairs facing his desk. He planned on attending an event later in the day that required him to wear the traditional forest green Bundespolizei uniform rather than his usual coat and tie.

He had spun his chair to stare at the building across the street when the phone on his desk jangled. As was his custom, he just used his last name.

"Starkeholz."

"Sir, how did the meeting go with the Justice Minister?"

Starkeholz recognized the voice of Polizeoberrat Grenfel, selected to lead the Red Hand investigation. The Diplomatic Protection Group, or SD Division of the Bundeskriminalamt, had been split to create the ST Division after the 1972 Munich Olympics massacre.

"Not well. The minister wants results now. He doesn't like the fact we don't have anything on Red Hand. I don't even have a good theory to give him. The one thing I could say with certainty is that more bombs will explode and more Germans will die, and that made him very, very unhappy."

"We are pressing all our informants. Interpol just delivered copies of all the terrorist groups likely to spawn Red Hand as a splinter group."

"Well, keep looking at all the possibilities. The minister says that he will provide whatever we need: money, resources, equipment, anything."

"Right now, we need a dozen more people to do research so we can work around the clock. We're looking into the cars, but since 1949 there have been over fifteen million VWs produced in Germany alone. Our research says about ten million are still here in Europe, and most of them are still being driven. We need to check each chassis' serial number and find its last owner, then ask them what they did with the car. What we do know is that each car so far has been assembled from parts. So if even if we do find the owners, we won't know much other than when the insurance company wrote them off. Once they go into a junk yard, there is no requirement to keep track of the serial numbers when parts are resold."

"Maybe we will get lucky." Starkeholz knew that if the killings continued for much longer, even his stellar reputation as an investigator would not prevent someone else from sitting in his chair. And Grenfel, one of the best, most intuitive investigator's he'd ever worked with, would be either relieved or shunted aside. "Send me the names of who you want, and I will have them transferred within twenty-four hours."

The Same Day, 1947 local time, Mainz

Mohammed al Jahani stopped on the steps of the nondescript apartment building that overlooked a segment of the A60 Autobahn. He surveyed the dark street and its shadows for anyone following him or anything unfamiliar along the block of similar gray-beige concrete buildings.

Satisfied, he began the six flight walk up the stairs to his flat. Even though the elevator was a model of German efficiency, he enjoyed taking the steps two at a time as a way of helping stay fit. Once inside his one bedroom apartment, Mohammed again scanned the street below, staying back from the window as he did. Seeing nothing out of the ordinary, he closed the curtains and turned on a light, illuminating a kitchen with a table and two chairs at one end, a couch and a TV set on a small table at the other.

He had picked the furnished flat because of its location. Most of his Albanian and Turkish neighbors worked in the nearby Opel factory and weren't nosy, so Mohammed had never had to test his cover. If asked, he would say he was waiting to be cleared to go back to work after a serious illness and that he came from the small town of Anatakya near the Syrian-Turkish border.

To learn about automobile production lines, Fatah had sent him to work at the Togliatti FIAT plant in the Soviet Union for six months. In Germany, Mohammed kept to himself to minimize the risk of a conversation that would expose his lack of knowledge about Opel and its production lines.

An old, well used typewriter he had bought second hand sat on the kitchen table. After making a cup of tea, Mohammed adjusted the worn roller so that the ends of the paper were level, then began typing.

Ahmed,

The past few days have been very good. Our friend has been very successful in his business.

My recommendation is that we should expand our support for his enterprise. He relies on our friends in the East but has concerns they may prove unreliable. We should provide him with more money and introduce him to our local friends.

He is such a good friend we may want to invite him to vacation with us. Please let me know what you think.

Mohammed

Satisfied that the content was innocuous to someone who didn't know the greater context, he hand wrote an Egyptian address on the envelope. He knew how many stamps to use because he sent such letters every week. In the morning, he would drop the letter in a post office box by the Mainz train station. With luck, he'd get a reply in two weeks. Last week's letter had listed newspapers that Mohammed had suggested Ahmed either find on a Cairo newsstand or read in a library.

Each letter was only one of millions handled by the Bundespost every day. The two men had been corresponding since Mohammed arrived in Germany three years ago as a doctoral student in political science at Heidelberg University. He had been sent to recruit Germans sympathetic to the Palestinian cause, and he had met Dieter, who wanted to do more than talk. When his student visa ran out, Mohammed had left and come back with the papers of a Turkish gastarbeiter.

Friday, May 21ˢᵗ, 1976, 2130 Local time, Zehlendorf

Dieter held up a bottle of beer in mock salute to the VW he'd just finished packing with explosives. This was a work of art. His!

It was his third beer. After a deep swig, he headed to the bathroom to clean up. His t-shirt was covered with a mix of dirt, oil, grease, and sweat. Carefully, he placed the bottle on the toilet seat as he washed his face and hands. When he looked up and saw his face in the mirror one word popped into his mind.

Why?

Because I hate my life.

Why?

Because until now, it had no purpose.

Why?

Because I didn't fit in.

Why?

Because no one believes the same things as I do.

Why?

Because I am a radical—an anarchist, a social revolutionary.

Why?

Because I like making car bombs and killing people, especially enemies of Germany.

Why?

Because I hate what is happening to Germany. The fatherland deserves better.

Why?

Because this is not right! Too many foreigners, too many Jews. I hate them all.

Why?

Because I am my father's son.

Dieter drained the beer bottle. *Red Hand is all about hate.* The thought pleased him.

Saturday, May 22nd, 1976, 0822 local time, Mainz

Mohammed was reading one of the Frankfurt newspapers and sipping his morning cup of aromatic Turkish coffee when his phone rang. He wasn't expecting a call, so the ringing phone early on a Sunday morning triggered a sense of alarm. The Israelis sometimes planted bombs in telephone handsets. He hesitated, then picked up the receiver carefully.

"Good morning. I understand you inquired about buying my car?"

The voice on the other end of the phone used the code words that meant someone from Fatah wanted to meet him.

"Yes, I am looking for an older Volkswagen. Can you tell me more about yours?" That was the proper response, and both men hoped anyone monitoring the call would not take note of the exchange.

"It is a dark green 1968 model that has never been wrecked."

Mohammed wracked his brain, trying to remember what 1968 meant. "Never been wrecked' was the code phrase to indicate that the speaker didn't think there was any danger of being arrested. "How many kilometers?"

"Just over fifty thousand. It has new tires. Would you like to see the car?"

This meant he had new information that he wanted to tell him in person. "Yes. Where and when?"

"Can you meet me at eleven o'clock today? There is a small parking lot opposite a café at the corner of Marienborner Strasser and Drechslerweg that is empty on Sunday. If you like the car, we can discuss a price."

"Yes, that is agreeable. What is your name?"

"Karim. Karim Bahamdan. See you then."

The café was a pleasant thirty minute walk from his apartment. Less than an hour later, Mohammed stood opposite Karim in the parking lot, which gave them a three hundred and sixty degree view to see anyone approaching. And the VW did have new tires! There were just a few cars in the large lot, which gave them a space to talk without fear of being overheard.

"Our leaders likes your idea of using Turkish immigrant identities as covers to bring more of our people into Germany. Some of them think we could hide a small army here."

Mohammed smiled at the veiled compliment. This was the first time he had met Karim, who was a legend in Fatah because of his ability to switch identities and move around the world at will. "I agree. A force that can create a lot of pain for our enemies can be based here."

"As for our primary mission, I have two questions. First, we know some Germans who might want to join Red Hand. Do you think Stiglitz might accept them?"

"Maybe. Dieter is very, very suspicious and will have to vet them himself. That will take time. He thinks most of the radicals are all talk. And we would have to recruit from those who have not come to the attention of the police. If you want, I can make the introductions, but they cannot know he is Red Hand, and it will be his decision, no one else's."

"We need to have more agents; no one man should be indispensable. So the second question is, do you or your friend know any Germans who will help us?"

Mohammed looked around his sector before replying. "The answer is complicated. The Neo-Nazis and ex-Nazis are well penetrated by the police, so we should stay away from them. My suggestion is we find people like Stiglitz who are anarchists or have a reason to hate Jews. We will have to be very thorough in our background check, or we will lose everything."

"I agree. I am sure our leaders will provide the resources. Tell me what you will need."

"First, I need money, documents, and a safe place for Stiglitz to go outside Germany. Second, we will need safe houses here. Three, I have to go back to school, because that is where a lot of the radicals are based. It is where I found Stiglitz. Some we can offer to Red Hand and help him check them out. Others we may decide to use elsewhere. In either case, I think it best if we stay in the background and not get involved in direct action inside Germany at this time."

"And if he doesn't want to expand the number of cells?"

"He will. He wants to create enough chaos so that the government will be overthrown and a new one will emerge, focused on keeping Germany for Germans. His has told me that Red Hand will have to grow if it is to accomplish its mission. Stiglitz's ego will drive him to add cells, so it will be a question of training and equipping them and helping him minimize the risk. I want us to be there to provide assistance and guidance. But, as I said before, we have to stay in the background."

"Why?"

Mohammed weighed his words. "It is safer for us if Germans are killing Germans, Americans, and Jews. If the authorities think we are involved, then the Israelis will find a way to get involved."

"I agree with your conclusion. How many people do you need to support Red Hand and you?"

"Five or six at first to set up and manage a logistic network to support cells, and then we can bring in people to help build and set off his car bombs. Right now, we just have to get explosives and guns into Germany. Stiglitz likes car bombs and he makes very, very good ones. We could learn from him."

"I will take your recommendations back to our leaders." With that, Karim got into the VW and drove off.

Monday, May 24th, 1976, 1426 local time, East Berlin

Grünewald was settling into his chair after a long lunch in the officer's cafeteria, followed by a short walk and a smoke in the warm late spring air. As the department head in the Main Administration for Reconnaissance responsible for covert operations in West Germany, he reported to the Director and to the Minister for State Security. No one else, unless approved by one of those two individuals, could tell him what to do, which gave him much more freedom than his fellow workers enjoyed.

The former Waffen SS officer was looking through the stack of newspapers, which were arranged by his assistant. *Die Zeit* and *Frankfurt Allgemiene Zeitung* were always one and two in the pile, followed by *Der Spiegel* and other newspapers and magazines. Every day, Grünewald marked articles that should be cut out and filed. The information gave him much more insight into the pulse of West Germany than the traditional Stasi reports, which he thought were colored to conform to the party's view.

After reading each article, Grünewald typed an index card, summarizing its contents, which went into a set of drawers. His decimal numbering system organized the articles by subject and individuals involved, and made the originals easy to find in the filing cabinets just outside his office.

Grünewald had no illusions about the differences between the prosperous West Germany and the country he served. He'd made his choice when he returned to what was then the East Zone in late 1945 to take care of his parents, who wanted to spend their remaining years in Dresden.

The ringing private phone interrupted his unfolding of the front section of *Die Zeit*. "Grünewald." That was all he had to say; this number was known to only a few people inside Stasi. Even his wife had to call his assistant.

"Colonel Grünewald, Steyer here." The lieutenant general, who was the head of the Main Administration for Reconnaissance, never used his rank, or his first name.

"Good afternoon, sir." Grünewald fished under the newspaper for a pad. Not finding one, he prepared to write in the paper's margin.

"I just left a meeting with the Minister of State Security, who told me to pass on his congratulations. Comrade Honecker is delighted with your operation and thinks the bombing of the synagogue in Frankfurt was a brilliant move. Jews are again being killed in Germany by Germans—and in what the capitalist Americans call a free country! He likes the irony. In fact, if the killings continue, which I am sure you will find a way to facilitate, our propaganda minister will have fun embarrassing our former countrymen in the Bundesrepublik about their inability to maintain law and order."

"Thank you, General, I will do my best." Grünewald knew that Markus Wolf, the head of Stasi, had fled the Nazis because his father was Jewish. Wolf had returned to East Germany as a protégé of Walter Ulbricht, and in 1950 had been directed to create a secret police agency known to all Germans as Stasi. Grünewald wondered how long Wolf would allow this mini-holocaust to go on, or if he had no choice but to watch in stoic silence.

"I am sure you will. Keep me informed."

Thursday, May 27th, 1976, 1743 local time, West Berlin

Dieter Stiglitz got out of his car at Checkpoint Charlie, the only gateway that allowed both Germans and non-Germans to cross the border of East Germany, and handed his East German passport and identify card to the Grenztruppen border patrol sergeant. The little red and white shelter had a neat line of stamps that the East German policemen used, depending on the documents presented. The sergeant scrutinized the photographs and held them up to compare them to the young man standing before him.

Going east or west, Dieter had a choice. He could use his East German papers that showed he worked as a mechanic in a Berlin VW dealership, which meant he was one of thousands that went back and forth across the border every day. Or he could use his West German passport and papers that showed he was a doctoral student. Both had the endorsements that let him enter or leave East Germany at will.

This was his second trip that day into West Berlin, each time using a different checkpoint. The West German police sergeant waved Dieter through after a quick look at his passport. Grünewald had informed him that the Grenztruppen logs would be sent to an archive and only inspected if the Stasi suspected him of a crime. He'd memorized the number the colonel said to call if he was detained by the Grenztruppen. It amused him that the Grenztruppen were only interested in looking for people hidden in the car attempting to escape, rather than inspecting the car itself, which would reveal the explosives and ball bearings lining the doors and interior.

After clearing the checkpoint, he drove the VW into the Bundesrepublik proper, and parked it in a garage with the battery disconnected. It would sit there until he was ready to place it and set the timer. He then took the train back to Berlin. It was a time-consuming process; it took a week to get three cars into West Germany from Zehlendorf.

Tonight he planned to spend the night in a drab East Berlin hotel before taking the local train to Teterow, and then the bus back Zehlendorf, which was about fifty-five kilometers south of Rostock. His Deutz truck was parked behind a gas station that was a short walk from the bus stop. He would need all of Saturday to assemble materials before he drove to Hannover for a family Sunday dinner with his parents and brothers.

Friday, May 28th, 1976, 2137 local time, Yeovil

Rebekah was sitting with her back against Josh's shoulder and her legs folded up, while Josh's were stretched out on the ottoman in front of the couch. With a flourish, she put a book mark in place and closed the Leon Uris novel. "When are you going to hear back from Marty?"

Josh stopped reading the latest issue of *Road & Track* and turned toward her. "I don't know. When Marty left, he said he was stopping in D.C. for a week or so before going back to San Diego for the Fourth of July weekend. He said he'll know more after that."

"Do you have a guess?" Rebekah the inquisitor wasn't satisfied.

"I don't; sometimes these things don't move very fast, and sometimes they happen overnight. I just don't know."

"My uneducated guess is that the next time a bomb goes off, you are going to get a call." Rebekah spoke with an air of certainty.

"I think you are right."

"Many of the wives I know say the bombings by the Provos went unchecked until the British government got serious and turned the SAS loose. It took a few years, and they don't think it is settled yet, but at least the pace of bombings has slowed. I can't see West Germany declaring martial law; there'd be riots in the streets, and the government would be accused of turning back the clock to the days of Adolf Hitler."

"When did you get so knowledgeable?" Josh leaned over and stroked her swollen belly.

"My love, when you are not around and Sasha is asleep, I get my reading in—and I talk to the squadron wives. World War II was a lot closer to the Brits than it was to us. Yes, many Americans were killed and wounded, but over here almost every family lost a loved one, and cities and civilians got bombed and strafed. World

War II decimated an entire generation of European men and bankrupted England."

"I love it that you are so smart and knowledgeable." They kissed for a few seconds.

"You do know that kissing is what started this." Rebekah pointed to the large bulge in her mid-section.

"I do, and I enjoyed every second of it."

Rebekah shifted, trying to find a position that was less uncomfortable. "These Red Hand guys are striking hard. My guess is that they have help."

"Are you now an intelligence analyst?"

"Yes. I have to be, because you are the father of my children and I want you to be around as they grow up. In Vietnam there was, as you say, a known threat. Red Hand is a big unknown, but I can give you a list of potential suspects and reasons why they would or could support Red Hand. To this very pregnant lady, that is scary."

Josh shifted to pull her back against his chest and rested his chin on her shoulder. "I understand your fears, but right now, all Marty is doing is planning. Nothing has been put into action, and as of the moment, I'm not involved. My hope is the German police or the intelligence community will find the bastards soon, so we can finish this tour and be back in the states next summer."

"I hope so, but something in my gut tells me that something bad is about to happen, and you know me and my intuitions."

"That is what makes me nervous. Let's hope this is one of the few times you are wrong."

"My intuition is never wrong."

Sunday, May 30th, 1976, 1826 local time, Hannover

The ticket counter and information kiosk was in the part of the train station that had survived the war. When the station was rebuilt, the engineers decided, rather than make it look modern, to repair the original glass and iron lattice work design from the 1880s, so that from the outside it looked as it had when it was built. Inside much was new, but there were walls that had gouges where shrapnel had dug out large chunks of concrete which were not going to be repaired, as a not-so-subtle reminder of the war.

Dieter slid a hundred Deutschmark bill under the grill that separated the clerk from the customer. The elderly clerk was counting his till at the end of his shift and continued counting a stack of twenty Deutschmark bills. He wrote 1000 on a small slip of paper and wrapped two rubber bands around the money before he used his forefinger to push the bridge of his bifocals back up the bridge of his nose and acknowledged Dieter's presence outside his window.

"First class ticket for Frankfurt am Main for tomorrow on the 1207 train."

Nestled in the heart of the business capital of West Germany, there is no parking at the station, only the taxi stand, bus stop, and extra lane so drivers can drop off passengers wanting to take a Deutsche Bahn train. Ticket in hand, Dieter walked to the taxi stand and gave a driver an address to an apartment building near the central business district.

After paying the cab driver and giving him a generous tip, he walked a few blocks before unlocking the passenger side of a VW with faded paint and two fenders in different shades of silver. To a casual observer, it would seem that Dieter put something in the glove box of the car before relocking the door. Satisfied, he crossed the street and hailed a cab from the taxi stand near the local Hertie's department store. The cab ride to his parent's apartment took less than fifteen minutes.

Dieter greeted his mother with a hug. He had to submit to an inspection at arm's length before he was allowed to help himself to a bottle of beer. Dieter knew his mother counted her life a success: they had survived the war; and her four boys, all educated, all well-mannered, and all destined for successful lives, were all out of the nest. Dinner was a quiet affair, and after dessert, his father pointed to the living room where the two of them, drinks in hand, settled in for a private conversation.

"Vati, I never did hear all about your trip to Argentina. All you said was that you had a good time and saw some old friends."

"That I did." Helmut Stiglitz occupied his favorite chair in a corner. Behind him were pictures of a younger man in a tight fitting uniform wearing a decoration that had silver swords just above the Maltese Cross. In another, the same man was in camouflage utilities, sitting on the top of a Tiger tank. Behind this photograph, almost hidden, was a more formal portrait showing the same blond-haired man in his black dress uniform with silver piping, wearing the unit badge of the 10th SS Panzer Division, a.k.a. the Frundsberg division.

"Well, what did you do? Who did you see? You were gone over a week," Dieter probed.

"I met with some friends from my division and other SS units from my days in the army." His father never referred to it as World War II, but always as his "time in the army."

"Why Argentina? You could meet here." Dieter's curiosity was aroused. This was the first time in recent memory that his father had mentioned meeting with his army friends, who had all been in the SS.

"We had a reunion at a nice place away from prying eyes. It was good to see old comrades in a place where we could talk freely."

"You don't need to hide. You were cleared of any war crimes." In his mind, Dieter was comparing his dual life to his father's.

"True. I am proud of my service. I followed orders, did my duty, was lucky and survived. Many good men did not." His father took a slow sip of his favorite schnapps before continuing. "Anyway, many of us think that this county needs new leadership. We have been living under the Americans' thumb for far too many years. They have been good to us, but Germany must be a world power, not a country to which they dictate their wishes. We must regain our position as one of the dominant countries in Europe."

Dieter gave his father a puzzled look. "You're not getting into politics, are you?"

"Not me, but some others I know."

"How? They have the same restrictions as you do." This was big news! Dieter fought to contain his excitement. *If this is going where I think it may be headed, it could be to my advantage, and Vati may approve. But I can't tell him about Red Hand! At least not yet.*

Dieter knew SS officers were discouraged from entering politics and were not welcome in the government, unless they were vetted by more than one agency. The process took months, even years.

"True. However, many of my comrades' children believe as I do that Germany should be one of Europe's great powers, and they want to get into a position to move the country in that direction. "

"I didn't know that." *This is the first I have heard of it!* Dieter finished his beer and suppressed a burp. "So, are you forming a new political party?

His father poured a measure of schnapps into a small glass and passed it to his son.

"Yes, Dieter we are. We have the funds and are building the organization. It is called the New German Party and we will have candidates in the elections in October. The government has approved our application and petitions. Our party platform is being developed by your generation with guidance from mine. We are confident that those who want a strong Germany will flock to our side. Your brother Erik has agreed to run."

"How are you going to be involved?"

"I am not. I have a struggling business to run which supports only three of my sons, which means you have to go out on your own, as you already have. If you need a job, we can provide one for you in the party. I have connections, and we have a need for educated people like yourself who share our beliefs."

Dieter sat back and sipped the schnapps. "So what will the New Germany Party's platform be?"

"We want a strong, independent Germany that has its own foreign policy. Right now, we can't fart without either the Tommies' or the Americans' approval. That's number one."

Dieter nodded for his father to continue. *Sounds familiar.*

"We want limits on immigration. Germany must be for Germans. Those living abroad should be allowed to come home. And we must get rid of the gastarbeiter. They are not Aryan or even European! They must go."

This was another way of saying that the party wanted to cleanse Germany of the non-Aryans and allow those Nazis who fled after the war to return without being charged with a crime. Again Dieter nodded his assent and approval.

"And, we want an end to all the reparations and the war crimes trials. My God, we were at war fighting for our survival! Enough is enough. Reparations bankrupted the country after World War I. We don't want to see that happen again."

Dieter held up his glass. Inwardly, he exulted. *The New German Party is aligned with Red Hand's manifesto!*

"All that money should be spent on *Germans* and invested in *German* businesses, not given to people who *claim* their families once owned a business in Germany, let alone given to the Israelis. It should stay at home!"

I knew it was going to come around to Jews. "Vati, if that comes out, the world will think the New German Party is anti-Semitic and anti-Israel. If that happens, many Germans won't vote for you, and the Americans won't let you come to power."

"Our plan will not be public, but is agreed to by the party leadership and its key supporters. Nothing of this will be said in any party communication." His father knocked back the last of the liqueur his glass. "What do you know about Red Hand?"

The change in topic surprised Dieter. "Not much. All I know is what I read in the newspapers."

"From what I read, Red Hand has killed several prominent Jews and bombed Jewish owned businesses. That is a good thing."

"True." Dieter finished his schnapps and admired the glass. "Vati, it has been a long day, so I am going to bed." He needed a way to end the discussion about Red Hand. He was not ready to tell his father. Not yet.

Monday, May 31st 1976, 1110 local time, Yeovil

Josh was tickling Sasha on the front lawn when their dark green Volvo 145S station wagon pulled into the driveway. Josh scooped up his son and went to help Rebekah get out of the car.

"How'd it go?"

"Good news and bad news. The doctor said I am farther along that he thought a month ago. Now, he thinks I may go into labor in early rather than late August. He also told me the swelling in my legs is normal and to stay off them as much as is possible. But he also doesn't want me to act like an invalid."

"Is that good news or bad?"

"Depends on how you look at it." Rebekah spun to get her purse out of the car. "He says both the baby and I are doing fine and there is nothing to worry about. And I am ready to be done being pregnant!"

Josh gave her a gentle hug. "I'm tired of you being pregnant as well."

"You're just horny."

"Guilty as charged. And the bad news is?"

"You'll be helping me change diapers sooner than you think. I need to write letters to both sets of grandparents so they can plan to be here earlier. Your mom and dad were planning to come right after Rosh Hashanah and stay for a couple of weeks, until my folks got here. They may want to come sooner, especially if you will be away. And who knows when my mother will be able to drag Stan away from his work? She knows the two of you will be at each other's throats forty-eight hours after he arrives, and he's barely civil to your parents. I think if he hesitates, she'll come by herself. All I have to do is tell her when."

"I'm sure they can come at different times. And I'll do my best to behave when Stan is around, if he comes."

"I know you will." Rebekah gave him a peck on his check. "You are far more tolerant of him than he is of you. What about your parents?"

"They've been looking for an excuse to come over sooner. My mother can drag my dad along to visit the few castles in England they haven't seen!" When he had been a kid living in Germany, his mother had taken him to every castle she could find. His parents lived in Sudbury, a small town outside Boston, and would be happy to leave from either New York or Boston.

"If I write them right now, can you mail the letter on your way back to the squadron?"

"No problem. My briefing isn't until 1430, so we have time for lunch as well."

"That will be lovely."

Monday, June 7ᵗʰ, 1976, 1247 local time, Selmsdorf

Late in the lunch hour, Dieter pulled into the line waiting on the East German side near where the A20 autobahn goes from East Germany into West. The Selmsdorf checkpoint offered the most direct route to Hannover, where his parents lived, but it was also the farthest from his targets in central Germany.

The East German Grenztrupper studied his West German passport for a few seconds before handing it back. "In ordnung." He waved his arm and the bar in front of the VW was raised.

A hundred meters down the road, the West German Bundesgrenzshutz officer held up his hand, signaling him to stop.

"Passport."

Dieter handed him his passport, identification card, and driver's license.

"What was the purpose of your visit to East Germany?" The officer was being curt, but polite.

"I was visiting friends in a town near Laage."

"Where do you work?"

"I don't, I am a doctoral student at the University of Marburg in Geissen."

The West German customs officer slapped his passport against his hand before handing it back. "Good, welcome back."

Dieter was proud of this particular Volkswagen because he had found ways to pack two more kilos of Semtex into spaces behind the rear luggage compartment and the chassis. After he refueled at a rest stop, Dieter waited until no one was using the pay phones before he dropped several one Deutschmark coins in the slot and dialed a number in Mainz. He looked around; no one was within five meters.

"Mohammed?"

"Dieter?"

"Where are you?"

"On my way south. I would like you to follow me to a location and then take my car back to Geissen."

"My pleasure. When?"

"Tomorrow. When I get closer, I will call you."

The Same Day, 1530 local time, Dinkelsbühl

Dinkelsbühl, with its historic buildings and the wall and towers from the middle ages, had survived the war intact. A walk around the old city was a trip back in time: most of the buildings had cornerstones laid in the 1100s.

Parking places on the narrow streets were hard to find, and Klaus von Ritter was delighted when he squeezed the Opel into a spot two blocks from his destination. The road was barely wide enough for a single car, and there were no sidewalk doorways to offer concealment, making it easy for him to check for a tail as he walked to the post office. Two letters awaited him. One envelope contained a credit card bill. The other was a large manila envelope; the address was hand written and there was no return address. He looked at it for a few seconds as his heart raced. One thought ran through his mind. Tasking!

Von Ritter returned to his car and sat in the driver's seat.

He opened his pocket knife and stared for a few moments at the manila envelope, which had been bent to fit into the letterbox, before he inserted the tip and cut the heavy paper. *First the money, now this. They—whoever they are—want us to do something in a hurry.*

He'd bought the used 1973 Opel Ascona four-door sedan for cash for this operation, and had registered it using a false address. He'd picked the plain looking silver car because there were thousands of them built and it had a reasonable amount of room for four adults.

Von Ritter pulled on a thin pair of deerskin gloves before he slit open the envelope the rest of the way and dumped out the contents. First was a single sheet of paper folded in thirds with the type-written command "Call 20 52 36 89 to acknowledge receipt and discuss tasking." He then pulled out two black and white pictures; on the back of each was a name and address.

At a Shell gas station he pulled up in front of the two pay phones. After selecting an orange soft drink, he gave the clerk a fifty mark bill and asked for plenty of change to use the pay phone. The teenager, whose pale face sported half a dozen or more pimples, gave him a handful of one, two and five Deutschmark coins and went back to reading Gore Vidal's *Myra Breckingridge* in German.

Von Ritter deposited far more money than he thought he'd need and dialed the numbers; the phone rang twice before a voice answered with a hesitant, "Allo."

"Twin silver lightning bolts." Von Ritter gave the code words his contact had instructed him to use whenever calling a number given to him for this operation. He would get a new set for each operation.

"Crooked cross."

"Identity confirmed," Von Ritter replied. "What do you want done?"

"I want to read about a fatal car accident no later than June twenty-first."

"Consider it done." Von Ritter hung up the phone and waited until his change rattled down.

Now they were going to have to start earning their retainer.

Tuesday, June 22nd, 1976, 1337 local time, Wurzburg

Von Ritter drove to Wurzburg and bought two copies of five different newspapers, each bearing the date of Tuesday, June 22nd. He noted that it was the anniversary of the Nazi invasion of the Soviet Union; all through the drive home he recollected events of the summer of 1941.

Von Ritter laid the papers in a row on the kitchen table of his three bedroom farmhouse, the cornerstone of which was dated 1589. The building, which was about ten kilometers southwest of Dinkelsbühl, had been expanded in 1724, and then again to its current size in 1870. He'd bought it, and the twenty thousand hectacres that came with it, in 1952 with surplus expense money from an African government that had hired him to lead a group of mercenaries to keep the rulers in power.

The farm was the perfect place for von Ritter to get away and relax. About a quarter of his land was neatly cultivated fields which one of his neighbors rented to plant wheat, barley, and cabbage. Most of the rest was wooded and hilly, which let him set up a gun range in a ravine that, with the help of the surrounding trees, muffled the sound. He kept the kitchen stocked and the electricity on and lived there when he could.

For security reasons, the four-man team he had put together would operate from rooms in one-star hotels, where cash customers were more welcome than those who used credit cards that cost the owners some of their profit margin. Now that the recent operation was accomplished, the other men had gone back to their homes with orders to stay out of sight and trouble. Von Ritter would call them when he got the next assignment. If they were smart, they would continue to live quiet lives and save as much of their pay as possible for a rainy day.

Von Ritter skimmed the liberal Frankfurter *Allgemeine Zeitung,* then in the more conservative *Die Zeit.* Both carried the obituary of a politician running for re-election to the Bundestag. He didn't even bother to read the other three.

He cut out the obituary from the Frankfurt paper, which had a picture of the dead man, and stapled it to an editorial which lamented the loss of one who had held a safe seat in the Bundestag for the Social Democrats. Now that he was dead, the writer observed that the race for the seat was wide open, and the New German Party might have a chance with voters who wanted a fresh face with new ideas to represent them.

The article on the accident noted that the police report said the dead man's car had run through a guardrail and plunged down an embankment. The reporter quoted a police officer, who speculated that if the victim had not died on impact, the fire that consumed the car would have killed him. The policeman stated there was no sign of foul play and that he would list the incident as an accident.

The two articles were placed in a manila envelope, which von Ritter sealed and placed on the seat of the Mercedes he had registered in his own name. Thirty minutes later, the envelope went into a safe deposit box at the Deutsche Bank branch in Aalen, about fifteen kilometers west of his property. At a nearby gas station, he dialed a number from the pay phone.

"Allo."

It sounded like the same voice he had heard before, Von Ritter thought, and went through the authentication process before he asked a question. "Have you read today's *Die Zeit* or the Frankfurter *Allgemiene Zeitung*?"

"I have."

"It has several articles that provide the information you require."

"Yes it does. I am glad to read that you were successful. We'll be in touch very soon. Excellent work. Good day." Dial tone.

Saturday, July 3ʳᵈ, 1976, 1030 local time, Wiesbaden

Dieter waited between the rows of cars until he found a parking spot next to one marked "Reserved for O-6 and Above" near the front entrance to the Armed Forces Exchange. The Volkswagen he exited had the U.S. style red plates with two groups of three numbers in white, and the letters USA where a state's name would go. To any casual observer, they were similar to other plates on cars owned by American servicemen in the parking lot.

Dieter, dressed in jeans and a golf shirt, looked like any young American serviceman out shopping on the day before a major U.S. holiday. He walked toward the far side of the parking lot where Mohammed was waiting in the driver's seat of his silver BMW 1800ti. "Let's go. We have about an hour."

No one paid attention to the BMW's wide, white German plates with black letters and numbers on the front bumper; these were almost as common in that parking lot as the American style, as they were driven by families of German women who married American servicemen.

Dieter waited until they were out of the parking lot before he spoke. "There's a café across the street from the Bahnhof in Wiesbaden that has excellent whipped cream cakes. We can sit outside in the park, eat, and talk."

Dieter looked at his watch, making a mental note of the time. In his experiments, Dieter had found that cheap mechanical kitchen timers were often off by as much as three minutes. They would know when the bomb went off, because even if they didn't hear the explosion, the sound of police sirens would tell them something had happened.

Mohammed sat down on the cement wall in the park a block away from the train station, in front of the city's famous casino that looked more like a bank than a gambling palace. He nibbled at the whipped cream cake in his hand before speaking.

"My friends are willing to help you expand. We have money, and we can help you recruit."

"You can't decide who will be let into Red Hand. That is my job." It was Dieter's oft repeated, non-negotiable position.

"Agreed. But we can make recommendations. We know how to recruit people who will be loyal to your cause. Fatah does this sort of thing all the time, and we can have resources that can vet them."

"How?" *I can't check anyone out if I don't know them.* "I have to be comfortable with a person before I invite them to join Red Hand. My trouble here is that if I let Stasi check out potential recruits, their loyalty may be divided between Stasi and Red Hand, which is unacceptable. How would it be any different if your people vetted my choices?"

"We have friends and sympathizers who would like to help you, who would be willing to follow your orders and do things your way. And we have our own sources of information."

"Are your sources Russian?" Dieter had never told Mohammed where he got the explosives, but suspected that he knew.

"No. They are ours, and they can be trusted."

"Why?"

"Because we use them to check on Europeans we are recruiting for our own operations. We are fighting a common enemy, Dieter."

"You mean Jews?"

"Yes. They stole our land, and the Americans and British helped them do it."

"I want this government to fall. Killing Jews is good because there will be fewer of them around to spread their influence, and it also embarrasses the government. So the more Jews I kill, the better for both of us. I am killing Americans so that they will get the message and leave. Germany should be for Germans."

"Dieter, that will be a very difficult goal to attain. I can see the Americans, British and French leaving, but not the Russians."

"East Germany is a shithole, Mohammed. I go back and forth, and I live there. The Russians are holding it hostage. Once we change the government of the Bundesrepublik, the DDR will be next. It will be harder, but the Russians will have trouble dealing with Germans wanting to unite their country to return it to its proper place in the world. They struggled to put down the uprising in 1953. The next time it will be much more difficult for them to maintain control!"

"Once the East Germans suspect that you want to unite Germany, Dieter, we think you will lose their support. That is why *we* want to help. We want to see you succeed, in *all* your goals. We can provide safe havens outside Europe where there are no extradition treaties, places you can rest, places you can train more followers."

A distinct, dull *thump!* was heard over the street noises, and Dieter looked at his watch. The timer was only a minute off. "I will find some candidates. Then we will talk more."

Two BMWs painted in the green and white of the Hessian Landespolizei went by with their two-tone warbling sirens blaring. They could hear others in the distance before an ambulance went rumbling by with its blue lights flashing and siren wailing.

"When will you be back?"

"Two weeks." Dieter stood up signaling that it was time to leave. "Maybe more, maybe less. I will call you as soon as I come back."

The Same Day, 1245 local time, Wiesbaden

Inspecktor Grenfel stood on the small hill that overlooked the end of the parking lot. A Leica camera hung by his side, but instead of taking photographs he was trying to picture what it had been like before the explosion. The ambulances carrying the injured were long gone. Those that remained were for transporting the bodies covered in white sheets, lying among the small fires that still crackled from the destroyed cars. The smell of burning rubber, burnt leather, gasoline, and charred flesh created a pall of smoke that hung over the parking lot.

The scene before him reminded him of the Germany of his childhood: burned out buildings, rubble in the streets, and the stench of death.

"How long have you been here?"

The voice of Friedrich Starkeholz was a welcome sound.

"About ten minutes. I was in Frankfurt visiting my mother when I got the call. I drove like a madman to get here as fast as I could."

"A helicopter flew me down from Bonn. I saw you standing here."

The two men stood in silence, watching the white uniformed technicians gently place corpses onto stretchers and then slide them onto racks in an ambulance. Grenfel grimaced when he saw a man pick up a leg that fell off the stretcher and stuff it under the sheet as they were carrying the stretcher to a van from the morgue.

"You never get used to the smell," Starkeholz said, staring straight ahead, his eyes fixed on the scene below. "And you never forget it. It stays with you like it is stuck to your skin. This is what is left after being bombed, or after an artillery barrage. You stand around wondering why and how you survived." The former Wehrmacht and SS officer took a deep breath. "The bastard who made this bomb built it to kill and maim as many people as possible, and he knew how. This is a skill one doesn't learn at a university or from reading a book and experimenting in a backyard. So either the bomb maker was trained by an expert, or he or she is a genius. I would bet a lot on the former and a little on the later."

"That would mean that the bomb maker has military training or has been trained by an intelligence agency."

"Yes. That is what I am saying. We should, based on the design, be able to figure that out very soon."

Grenfel stood staring. "Herr Hauptpolizeidirektor, this goes beyond terrorism. With this action, Red Hand has declared war on the Bundesrepublik and our allies. We must find the bastards—and soon."

"I agree." Starkeholz put his arm on his subordinate's shoulder. "Come, let's take a closer look. Others will take excellent pictures that we can examine later."

Chapter 8
Manifesto

Monday, July 5ᵗʰ, 1976, 0930 local time, East Berlin

"The boy has outdone himself this time," Grünewald said out loud, as he read the *Frankfurt Allegeime Zeitung* spread out on the top of his desk at Stasi headquarters. He dumped the ashtray full of spent cigarettes in the trash before placing it out of the way on the corner of his desk.

On page two, he found four pictures of mangled, burnt out cars, and corpses under white sheets in front of the shattered Armed Forces Exchange shopping mall. At the bottom, a diagram of the complex showed where the bomb had been placed and the locations of twenty-one bodies. Page three had interviews with police, paramedics, and several witnesses of the blast that had sent almost one hundred people to the hospital.

The surprise, on page four, was in a black box titled "Red Hand Manifesto." In a bold face disclaimer, the newspaper said that it had printed what arrived in the mail without comment or endorsement.

RISE UP GERMANY!

We must take our country back. It is time for the occupiers to leave and take their nuclear weapons with them. We don't want their soldiers on our soil nor do we want to be ground zero of a nuclear exchange. The government must do more to enable Germany to once again be the economic and cultural leader of Europe. And it must provide more for its citizens.

We will change the government, through elections or by violent revolution. Red Hand's campaign of violence is underway.

Red Hand attacks the occupiers and the internal enemies who hold Germany back. We will continue attacking until Germany is unified under a new strong government led by new people with new ideas that:

• Force businesses to cap executive pay and redistribute the profits to the employees. Shareholders will get paid after the workers who create the products get their fair share. Equal pay for equal work for equal value *must* be enforced.

• Provide equality for us all. There can be no privileged or ruling class or professional politicians.

• Put limits on the time guest workers can stay, and eliminate the path to citizenship. Those here longer than ten years must leave. If they don't leave on their own, we will force them out. Only native born Germans and their descendants can be citizens.

• End reparations. We have suffered enough from losing World War II. It is time we stop paying the Americans, the British, and the French. That money should be used to benefit Germans.

Red Hand is the action arm of the New German Workers Party which we will form as our movement grows. We intend to change Germany for the better, and will do so by force if necessary. We want to return Germany to the Germans and restore Germany to its historic place in Central Europe. The New German Workers Party will succeed because Red Hand will succeed in forcing the government to change. Hail Germany!!!

The article said that the latest bombing came the day after a similar one in Hannover that destroyed a department store. Grünewald noted that this was the third Hertie's that was attacked, and wondered. Was it an anomaly or was it deliberate? If deliberate, he wanted to know why. Patterns were dangerous. They could be analyzed.

The Stasi colonel knew this attack was going to piss off the Americans. Right now, Dieter Stiglitz was an asset who was giving the West Germans a migraine headache. *Will he give me one?*

Chapter 9
Who's in the Zoo

Tuesday, July 6th, 1976, 0330 local time, San Diego

Marty heard about the bombing first on the radio. For three days he read every newspaper he could find and watched the news coverage on TV. By Monday night he was surprised that he hadn't been summoned to DC; he kept telling himself that the loud silence meant that what was going on was well above his pay grade. And, he admitted to himself, the timing had been perfect to catch the USA government off guard. It was the Bicentennial 4th of July weekend, for Chrissakes! Every politician and higher echelon officer who could arrange time off was away at their favorite family place, if they weren't participating in the nation's capital's celebrations. After tossing and turning, Marty gave up. He could not sleep, so he got dressed and headed to the SEAL base in Coronado, the peninsula that protected San Diego harbor from the Pacific. It boasted three Naval facilities: Ream Field, where helicopter squadrons were based; Naval Air Station North Island, home to many fixed wing squadrons; and the Amphibious Base, where the headquarters of the SEAL community was located.

Soon Marty was sitting at his gray steel desk in the bullpen. There were no partitions, but at this hour in the morning, the only noise was the bubbling of a coffee pot as he started writing questions on a pad:

Why are the Soviets not mentioned as occupiers? Does this mean that Red Hand is supported by them or the East Germans?

Is the leader of Red Hand a radical socialist? An anarchist? A communist?

What is his background? Is he a native German?

Where and how was he radicalized? University? Or is he a trained agent?

How many cells does he have? Or, is he a lone wolf?

Does the New German Workers Party already exist? If so, where is its headquarters? Who are its members? Where do they recruit from? Where does it get its money? How is it linked to Red Hand? What election is he referring to?

Who are the real targets—Americans, Germans, Brits, other?

Why is he picking on the guest workers?

Who—countries, people, organizations—are getting reparations? How much are the reparations costing Germany? This sounds like Hitler, who often pointed out that payments dictated by the Versailles Treaty had bankrupted Germany.

Who is helping him—Stasi, KGB, other, combination—and supplying him with Semtex?

Where does he buy the ball bearings?

Where is his workshop to build the bombs? Inside West Germany, East Germany, or in a neighboring country?

How does he pick his targets?

As he wrote, Marty realized he had many more questions than answers. Frustrated, he took a run down the beach to clear his brain before the workday began.

Forty minutes later, at 0545 in the morning, Marty reentered his office to hear a jangling phone at a desk in the cluttered, but still unpopulated, bullpen area. Wondering who in D.C. might be calling, he picked up the receiver. "Cabot."

"Good morning, Marty. Josh here."

Marty waited a few seconds to allow for the transatlantic lag. "Hi, you know this is not a secure line."

"Yup, just wanted to make sure you've been following the news. I figured that when I didn't wake you up at home at oh dark hundred, you'd be in the office."

"Am I that predictable?"

"Yes. Remember, we've planned a lot of ops together. It starts with research and intelligence, and my guess is that you are reading everything you can find."

"Guilty as charged." Marty settled his sweaty body into his chair. "It has been tough to get ahold of anything that's of use." Marty stopped for a second. "Are you calling from home?" It was a way to ask if he was using a phone at the base without actually asking.

"Yes, Rebekah made rigatoni and the house smells wonderful. Here's a hot flash from the local press: the Germans have red faces. From what we can tell from the Brit TV stations, the Krauts still don't have a lead."

"I hope they catch those guys and string them up by the balls!" Marty said heatedly.

"I airmailed you the *Stars & Stripes*, the *Times*, and a couple of other English language newspapers and magazines from the past few days. I'll send another package at the end of the week with any other pubs I can find. SACEUR"—Josh pronounced it as 'sack-yewr'—"you know, the Supreme Allied Commander, Europe, was interviewed on German television yesterday, and you could tell by the tense look on his face that he is pissed off big time, but he can't show it."

"That doesn't surprise me. I would be in action mode if they were my people and their families."

"You and me both." Josh paused for a second. "Any other news?"

"Nope, not a peep." Marty took a deep breath. "Tell Rebekah that Ma'i and I have separated. She demanded I resign, and I said no. She then said, 'We're done' and handed me the divorce papers. It's over. She's not going to change her mind and neither am I. I moved into an upstairs two bedroom apartment in a duplex for a few months until the settlement is done, and then I'll find someplace more permanent. Ma'i is off with her mother, so that's why no one answered the home phone."

"I'm sorry to hear that."

"I'm sorry too." Marty paused for a few seconds. "I'll let you know if anything changes. But right now, I'm here in San Diego doing my SEAL thing and commuting to D.C. I don't have approval for my next trip, but I suspect it will arrive soon."

"Cool." Josh knew that with Marty doing the planning, things would start to move as soon as he was given the green light. He was sure there were others besides himself on stand-by. "The doc says Rebekah is going to be early rather than late. After Rebekah gives birth, I go out next month on H.M.S. *Fearless* to cruise up north for three weeks. My parents will be here to help out for a few weeks."

"Have fun. Give Rebekah a hug for me." Marty hung up, knowing that the conversation couldn't continue about their military careers without violating a bunch of regulations.

When Marty came back from his shower, the duty officer handed him three pieces of paper. One was a set of temporary additional duty orders for six months, which in itself was unusual; prior sets of orders had been for two to three weeks. The second was a ticket on the red-eye flight from L.A. to Dulles that left that night, and the third was a phone message asking him to call Vice Admiral Hastings as soon as he could.

Wednesday, July 7th, 1976, 0730 local time

Marty had changed into summer whites in a bathroom at the Hertz rental car location at Dulles. He did a quick check of his appearance before Admiral Hastings' administrative assistant met him at the main entrance to the Pentagon. On the way to her boss's office, she told Marty that she had found an empty, secure office in the basement for him; but before he could use it, the code in the cipher lock had to be changed. In the meantime, he was to wait in the admiral's private conference room, where the Admiral had some reading material for him. When Marty walked in, he saw this consisted of a foot-thick stack of documents, which he began to look through and organize.

"Good morning, Marty. You look like shit."

Marty almost knocked over the chair as he stood to attention to greet Admiral Hastings. "Good afternoon, sir. I didn't get much sleep on the plane."

"At ease. I can't sleep on planes either. Anyway, I'm glad you're here." The two officers shook hands, then Hastings continued.

"Nothing has changed. As the general commanding our troops in Europe, SACEUR's public position is that he wants to let the German authorities find Red Hand. However, yesterday he suggested to the chairman of the JCS that it might be a good idea to have a military planning cell outside his command prepare some options. He thinks that would be good for security as well as deniability." Admiral Hastings paused to add three thick folders to Marty's pile.

"I wanted you here so that you would have access to all the data. We're getting stuff from everybody—FBI, BATF, NSA—and still nobody knows who is behind Red Hand. Everyone has a theory, but no one has facts. You're here because I want your ideas on how to find the bastards. I know your objectivity won't be colored by anyone's, or any agency's, political or budgetary agenda. And I know you'll be able to answer the question, when asked, of how to take them out."

"How much time do I have?"

"I'd like a first pass by noon on Friday. Can you do it?"

"I'll do my best, sir. It will be preliminary and not very deep, but I think I can have something that is directionally accurate. It will have holes, but at least I will know where they are. I'd like some help."

"Good." Admiral Hastings referred to a sheet of paper. "Who do you want first? Josh Haman?"

"Yes, but his wife is due early next month, so not until she's had the baby. That's my call, not his. He'd be on the first plane if we asked. Until we are doing more than research, I can wait for him. You never know what will come out of his brain if we give Josh some facts to chew on." *And if anything has to be flown, he can fly it!*

"Amen," Admiral Hastings chuckled, and he nodded his head in agreement.

"Sir, I'd like Senior Chief Gary Jenkins from SEAL Team Six out here as fast as he can get here. He's on the list I gave you after my trip in June."

"The orders are in process. I'll check on where they are and light a fire under someone's ass to get him here ASAP. After that, we'll determine whether or not you stay here, or, as you suggest, go to the U.K. Go take a nap. By the time you get back, the Senior Chief will be on his way."

"Yes sir. I'll get started right away."

"Sleep first. The office will be ready when you get back." Admiral Hastings stopped by the door that led to his office in the E ring. "One last thing; come straight to me for what you need. If I can't get it, I'll get either CNO or the chairman to make it happen. We don't want anyone or any other agency to know what we are doing. The leaks from your days in Vietnam still have not been plugged. We don't know if they are in the Navy or the intelligence community, so until we find those bastards everything is close held amongst your team, the CNO, and me. I'll broaden the audience as needed. Is that clear?"

"Yes sir." Marty liked the idea of keeping those involved to a small, trusted group.

"As you can imagine, there is a lot of gnashing of teeth and flailing going on in this town, and I don't want you involved or compromised in any way by the politics. The fact that we know nothing about Red Hand is ugly news that the administration doesn't want the public to know. For the moment, the president is hanging his hat on letting the German law enforcement do their job. But if more American military service members and their dependents die, then all hell will break loose around here. That's when we can step up to the plate and say we have a plan, one we are ready AND able to execute, to bring this fruitcake and his friends down."

Thursday, July 8th, 1976, 1317 local time, Frankfurt

Four men were in a small hotel room, two on each of the two beds facing each other. An open briefcase was on the bed behind von Ritter, along with several folders.

"We have another mission. This one is a little different. Same rules—we leave nothing behind in our rooms, and that includes nothing in the trash. Clean anything you touch with alcohol and then rinse the wash cloths. When we are done, I will, as I did last time, give you money to pay your bills. We check out one at a time and do not acknowledge each other. Before we walk out, all our material is folded up, put in my briefcase, and we take it with us. Understood?"

The three other men in the room looked at von Ritter and nodded in agreement. All were native Germans and, in addition to being fluent in English, all spoke at least one other language. The most common one was French, although one of the men spoke Russian as well.

Von Ritter had picked Ernst Hofschlanger for his number two because he had watched him come up in the ranks of the parachute regiment. When Hofschlanger retired from the Army he had contacted von Ritter, asking if he knew of any places he could see action. After surviving several mercenary contracts in Africa, the former Oberstabsfeldwebel had been back in Germany looking for work when his former teacher called.

The other two men von Ritter had vetted through his friends, who still funneled qualified people into mercenary contracts. Manfred Goetz had retired after twenty years in the French Foreign Legion; he was recommended for his expertise in making and defusing bombs. The last man—Wilhelm Zweibel—had retired as Stabsfeldwebel, which is the equivalent of a Senior Master

Sergeant in the U.S. Army, after twenty-two years in the Bundeswehr. After an expensive divorce gobbled up most of his pension he needed money, and von Ritter was paying much more than any other potential employer.

"This time, our employers want a botched burglary to turn into a murder. This one makes me uncomfortable because a burglary takes longer and we have to be out in the open. So let's find out more about this person—where he lives, what his habits are, et cetera, before we decide what we are going to. If a burglary is too risky, then I get the pleasant task of going back to our employers and with an alternative plan."

Three heads nodded in agreement.

Tuesday, July 20ᵗʰ, 1976, 2125 local time, Zehlendorf

Each time Dieter turned his head, his armpits told him he needed a shower. He reeked of sweat, oil, and grease, and after three nights of sleeping in his truck and visiting truck stops to wash his hands and face, the cab of his truck smelled too. Now, after eight buying trips in two weeks, he was exhausted but not worried.

On top of the small table that served as a desk, he had an article with the latest Volkswagen production figures he'd gotten from the library at the University of Marburg. Another hundred thousand this year, added to the millions already built and driven in every European country, making Hitler's dream of a people's car come true. Ferry Porsche's design was ideal for his purpose: VWs were inexpensive to buy, economical to operate and cheap to repair. Best of all, most of the parts from one year fit another, and even if they didn't, they could be banged and then spot welded into place. It made sense to pick the most popular car, because it also made for the most wrecks. His work didn't have to be perfect, just good enough to get the car to the target. Then it didn't matter.

The sight of a dozen wrecked VWs lined up in the compound assured him that he could create five, maybe six car bombs, in addition to the two in the workshop that were nearing completion. He held up his bottle of beer and then drained it, thinking as he went to bed about how he was going to create an assembly line.

The next morning, Dieter made notes as he examined each wreck and created six new columns of seven-by-twelve centimeter note cards on a bulletin board above his work space. On separate cards he wrote the serial numbers of an engine, the transmission it was to be mated with, and the chassis on which they would be mounted. Dieter added other cards to the columns until he knew which component was to be mounted in which chassis to make a complete car.

Satisfied that he had a good plan, he rolled the dolly with the first engine on the list next to the transmission. Off to the side, he placed the front axle assemblies, and with another dolly headed into the courtyard to find the chassis.

It was almost 2200 and the northern summer twilight was fading to darkness when Dieter surveyed his day's work. The car was ready for the plastic explosive. He had to stop, not because he was tired, but because he was out of gas for his cutting and welding torches. He cursed the East German supplier, whom he suspected had charged him for full bottles but given him only about seventy-five percent of the gas he'd paid for. Either that or the quality of the gas was so low that he had used more than normal.

Knowing he was running low, he'd called Grünewald's assistant around noon. The man had said he would make the arrangements for a pick-up the next day.

Right after he woke up Wednesday morning, Dieter put the fence-like sides into the slots on the bed of the Deutz truck to turn the flat bed into a stake truck. By ten, he was at the back door of the Stasi office in Neurippin. Two Stasi officers helped him lift four boxes, each of which had twenty-four one-kilo bricks of Semtex, onto the truck bed; then one handed him a fifth box with two dozen fuses in individual metal containers, which he tied down on top of the others. When they were done, he went inside and signed for the smallest box; it held five hundred thousand West German deutschmarks in cellophane bundles of fifties and hundreds bound with rubber bands. That box went on the floor in front of the passenger's seat.

The army depot outside of Neurippin that repaired East German and Russian army vehicles was about fifteen kilometers away. Lifting the ten twenty-kilo boxes of discarded ball bearings onto the bed was sweaty, exhausting work. By the time Dieter and the depot workers finished, his two acetylene and two oxygen tanks lashed to the stakes had been filled.

Dieter wasn't worried that any of them would question the cover story that he had a contract with the army to pick up scrap ball bearings for disposal. If they did, they would get a visit from Grünewald, and it might not be a pleasant one.

Friday, July 23rd, 1976, 0748 local time, Wiesbaden

For the second time this morning, Friedrich Starkeholz popped two aspirin into his mouth. The blinds on his windows were drawn to keep out the sunlight that felt like lances in his eyeballs.

He rubbed both temples with the tips of his fingers, thinking, *Damn, I shouldn't have gone out with 'die Alte Kameraden' last night. I can't drink like I used to.* His eyes fell on the row of pictures on the credenza. They were from a long time ago, a past that was just there—not forgotten or hidden in the recesses in his mind. They were also a reminder of how different the Germany of his twenties was from that of his fifties.

Starkeholz closed his eyes as he could still see, smell, and hear in his mind the battle for Kursk as a member of the 2nd SS Panzer Division, also known as the Das Reich Division. *It was a blur then and now. For the first eleven days, it was attack, attack, attack. Don't worry about the cost, keep attacking. Then, for twenty-one days, it was stop them, stop them, don't give up ground. What a gottverlassen waste! Too many young men gone.*

Without realizing it, he was sweating as he remembered the small wooded area on the top of a hill that the battered remnants of his panzer grenadier held. They stopped at dusk and used the abandoned log cabin as a place to treat their wounded. Outside, hidden amongst the trees, along the barrel, they sighted their two last eighty-eight millimeter anti-tank guns so they had clear lines of fire out over the grass field between them and the Russians. Logs the prior owner had cut, probably to build another cabin, were hauled into a U shaped perimeter to provide cover just inside the edge of the wood.

At the end of that day, he couldn't believe he could be any more tired. They'd started the battle with over six hundred infantrymen, thirty half-tracks, six eighty-eights and a dozen other vehicles. Now they were down to two guns, three hundred men and twenty vehicles. As they had retreated, they'd stripped the dead and immobile vehicles for ammunition, food and fuel.

Ammunition was more important than courage. Without it, all courage meant was that you were going to die. With it, you had a chance to survive.

The clanking of tanks churning through the grass field woke them. Russian tanks. With the other officers, he ran to the edge of the woods, only to pull back at the sight of so many of them that they knew they couldn't kill them fast enough. Thousands of

Russian soldiers darted around the tanks. At two thousand meters, they opened fire with the eighty-eights and the Russians kept coming and they kept killing them. Each day was the same, shoot at the tanks, watch them blow up, shoot at the men with machine guns and rifles and watch them topple into the grass. It went on for four days and then stopped. When they got orders to pull back, there were only two hundred men left. *Why was I one of the lucky ones to survive?*

Starkeholz smiled when he remembered how he, along with the rest of the division, was sent to France to recover. *I was done with the Eastern Front, and for some stupid reason promoted to Sturmbahnführer and awarded the Knights Cross of the Iron Cross. Wunderbar! What about all the men we left there in the woods? What did they get other than an early grave?*

Starkholz picked up one of the pictures. Here he was, not even thirty and the equivalent of an Oberst in the Bundeswehr.

Ahhhh, la belle France. Good food, good wine, and it wasn't very cold. We knew the war was all but lost and it was a just matter of time. The only people who didn't know were the fanatics in Berlin. But I survived.

Starkeholz's subconscious wouldn't let go as he stared at the picture of the muddy Hanomag 251 half-track that was his command vehicle. He tapped the picture, one of the last ones he sent his wife.

We were the lucky ones, which is why we drank so much last night. There were five hundred men left in my regiment when we got orders to keep the Americans and British from cutting the rest of the division and the Fifteenth Army off so they could escape. If it were not so serious, it would be a joke. The good news is that one hundred and ninety-four of us were marched into captivity and I got to spend the rest of the war in Texas.

The Fifteenth Army did escape the British American pincer at Falaise, but it was badly mauled. Much of its equipment was destroyed and only about 30,000 escaped.

The bastards never told my wife that I was captured. Nor did they deliver my letters. Instead, they gave me the Knights Cross with Oak Leaves posthumously and told her I died gloriously in the service of the Fatherland. What fucking bullshit! After the war, I found my lovely Else picking through the rubble of a bombed out apartment building in Cologne that summer. It is a miracle that we both survived, and we celebrate it every day!

His musings were interrupted by a sharp knock on the door. Before he said anything, he used a Kleenex to wipe his cheeks. "Come in."

Grenfel stuck his head in the door. "Good morning, sir. May I have a word with you, Herr Hauppolizeidirektor? It is important."

"You are here to tell me that Red Hand has gotten bored and announced it is stopping its bombing campaign?"

Polizeioberrat Grenfel ignored Starkeholz's sarcastic remark and walked in. "No sir, I am not." He didn't feel it necessary to state Starkeholz's full title because of their working relationship.

"Please sit down. What do you have that is so urgent?"

"We are making progress. First, the American, British, and French intelligence agencies all denied that it is someone they trained. I believe they are telling the truth because if it came out that Red Hand was trained by one of their agencies the political shit storm would send people to jail."

"We had to ask the question and I agree with your assessment. What's next?"

Grenfel picked up where he left off. "Second, we know where the bomber bought some of the cars he turned into bombs and have or will have a sketch Monday. This should make the minister happy."

"You do know that the only progress that will make the justice minister happy will be a report that we have made an arrest? But go on."

Grenfel didn't need the reminder, but understood the pressure Starkeholz was under. "We were able to trace the wrecked cars and contact the owners. They gave us the details about each car and the insurance company names. From the insurance companies, who were most cooperative, we were able to find where the wrecked cars were taken, and we interviewed the salvage shop owners. All sold salvaged parts, but only a few sold whole wrecked VWs. They don't remember the name of the man who purchased them, but all agreed to work with one of our sketch artists. All they could tell us is that he was—" Grendel consulted a notepad —"young, Aryan looking, about six feet tall, skinny, with light sandy brown or blond hair, and appeared to be well educated. His accent indicates he grew up in the Hamburg/Hannover area." Even the very reserved Grenfel couldn't help but be excited.

"Excellent work. The minister will be pleased." *I hope it is enough, soon enough.* Starkeholz wanted this man found and stopped before any more bombs went off.

Tuesday, July 27th, 1976, 1623 local time, East Berlin

Colonel Krasnovsky held out his hand to his Stasi counterpart. He'd been sitting on a bench in Volkspark Friedrichshain reading a newspaper when the East German walked up. "I do enjoy these afternoon walks, comrade colonel. They are better than lunches."

"Yes, and much more private." They both knew that Grünewald was referring to the well founded suspicion that Stasi recording devices were everywhere. Some conversations could lead to a very uncomfortable interview, in which the speaker's words were played back and each nuance or pronunciation questioned. "It is a very nice day."

"Shall we?" Krasnovsky pointed in toward a path in the wooded park that had recovered from the pounding it took during World War II. The first time Major Krasnovsky had entered Berlin in late April, 1945, he had been peering out of the commander's periscope of a tank. The two men had fought in opposing armies in the same battles. They respected each other because they had shared the same miseries and similar experiences.

In 1943, Krasnovsky had been a young intelligence officer right out of school, assigned to a tank battalion in the 90th Guards Armored Division. During the battle of Kursk, artillery shells killed all the battalion's senior officers and he took over, directing the unit from the back of a small truck. His actions halted the German attack in their area and, on his own initiative, he ordered a counter attack that regained their former positions and destroyed over twenty German tanks. For his bravery and initiative he was awarded the Hero of the Soviet Union, its highest medal, and promoted to captain.

"What helpful tidbit of information do you have for me?" Grünewald decided to let the Russian go first and see what he was willing to share. He knew that in their respective countries and agencies, information was power. One could use it to accomplish a mission, gain a promotion, or ruin the career of a competitor.

"Well, my good friend, after our last chat, during which you confirmed that your government's propaganda ministry is having fun with Stiglitz's operations, I did some research." Krasnovsky was smiling as if he were about to share a juicy tidbit.

"Just as Stasi has very good intelligence on what is happening across the Oder," Krasnovsky went on, "we have very good information on what is happening in Washington. I was assured by a close friend in Moscow, who visited me a few days ago, that we will know if the Americans start any kind of investigation on their own."

"What about some kind of covert operation by the CIA?"

"We will know that too."

Grünewald looked at the Russian colonel and understood the implication. He'd heard through the Stasi grapevine that the Soviets had sources in the FBI's and CIA's covert and counter intelligence operations. "So, right now, what you are telling me is that the Americans are not involved?"

"Our sources tell us that they are letting the Germans handle it. That may change, but right now, they are, as the Americans say, hands off."

"But, if Red Hand continues killing Americans, they will get more involved. We know they are being briefed on everything that is happening." Grünewald wanted to press the issue.

"We think that they will increase the pressure on the Germans to find Stiglitz, but they will be reluctant to take an active part. The Americans are very squeamish about conducting an investigation on their own in an Allied country. After all, if they find your Stiglitz, what do they do? Capture him and turn him over the German police, or bring him to the U.S. for trial? How are they going to explain how they found him when the locals could not? The Americans are in a very difficult position."

The two men walked in silence as they passed couples walking hand in hand. Lovers gave the two uniformed officers a wide berth.

"Do you think Stiglitz will be able to recruit others, or will it continue to be a one man show?" Krasnovsky was asking because Moscow wanted to know. He himself didn't care one way or the other.

"Let me give you the official Stasi opinion," Grünewald replied. "Our experts in the Main Administration for Reconnaissance tell me that the radicals in West Germany are all talk and no action. They are not, by our estimation, true revolutionaries. But I think these answers are tainted by the DDR's own propaganda."

Grünewald was sure Krasnovsky didn't believe the official answer either. "As for our zealous bomber, all he has said is that more cells will be formed in time. I think he likes making car bombs and killing people. And I think he likes being a lone wolf. The political message is an intellectual afterthought. In other words, he is having fun doing what he is doing, as sick as that sounds, and he doesn't trust anyone."

"Even you?"

"Even me." Grünewald smiled and knew he was going out on a limb with what he was going to say. "I provide him with papers, explosives, and lots of money; so he tolerates me and is grateful for my help. But as far as trusting me, no, I don't think he does. We co-exist because we have, at least for the moment, similar goals. That can change. He knows it, and I know it."

"Sounds like a smart operator."

Grünewald laughed at the inference. "Yes. He is smart. He knows expansion means more people, and that opens the organization to penetration by the police. He is not a recluse, but we have no evidence of any romantic entanglements either. He's too engrossed in what he is doing. I don't even think he has visited a prostitute."

"I gather you have followed him in West Germany?"

Grünewald didn't want to give Krasnovsky the honest answer, which was that they had searched and bugged his apartment in Geissen, but didn't know much about what Stiglitz did once he left the DDR. The young man had a knack of disappearing for days on end. "We know of his whereabouts, but not specifics of his operations. And, of course, he checks in with me when he comes back into East Germany."

"You don't approve each attack?"

"No. He wouldn't allow it, and that much contact could leave a trail right to Stasi," Grünewald said flatly. He didn't know how his answer would square with the KGB's need for control. "In many ways, he's just like the Palestinian terrorists *you* support. We give him money, a safe haven, and equipment, and let him do what he wants. As long as it doesn't hurt us, we give him a free hand. If that changes, we can either cut him off or turn him over to the police."

"So, you are going to let him continue with the bombings?"

"Oh yes, my government wants the carnage to go on." Grünewald knew he wasn't telling Krasnovsky something he didn't already know. "The propaganda minister likes being able to point out that the West German authorities can't protect their citizens.

And the results make for fascinating reading. Stiglitz is a unique asset that we may be able to use later. And, most importantly, our president, Herr Honecker, likes him."

"That's what I thought. There are people in Moscow who have a different opinion, but for now they are telling Honecker to let this to continue as long as it doesn't affect Soviet–U.S. relations."

Saturday, July 31st, 1976, 1049 local time, Heidelberg

Von Ritter was leaning against the fender of his rental car, which was registered to a fake name and address and bore different plates. At just over a meter and three quarters tall and a trim ninety kilos, the blond-haired, blue-eyed ex-paratrooper was the perfect image of what a middle-aged German should look like. As the lookout, he was peering over a paper, watching the entrance to a small food store and hoping that the rain would not start again. His view through the floor-to-ceiling glass windows was obscured by posters advertising sale items. Their quarry was filling a last minute grocery store order from a list his wife had given him before the stores closed for the weekend.

Inside, Hofschlanger was observing the target while Zweibel and Goetz waited in the parking lot, in a small panel truck stolen earlier that morning that now had fresh magnetic graphics of a made-up company and fake license plates.

At last their target exited the store. The short, overweight man stopped at the door to shift his bags to one hand and looked up at the low, dark gray clouds. He had just fished out his car keys when Hofschlanger stuck the barrel of a Walther PPK pistol into his back. "Into the van."

Inside the tinny empty interior, the former Foreign Legionnaire hit the man with a flat blackjack on the side of the head. Goetz then pressed a finger into the man's neck to check for a pulse. Feeling none, he tapped the Zweibel on the shoulder. "*Fertig*. He's dead."

Ten minutes later, the van stopped in an empty parking area on Bergweg Strasse which led to the top of a hill overlooking the city. Zweibel and Goetz dumped the body on the other side of the guard rail and tossed the groceries along with his ransacked wallet down the embankment. At a nearby car-wash, the interior of the panel truck was hosed out using a pungent solvent after all the controls were wiped down with rags soaked in alcohol. The magnetic signs and fake plates were dumped into separate trash bins about two kilometers away before the van was abandoned in a parking place on the Ring Strasse in Heidelberg.

Zweibel walked the two blocks from the van to the train station for his trip home. Von Ritter dropped Goetz at the train station in Heilbronn, and Hofschlanger boarded in Ludwigsburg. Both cities were to the southeast of Heidelberg and on the way to his farm.

By 1630, von Ritter was sipping a beer and had potatoes roasting in his oven while he cooked bratwurst in sauerkraut. Tomorrow would be spent scanning newspapers looking for proof that a potential member of the Bundestag who was leading in the polls had been kidnapped, robbed and then murdered. Once he found them, he would find a pay phone and report in.

Monday, August 2nd, 1976, 1411 local time, Selmsdorf

Before leaving his compound, Dieter surveyed the results of his work. He had come to a decision at 0335, as he was disconnecting the batteries on three finished cars to reduce the chance of a short setting one of them off before he returned to stash them around Germany. It was time. He would call Mohammed, but not from here.

Dieter timed his arrival at the East German checkpoint for late in the morning shift, hoping they would be bored, hungry, and less vigilant.

While sitting in line at the checkpoint, Dieter reviewed his plan. Once the last car was positioned, he would return to his flat in Geissen for a few days before looking for his next targets, which would be British military installations in Hoehne and Bielfeld, as well as two Jewish-owned Stern's jewelry stores.

By noon, Dieter was south of Hamburg headed for Frankfurt, where he knew he could park the car in a public garage and catch a train back to Berlin. From Berlin, it took a half-day to get back to Zehlendorf.

After the next car was stashed in Kaiserslautern, Dieter dialed Mohammed's phone from a pay phone at an autobahn rest stop and let it ring four times, then he hung up and redialed. This time, he let it ring twice before hanging up. On the third call, he let it ring until it was answered.

"Hello?"

"It's me."

"I haven't heard from you in weeks."

"I have been busy. Can you meet me at the usual place in about an hour?"

"How much time will you have?"

"Assuming you can be there when I arrive, about an hour."

"Yes."

"Perfect."

Despite its size, there were still bottlenecks where crowds gathered in the Frankfurt Hauptbahnhof, the major nexus for travelers in Germany. One was the row of lockers with wide benches in front which many travelers rummaged through their bags, laying out items, repacking, then storing some in a locker. Near the platform for the train to Berlin, Dieter stuffed his duffle bag into one the largest of the three sizes of lockers in the lower corner, then he went outside and leaned against a railing where he could watch the main entrance.

Mohammed was carrying a windbreaker, rather than wearing it, as a signal that he didn't think he was being followed. Dieter waited until they were out of the noisy area in front of the train station before coming right to the point.

"I want to meet your friends, and I want to recommend some recruits." There it was, he'd said it.

"Here in Germany?"

"No, someplace where it is safe for us."

Mohammed knew what Dieter meant by us. It also meant that he would have to make arrangements, which would take time. "When do you want to meet?"

"I want to leave on September 26th, so after that."

"Good, that gives us some time. Do you have a preference where?"

"Someplace warm and safe. I want to be there for at least a month." Not only did Dieter wish to lie low after the next two series of car bombs, he had realized that a single pair of cold hands working through a German winter simply could not inflict the scope of damage he wanted.

"What do you want to do?"

"Train, and rest away from prying eyes. I have a list of names I want checked out. Can it be done in a month, and then can you arrange for them to join me?"

"I believe we can. I'll have to check to be sure. When can we talk again?"

"How long will it take you to make the arrangements?" Dieter wanted to find out how fast Mohammed and his people could react, and how much influence he had.

"Give me a week."

"Perfect. I will call in two weeks, when I am back in West Germany. When we talk again, I will give you the names."

"How many people will we have to vet? It makes a difference."

"Five or six."

"That should not be a problem in the time you are giving us."

Same Day, 1326 local time, Aalen

The woman who controlled access to the safe deposit boxes in the branch's vault recognized von Ritter as soon as he walked into the bank and headed to the large, polished steel door that controlled access to the vault. She also knew that he had a checking account with an average monthly balance of forty thousand deutschmarks.

"Both boxes, Herr von Ritter?"

"Yes, Frau Grafner, please."

He signed the form and followed a step behind the well dressed, middle-aged matron. Von Ritter guessed she had been managing the branch and access to these boxes for a couple of decades. His two boxes, the largest available, were next to each other in the bottom row. "Frau Grafner, I'll take them out."

"Thank you Herr von Ritter. I'll leave the bank's keys in the boxes and you can give them to me when you are finished." The woman bowed at the waist and left von Ritter alone. Once she was out of sight, he pulled out the heavier of the two drawers just far enough to open the lid.

Von Ritter placed his briefcase on the floor next to the metal drawer and popped open the latches, taking care to minimize the noise they made. He pulled out three stacks of one hundred Deutschmark bills, each wrapped with a yellow paper ribbon noting the total, and placed them in a neat row. On the ledger sheet that sat on the bills, von Ritter crossed out the total and wrote a new number that increased the total by thirty thousand.

Satisfied, he made a mental note that it was time to make another trip to Switzerland to turn the cash into investments. The remainder—about half a million marks—had to stay here and not grow.

Finished with the box of cash, he slid it back in place and locked the door with both keys. He carried the second, lighter box to a small desk in the back of the vault. It too had a log detailing the contents. Yellow envelopes of varying vintages and shades were in order by date, and each contained his notes, photos, and documents from his mercenary contracts. The oldest, way in the back with the Wehrmacht emblem, contained operational reports from World War II. In a separate envelope, he had a copy of his Wehrmacht personnel file provided by the Bundeswehr.

Just before he'd surrendered at the end of the war, von Ritter had stashed the reports of his military actions deep in a cave in Italy, as protection against war crimes accusations. On a warm June day in 1946, he had made his way back to the mountain top to collect them and other material he'd hid in the cave.

Von Ritter removed papers from his briefcase. Before placing them into the newest envelope he reviewed them one more time: his handwritten narrative of what happened, who was involved, photos and negatives, and documents he collected during the operation. He viewed the mission report as a catharsis to clean his mind, as well as evidence he could trade if he were ever arrested. Satisfied everything was in order, von Ritter entered the event, the day, and time on the log with his fountain pen before the closed the box and slid it back into place.

Wednesday, August 4th, 1976, 2122 local time, Yeovil

A ringing sound interrupted Josh's diaper folding. On one side of the table he had a pile dumped there after they came out of the dryer; on the other side, a neat stack. "I'll get it." The one phone in the house was a few steps away in the living room.

"Lieutenant Haman here."

"Josh, it's Marty."

"Hi, how are you?"

"Great! Congratulations! You left the message at my San Diego office and I just got it. Sorry. All I got was, 'Sara Hanna arrived healthy and loud at six pounds fourteen ounces on July 31st.'"

"No worries. Sara is fine. Rebekah is upstairs feeding her, and Sasha is supervising."

"Josh, is everyone OK?"

"Yup. Rebekah was in labor for about two hours. Sara was about three weeks early, but looks and sounds like her mother. My parents should be here in two days to help out. The *Fearless* is leaving in two weeks and I'll be on it."

"I'm happy for both of you."

"Thanks." Josh paused. "Where are you?"

"Pentagon."

"That's a change."

"Yeah, Senior Chief Jenkins and I are spending lots of Hastings' TAD dollars. By the way, Admiral Hastings said to say hello. "

"Marty, being in D.C., that's serious."

"Yeah. Bombs keep going off. The last one killed and injured about thirty people in Hohne and destroyed a couple of retail stores. There is still a lot of flailing around here but no action. I'm here doing research."

Josh knew his friend couldn't tell him anything more. "How's being a bachelor?"

"It gives me more time to work, but my social life sucks."

"Sorry to hear the latter. Look at the bright side. You have a lot more spending money. No kids means no child support or alimony! You're a workaholic; now you don't have to feel guilty about it."

"It takes one to know one. Enjoy your time on the *Fearless*. By the time you get back, I should know something. Anyway, I'll know where to reach you."

"Thanks."

Josh replaced the phone receiver and thoughtfully resumed folding the thick, soft white cloth diapers.

"Who was that?"

Josh turned around to see his wife emerging from the stairway. He smiled his appreciation of the sight.

"Marty. He called to say congratulations. Also, there's no news." Josh pulled his wife close to him. "How come you are all sweaty?"

"Both kids are asleep." She took a sip of the bottle of water she had been holding by the top between her fore and middle fingers. "I spent fifteen minutes on the stationary bike and it was all I could do; I am weaker than I thought. I need to get my strength back so we can go skiing this winter."

"You have plenty of time."

"Yes, but I also want to get all this extra weight off."

"You have plenty of time for that as well."

"But I want to look sexy for you."

"You always turn me on." Josh began caressing her bottom.

"Not yet, you still have a few more weeks before you can play with your pleasure palace." Rebekah pushed her husband back a bit with both hands, but he persisted and they French kissed for a few seconds. "Mmmm. Maybe the best place for you *is* out on the *Fearless*. That way I can be ready when you come back."

Josh nuzzled her ear and whispered, "Good things are worth waiting for."

Friday, August 6th, 1976, 1230 local time, East Berlin

From the vendor at the Volkspark Friedrichshain's entrance, Grünewald handed a cup of soft chocolate ice cream to the Russian colonel, who was ogling two young blonde and braless joggers.

"Ah, the sights of summer!" Colonel Krasnovsky smiled as he enjoyed his first spoonful.

"Those two are young enough to be your daughters!"

"True, but one can always dream..." He moved a few steps so they couldn't be overheard. "So, what is it you want to tell me?"

"I was just briefed by the people who keep an eye on our countrymen to the west. We have word of a meeting last week in which Hauptpolizeidirektor Starkeholz, the man in charge of the investigation, briefed the Minister of Justice and key members of his staff."

"So soon." Krasnovsky was impressed.

"Yes. Well, Starkeholz is a former grenadier from the Second SS Panzer."

"He's allowed to be a policeman?" Krasnovsky's eyebrows shot up in surprise.

"He was training to be a policeman when the war started. After the war, he was cleared of any possible war crimes and allowed to rejoin the police force. He is very good, and advanced quickly."

"So you know a lot about the man?"

"Yes, we have a copy of his SS personnel file as well as the one the Gestapo kept. He is a loyal, hardworking German. For about five years running, he had the highest conviction rate of anyone."

"I see." Krasnovsky wasn't sure what Grünewald meant by his "loyal German" comment. He, like many of his Soviet countrymen, didn't trust the DDR's Volksarmee and often wondered how long the East Germans would fight their countrymen if the Soviet Union went to war with NATO.

"They have found one or two junkyards where Stiglitz bought cars for cash, but don't have his name. The Bundeskriminalamt now has a description and a crude sketch that will be released to the public and the press on Monday. But from what I was told, it could be any one of a million German youths."

"So they are making progress."

"Yes and no. All they can confirm is that a native German speaker is buying wrecked cars in Germany and turning them into bombs."

"So what are they going to do?"

"What any good investigator would do--keep digging."

"Anything else?"

"Yes. Special agents from the American FBI and Scotland Yard now attend every briefing by Starkeholz. The Americans have full access to the investigation, but the Minister of Justice made it clear to everyone in the room that Starkeholz is still in charge."

"Do you know what the Americans are doing?"

"Our sources say they are making suggestions, but so far their offers of help have been turned down. When they go to the bomb sites, they are escorted by members of the Bundeskriminalamt. Our analysts think the Americans are about to increase the pressure."

"I'll check with Moscow and see what they know."

"Thank you." Krasnovsky's answer was what Grünewald wanted. "Anything you can tell me will be most helpful."

Sunday, August 15th, 1976, 1923 local time, Hannover

Dieter sat in a crowded dining room next to his mother at the end of a worn polished oak table that, with the extensions, protruded well into the living room of his parents' three bedroom, sixth floor apartment. His two oldest brothers sat on either side of his father, with their wives next to them. As the younger sons, he and Erik were expected to help carry food from the kitchen.

Anna Liese Stiglitz was beaming as she sat down. The nest was full with all her sons—Gunther, Georg, Erik and Dieter—and two daughters-in-law: Greta, who was married to Georg and was six months pregnant; and Gunther's wife, Helga. Almost equally important, the table was full of food she'd spent most of the day cooking.

Dieter was glad to be far from his father; he didn't want to get drawn into a discussion about Red Hand. Although Helmut Stiglitz was the CEO of Stiglitz Warenhaus Atkiengesellschaft, Dieter knew from talking to his mother that he was spending a lot of time helping the New German Party and letting Gunther run the business.

Helmut swallowed the last piece of the thin rolled beef, bacon, and pickle dish known as rouladen, and addressed his son. "Gunther, how many seats do you think we will win?"

"It is too early to say, but the party believes it will win between eight and twelve seats, maybe more. Our polling supports that number. We are getting stronger in Bavaria, where many Germans support our call for a stronger, united Germany."

"Excellent." His father pointed a fork at Erik. Blond and blue-eyed, Erik was the most Nordic-looking of the four brothers. He had been a professional football player for FC Augsburg in the second division of the Bundesliga before suffering a serious knee injury and a broken leg in a motorcycle accident.

"Erik, what are your chances?"

Erik, who ran the StiglitzHaus hardware store in Kassel, finished chewing before he spoke. "Father, I don't want to make any predictions, but I have a very good chance of winning."

"Your campaign is not wanting for money or assistance?"

"No, I have all I need."

"Excellent. If you need help, please let me know and the party will provide it."

"Yes, father, I know that." Erik was the quietest of the four brothers. He had told his younger brother that their father had pressured him into running.

"We do have one problem that may be hurting us." Gunther, who was sitting at their father's right hand as the eldest, would be their father's successor. His store in Kiel was the most profitable.

"What is that, Gunther?"

"These Red Hand lunatics are killing Germans. On the one hand, they are helping make our case for German independence; but on the other, they are murdering our people. There were three bombings last week and another hundred or so Germans were killed or maimed. Someone has to put these idiots behind bars. This would not have happened under..." He decided not to use the words that were about to come out of his mouth. " ...before 1945."

Helmut Stiglitz took a long swig from his glass of beer. "From what I understand from one of my former comrades, the police have no leads. They have the sketch we have all seen on TV and in the newspapers, but it could be any German that has blond hair and is between twenty and forty. You could all be suspects!" He waved his beer glass in a sweeping motion.

Dieter looked down, determined not to say anything.

"Dieter, you are the political scientist, or at least that is what you are studying. What do you make of this Red Hand group?" His father gestured in his youngest son's direction as if to say, *speak up*.

Dieter took a long sip of his beer to buy time. "Whoever they are, they want to show that the current German government is weak and cannot protect its citizens. I think there is also an anti-American and anti-occupier flavor. And after their fiasco in Vietnam, I don't think the Americans have the stomach for another long war and thousands of casualties. My guess is the leader of Red Hand thinks if he kills enough Americans, they will go home."

"Dieter makes a good point." Helmut put his knife and fork down as he finished the last roasted potato on his plate. "Red Hand wants the same thing the New German Party does, which is a strong, united Germany free of any occupying forces."

"Has anyone of you noticed that Red Hand is not hurting this family?" Greta, Georg's wife of two years, who was six months pregnant and a pharmacist, folded her napkin into a very neat and precise rectangle before placing it on the table. "Six of the bombings damaged Hertie's stores, but none targeted StiglitzHaus."

"Hertie's shouldn't be in business," Helmut stated flatly.

"Why?" Greta persisted. "They have every right to be in business. I think the government did the right thing by giving the survivors money to help them reopen the businesses that were seized by the Nazis. It was the least that Germany could do. And then a synagogue was bombed, for God's sake. If I didn't know Hitler and Himmler and their ilk were dead, I would think that they were behind the bombings."

"The billions of marks in reparations money could have gone to loyal Germans who did their duty during the war and needed financial help." Helmut was trying to conceal his anger at his daughter-in-law. He had suspected after he met her for the first time that she was a Jew lover, and told his other sons to be careful around her. When he confided his suspicions to his wife of thirty-plus years, she told him to keep his opinion to himself and not object to the marriage. She adored the young woman. The former SS officer knew an order when he heard one!

"We Germans will be paying for what the Nazis did for generations." Greta shot back. "Giving them money is the least we can do when you consider that we murdered at least six million Jews. What else can we do, bring them back from the dead? Give back the years of suffering and torture these people and others spent in the camps? The Holocaust was…" Greta struggled for a word, "unconscionable, and we as a nation and as individuals should be ashamed of what we did to innocent, loyal Germans who happened to be Jews. If asked, they would have, just as they did in the Great War, defended and died for their fatherland; but no, they were herded off into concentration camps and exterminated like bugs."

"That reparations money could help our family business." Helmut wanted to say something else, but restrained himself. He knew pregnant women could be emotional, and the father she had never known had died when the field hospital where he was a doctor was bombed by the Russians during the battle of Minsk.

"When the German people find out who is behind the New German Party, they will be horrified." Greta's face flushed with anger. "The thought of bringing anyone associated with Hitler back into our government in any way is … is disgusting and frightening at the same time. Too many families were destroyed by the war. And you think Germans will bring you back into the government once they know your plans? You have to be nuts. The Allies who brought us the prosperity we now enjoy will not allow anyone associated with the Nazis to come to power!"

"Greta, I think you are very wrong." Helmut's tone was soft, but not condescending. He had assumed that his beliefs were supported by everyone at the table. "Germans like strong leaders. The New German Party will provide them, and we will create a Fourth Reich that will be more democratic than the Third and will make us true Germans proud."

"Strong leaders! You mean like Hitler or Goebbels or Himmler or Goering? A Fourth Reich?" Greta looked around the table with her green eyes flashing. "You have to be crazy. No one wants to return to those days. My grandfather filled in for the father I never knew because Hitler and his so-called leaders started a war against Russia we could never win. As I was growing up he told me many times that he couldn't believe what Hitler did to the Jews. He, and my father, went to medical school with many of them, and he often said Jews were some of our best doctors and scientists. Some were fortunate and got out before the war … the rest died in the camps. As loyal Germans, men like Einstein, Teller, Oppenheimer and others could have helped develop weapons for Germany, not the Allies. And what did Hitler and his Nazi friends do? They massacred the ones that did not get out. For what reason? Because they were Jewish! That was their sole justification. Just talking about a Fourth Reich makes me want to throw up."

"Greta, there was much more behind Hitler's actions against the Jews than just their religion." Helmut realized he was allowing himself to be drawn into an argument. "They were the bankers and politicians behind the Weimar Republic and were the cause of much suffering by the German people. Jewish bankers and lawyers profited from the collapse of the Weimar Republic and didn't care about Germany. All they wanted to do was get rich. As such, they were traitors to Germany."

"That's bullshit and you know it." Greta's eyes flashed as she looked around the table for help. There was none, yet she continued, unafraid. "Respected historians and economists say that the collapse of the Weimar Republic was brought on by the burden of the reparations for a war that we started and lost, and by an economic collapse in America, France, and Britain because bankers and investors got greedy."

"Most of whom were Jews," Helmut stated without emotion when he interrupted to make this point.

"I'm sure there were some who were. But most were Lutherans, Catholics, Episcopalians, and other religions. Were *they* sent to Dachau or Buchenwald or Bergen Belsen and gassed? No. Hitler and his cronies blamed the Jews for Germany's troubles, and many believed him." Greta restrained herself from saying, 'many like you.'

"It was a few fanatic Nazis who did that. And, the number of Jews killed in the camps is vastly overstated," Helmut persisted.

"That too is bullshit. As good Germans, the Nazis kept detailed records, so the world now knows by name how many Jews and others were exterminated in the camps. It was so systematic that numbers were tattooed on their arms and recorded in ledgers! Everyone in this room as well as the rest of the world knows that the SS was involved up to its Aryan neck. What we don't know is how many Jews were killed elsewhere in Europe. Don't forget, there were Poles, Russians, Romanians, Hungarians, and Austrians who helped the Nazis exterminate Jews in their countries. And if the mass killings in the concentration camps weren't bad enough, the experiments the Nazis performed on people in the camps was disgraceful and beyond inhuman. There are no words in any language to adequately condemn that barbaric behavior. As a country, we will be tarred with this guilt for generations to come."

Greta, flushed with a mix of anger and defiance, took a deep breath. "Helmut, I am told that you were not involved in any of the atrocities. I hope to God that is true. I understand that war is a hell unto itself and men behave on the battlefield in ways that are not always honorable." She paused and then looked at each male at the table for several seconds before stopping to stare at her father-in-law. "Out of my loyalty to my husband, I am not going to share my thoughts and suspicions with anyone outside this family. However, if you, Helmut, are ever charged with war crimes of any kind, or if anyone in this family is charged with hurting or killing Jews..." Greta was enunciating each word to make clear what she had been thinking for many months, ever since Gunther had first told them all about the New German Party, "... the next day I will file for divorce from Georg. And I will do all I can to make sure that person is sent to jail with all the other monsters still alive from the Nazi regime, never to come out."

Greta bobbed her head and pushed back from the table. Dieter, who was sitting next to her, stood up and moved his chair to let her out. "Georg, you can stay here. I am going for a walk alone to calm down and then take a cab home."

No one said anything as the table was cleared. While Helga was in the kitchen helping her mother-in-law with the dishes, the men sat the table sipping coffee, waiting for the whipped cream chocolate cake they all knew was coming. But for a good ten minutes there was no conversation.

"I think that Red Hand may be good for us." Helmut said to no one in particular, breaking the silence. He'd already made a mental note that Greta was a threat. *If the New German Party gains momentum, she may need to have a fatal accident.*

"Why?" Erik was curious. The New German Party had struggled to get the minimum number of signatures on the required petitions to contest just twenty seats, rather than the fifty or so that had been targeted. Party organizers dismissed the failing based on the fact that this was their first election.

"Because Red Hand is showing everyone that the government can't protect its citizens. That supports our law and order platform." The head of the family finished his coffee.

"Dieter, can you do some research on Red Hand for me? I have to believe they are being discussed at the university. Is that true?"

"Vati, I told you before, radical students like Red Hand's methods and message, but for most of them it is just talk, no action. They are socialists and anarchists who want corporations to share their earnings with their workers before their shareholders get paid. Red Hand's manifesto says investors should get paid, but most of the dividends should go to the people who create the wealth, who are the workers and not some distant stockholders. Also, they want a limit on executive salaries."

It was almost nine when they finished dessert, and Dieter was on his way out the door when his father caught up to him.

"Dieter , find out what you can about Red Hand. Where are they getting their money? Who is supporting them? I like what they are doing because they are killing Jews. See if you can get me a name; I know people interested in helping them."

"I'll do what I can, Vati," Dieter said seriously.

The Same Day, 2319 local time, Ingolstadt

They were sitting in a back booth of a noisy restaurant with no one around them when von Ritter leaned over and spoke so that just the other three men could hear. "Ok, Goetz, what's the entry plan?" It was time for one last review.

Goetz had joined the French Foreign Legion after completing his compulsory service in the Bundeswehr because he wanted more adventure. Twenty years later he'd retired as an adjutant chef or senior warrant officer, only to find he missed the camaraderie and excitement of military life. He realized that he was born to be a mercenary and would die as one. He understood the importance of clear instructions.

"Zweibel is with you in the car, watching the office. Hofschlanger and I act like drunks, stumbling home from the bar down the street, which for us should be easy to do, eh, Hof? We stop in the doorway so Hofschlanger can pick the lock. You and Zweibel follow us into the offices with the four bags. Once inside, Hofschlanger and I go into the offices on the left side of the hallway, Zweibel and you take the ones on the right. We ignite the thermite bombs in file cabinets, close the office doors, and should be in and out in less than two minutes."

"Good. That's the plan. Now, Goetz, how sure are you that the thermite will work?"

"Very sure. It is a mixture of aluminum oxide, powdered iron, and barium nitrate that was molded into the modeling clay to make it easy and safe to transport. We tested it yesterday and it generated enough heat to split a large rock. Once the thermite starts going, it generates its own oxygen and burns at around twenty-five hundred degrees Celsius. Trust me, it will work. The bundled match fuses will give us between ten and fifteen seconds before they set off the thermite. Each bag has spare fuses. I suggest that everyone waits for the bombs to start burning before leaving your room to make sure the fires are started."

"And you are sure that no one can associate any one of us with buying the material?"

"We each bought an item for the thermite mix at a different place, so it will be difficult to tie us together. They were legal purchases made with cash in small enough quantities that there should not be any questions, and our names are not on any of the receipts. I made enough for ten bombs, so each of us will have two, and I will carry two spares that I will light for good measure."

"Good. Zweibel, what's the exit plan?"

"Sir, once we are out, we go to the public bathrooms at the train station. There are four and we go to different ones. There, we take off our gloves, wash our hands, change clothes and put the ones we took off in our duffel bags. Then we go to our separate hotels, where we spend the night. As soon as we are in our hotel rooms, we take the new clothes off, stuff them into the bags, take a shower and then get some sleep. In the morning, we put on fresh clothes, meet you at 0900 in the public parking lot opposite your hotel, give you the duffel bags with our worn clothes, and go home."

"That is correct. Goetz, what about weapons?"

"Sir, we are each carrying a Walther PPK with four spare magazines, each with seven rounds of nine millimeter Kurz ammunition. All have been wiped down so there are no fingerprints on the guns, ammunition or magazines. The suppressor will be screwed onto the barrel and we will have a round in the chamber and the safety on when we go in, but we are not to use them unless we are threatened. We do not want to harm anyone, but if we get into a fight, we are to kill our attacker as quickly and quietly as possible."

"Correct."

"What if someone is in the office?"

"We kill him or her." Zweibel said it as if executing another human being was routine.

"Hofschlanger, what do we do if the polizei show up?"

"We run in different directions and dump the guns and magazines. If we are caught, we are on our own. However, we have been given a number—three-six-one, two-one, four-six—to call. The person we call is supposed to provide and pay for an attorney. But I think they will say reassuring things and then hire an assassin!"

They all chuckled at Hofschlanger's black humor. "Good luck to us tonight. All we have to do now is finish dinner and execute the plan." Von Ritter held up his beer glass, and they all clinked their glasses together before draining the amber liquid.

In the morning, Von Ritter dropped the duffel bags off in trash cans one by one at gas stations along the way to the airport in Nuremberg, where he turned in his rental car and walked out to the long stay parking lot to his Mercedes. By the time he got to his farm near Dinkelsbühl, he had a collection of newspapers on the front seat along with food for lunch. One had a front page story on how the Social Democrats' local party office in Ingolstadt was destroyed by fire, while the apartments above the third floor offices had only minor damage. Von Ritter had completed two objectives: the mission set by their employer, and his own goal of minimizing damage to the building and loss of life

Chapter 10
Stewart House

The crystal decanter with the Royal Navy crest was rocking like a slow moving pendulum in its holder at the forward end of the wardroom. Dinner and flight operations were over, and Josh had just poured a glass of port when he heard a familiar voice from behind him. "Lieutenant Haman, sir."

He turned to find one of the stewards from the officer's mess. "Billers, what can I do for you?"

"Lieutenant Osborne sends his respects, sir. Your squadron CO wants to see both of you in his cabin as soon as possible."

"Now?"

"Yes sir. I'll take your glass to your stateroom, sir."

"Thank you, Billers."

John Osborne was waiting outside the Commander's cabin when Josh stepped over the polished steel frame known in the U.S. Navy as a knee knocker, because if one wasn't careful, one could bang one's shin or knee on the steel and get a nasty bruise. "What's up?"

"Haven't a clue, mate. I was doing paperwork in our stateroom when the boss's yeoman rang and asked that the two of us come straight away." With that, he rapped on the door.

"Come in." The Commander's heavy Scottish accent was noticeable even in the two simple words.

"Lieutenants Osborne and Haman reporting as ordered, sir." As the senior officer, Josh spoke as they entered the tiny cabin, which had a single bunk and a chest next to a closet. There were two chairs on the other side of a table that jutted out from the wall.

"Take a seat, gentlemen." Even though the man had short, close cropped hair, one could see the red turning to gray at the temples. The commander spun the dials on a safe and pulled out an envelope. "I was told to give this to you, but all it says is you are being ordered to report to the U.S.S. *Independence* for a special mission as soon as we get in range, which, by my estimation, is two hundred nautical miles. We should be rendezvousing with the carrier tomorrow afternoon. Be ready to go at 1300, and we'll take you two over with your flight gear and some spare clothes as soon as we can."

He handed Josh the opened envelope and the single sheet of paper and waited until he finished reading it. "My orders were to open it as soon as we were outside territorial waters and on our way north. The *Independence* and its battle group are going to support our exercises."

"Sir, any idea what they want us to do?"

"Nary a clue, lads. We'll get on without you on the rest of the exercise, so don't worry about us. Tonight, turn over anything left to be done on the cruise to your assistants. If anyone asks why, just tell them that you are going over to the *Independence* for a few days as liaison."

"Yes sir." Josh paused for a second. "Sir, I think it best if we leave most of our clothes on the *Fearless*."

"Good idea. If you're not back by the time we dock in Plymouth, I'll have them packed, brought back to Yeovilton, and dropped off at your houses."

"Thank you, sir."

"Good luck to both of you. See you when we get back."

H.M.S. *Fearless* was just passing east of the Orkney Islands when the klaxon sounded, announcing the ship was going to flight quarters. Before engine noise drowned out conversation in the back of the helicopter, Josh shouted at his friend, "It feels weird sitting in the back!"

"I know!" John bellowed in reply. "I'm used to the view from the cockpit!"

Two hours later, the HC.4 touched down on the American carrier's deck. The admiral's aide was waiting and led them to the *Independence*'s flag conference room. When the aide announced, "Attention on deck," both young officers stood up with their hands at their sides.

"At ease, gentleman." The speaker was wearing two stars on each collar of his long sleeve khaki shirt, signifying his rank as rear admiral, upper half, which meant he was the equivalent of a major general. His name tag read Spencer. He was followed by a captain, wearing the wings of a Naval Aviator, and a commander with no warfare insignia over his ribbons. "Welcome to the *Independence* and please sit down, gentlemen."

He placed a sealed envelope that was at least three inches thick, stamped Top Secret/SCI, on the table. "A courier from the Pentagon flew out two days ago and handed this to me." He slid the package across the table. "Taped to the outside was a personal letter from my good friend Vice Admiral Hastings, who asked me to personally deliver it to you, and to have my battle group provide whatever support you need to help you execute the mission. It also said that the extra SH-3A on the hangar deck was to be given to you in the best possible condition, and if we needed any parts for it, they would be expedited to the *Independence*. The cover story is that the H-3 is being given to an allied nation, which is why it has been stripped of all its ASW gear and painted in a non-standard paint scheme.

"Captain Sam Ricker here is my chief of staff, and Commander Julio Hector is my intelligence officer. Reading between the lines and the short unofficial note from Admiral Hastings about you, Lieutenant Haman, leads me to believe that this op is in good hands."

Josh waited for a few seconds to make sure that the admiral was finished. "Thank you, sir. If you should get a chance to talk to Vice Admiral Hastings, please thank him for his confidence in Lieutenant Osborne and myself."

"He speaks very highly of you."

"Please, sir, thank him for his kind words."

"No need; from what he wrote, you earned them." The admiral looked around the room. "Our job as delivery boys is done. Off this room is a small office with a new combination which Commander Hector gave me a few minutes ago." The admiral slid a slip of paper across the table with four two digit numbers. "Your passengers are already on board and should be up here in a few minutes. I suspect you'll find the secure space useful, and if you need anything, start with the staff's command duty officer. Everyone on my staff knows that if you come calling, he is to get what you need as soon as possible." The admiral stood up. "Gentlemen, I suspect you have work to do."

The two junior officers stood at attention until the Carrier Group Six officers filed out of the room and closed the door.

"My my, it is not very often that you find an admiral in awe of the accomplishments of a mere lieutenant. Some day you have to tell me more." John couldn't resist mocking his friend, knowing how sensitive he was about the topic.

"Most of it was in the briefings I gave you guys. Admiral Hastings pinned a Navy Cross on my chest and signed off on two of my three Silver Stars."

"My guess this is going to be one of those adventures!" John was smiling as he unsheathed a Fairborn knife from his flight suit and handed it, hilt first, to Josh. The first thing that slid out of the package was an envelope with "Read this first!!!" in Marty Cabot's precise block printing.

JOSH,

IF YOU ARE READING THIS LETTER, IT MEANS THAT YOU ARE ON THE INDEPENDENCE HEADING NORTH. BEFORE THIS PACKAGE WENT OUT, I HAD TO MAKE SURE THAT YOU WOULD BE ON THE FEARLESS, WHICH WAS ONE OF THE REASONS BEHIND MY CALL LAST WEEK. I COULDN'T TELL YOU THAT BECAUSE OF THE SECURITY LEVEL OF THIS OPERATION. ALSO, I WANTED TO LET YOU KNOW THAT ADMIRAL HASTINGS ASKED ME TO COME UP WITH THIS PLAN. HASTINGS SAID THAT IF ANYONE CAN FIGURE OUT HOW TO PROVIDE A SAFE TAXI RIDE THAT MAXIMIZES THE TEAM's TIME ON THE GROUND, YOU COULD. WE PROVIDED THE H-3, NOW YOU NEED TO DO YOUR THING!

LT DICK CARLSON WAS PICKED BY ME TO HELP PLAN AND THEN LEAD THE GROUND PART OF THE MISSION. YOU SHOULD BE MEETING DICK ON THE INDEPENDENCE ALONG WITH COLOR SERGEANT RON CALHOUN AND TWO OF HIS FELLOW MEMBERS OF THE SAS. CALHOUN WILL BE DICK'S NUMBER TWO. CALHOUN SPENT A COUPLE OF YEARS WITH US IN S.E. ASIA. AND WAS MY INSTRUCTOR AT THE BRIT'S JUNGLE WARFARE SCHOOL IN BORNEO. HE IS A FIRST RATE SOLDIER AND COOL UNDER FIRE.

THE MISSION DETAILS ARE IN THE PACKAGE. THIS MISSION HAS A VERY HIGH PRIORITY AND

INTEREST ON BOTH SIDES OF THE ATLANTIC. DICK HAS A DEGREE IN NUCLEAR PHYSICS FROM CANOE U. AND CAN GIVE YOU A LOT MORE DETAILS ON WHY THIS IS SO IMPORTANT. I KEEP TELLING CARLSON THAT HE IS WAY TOO SMART TO BE A SEAL!

WHEN I WAS IN THE U.K. EARLIER IN THE SUMMER, PART OF MY JOB WAS TO GET THE BRIT'S OK AND ASK THE SAS TO PICK THE BEST FOLKS FOR THE JOB. AT THE TIME, I WASN'T SURE IF WE WERE GOING TO GET THE OK FOR THIS MISSION. WHEN ADMIRAL HASTINGS TOLD ME HE WAS SENDING THE BRIEFING PACKAGE, I THOUGHT I WOULD ADD A QUICK NOTE.

GOOD LUCK, AND GOOD HUNTING. TALK TO YOU WHEN YOU GET BACK.

MARTY

Three days later, the two pilots were standing in front of the H-3 that, after a short test flight, they had flown over to the Royal Navy destroyer H.M.S. *Antrim*. The helicopter was tied down on the helo deck, as it was too big to fit into *Antrim's* hangar. The bright evening of late Arctic summer, one hundred miles north of the Norwegian coast, was turning to twilight, but it was still bright enough to cause a dull glint from the helicopter's flat blue-gray paint scheme as the ship pitched and rolled in the five foot swells.

John turned to his friend and co-pilot. "This is my first time this far north and I keep thinking about how we're sailing through strategic waters. Thirty-five years ago, the Royal Navy was escorting convoys up here to the Soviet Union, and the Germans were trying to sink them. Now NATO navies have to prevent Soviet ships and submarines from getting into the Atlantic."

"If we go to war with the Soviets, the war plans say we have to get the Royal Marines to Norway no matter what the weather. That's the purpose of the exercises."

From where he was standing on the County class Royal Navy destroyer, Josh could see the two Norwegian frigates a mile or so to either side, with one about half a mile ahead and the other the same distance behind. "Weather is supposed to be good for a few days."

"Yes it is. It is going to be lovely. A month or so from now, it starts to get very ugly."

Wednesday, August 25th, 1976, 0846 local time, Barents Sea

They had been flying a constant heading at one thousand feet and one hundred knots into the Arctic morning twilight for almost three hours when they sighted a red flare fired by a Norwegian fisheries patrol vessel as a recognition signal. Josh descended in a wide circle to give the small ship a chance to turn into the light wind.

After hoisting the refueling hose up from the flight deck to the H-3, Josh kept the helicopter thirty feet off the water and about thirty feet abeam off the right side while the ship steamed northeast into rolling swells at a steady twelve knots. It took twenty minutes to take on twenty-four hundred pounds of jet fuel. With internal and external tanks full, Josh eased the helicopter over the deck while the hose was lowered and detached before he dumped the nose and continued heading east with all the helicopter's radios and navigational aids turned off.

The plan was that they would switch roles every twenty minutes during the flight to share navigation and flying duties. Now that the refueling was finished, it was John's turn to fly. Josh keyed the intercom with the tip of his forefinger. "You know, John, this is the most alone I have ever been in a helicopter."

"What do you mean?"

"Think about it. The safety net is gone. We can't just call for help if something goes wrong. In Vietnam, if the shit hit the fan, we could call someone on the radio and help would arrive in minutes, or at least we would know it was on its way. Where we're going, we may not be heard. And a more sobering question is, who could come to our rescue?"

"Well, the operation tasks a Norwegian P-3 to be on patrol. They should be able to hear any call for help."

"True. But we've not communicated with the P-3. We don't know where it is. And we can't tell him where we are going or where we've been. If we go down, it will be a race between the good guys and the Russkies!"

"True enough, but as we Brits like to say, I'm confident we'll muddle through."

"This kind of independence is one of the joys of missions like this. We are on our own. We make our own decisions, and that means we have about as much control over what will happen as anyone could have. So let's get in and out as fast as possible."

"Agreed." Josh scanned the gauges for the umpteenth time, making sure everything was normal. He wrote down the readings on a kneeboard card they passed back and forth, depending on who was flying, so they could track a trend if needed, rather than rely on memory.

Josh looked at the chart and then the clock. "Ok, time to adjust the heading. Deviation here is twenty-five degrees east. We're approaching the point where we need to drop down to one hundred feet. The Soviets have a radar station on top of the five thousand foot mountain just west of the town of Belushya Guba on the southern end of the island. Our radar warning system hasn't picked up any transmissions, so it may not be on the air. They shouldn't be able to pick us up out here at one thousand feet, but let's not take any chances." Josh checked the handwritten details of their flight plan. "Fuel burn has been better than planned, so let's stay at one hundred knots. We should see the mountains of Novaya Zemlya in about twenty minutes. And so far the weather guessers were spot on with their forecast of light winds, but this is the Arctic, which is known for its unpredictability."

Josh's reference to the helicopter's fuel consumption was based on meticulous fuel burn calculations that had been part of their planning. They had used the charts in the flight manual to compare ninety, one hundred, one hundred ten, and one hundred twenty knots; and settled on one hundred as the best compromise between ground speed and fuel burn.

"Descending now."

As they came down, the long rolling swells of the gray-blue Barents Sea became clearer. Josh kept thinking how lucky they were; today's weather was in marked contrast to what he'd read about World War II: convoys of ships coated with ice battling heavy seas as they steamed to Murmansk.

"Land. And it isn't a mirage. Those are snow-capped mountains." John's voice was matter-of-fact.

Josh studied the distant peaks. "Well, we're about to see how good our navigation is. Flying a heading that is between twenty-five and thirty degrees off what the magnetic compass says is weird."

"Everyone, keep an eye out for other planes." Josh pulled the tactical pilotage chart of the island out of the navigation bag next to his seat, along with several satellite photos. "Intelligence says the Russians have a squadron of twenty-four twin engine YAK-28P fighters, along with about a dozen MI-8 helicopters based at Rogachevo, which is the airfield right by the town. The helos carry technicians up and down the island as needed, so they fly on an unpredictable schedule. Let's hope they're not flying today. Also, we had a report that a KGB Grisha frigate pulled into the port at Belushya Guba, and the Soviets have several small patrol boats. We should be well north of the port, but you never know whether they decided to go for a sail in this delightful weather!"

Josh felt the rush of cold, forty-five degree air through the cabin as the top of the passenger door and the cargo door were opened to allow the air crewmen to scan the sky to the left side and rear. "Dick, we think we're less than thirty minutes out, assuming we are anywhere near where we think we are."

The barren, grey-black rock cliffs that marked the shoreline of Severny, the northernmost island of the two that make up Novaya Zemlya, loomed in front of them. The island was home to a large settlement called Beluysha Guba. Most of the town's residents were workers assigned to support the Soviet nuclear tests on the island that began in 1954. In addition, the intelligence data suggested there were about two hundred local natives, called Nestenes, who roamed the two islands, trapping and fishing for food.

To the H-3's left was a large, dark green, flat area, looking like either moss or some type of grass, coming into focus as they closed in on the island. John keyed the mike. "I think we're one valley north of where we thought we would make landfall. My suggestion is that we follow the canyon in front of us over the mountain, then come down on the other side and go where we want to land. Josh, it's time you took over the flying."

"I've got it." Josh slowed the helicopter to about ninety knots before they crossed the coastline and added power to keep the helicopter about forty feet above the ice as they climbed over the glacier. Cresting the mountain, they saw black hulls of anchored barges contrasted with deep, blue-gray water and the chunks of last winter's ice floating in the bay and the Kara Sea. The barges with the nuclear reactors and drums of spent fuel were nestled along a narrow peninsula right where the satellite photos had shown them to be.

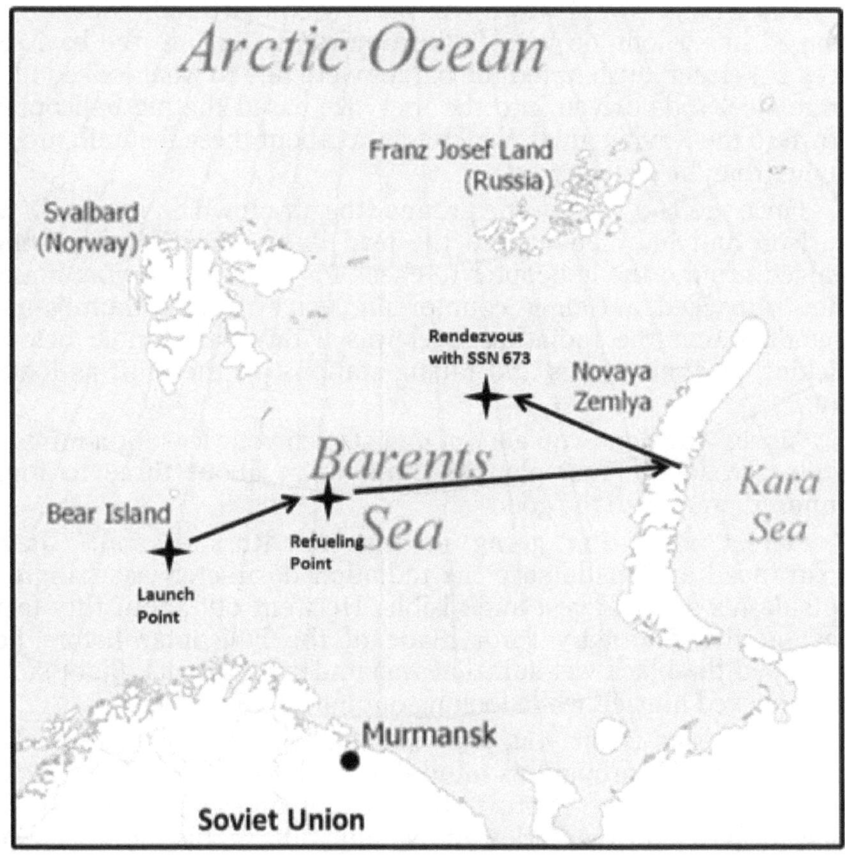

"Dick, five minutes to touchdown. You've got an hour—no more. Thirty minutes or less would be better."

"We're ready. It shouldn't take that long. We want to limit our exposure as much as possible. Both of you make sure you have your dosimeters where you can see them. I've checked the three guys back here. We're all set."

Josh turned around and saw the SEAL and members of the Special Air Service, already in their white anti-radiation suits and holding their masks. The tie downs for two gray, lead-lined plastic boxes that looked like large ice coolers would be removed when they land.

"John, as soon as they exit the airplane, let's shut down everything except the number one engine to save fuel and recalculate our fuel consumption."

"Right oh."

The SH-3A swept down the narrow spit of land, which was shaped like a lollipop with its head sticking out into the bay. As they got closer, Josh noted the barges were tied to what looked like large steel rods driven into the rock. He eased the big helicopter down to the waving grass, which was, at about three feet tall, much higher than he'd suspected.

Once the H-3 was on the ground, the air crewmen helped Dick Carlson and his men unload the lead lined coolers before they walked around the helicopter to check for damage. Finding none, they unpacked a Geiger counter and gave Josh a thumbs-up, signaling that the radiation level was within safe limits, before picking up their M-16s and taking stations on the bluff as lookouts.

"Josh, why don't you get out and stretch your legs for a minute while I redo the fuel plan? I think we're about three to four hundred pounds to the good."

"Great idea; I'm going to piss on Russian soil!" Josh unstrapped and made sure the radiation dosimeter was hanging outside his survival vest and visible. He went out about fifty feet beyond the stationary rotor blade of the helicopter before he unzipped the black wet suit that was under his Nomex flight suit, and relieved himself while looking out into the Kara Sea.

"Artur, this is for you," he said out loud, and smiled as the thought passed through his mind that his late father-in-law who'd hated Stalin would approve his pissing on Soviet land. Josh pushed pleasant memories of Natalie out of his mind as he reached down and picked up a tuft of grass and a few rocks and stuffed them into a plastic bag that went into a boot pocket of his flight suit.

Josh was writing a note with the time, place, latitude and longitude to stick in the plastic bag when he heard a yell from one of the air crewmen, who was running past the H-3's nose and pointing toward the bay. Josh thought he was pointing toward Dick Carlson and the three others struggling uphill toward the helicopter lugging the lead lined boxes, until he saw a patrol boat with what looked like a small cannon on the bow, headed in their direction.

"Go help those guys get on board ASAP!" he yelled to the air crewmen. "We need to take-off as soon as we can!"

As quickly as he could, Josh climbed back into the pilot's seat. The dull thuds of the two containers landing in the cabin were distinct from the increasing whine of the number two engine starting. As soon as it was up to speed, Josh released the rotor brake while John finished the engine startup and take-off check lists.

"Everyone's on board, boss. We're ready to go in the back," the senior air crewman reported over the intercom. Josh hooked his shoulder straps into the seat belt and pulled them tight.

"Lifting. Everyone keep a sharp lookout. We're almost in range of that gun, and the ship may have called friends who will be here any minute." With that, he pulled up on the collective. As soon as the helicopter was ten feet in the air he dumped the nose, called for the gear to be retracted, and began to accelerate up the mountain at full power.

John pointed to the right. "Let's go up that valley. It gives us a shorter route to the other side of the island and we should be hard to see or hear outside the valley. The Soviets now know we're here and where we've been. The question is, what are they going to do about it?"

"My guess is they'll try to shoot us down! We're going to go as fast and as low as we can to make it hard for them to find us. But that will eat up some of the fuel we saved."

"That's O.K! It's about two hundred miles to the rendezvous, and based on my recheck, we have about two hundred pounds more fuel than our plan, so we should arrive with nearly fifty minutes of gas to spare."

"Optimist." Josh grinned at his co-pilot. "You are assuming of course, that (a) the sub will be where it is supposed to be; (b) we can find it; and (c) we don't get shot down."

"I am. You don't survive very long in this business unless you are an optimist. Have faith, Yank!"

The helicopter was nose down and close to one hundred and twenty knots when it began to shudder. Josh lowered the collective and pulled back on the cyclic until the vibration lessened, noting that at their current weight one hundred and ten was as fast as the helicopter could go before it either shook itself apart or the blades stalled. "I'm going to keep us at one hundred and ten until we are sure we are out of danger."

"Good idea. When we slow down, I'll recalculate our fuel plan. And, oh by the way, I never got to take a piss!"

"When we get out to sea, you can use the relief tube! I'll hold it nice and level for you."

John made a rude gesture in response.

"Josh, John; Dick here. Mission accomplished. We got what we came for, and that's parts from reactors taken from an Alpha and what we think was a Victor II. They should give us great data on their subs' nuclear fuels, metallurgy, and the materials the Soviets are using in the Alfa class submarines. I'll tell you more when things calm down."

"Thanks, Dick."

"Going feet wet in about three minutes." John rechecked the notes on the chart. "Steer three-four-zero when we go feet wet."

"Give me another heading more to the west. I don't want to lead them to the rendezvous."

"Fly two-nine-zero for fifty nautical. We should be O.K. I'll work out the track and the new heading to the rendezvous when we turn northwest again."

"I'll use two-nine-zero as a base course in case I have to do some violent maneuvering, but we will have to figure out how far off we are from tracking three-four-zero."

"Right. Got it."

"Josh; Dick."

"Go."

"If you need to lighten the load, we'll take the food and medical stuff out of our packs and then dump the guns, ammo and the rest in deep water. It'll save us about three hundred pounds. Will that help?"

"Yes, but don't do anything until we get over deeper water and I tell you to toss it out. As of now, we shouldn't have to dump your equipment."

Josh kept the helicopter at one hundred and ten knots and eighty feet over the water, it was high enough so that the rotor wash wouldn't leave a wake and low enough that airborne radar would have a hard time distinguishing the rotor disk from the reflected sea surface.

"Boss, we've got company! Two bogeys, seven to eight o'clock and very high. It looks like they are crossing from eight o'clock to four o'clock."

"I can't see them." John craned his head to the left, trying to look aft and high. "Let me know if they start down."

Josh rolled the helicopter and changed the heading so that he could watch the incoming jets and still head seaward. "They're Yak-28s. John, how long to the twelve mile limit?"

"We're there now, but the Russians don't always honor it. Up here, it'll be hard to prove where we were if they shoot us down."

"If they follow the rules, one jet should come down to identify us to make sure we're not one of their own. But they already know that, because we were not on their flight schedule. Once they see the star and bar on the side, they're supposed to encourage us to turn toward their base. Since I don't think any of us want to be long term guests of the KGB, we won't cooperate, which is when they will try to shoot us down."

"You sure?" John loosened his harness and pulled himself forward to get a better view of the YAK-28s.

"No; who knows what they'll actually do." Josh checked all the readouts before continuing. "International rules of engagement say they are to fly by us to make a positive identification first, then contact us on the radio on one of the two international distress frequencies. Then they are supposed to encourage us to land at the nearest airport by making a pass with their wheels down, and after they pass in front of us, turn in the direction they want us to go. Of course, that's risky; no one wants to be shot from behind, so it's protocol to return to a rear position. The next escalation is gunfire parallel to us, followed by another wheels-down pass. Then, if we are still in their territorial airspace and not responding, and/or if we do something that appears to be hostile, they can shoot us down. So the game plan is: we are an innocent and very lost unarmed helicopter!"

"Do you believe that?" John wasn't sure if Josh was being sarcastic or serious.

"Innocent, no. Unarmed, yes. Lost, that's to be determined. Their response is the unknown."

"You do realize that the Soviets don't follow international law unless it is convenient for them." John had his head locked on the two Yak 28s, now in a loose trail formation. "When they think their airspace has been violated in sensitive areas, they tend to shoot first and ask questions later. And Nova Zemlya is a sensitive area!"

"I was just reciting the international rules of engagement!" Josh changed to a more serious tone. "But you're right, and my bet is that they'll try to shoot us down. That way there is only one side to the story. They can deny anything ever happened. Our families will be told we are missing, presumed killed, and never know the truth." Josh craned his head to the right to get a better view of the Soviet aircraft at the same time he flexed his fingers. He could feel the fear grow in his stomach; he reminded himself this was not the time to let it govern his actions.

"I'm not ready to let them tell the only version of the story! I'll turn on the HF and UHF radios in case the try to contact us."

Josh stared at the black radome on the descending twin engine fighter. From the two black plumes of jet exhaust, he could gage the corrections the Soviet pilot made to make sure the diving twin-engine fighter passed behind the SH-3A. *O.K. asshole, what are you planning to do? It's time to take the initiative and make you change your plan.*

"Hang on everyone. Turning hard left now, and then we will be coming hard right." Josh pushed the cyclic to the left and pulled up on the collective to maintain one hundred plus knots as he stayed in the sixty degree bank, then, without pausing, after thirty degrees of turn he rolled it the other direction and let the g's increase a bit. The SH-3A uttered the usual shuddering and vibrating protests that all helicopters give out as the blades led and lagged and flapped as they adjusted.

"Holy shit! Sir, the Yak crashed into the ocean at about our five o'clock!"

"Whaaaaat?" Josh watched the horizon as he spoke and rolled the helicopter right.

"Sir, as soon as you started your turns, the Yak tried to pull out of his dive but plowed right into the water!"

Josh could see an oily black plume of smoke from burning jet fuel off to his right. "Where's his friend? Anyone see him?"

The two "No"s were drowned out by the screeching of the radar warning receiver, which went right to the warbling tone that indicated they were targeted. "John, are the chaff and flare dispensers armed?"

"Yes, they're ready," John responded as he checked the switches to make sure.

The tone in Josh's headset kept rising and falling in volume as the Yak pilot tried to keep his fire control radar on the turning helicopter.

"O.K. gang, I'm going to complicate his firing solution." Josh pulled back on the cyclic and the helicopter climbed. "John, as soon as we are level at one thousand feet and seventy-five knots, pump out four chaff bundles and four flares in that order as fast as you can."

John clicked the mike switch twice. As soon he saw a thousand feet on the altimeter and seventy-five knots on the airspeed indicator, he pushed the decoy fire button four times, rotated the switch to flares and counted four more bangs. "Chaff and flares away."

"Going up to one hundred plus knots for about ten seconds. When I reach one hundred knots pump out four more chaff bundles, and then we're going down to forty feet and sixty-five knots."

"Sir, he's at our seven o'clock and diving!" The air crewman's voice was at a very high pitch. "Oh my god, sir, he shot a big-assed missile at us!"

Josh saw the plume of the white Kalingrad K-8, also known by its NATO air-to-air missile designation as an AA-2 Anab. He wondered if the Yak-28 had shot the radar guided version or the infrared one. Their intelligence briefing said they flew with one of each. The nose of the Soviet fighter was still pointed at the SH-3A, which was now just forty feet over the water and running at seventy knots. Just before the nose of the two-seat fighter began to rise, a second large missile began to corkscrew toward the helicopter.

The first Anab was well astern and went right between two chaff clouds before slamming into the water without exploding. "When I tell you, pump out four flares as fast as you can!"

"You've got a plan?"

"Yeah, sort of. I hope the flares float for a few seconds." Josh glanced at the water and then looked over his shoulder at the incoming missile. "Now, NOW, NOW!!!"

As the flares went arcing out of the port launcher, Josh turned to put the missile on the H-3's nose. When it was about one thousand yards away, he pushed the nose down so hard that everyone felt almost weightless. "Four more flares. Now, *NOW, NOW*!"

Seconds later, the blast from the missile's eighty-eight pound blast fragmentation warhead shook the helicopter.

"Any damage? And can anyone see the Yak?" Josh didn't feel anything unusual as he rolled the helicopter to three-four-zero in a gentle ten degree angle of bank. A glance at the instrument panel confirmed why John hadn't said any caution lights. There were none, and all the gauges were in their normal ranges.

"Yes, and he's climbing. It looks like he's returning to base, now that he has nothing left to shoot us with."

"I'm hoping that by the time his friends come out, we'll be far out to sea and hard to find." Josh took a deep breath and flexed his hands. "I don't think we went far off course."

"We meandered about a bit, but I think we're all right."

"Good, you fly for a while. Stay at fifty feet and fly three-five-zero at a hundred knots for five minutes and then come back to three-four-zero. I'll try to figure out how much fuel we have left." Josh took his hands off the controls. His left leg was shaking so bad he had to rest his left hand on his knee to stop it. *Fuck, that was close!!!*

Two uneventful hours later, Josh double-checked to see if the UHF radio was on and set to the proper channel. The SH-3 was cruising at one thousand feet and one hundred knots with twenty-five minutes of fuel left, and he was wondering how soon the low fuel lights were going to come on when he keyed the mike. "Peter Pan, this is Jolly Roger broadcasting in the blind. Repeat, Peter Pan, this is Jolly Roger broadcasting in the blind. If you are up, give us a short count."

Josh repeated the radio call three times at three minute intervals. After the fourth, and just as the low fuel warning lights came on, he heard the "One, two, three, four, five, four, three, two, one," he had been seeking. The number 1 needle on the radar magnetic indicator linked to the UHF radio flickered, spun around the dial twice, then stopped at a position ten degrees off to the right.

John, who had been flying for over an hour, nodded his head as he adjusted the heading so that the needle was vertical

Josh keyed the mike. "Jolly Roger authenticating. Apache, repeat, Apache."

"Peter Pan authenticating. Teepee, repeat, Teepee."

"Guys, it is show time." Josh reached for the controls. "John, I've got it. Everyone get ready for a water landing. I hate to say it, but aside from our little incident on the way back, this next part is the most dangerous."

John was stowing gear in the cockpit when something made him glance up and to the right. "There's the sub." The white numbers six, seven and three were visible on her conning tower. A sailor held a flare over his head that billowed orange smoke as

Josh passed astern of the sub. He could see two sailors inflating a boat on the deck as he turned the helicopter into the light wind.

The option of taking on fuel from the nuclear powered sub had been discarded in the planning process for two reasons. Subs rarely practiced the technique, and even if they could fill the tanks, they would need to refuel a second time to make it back to a Norwegian base. Not impossible, but by then they would have been airborne in a helicopter that was near the end of its service life for more than twelve hours. The most logical thing to do was not push their luck, but ditch then sink the helicopter once everyone was safely off.

"How many times have you landed one of these things in the sea?"

"In the ocean, never. In a lake, dozens. We were taught water landings in the H-3 RAG in San Diego and I was supposed to be the resident expert. We used a lake so we didn't have to deal with the corrosive effects of salt water. Anyway, as an instructor, I had to qualify with six landings; and then each time I took a student out I had to demonstrate the technique. But we didn't have the rolling swells of the Barents, and the water, even in the winter, was in the sixties."

"I'm glad someone on this helicopter knows how to make a water landing!"

Josh laughed. "Prepare for ditching."

"Ready in the back. Ditching checklist complete, we're all strapped in, cargo is tied down. The cargo door and windows have been jettisoned." All was ready and everyone had a clear path to a door.

"John, let's get rid of the cockpit windows." The helicopter was slowing below seventy knots.

John nodded and both of them pulled the release levers and pushed the windows into the slipstream with their elbows.

After the windows fell out, Josh eased down on the collective to let the SH-3A settle toward the water about two hundred yards from the sub. At twenty feet, white spray enveloped the helicopter, making it almost impossible to see. John called out the height above the water, as indicated by the radar altimeter, in five foot increments and then stopped as the H-3 transitioned from a flying helicopter to a boat.

"Boss," the senior air crewman said over the mike, "the boat from the sub is coming alongside. If it's OK with you, we'll transfer the containers and the passengers first."

Josh applied a little forward stick and taxied the H-3 through the water at about three knots, which made it easier to control and more stable. "Do it, and tell the boat driver that on the second trip he's to take everyone off but me, then wait outside the rotors on the starboard side until I get it shut down. Then he can come pick me up. If it starts to roll over, I'll get out somehow and you can fish me out of the water."

"Yes sir. Got it."

"John, go ahead and unstrap and get back to the cargo door with the rest of the crew. This thing is top heavy, and if it turns turtle I don't want you trapped in it. I can shut it down by myself." Josh looked back in the cabin.

John was half out of his seat. "Water looks very cold."

"It is a balmy forty degrees Fahrenheit. Help me get out of my vest. You take it with you. Don't worry, I'll float in my wet suit, and this will reduce the chances I'll snag something if I have to go out the window."

Josh leaded forward and, with John's help, shrugged off his survival vest, at the same time keeping a slight forward pressure on the stick to keep the H-3 moving through the gentle swells. Once out of the vest, he glanced over his shoulder in time to see the heavy box manhandled into the boat.

While he waited for the boat to come back, Josh eased the cyclic back so the helicopter was barely moving through the water. He didn't want to get too far from the sub.

When John called out that he was getting into the boat, Josh waited until he saw the raft was clear before pulling the two speed selectors straight back to the idle cut-off position. As the engines wound down, he applied the rotor brake with constant pressure to minimize the effect that the decrease in torque had on the helicopter's stability in the water. Without the rotor system to stabilize the helicopter, the H-3 began a sickening pitch and roll in the three foot swells; water began to splash into the cockpit through the open side windows.

The rolling helicopter almost tossed Josh into the water before the boat returned for him. The helmsman took hold of the cargo door frame to keep the boat against the side of the helicopter. Josh pulled the pin on the detonator, which was set for two minutes, and tossed the two pound brick of C4 up into the fuselage as the rubber raft backed away. They were almost to the sub when the explosion broke the H-3 in two, sinking it in six hundred feet of water.

Saturday, August 28th, 1912 local time, 1946, Holy Loch

The black acoustic coating of the U.S.S. *Flying Fish* glistened in the yellow arc lights along the pier at the U.S. Naval Base in Scotland. Like the others from the helicopter, Josh was wearing blue submarine coveralls lent him by the crew. In recognition of his designation, there was a pair of gold Naval Aviator wings above the right pocket. In his pocket was a card that said he was now a member of the Order of the Blue Nose, which meant he had been above the Arctic Circle. The submarine's administrative officer assured him that a letter noting that fact would be sent to the Bureau of Naval Personnel and the Royal Navy for inclusion in all their service records.

He was carrying his olive-drab helmet bag, holding his flight suit stuffed into his helmet, as he approached the enlisted man on the makeshift quarterdeck.

"Sir, at the end of the gangway there's a passenger van. Behind it, there's a small van for your gear. The truck taking the radioactive material to the airport for the flight back to the States is the last one in line."

Josh looked around. The *Flying Fish* was the sole submarine on the pier. Behind the two vans, there was a large stake truck from which sailors were already unloading fresh fruits and vegetables. Lined up behind him were the nine men from the mission to Novaya Zemlya. "Thank you, petty officer Henderson. Again, that was good work with the boat."

"Thank you, sir. Glad you had a successful trip." The boatswain's mate who'd handled the rubber inflatable boat smiled and saluted.

After tossing his bag into the back of an empty British-made Bedford CA panel truck, Josh looked into the passenger van, seeing three bench seats in the back, plus the ones for the driver and passenger, making it a tight fit for the nine of them.

"Everybody's aboard, sir." Colour Sergeant Major Calhoun slid the side door shut as Josh got into the passenger's seat

As they exited the naval base, Josh turned to the driver, who was wearing the fatigues of the Royal Marines. "Private, where are we going?"

"Off base, sir." He then went back to his driving, so Josh turned in his seat. "Colour Sergeant Calhoun, what's going on? Why are we leaving the base?"

"Don't know, sir, but after these hush-hush ops, they often take us to some secluded place to debrief. Some are very posh and some are, well, let's just say they are a bit Spartan. Anyway, we'll spend the next two or three days being poked and prodded by the medical types and then be asked the same question in seven different ways until the intelligence boffins are convinced that they have gotten everything of value out of our brains. Meanwhile, they'll feed us pretty well. Might even a have a drink or two, and all on the Queen's shilling."

As they headed into the moors of Western Scotland, Josh couldn't help thinking of the eight years he spent at Gordonstoun, an English school in Moray, about one hundred and fifty miles northeast of Holy Loch and about twenty miles east of Inverness.

When Rebekah and he were exchanging stories about their childhood, he told her how at age eight he was bundled off to Gordonstoun because his mother, a teacher, wanted him to have a proper British education. There Josh was the only American, and of "modest means"—which was a polite British way of saying he was middle class. His classmates often kidded him by referring to him the "damned Colonial".

At Gordonstoun he learned to play polo, and became a pretty good soccer player, but his favorite sport was fencing. He was much better at sports than in the classroom, and often told his fellow Naval officers he learned American history from the Scottish perspective. And oh, by the way, in a class four years behind him there was a lot of hubbub surrounding a chap by the name of Prince Charles who someday would be the king of England.

Before he reporting to 846 Squadron, he'd driven Rebekah, who'd just found out she was pregnant, along the narrow, windy, twisty roads to show her Moray. The rugged drive had made the nausea and morning sickness worse, but once there she fell in love with the castles and the hills that surrounded Inverness and Beauty Firth. Every time a Scotsman with a heavy brogue had spoken to her, she'd give Josh a look that said, "translate please."

The crunching through the down gears and the slowing of the van brought Josh back to reality. There were no lights along the humpbacked road lined with low stone fences, and the van's headlights didn't go far enough to show much, but the driver seemed to know where he was going.

The van slowed to a crawl as the driver turned into a gap in the low stone wall and onto a gravel road that led off into the darkness. When it stopped, Josh saw one man and then another appear alongside.

"Evening, sergeant," the private said through the rolled down window.

"Evening, gentlemen." The sergeant was carrying a clip board and had a British-made L1A1 rifle slung over his shoulder. Josh noted that a magazine was in the rifle. Another Royal Marine, with camouflage paint on his face, was also carrying one of the Belgian-designed rifles, manufactured under license in the U.K, cradled in his arms. "Would you gentlemen mind stepping out and standing in a line? This will take just a moment." While the speaker made it sound like a request, it was an order. The men lined up by the side of the van.

"Like lambs to slaughter," Colour Sergeant Calhoun mumbled, and the men, who had sorted themselves into a line based on their rank, chuckled.

"The chaps in the big house are very picky about who we let in." The smiling sergeant looked at the picture of each man on the clipboard and then at the man. When he had finished, he came to attention in front of Josh and saluted. "Sorry for the inconvenience sir, but we have to make sure we keep the riffraff out."

Josh returned the salute from the position of attention. "No problem, sergeant."

They re-entered the van, were driven around a hill, and stopped in front of a wide set of steps leading up to the red-painted double door of a three-story manor house. In the shadows, Josh saw two more two-man fire teams. A tall skinny man wearing civilian clothes was waiting on the steps. He didn't say anything until all of them were out of the van.

"Good evening, I'm Jack Donaldson from the U.S. Office of Naval Intelligence. Welcome to Stewart House. When you go inside, please go into the first room on the right, where you'll talk to a doctor for a few minutes and a corpsman will draw some blood. The submarine crew has already tested you, but we want to make absolutely sure that you have not been over-exposed to radiation. After the exam, you'll be shown into the study where we have a small bar and some refreshments. Please feel free to help yourself, courtesy of Her Majesty's government." He looked at his watch. "It's 20:49 and we should be wrapped up with the medical stuff in less than an hour. When we're all in the study and have had a drink or two, we'll show you to your rooms, where your respective governments have provided you with proper uniforms. Breakfast is served between 06:30 and 07:30 in the dining room, and the debriefings start at 07:45 tomorrow morning."

Josh waited until everyone was in the study and had a glass. "Gentlemen, Her Majesty the Queen."

"The Queen" chorused the assembled men.

He took a swallow and enjoyed the mild burning in his throat, while his other senses savored the smoky Ardbeg scotch from the island of Islay.

John held up his glass. "The President of the United States."

"The President."

After each man took a sip, Dick Carlson looked around the room and realized it was his turn to make a toast. "To the two greatest navies in the world."

"U.S. and Royal Navies."

The Colour Sergeant waited until everyone who needed a refill was accommodated. "To the 22nd Special Air Service Regiment, Her Majesty's Special Forces, and our American counterparts!"

With the informal, unofficial, but to Josh's mind, necessary toasts completed, he turned to the senior SAS enlisted man. "Colour Sergeant Calhoun, why did they pick this place for a debrief? Didn't they have a secure facility at Holy Loch they could use?"

"Sir, they like to get us away from everyone for security reasons. It also keeps us together. At the base, the enlisted would have been segregated from the officers." He swirled his glass, which had started with four fingers of the same scotch Josh was drinking and was now well below one. "Good stuff this, sir." He took a sip. "Been on a couple of these ops, and they set up a security perimeter as part of a training exercise. My guess is that this place was picked because the owner was behind in his taxes and Her Majesty is using this place for a few days to offset what is owed. It's been done that way before."

"That is an unusual way to handle the payment of back taxes. Our IRS could learn a lesson or two from you."

John waved his finger at Josh. "You don't want that!"

Sunday, August 29th, 1503 local time, 1976, Scotland

Josh was browsing through the shelves that lined three walls of the library on the second floor of Stewart House when Jack Donaldson came into the room, followed by John. Their entry interrupted Josh's perusal of an old edition of poetry by Robert Burns.

"Josh, there's a man from the State Department who is not part of the official debriefing team in the sitting room at the end of the hall. He wants to talk to both John and you." Donaldson looked at his clipboard. "He's the last person on your schedule. Tomorrow, you're going back to Holy Loch, where you'll be flown to the *Independence* and then to the *Fearless*."

"By 'not part of the official team,' do you mean that he doesn't know a lot about the mission?"

"Correct. His name is Brent Gibson and he is not cleared to know why you went to Novaya Zemlya. He knows that you flew around up there, but nothing else, and he is not cleared for this operation, nor will he be. We were told to allow him to come here. Gibson was brought here blindfolded and as soon as you finish, we'll send him back to Holy Loch where he can take a train back to London."

"Understood. I'm guessing the blindfold made him very happy!" The other two men chuckled. "Let's get on with it." Josh slid the leather-bound book back onto the shelf where he had found it and followed the other men down the hall.

"Enjoy!" Donaldson's sarcasm was plain as led them to another sitting room and closed the door behind the two officers with a soft click. Ensconced on a couch at the far end of the small room was a man wearing a three-piece suit and a red and blue striped tie. As he stood up he flashed his cuffs, and for some reason Josh took an instant dislike to the man even while shaking his well-manicured hand. *Why the fuck are you here?*

"Brent Gibson, State Department."

"Josh Haman." He didn't bother to use his rank because he assumed it was already known.

Gibson, who if he wore elevator shoes might make it to five foot six, motioned to two chairs positioned in front of a coffee table on which sat a reel-to-reel tape recorder. Again flashing his cuffs to display what Josh presumed to be diamonds decorating a pair of silver cuff links, Gibson unsnapped a leather briefcase and took out a yellow legal pad.

Both aviators sat with their feet crossed and their hands in their laps waiting for Gibson to proceed.

"Do you mind if I tape this interview?"

"Not at all, as long as there is a second tape recorder and John and I get one of the original tapes." *I've been down this road before!*

"Interesting request. Redundancy. Good idea. As a matter of fact, I have a cassette recorder with me as well. I use it to record my notes. We can use that as a back-up."

"Excellent. Then Lieutenant Osborne and I can have the tape reel when we are done, and you can drop the cassette in your briefcase. Be easier for you to carry that way." *And, asshole, if the other recorder is a dud, I have the original.*

Gibson looked at Josh for a few seconds and then smiled. "Fair enough." He put the cassette recorder on the table next to the microphone, pushed the start buttons on both machines, and began to speak.

"This is Brent Gibson, a senior executive service State Department employee on the staff of the Assistant Secretary of State for Military Affairs. It is Tuesday, August twenty-ninth, nineteen hundred and seventy six, and I am interviewing Lieutenant Joshua Haman, United States Navy, and Lieutenant John Osborne, Royal Navy. The reason for the interview is a recent flight in the Barents Sea. For the record, will both of you gentlemen identify yourselves so we can distinguish your voices later?"

Each officer enunciated his name, rank and service in turn.

"Thank you." Gibson let a few seconds pass. "Lieutenant Haman, I understand that you were the helicopter aircraft commander who flew an SH-3A helicopter on a mission on August 26th in the Barents Sea."

"Yes, I did. Lieutenant Osborne was my co-pilot."

"Who was on board?"

"We had a crew of four and four passengers."

"Can you give me more details on who was on board?"

"Four members of the U.S. Navy and four members of Her Majesty's forces. Why?"

Gibson flashed an annoyed look as if to say, *I am asking the questions.* "Can you at tell me their names?"

"You have ours. That is enough. Again, why do you want this information?"

Gibson looked at his list of questions. "Why were you in the vicinity of the Soviet Union?"

"We were on a classified mission. The mission was authorized by the president of the United States and the prime minister of the United Kingdom and assigned to me as the mission and aircraft commander."

"Were you given written orders, Lieutenant?"

"To fly the mission?"

"Yes."

"Yes, Mr. Gibson. I had written orders and tasking detailed in a briefing package that was couriered out to the U.S.S. *Independence* and given to me. We planned the mission on the carrier. Again, it was classified at a very high level and the code words for the mission itself are classified as well, so you won't find the mission on the carrier's air plan." *And, classified well above your level of access, asshole.*

"Do you have a copy of those orders?"

"Not with me. We left the planning documents on the U.S.S. *Independence*." That wasn't a lie, even though the orders were now in a room on the third floor. "I don't believe that the State Department will be given access to them or to our after-action report."

"We'll see about that." Gibson consulted his notes on a yellow legal pad. "Do you know who has custody of the documents at this time?"

"No, I do not. I signed them over to the carrier battle group's intelligence officer before we took off."

"What happened on this classified mission?"

"We took the team to where they were supposed to go and brought them back. It went as planned." *I wouldn't call it routine, unless you consider crossing two hundred miles of ocean above the Arctic Circle using dead reckoning, dodging two air-to-air missiles, finding a submarine in the middle of the Barents Sea, and then ditching a helicopter routine.* "More I can't tell you."

"Did you encounter any member of the armed forces of the Soviet Union?"

"Are you asking me if we had a conversation over a glass of vodka with them or engaged in battle, then the answer is no. We were fired upon by the Soviets and did not carry the types of weapons needed to shoot back. So by definition there was no battle, because to have a firefight, both sides have to shoot. We never fired a shot."

"Don't fence with me Lieutenant. I know what happened."

Do you? Josh counted *one one thousand, two one thousand,* and then spoke. "Then suppose you tell me, because, if you do, I am at a loss as to why we are having this conversation." John turned away with his hand over his mouth to keep Gibson from seeing his smile.

"I gather you are not aware that the Soviet Union has filed a diplomatic protest with the United States and another in the United Nations saying that one of their fighters, which was unarmed at the time, was shot down over the Barents Sea by a U.S. helicopter. Based on queries by the Secretary of State to the Department of Defense, we determined that the only U.S. helicopter that was flying up there on that date was yours. So, would you care to tell me what happened and how you managed to shoot down a Soviet fighter from a helicopter?"

"No, neither John nor I were aware of any protests. I would prefer to hear more about what the Soviets claimed. Their creativity should be entertaining."

"Very well." Gibson cleared his throat as he fished a sheet from his briefcase. "Their diplomatic note says that an American attack helicopter shot down one of their fighters, something they call a Yak-28 interceptor, which I was told had the NATO code name of Firebar. The incident happened northeast of Murmansk, and their airplane was on a routine training mission when it was downed, killing both crew members."

"Fascinating." Josh paused for a few seconds, hoping to refrain from laughing or sounding sarcastic or as if he were talking down to the State Department twit. "Did they say how this attack helicopter shot the Yak-28 down?"

"Yes, the Soviet report was very detailed. Their protest included this information and our experts said, based on this, it is very authoritative." Gibson snapped the paper as he handed Josh a copy of the write-up from *Jane's All the Worlds Aircraft 1975* on the H-3. "The Soviet note to the State Department had very strong language and has a lot of important people asking questions. According to the Soviets, the pilot of a second jet that survived the attack said the helicopter used a fast firing cannon and flare decoys when it shot down his flight leader. It also states that the Soviet airplanes were following international rules regarding unauthorized penetration of a country's airspace when the Yak-28s were attacked."

Gibson rummaged through his open brief case and pulled out two black and white pictures. "This is the model of the helicopter they said shot down the Russian jet, and this one was taken by the second Yak-28 who observed the shoot down."

Josh looked at the first picture and started to laugh as he handed the eight by ten inch photo to John. "This is a publicity photo of the HH-3A prototype on the ramp at Sikorsky! Those turrets made the helo too heavy and the mini-guns were hard to aim, so it never even went into production. Even if it had been put into production, it would be very difficult to shoot down a YAK-28 with 7.62 millimeter mini-guns unless it got very close and was moving very slowly. Anyway, at no time did any of the twelve HH-3As made, at least to my knowledge, ever carry a cannon of any kind. They did have a mini-gun in the cargo door, but there was a mechanism on the gun that prevented it from shooting upwards through the rotors. So, to shoot at another airplane, one would have to either be level with or above the target."

"How can you be sure of that?"

"I've flown almost all of the HH-3As in existence, either in Vietnam or when I was a tactics and transition instructor."

"That was not in my brief." Gibson made a note on his yellow pad.

Josh then held up the second picture. "This second picture is not of an H-3; it is a Mi-14, which is a Soviet-built helicopter with the NATO code name Haze. How do I know? The Haze has sponsons on the side that are significantly larger and farther aft than those on the H-3. And, if a trained photo interpreter spent some time with the photo, he could tell you that the Haze is much larger than the H-3. So, Mr. Gibson, the picture in the helicopter wasn't us. It is a Haze." *If the State Department had done their homework they'd know that.*

"So, Lieutenant, what did happen? This is your chance to tell your side of the story."

"How about the truth?"

"That would be welcome as well."

Josh wasn't sure how to interpret that "as well", so for the moment he decided to ignore it, thinking Gibson was just being sarcastic. "We saw two Firebars. One remained at about ten thousand feet while the other dived on us and lit us up with his fire control radar. That in itself is considered a hostile act. Anyway, he failed to pull out of his dive and hit the water. That is when the second one dived on us, and when he fired the first missile we flew evasive maneuvers and dropped chaff and flares. Neither Soviet fighter attempted to communicate with us or to follow any, repeat any, of the international rules concerning unauthorized flight into another country's airspace."

"How do you know you were, how did you say, lit up? What do you mean by he fired the first missile? Were there more than one?"

Josh thought for a second, deciding how much he was going to say. "In the helicopter, we have a piece of equipment known as a radar warning receiver. If we are hit by a radar signal we can tell by the tone in our headsets what mode the radar is in, i.e. search, targeting, or even if the terminal seeker of the missile has activated. That's what I mean by "lit up." We heard all three tones so we knew we were targeted and the missile was aimed at us."

He put the photo of the Mi-14 on the coffee table. "When we saw the first missile, we knew it was a radar guided missile because of the tones we heard. So we dropped chaff and maneuvered to make it hard for the missile to keep tracking us. We were lucky because the tactics worked, but the diving Yak fired a second AA-2. Because we did not get the same tones, we assumed that it was the infrared version. Again, we maneuvered and used flares to decoy this second missile. To make a long story short, the second Yak flew away after launching the missiles. At the time of the attack, we were well beyond the twelve mile limit and in international waters."

"That's not what the Soviets say. They claim you were inside the three mile limit near the island of Novaya Zemlya."

"Oh, so we were not northeast of Murmansk? That's a contradiction."

"The department assumed the Soviets were using Murmansk as a point of reference known to many."

"As a point of fact, we were more than seven hundred miles from Murmansk, so we were not even close to the Soviet port."

"Where were you then?"

"That's classified."

"What were you doing there?"

"I can't tell you that." Josh was enjoying the jousting.

Gibson was acting like an attorney in a courtroom. Nothing was going to change his line of questioning. "What kind of weapons did you have on board the helicopter?"

"Nothing that could shoot down a Yak 28."

"So you did have guns on board?"

"Yes, we had rifles and pistols. None of which, unless we were very, very lucky, could shoot down a jet."

"So how could a helicopter shoot down a Yak-28?"

"You need an air-to-air missile. We didn't have one on board, nor is the SH-3A equipped to carry one."

"Then how was the first Yak-28 shot down?"

"It wasn't. As I said before, the pilot flew it into the water. My guess he had what is known as target fixation."

"What is target fixation?"

"I am not a fighter-bomber pilot, but from what I understand, it means that in a diving attack the pilot, in his desire to hit the target, focuses so intently on the target that he stays in the dive too long. Then, when he tries to pull out, he is too low and crashes."

"So your position is that the Yak-28 pilot suffered from 'target fixation' in his desire to shoot you down and as a result, crashed into the sea?

"It is not my position, it is the truth."

"Is it in your debrief?"

"Yes, with a lot more detail on what we did to avoid being hit by the missiles."

"I'll ask for a copy of it before I leave."

"I doubt that you will be given one because I was told you don't have the necessary clearance." Josh regretted the words for a second until he saw the fiery look in Gibson's eyes. *Got you, asshole! You thought you were coming up here to fry my ass and now you are going to leave here blindfolded with a record that is the truth. And, you won't be able to doctor it because I'll have a copy, as will the Navy. It is not what you wanted to hear, and now someone in the State Department is going to have to get some backbone. Maybe they'll even tell the Soviets to piss up a rope.*

Gibson shut of both tape recorders and started to put both recordings in his brief case. "We'll see about that."

"I believe the reel to reel version is the Navy's copy."

"Oh, sorry."

Josh ignored the insincerity of the response and handed the box to John as a gesture of trust. "Are you a lawyer?"

"As a matter of fact, yes. I graduated from Harvard Law and specialize in the legal aspects of international incidents." Gibson made a small ceremony of putting the cassette into his briefcase and then looked down at his notes. Again, the bright flash of his cuffs showed beyond the end of his suit coat. The way he said 'Harvard Law' convinced Josh the man was a snob.

"Lieutenant, do you have any idea of why I am here?"

"Don't have a clue, other than that you wanted to find out the truth of what happened over international waters in the Barents Sea."

"Let me give you, as they say, a clue. You've created an international incident that has upset the apple cart at a time when the Secretary of State is trying to keep the Soviets happy so they don't come charging through the Fulda Gap in Germany. The president told Kissinger to keep things quiet and avoid any incidents until after the election. This doesn't fall into the quiet category. Based on their note, the Soviets are pissed that we shot one of their unarmed jets down. And we don't have any good answers. In fact, we don't have any proof to the contrary."

"You could tell them the truth. Here are four facts that the Soviets ignored because it blows their protest out of the water." Josh was struggling to contain his anger. "One: their pilot flew the Yak 28 into the water. He was not, repeat *not* shot down. Two: SH-3As don't carry cannons or missiles. Torpedoes, yes; depth charges, yes; light machine guns, yes; but cannons or missiles, no way, and if you read NATOPs manual—that's the pilot operating handbook in civilian terms—or ask someone at Sikorsky or in the H-3's program office, you would learn it is impossible to fire air-to-air missiles from any current model H-3. Three: the Soviet pilot didn't follow any of the agreed upon international rules regarding unauthorized penetrations. Instead, they dove at us with their fire control radars on, which is a hostile act and allows us to fire back in self-defense. They committed a second hostile act when they fired not one, but *two* missiles at us. And last, but not least, four: firing the missiles first is a direct violation of those same warning procedures, which require making an attempt to contact by radio before flying by with wheels down as a signal to land, and then to fire tracers in parallel of the offending flight before you try to shoot down the plane. Oh, and the Soviets know what frequency to use to call a U.S. military or NATO aircraft because it is an internationally known frequency called 'guard', which on the UHF band is two-forty point three. The VHF distress frequency is one-twenty-one-five."

"Ok, where's your recording or do you have photos?"

"We don't have either. We weren't carrying cameras, and even if we did, they would be classified and you wouldn't have access to them."

"That's the problem. We don't have any *proof* that their charges are false. They have photos."

"Their evidence is bogus and you and I both know it. Mr. Gibson, who do you represent, the U.S. or the Soviet Union?" Josh queried, knowing in the back of his mind that his mouth could ruin his career, but also that at this point, he didn't care. "It is your job to present the facts, not mine. You're a lawyer, go figure it out, and with your help, the State Department will get some balls and tell the Soviets to fuck off. They've shot down a lot of our planes and now they've lost one because their pilot was incompetent. Sorry."

"So you admit shooting down the Yak 28."

"I did nothing of the sort. The Yak flew into the water and there are seven witnesses who heard the conversations on the intercom, saw the missiles, or watched the Yak fly into the water. Their testimony will hold up in any U.S. board of inquiry."

Gibson sat back with a thin smile on his face. "Right now, there are a lot of very senior people within the State Department who want your head on a silver platter. They think you are a cowboy and a loose cannon who for some personal reason is determined to start World War III. This interview only reinforces my view that you should be cashiered out of the Navy and possibly face criminal charges."

Josh didn't answer. *If the bastard only knew.*

The State Department official turned to John. "My guess is that this cowboy hasn't told you that this is the *second* international incident in which he was involved that killed members of the Soviet armed forces."

"I'm sorry, Mr. Gibson, again, you have your facts wrong," Josh cut Gibson off. "This is at least the *third* time that my actions have resulted in the death of members of the Soviet military. I just want to make sure that you and your associates in the State Department know that, in order to ensure that the next time you point this out, you at least have an accurate number. And, again for the record, I want to make sure that you know that each time I was on an authorized mission acting within the rules of engagement in the execution of lawful orders." Josh turned to John, who was smiling.

"As I was saying, *Lieutenant* Osborne," Mr. Gibson continued icily, "your aircraft commander was about to be court-martialed for an incident in which his helicopter attacked two neutral freighters in Haiphong harbor. He was saved from a long, well deserved visit to Leavenworth by the intervention of several flag officers who supported his gross violations of the rules of engagement. Considering your station in life, you should consider carefully with whom you associate. He will get you killed, or bring down your good name."

John stood up. "I've had enough of your poppycock, Mr. Gibson. Again, you have your facts wrong, and your State Department needs some back stiffening. The ships in Haiphong were not neutral. They were Soviet ships bringing arms to the North Vietnamese, and you should know that makes them combatants. As I understand international law, the U.S. had the right to attack them, but chose not to unless they fired on American aircraft or ships. And if you had studied the incident, as I have, you would know that the Russians fired first." John paused for a second or two to let his point sink in. "This interview is over." After he got to the door, he turned to face the civilian. "Gibson, the next time we meet, if we ever do, you will address me by my *proper* title, which is... Your Lordship."

The Same Day, 1850 local time, Harz Mountains

Herman Werfel down shifted his Mercedes from third to second and then double-clutched to drop the 220SE into its unsynchronized first gear when he saw the familiar stone columns with the family crest and "Schloss Theissen" on a brass plate. Nothing much had changed since 1938. As the Luftwaffe ace waited for the gate to open, he folded the map he was using that showed he was about fifty kilometers southwest of Bonn and slid it between the passenger seat and the center console.

A man approached the car wearing the traditional green loden cloth coat and black lederhosen with his hands clasped behind his back. What was unusual were the black boots, which he recognized as similar to those issued to members of the Bundeswehr, laced to the top over dark grey socks that came up to just below his knees.

The man looked at him for a second through the rolled down window, "Ahhh, Brigadier General Werfel, welcome to Schloss Theissen. Herr Baron is waiting for you. The road is wet and narrow, so please be careful."

"Danke." Werfel left the window open to take in the resinous smells of spruce and pine. In the fading summer light, the asphalt glistened from the rain. He was trying to remember the elevation of the house and had settled on about one thousand meters when the road opened into a wide cleared area in front of a large stone building that looked more like a hotel than a house.

As he got out, he saw that two of the eight garage doors were open, giving him a glimpse of the baron's collection of exotic sports cars. A man was polishing a rare Porsche Abarth Carrera, of which, as a racing fan, Werfel knew just twenty-one had been made.

"Good evening, Herr Brigadier. The Baron is waiting." Hans Sturmer, Von Theissen's majordomo, bowed at the waist and gestured toward the open door. He too was dressed in traditional loden coat, but this one was gray and he was wearing long pants and more traditional shoes.

Von Theissen strode out from the hallway and passed Sturmer, who stepped aside. Baron Albert von Theissen put his left hand over Werfel's right as they shook hands. "Herman, it is so good to see you. It has been too long since the last time."

"Albert, it is good to see you again. How is the racing team doing? I don't see your name listed as the driver very often anymore."

"Ahhhh, I am glad you noticed. At least someone is paying attention. Alas, I spend most of my time testing and managing the team and only race in the long distance events. My young drivers are a lot faster than I am. You ought to come visit our new shops in Adenau, just a few kilometers from the Nurburgring. The police let us drive our race cars back and forth during the day."

"I may take you up on that someday. Maybe we could swap visits. I visit your team and you can spend time with my air wing."

"I look forward to it, and I will make sure that you can drive some of the cars on the ring." Von Theissen beamed.

"That sounds like fun. I will bring my boys, but I don't think I can arrange a ride for you in one of our fighters."

"If you could, it would be splendid, but just being around fighter pilots again would be wonderful. I will not let you forget that promise." Von Theissen changed his tone. "You know, they are going to stop using the north course for Formula One next year?"

"No. Why?"

"The Formula One drivers think that one hundred and seventy-plus turns over twenty-two kilometers is much too difficult and dangerous. The cars are much faster and lap times are down to about seven minutes for the Formula One cars and about nine for sports cars."

"It was not so long ago when the lap times were fourteen minutes for Formula One. So, where will they have the German Grand Prix?" Werfel's memory flashed back to when his father took him to races at the 'Ring, built in the 1920s, to watch Mercedes and Auto Union teams race Italian Alfa Romeos. Earlier this year, he had taken his own family to watch the Nürburgring 1000 Kilometer race from inside a turn called the Carousel.

"They plan to use south course and Hockenheim, which is flat and doesn't have the character of the 'Ring. But don't worry, they will still let private cars on the course for testing, and still have sports car races there."

Werfel let his mind wander. More than once, he, like many Germans, had paid four deutschmarks for a lap around the Nürburgring. You were, of course, on your own, and if you bent your car the track had tow trucks to bring it back to the garage area. If you were hurt in the shunt, you hoped someone else on the track would stop, go to one of the many phones along the fence, and call the office to dispatch an ambulance. "Too bad; it is the end of an era."

"Yes it is. Times do change. But some things do not." Von Theissen's tone lightened. "An excellent dinner awaits us. Schnitzel a la Holstein along with a fine 1972 Reisling from my vineyards near Bad Kreutznach. Shall we?" Von Theissen motioned toward the door, where a member of the household staff in a white jacket was standing.

"Sturmer, just serve the salad and the main course and I'll call you when we are finished. I think we can manage cutting the cake for dessert."

"Jawohl, Herr Baron." The man bowed and closed both sets of doors to the dining room.

Herman Werfel suspected that it was the signal that the evening's real conversation was about to begin.

"I am sure you know by now that the New German Party collected enough signatures to ensure that it will be on the ballot this November. We are contesting twenty seats in the Bundestag where voters are receptive to the party's message."

I have not heard about the New German Party. And why, Herr Baron, are you telling me, a Luftwaffe general, this? Because you are involved up to your neck. Von Theissen was not a member of the Hitler regime's leadership, so I am not duty bound to report the conversation.

"I donated the legal limit and have encouraged others to do the same. My role is mostly raising money."

Werfel didn't answer, just listened, trying to hide his growing discomfort. *I don't like politics.*

"The New German Party stands for returning Germany back to its rightful place in Europe as a strong, independent power not aligned with the Americans or the Russians. As part of that, *when* we come to power we will be asking the German people to ask the Americans, French, and British to leave. Not today, but on a negotiated schedule over a few years. The New German Party stands for a united Germany and we think if we are not a threat to the Soviet Union, they will eventually allow it to happen. We also want Germany to send the gastarbeiter back to their native countries. If they have married a native German, then we will allow them to stay. Otherwise, the longer they are in this country the harder it will be to send them home, and the more they will change Germany in a way that we native Germans may not want."

Werfel was never one to question his World War II squadron mate, but von Theissen was taking him into dangerous waters. "Herr Baron, why are you telling me this? You know that as officers in the Bundeswehr we cannot participate in politics until we leave the service or retire."

"I know that, but you can point out and discuss the issues with others. You can educate your men in the hopes that they support our candidates."

"No, Albert, I can't and we can't, because that will lead to questions about our personal preferences. The ban for officers, particularly generals, is quite clear." Werfel decided to drop the formal title and use the baron's first name; he'd earned the privilege. Years of flying missions together against the Poles and Russians made them equal despite the wide gap in blood line and wealth. "The Russians will never leave East Germany, even if the Americans and British pull out. And we are integrated in the

NATO command structure as an equal partner; we will not, as the French did, pull out. The Bundewehr is a large portion of the NATO ground forces. Our pilots train in America. Expecting the Americans or British to leave on their own in our lifetimes is a pipe dream." Werfel put a piece of a white cake topped with whipped cream and strawberries in his mouth.

"Herman, my good man, I have reason to believe that a strong, neutral Germany is in Russia's best interest. We can play the Americans against the Russians and profit on both the diplomatic and economic fronts. NATO is just an alliance, and such things come and go with the times."

"I couldn't disagree with you more. NATO is a unique political, military and economic alliance." Werfel laughed. "As for the Russians, the words 'strong Germany' sends shivers up their spines. We invaded them twice in this century." He paused to choose his next words with care. "You do know that you are playing with fire?"

"How so?"

"During the war, you were known to be a very ardent supporter of Hitler after you left front line flying. The fact, which is well known, that you were banging Hitler's favorite pilot, Hanna Reitsch, doesn't help you. Even today, she still champions National Socialism. While you were not a member of the SS or charged with any war crimes, my guess is that you are on a watch list somewhere. If you enter politics, someone from the government is going to pay you a visit and ask a lot of difficult questions. The question is, will they ask you to stop, or arrest you?"

"I did nothing wrong during the war," Von Theissen insisted.

"Albert, I believe you, but you were already a party member when we were in flight training. You thought the sun rose and set on Adolf Hitler. My guess is that somewhere in this house you have all your medals and photos taken with Hitler displayed. Other than a few pictures of me by airplanes or with a few close friends, the rest of mine are in a vault to be given to a museum when I am dead and gone."

"They are in my private office, and yes, people who are invited into the office see them. I am not ashamed of them because, like you, I earned those decorations."

"So again, why am I here besides to reminisce about old times?"

"The New Germany Party wants your help. We need you to reach out to other members of the military and encourage them, as private citizens, to support our party. Germans know and respect you and will follow your leadership. And, if we have a candidate in their district, ask them to vote for our candidate."

"I am not sure I can do that." *Albert, are you insane? We may be friends and old comrades in arms, but there is no way in hell I will risk my career to help your party.*

"Please, think about it."

Chapter 11
Happy New Year

Sunday, September 26th, 1976, 1926 local time, Yeovil

Something made Josh stop and watch the slim, familiar looking man with a slight limp who walked up to the white picket fence bordering his front yard. He stood up, wondering where he'd met the man, while Sasha toddled after the size one soccer ball. The stranger was average height, had close cropped, graying hair, and wore a white shirt under a blue sport coat. He tapped a manila envelope on his thigh in cadence with his steps.

"Lieutenant Haman?"

Josh couldn't place the accent, which wasn't German or Dutch. His memory went into overdrive trying to associate the accent and face. *Who are you?*

He quickly scooped up his son and carried him into the house before returning to the uninvited man. "And you are?"

"Excuse me, Lieutenant Haman, I am Lev Mogen. Please, let me show you some identification." The man used the tips of his fingers to pull two documents out of a folder that was so battered the black leather was turning gray from wear. "This is my passport and this is my identification." Without ceremony, he handed them to Josh and stepped back as if he didn't want to intrude.

"These say you are Israeli. How did you know my name?"

"We have met before. I was part of the Israeli liaison team at the Naval Strike Warfare Center in Fallon and we worked with your SEALs on desert operations and search and rescue tactics. You came up with student pilots several times while I was there. I believe you were an instructor in the H-3 helicopter."

"I don't remember working with Israelis."

"That's because we were all in civilian clothes and our nationality was kept quiet. You attended our briefings on tactics used by Arab nations, including one I gave on how they try to counter helicopter insertions."

"Yes, now I remember." Josh relaxed a bit. "I thought you were very exposed over the desert and anyone with a portable missile could stand up and fire one up your ass. It was also like flying over water because there were so few landmarks."

"I am glad you remember. By the way, happy new year!" Lev paused, coming abruptly to the point of the visit. "I would like half an hour of your time. My country needs your advice."

"Advice?" The word caught Josh off guard. What kind of advice? He knew he was treading on unfamiliar ground and had to report any contacts with members of a foreign government or military that were not in the "normal" performance of his duties as an exchange pilot with the Fleet Air Arm.

As he replaced his identification, Lev opened his coat wide as if he wanted to show Josh he was not armed. "I apologize for the direct approach, but my superiors asked me to talk to you in person. This is a very important conversation."

"Why couldn't we talk on the phone?"

"The Israeli government believes, as do I, that it is best not to use the phone for this discussion. I am sorry that was not communicated to you."

"What is going on out here?" Rebekah skipped a step as she came out onto the lawn.

"This is Lev Mogen from the Israeli embassy."

Rebekah looked at the man and then back to Josh. "Josh, don't be so suspicious. I knew he was coming and I distinctly remember telling you after the Israeli embassy called. You even said O.K. Don't you remember?" Rebekah turned back to the Israeli. "Lev, please come in, and I'm sorry if my husband was rude."

"Not rude, cautious. In our business, that is a good thing."

Rebekah led the way inside. "Mr. Mogen, something to drink?" She started to speak in Hebrew but decided against it. The Israeli embassy already knew that she still spoke her native country's tongue.

"Tea would be perfect."

"Coming right up. Happy new year." Rebekah headed for the kitchen.

"Happy new year to you, Rebekah." Lev also refrained from using the Hebrew words.

"Thank you." Josh spoke for both of them, and waved their guest over to a couch. "But I am afraid it is not a happy new year. We were watching the Armed Forces Network and then the BBC. We just learned that Red Hand set off a bomb outside one of the chapels on the Frankfurt Army base they were using for Rosh Hashanah services and killed about fifty people, with another sixty or so injured. There were other bombs. One outside a park in Stuttgart, and another exploded in Karlsruhe at a building used for the high holidays as a synagogue. Total dead is around a hundred, and with many more hurt."

"I heard about the bombs, but didn't know the number killed." Lev said with a frown.

"It is very, very bad. The chapel in Frankfurt collapsed, so it may be a day or so until they pick through the wreckage and get an accurate count of how many were killed." Josh looked at the TV as if it were still on. He'd sat in shock through two news broadcasts before he couldn't take it anymore, so he'd gone outside with Sasha. "Mr. Mogen, why do you want to talk to me? I'm just a lieutenant assigned to spend a couple years flying with the Royal Navy."

"They told me you would be direct."

"Sorry." Josh didn't make it sound like an apology.

"I like people who are blunt. Before we get to why I am here, please let me tell you a bit about me so it will make you more comfortable. I was a paratrooper before I joined Sayeret Matkal, which is the Israeli special forces unit subordinated to our military intelligence organization, called Aman. We're very similar to the British and Australian SAS, and two of our missions are counter terrorism and hostage rescue. After I was wounded in the '73 war, I was transferred to Mossad. I learned about your experiences in Vietnam from the SEALs I met at Fallon, who had lots of very nice things to say about you. With them you have an enviable reputation. And you are Jew. We had records of who attended our briefings, and your Navy was kind enough to tell my government where you were stationed."

Rebekah joined them in the room, bearing a tray with a tea set. She put a cup before their guest and took a seat.

Lev looked at Josh and hesitated, expecting Josh to say something. When the American didn't, he continued. "I came for two reasons. For the first one, I apologize in advance because it may bring back some unpleasant memories..."

"What unpleasant memories?" Josh first looked at the Israeli and then his wife as alarm bells went off in his head.

"Again, please accept my apologies in advance. This is difficult for me as well. May I continue?"

Josh looked at his wife, who nodded. Both instinctively guessed the topic.

"As you can imagine, Israel is very interested in Jews who have emigrated from the Soviet Union. In most cases, they just wanted to get out and have a better life. Before they can leave, the KGB investigates them and has to decide that they have no value to the Soviet Union. Sometimes, however, the KGB uses emigration as a way to get rid of criminals or undesirable people that, for any number of reasons, it does not want to prosecute. Israel, and I am sure the United States, has been stuck with some of these bad people. But the scenario that scares us the most is when the KGB uses emigration to get agents posing as Jews situated in the west. It is a wonderful way to have Western governments help deepen their cover, to accept them as refugees from a hated rival power...."

Rebekah and Josh were sitting next to each other holding hands, as though they were expecting horrible news. Rebekah didn't know, and Lev wasn't going to tell her, that her father Meier Shalaf had been his company commander when he was killed.

"The first and third possibilities are what bring me here today. The Soviet Union has officially approved exit visas for Dov and Lev Vishinski and will allow them to emigrate sometime this fall, most likely in November. Josh, if you remember, they are the brothers of your first wife's father. We know, and you may know, that they tried to emigrate once before, but the permits were pulled back at the last minute. And we both know that Artur Vishinski was assassinated by a KGB agent."

Josh squeezed his wife's hand. *Why can't they let my memories of Natalie and her parents stay in the recesses of my mind?*

"One question that we are asking is: do Dov and Sol know Artur is dead? If they do, how did they find out? The Soviet Union censors communications very effectively. But the big question is, are Dov and Sol Artur's real brothers, or are they impostors who are agents? Even if they really are the brothers, they could be suborned. What complicates everything is we have been told by trusted sources in the Soviet Union that Dov and Sol are supposedly carrying something that will be very valuable to the United States, its allies, and Israel. So, we want to know if the individuals are really Artur's brothers, and if what they are bringing is not disinformation. Does that explain why I am here?"

"Sort of. But what would my late wife's uncles know that is so important? If I remember, they are university professors and not involved in any defense work. That's why their application was approved years ago."

"Your memory is correct, but Dov is a professor of biology, and Sol is a physics professor. Both are sciences that can have, indirectly or directly, strategic significance. The Israeli government has been following their application because of their education, and because they listed their desired country of residence as Israel or the United States."

"I've never met them. You do know that my former father-in-law hadn't seen or talked to his brothers since the war. All they did was exchange letters."

"We suspected that, but weren't sure."

"Then why are you coming to me?" Josh was trying very hard not be annoyed. Yet the mention of the KGB intrigued him. *God, I hate the KGB and everything they stand for! If I can stick a sharp stick in their eye, I will.*

"We think you may be able to help."

"How?"

"We would like to know what you know about Dov and Lev Vishinski. We would also like to know if you have any correspondence or photos that we could use to make sure we are not dealing with impostors. And, we would also like to have one of our researchers interview you."

"I don't know much more than what I told you, but I might be able to be of help. When I cleaned out my in-laws house, I collected a lot of scrapbooks and letters and put them in boxes. Besides the ones of my late wife and me, there are photos that my father-in-law's brothers sent to him over the years. They are all in albums with the dates they were taken and some other notes. Each time he got a letter it was a cause for celebration, and he would put it away in a file in the order he got them. I emptied the fireproof file cabinet and put the letters in marked boxes. I haven't had the stomach to go through them since. My intention was to someday donate them to the Jewish Heritage Museum in New York in their memory."

"I understand." Lev paused before asking the next question. "Where are they, the boxes, I mean?"

"In a locked, climate-controlled storage facility in San Diego. Why?"

"Can we have someone collect them?"

"I suppose so." Josh was hesitant.

"What do we have to do to get to them? I promise, we will not destroy or harm them in any way. What we are looking for is information we can use to determine whether or not the people coming out are who they say they are."

"I understand. I have a good friend in San Diego who has a key to the storage facility. If you and I can work out details so that he can be assured whoever you send is indeed someone from Mossad, I will call him and make the necessary arrangements."

"How many boxes are there?"

"I am not sure, but if I remember correctly it's six. It could be eight. All are the size you use to pack books, and all are full."

"Excellent. That is good to know. What is your friend's name?"

"Jack D'Onofrio. He was my co-pilot during my second tour in Vietnam."

"Again, I am sorry to bring up a difficult subject," Lev sipped his tea, although by now it was quite cold, "but I think you'll find the second reason for me coming to be much more timely."

"Before we go on, I have a question. Why don't you use your connections with the CIA to pass the information Dov and Sol Vishinski are carrying straight to them?"

"We have told the CIA and the FBI that they have leaks in their counter terrorism and counter intelligence organizations; so far, they have not found the traitors. Therefore, we decided not to tell them about Dov and Sol until they are safely out of the Soviet Union. We do not want to risk the Soviets finding out and canceling their exit visas, or worse, to begin interrogating them. We want someone senior officers would listen to. We think that may be you."

"Message delivered. But I am not sure that that person is me." Josh looked at his wife sitting next to him. Josh didn't realize it, but he had moved to the edge of the couch cushion. Josh was already convinced, from his own experiences in Viet Nam, that the Soviets indeed had access to classified information, and that this had led to the deaths of some of his friends.

"And the second reason you came?"

"We believe we have some information on Red Hand that we want to pass on to your government."

"Like what?" Josh leaned forward.

Lev opened the envelope he had carried into the house and pulled out a stack of black and white pictures. "This is a photo of one of Fatah's top officers who is responsible for recruiting and training terrorists. He is a Palestinian by the name of Ahmed ibn Khaldun, and we are pretty sure he is running an agent named Mohammed someplace in Germany. We don't know if that is the agent's real name or his cover. Fatah has been asking a lot of questions about these five German citizens—Gerhard Wolff, Ludwig Kammer, Reinhard Dorf, Anna Schlemmer, and Karina von Berg." Lev laid eight by ten enlargements of several surveillance photos of each individual on the coffee table as he spoke their names.

"We know they arrived at a training camp in Libya about a week ago. We don't know if these are their real names or covers, but the West German passports they used are genuine. However, we suspect Fatah has agents in immigration offices in several European countries to give them access to passports, so we wouldn't be surprised if these were genuine with bogus backgrounds. We think all five are Red Hand, because there were references to someone arriving in Libya in late September whose code name is 'Mechanic'."

Josh knew better than to ask how the Israelis got this information. "Why don't you pass this on to the Germans? They'd love to have it, because from what I hear they don't have any solid leads."

"For the same reasons I gave before. Leaks. We know the German police force and their intelligence agency has been penetrated by both the Stasi and the KGB. And if we gave this to the American law enforcement agencies, they would give it to the Germans, and we are sure it would wind up in East German hands. If Stasi has it, the KGB will have it soon after, and they might tell their Arab friends, which would endanger our sources." Lev stirred the tea before taking a sip and continuing. "We don't trust the German government because they have been playing both sides by supporting us while at the same time being pro-Palestinian. However, right now they may be getting desperate and might agree to the conditions we would attach to any assistance we would provide. But that is a decision someone else must make."

"Why should I believe you?"

"Because you believe the U.S. has a leak in its message system which has not been, as you Americans say, plugged. One of the people we spent some time with at Fallon was a Russian by called Alexei Koniev. He helped us develop tactics to defeat the new Soviet missiles the Syrians and Egyptians were buying. I believe the two of you know each other."

Josh suspected he hadn't been able to maintain his poker face when he heard the name of the former Soviet Army colonel who had worked as an advisor to the North Vietnamese on Soviet missile tactics and doctrine. "So, what do you want from me?"

"A name of someone we can talk to who can use this information, who is trustworthy and who can help put Red Hand out of business."

"I know the perfect person." Josh reached over to the coffee table and began to dial Marty's office number.

Chapter 12
Bastards in the Service of the King

Monday, September 27th, 1976, 1952 local time, Genoa, Italy

Dieter saw the words *Blue Crescent* in white letters below the flag with the red, white, and blue squares on the stern of the Panamanian registered freighter. Where large flakes of the hull's black paint had peeled off, rusty steel was visible. A crane groaned as it hoisted a large wooden crate from the pier and whined as it lowered it into the hold. When the crate, marked with the logo of the heavy equipment manufacturer Fiat Allis, disappeared from sight, he pulled his West German passport out of his backpack, along with a sheaf of other documents, picked up his small duffle bag stuffed with clothes, and headed up the gangway.

A man with a three day beard and a dirty white bridge cover ambled over. "You must be our passenger, Wilhelm Gestner."

"Yes, that's me. Here is my ticket, my passport, and a Libyan visa."

"These look like they are in order. Keep your documents until we get to Tripoli, where a customs officer will inspect them. I hope you have someone meeting you, because where we dock is a long walk to where you can get a cab, if you can get one at all. I will show you to your cabin. I am Nicholas Andros, the ship's engineer. The captain said you are to eat with the officers."

After winding through a maze of passageways covered with faded, peeling beige paint, Andros took a key from his pocket and unlocked a door. "This is your stateroom. The bathroom and shower are down the hall. Please feel free to walk around, but do not go below decks without an escort. You may get lost and we'll never find you!" Andros laughed at his attempt at humor and tossed the key on the bed.

"When do we leave Genoa?" Dieter had been assured by Mohammed that he would be out of Europe within twenty-hours.

"We are leaving sometime late tonight, once we finish loading. We are behind schedule because the bulldozers arrived late. If we get underway by midnight, we should be in Tripoli by Saturday. The ship's estimated arrival time is posted by the port captain in the local newspapers, so the people meeting you will know when we are to arrive."

Dieter imposed a calm he didn't feel on his features, and thanked the engineer. Four hours. A lot could go wrong in four hours, but he had made it this far. He was determined to see his plans for expanding Red Hand carried out properly. He didn't trust anyone else to do it.

Wednesday, September 29th, 1948 local time, Yeovil

Josh and Rebekah were the first to arrive at the small restaurant known for its authentic menu. The owner, knowing his guests included the future Duke and Duchess of Leeds, who were regulars, had set up a table in a quiet corner.

"How was your flight?" Josh waited until Marty, the last to arrive, hugged Rebekah and shook hands with John.

Marty took a sip of single malt scotch before answering. "Jenkins and I hopped over on an Air Force Special Air Mission JetStar. With all the classified stuff I was carrying we couldn't fly commercial, and it was better than a MAC flight into Mildenhall."

"Where do you think Senior Chief Jenkins and Colour Sergeant Calhoun are now?" John Osborne asked.

"Lord only knows. I'll bet that they went to at least one pub to celebrate working together again before they got down to creating two lists—people and equipment. Whether or not they are still in a pub is anybody's guess."

So far, as a courtesy to the wives, the naval officers had managed to keep from talking shop and Marty wanted to keep it that way. "So John, tell me about your father and how he got his title back. I'd like to hear the story."

John looked over at Josh, who was looking down at the table with his face buried in his hands.

"I swear, I didn't put him up to it!" Josh raised his hands in an 'I surrender!' gesture.

"Do you want the truth or the official version?" John asked.

"I've never heard the truth," Rebekah chimed in, "not even from Gwen!"

"You'll love it," Gwen Osborne, the future Duchess of Leeds, smiled as she took a sip of her wine. "But it's John's story to tell, not mine. Go ahead, John, the colonials love a good yarn about English royalty!"

"OK, if you insist...." John glanced around the table to make sure everyone had a well-filled glass before beginning. "Well, at one time, it was thought that the 12th Duke of Leeds—Charles Osborne—had never produced a male heir, and lord knows, from what I was told, he tried. The man married three times and had numerous mistresses, but no children. So when he died in the early sixties, the title went with him to the grave, so to speak, because there were no heirs! The reality is that the peerage goes back to the monarch, who can award it to someone else as a reward for service to the crown and country."

Josh filled the wine glass that John held out from the bottle on the table. "My father, a commoner borne as William Bishop, developed an intense interest in heraldry after the war, for reasons that I will go into in a bit. By the way, during the war, he flew Bristol Beaufighters, then Mosquitoes with the Coastal Command's 143rd Squadron on anti-shipping missions in the channel, the North Sea, and off Norway. Despite his best efforts, my father managed to stay alive, even though he got bagged twice. One was a crash landing in a farmer's field in Kent, and the other a ditching in the Channel. Both times he managed to hang on to his radio operator/gunner, so each time he got shot down it was a jolly good show."

"Marty," Josh jumped in, "his father was awarded the Distinguished Service Order, which is the equivalent of our Navy Cross, plus a couple of Distinguished Flying Crosses. The Beaufighter was a twin engine plane that the Brits used as a night fighter, a torpedo bomber on anti-shipping missions, and a long range interceptor looking for German patrol planes. John's dad bought a Beaufighter that he is restoring to flying condition. It is about a year away from its first flight." Josh took a sip of his wine. "Sorry, John, but I just wanted pass on that info. Go on."

The future duke nodded. "My dad can't wait to fly a Beaufighter again, and it will be part of the Royal Air Force's Battle of Britain flight that maintains historic British aircraft." John raised his glass in a half-salute. "Back to my father's quest! After the war, he did quite well as a ship and cargo broker, and then as a lessor of ships. He was one of the first who saw the value in containerized freight, and to my very good fortune, he made a large one." John chuckled. "But there was something missing in his life, and it was a father. His mother had told him that his father died right after he was born and left them a trust fund that more than met her needs. Other than that, she was silent on the subject, other than vague answers to his questions. The solicitors—that's lawyers to you Yanks—were all mum on the subject of the fund, saying that the attorney-client privilege prevented them from divulging the source of the money or their client. All this aroused my father's curiosity. So, after his mother died in the late forties from injuries she suffered in the Blitz, my father started digging through his mum's personal stuff and found papers, love letters and others, many of which bore a heraldic coat of arms. Reading these convinced him that his mother and Charles Osborne, the 12th and last Duke of Leeds, had conducted a long running affair. But by the time he had sorted all this out, the old man had died."

"To make a long story short," Gwen interjected, "his father was a bloody bastard! For centuries, members of royalty have be impregnating commoners and walking away. At least Charles Osborne had some scruples and left Mary Bishop a nice pot of money." Gwen giggled and cast a roguish smile at her husband. "Go on, John, I just wanted to make that important point."

"Ah, yes. Anyway, he began to research the life of Charles Osborne. It was a bit of a cold trail, with the time that had elapsed and the absence of surviving family. I think he would even admit it bordered on an obsession. He hired private investigators. They found more and more evidence that Charles Osborne was indeed his father, and had arranged to support his mother until she died. My father thinks she was waiting for him to be free to marry her, but to be perfectly blunt, the likelihood of that was effectively nil, and perhaps she knew that. My father thinks that the old man liked to play around and didn't want to be tied to one woman. The trust fund was the old man's way to keep my grandmother quiet. You would think that having a war hero son, even one born out of wedlock, would bring them together. But it didn't."

"John, I keep telling you that it would make a tear jerker of a novel!" Gwen got the giggles when she drank wine.

John emptied his glass, and Josh divided what remained in the bottle into both their glasses. "So, with the evidence in hand, my father began to petition the crown to restore the title and lands. Since most of the property had been distributed to other peers of the realm, or sold off and the money kept by the crown, this was a bit dicey. My father, now a very wealthy man, told a chap in Central Chancery of the Orders of Knighthood during a formal interview that he would be happy to pay the owners of the house and grounds whatever it was worth to get them back." John stopped for a second. "For you colonials not familiar with this part of our government, the taxpayers support the chancery, who report to the Lord Chamberlain, who is charge of matters of peerage for the Queen. Such a purchase would mean that the government would get a tidy sum, which always makes them happy."

John toyed with the stem of his wine glass, turning it around as he mulled over what to say next. "It took a few years before my father was able to purchase the house in which his mother was impregnated. Then, in a ceremony at Buckingham Palace, his title was restored by the queen, and he changed his name to Tom Osborne. My mother became Katherine Osborne, Duchess of Leeds. So, as his oldest son, when he passes away, I become the 14th Duke of Leeds. I have two brothers who help run the family business who will be getting their own titles once the chaps in the chancery decide what they should be. Anyway, to make a long story short, if I don't produce a male heir, the next oldest brother in line, James, will inherit the title."

"Dear, you left out the best part of the story," Gwen said as she put her hand on his arm. "Tell them what the Queen said in the private meeting before the investiture ceremony.

"Oh yes..." John grinned. "Before the ceremony at Buckingham Palace when the queen awards titles and knights people, she has a private chat with each new peer. My father walks in, and the queen asks him to sit down in a chair opposite her. Then, regally sitting there in her formal dress, she says to my father with a broad smile, 'Congratulations on recovering your peerage. The crown and the nation owe you a debt of gratitude for your outstanding service to your country, both during and after the war. And by the way, you're not the first bastard with a title who has served this country well!'"

Thursday, September 30th, 1976, 0900 local time, RNAS Yeovilton

Marty Cabot swung into the large room which had become their operations center. It was windowless and had an organized clutter of reports in stacks on a large table, as well as photographs and maps pinned to the plaster walls. The solid brick exterior of the small two story building, built between the two World Wars, kept prying eyes from seeing anything the team was doing. And the small sign by the door, which read 66th Joint Observation Group, was vague enough to describe the comings and goings of men wearing uniforms from different countries and civilian clothes.

"Gentlemen," he said without preamble, "I have some good news." Marty waited until everyone in the room was facing him, either standing or sitting in one of the metal folding chairs. "We are getting two new team members. Both Lieutenant Haman and I served with Petty Officer First Class Derek Van der Jagt in Vietnam. Colour Sergeant Calhoun and Senior Chief Jenkins agree with my estimation that he will be an asset to the team. If something is broken, this man can fix it. And if it needs to be found, Van der Jagt will find it. He started out working on radial engines but is also qualified as a jet engine mechanic. I can attest that he is also a very competent shooter and a good man to have around when things get difficult. He should be here Monday."

Marty looked around the room. "As you know, we have been provided intelligence that may link Red Hand to Fatah, which leads me to the next man joining our unit. He is Major Lev Mogen, an ex-paratrooper and combat veteran who was selected to join the Israeli Defense Force's elite Sayeret Matkal unit. He's participated in many operations outside Israel. After being wounded in the '73 war, he became an intelligence officer specializing in counter terrorism operations in Europe. I talked to him this morning and he should be here for lunch. He will be our intelligence officer."

"Just what we need, a fucking Jew." Sergeant Rockwell of the Special Air Service muttered under his breath to no one in particular.

"What did you say, Sergeant Rockwell?" Josh was sitting just behind the slender, hawk-faced member of the Royal Army and forced himself to keep his voice calm and level. Rockwell was a sniper and the team's shooting instructor.

"Nothing, sir."

"Sergeant Rockwell, join me in the office at the end of the hall. Right now." Josh spoke the words in a measured, even cadence which made it sound like an order without his having to say it was. Marty stopped talking and heads turned toward them, but no one said a word as the two men rose and walked from the briefing room.

Josh followed three steps behind the sergeant and closed the door before he moved to stand face to face with the veteran from Manchester. He spoke first. "I heard what you said. So don't try to deny it. I want to know why you said it."

"I don't like Jews. The Nazis were doing the world a favor by getting rid of them. There are times I wish they killed them all." Sergeant Rockwell looked Josh in the eye.

"You do realize that our intelligence indicates that Red Hand is targeting Jews as well as British and American citizens."

"I do." Sergeant Rockwell almost said, *That may not be a bad thing*, but held back.

"So do you have a problem working with Jews?" Josh wanted to understand why.

"I didn't say that, sir. I said I don't like them."

"Sergeant, you didn't answer my question."

"To be honest sir, I think I would."

"Sergeant Rockwell, I admire your honesty." Josh took a deep breath. "Tell me why?"

"Long story, sir, but the short version is that a Jewish banker took everything my family had and forced us on to the streets because we couldn't pay our loans for our house or what my father borrowed for the store. He lost our family grocery business and it drove him to putting a gun to his head."

"And you blame a Jewish banker, and Jews in general, for the failure of your father's business and his suicide?"

"Yes." Rockwell said it with conviction reinforced by a lifetime of hatred. "I blame them along with the Jewish lawyers they hired who did all the dirty work to take the store from our family. They wouldn't give us a break. It was tough times. A lot of the factories in Manchester were laying people off. Many of our customers were on the dole and could not afford to feed their families. My father gave them credit, cut his profits, and told the bankers what he was doing. To him, it was important that his customers could feed their families. In the end, we couldn't make ends meet, just like our customers. The bankers didn't give a rat's ass what happened to us or to our neighbors. All they wanted was their goddamn money. Those Jewish bankers and their lawyers screwed lots of other businessmen in our neighborhood who couldn't make their payments. They got rich, and the rest of us suffered for it. It was not fair."

"Sergeant Rockwell, have you ever worked with a Jew in the Royal Army or since you joined the SAS?" Josh was asking questions to give himself time to figure out what he was going to do next.

"No sir, I don't believe I have."

"Sergeant, what would you have done if you knew they were Jewish?"

"Not sure, sir."

"Did you ever meet any of the bankers and lawyers your father dealt with?"

"No sir, I was too young."

"Sergeant, did you met any Jews before you enlisted?"

"No, sir, I don't believe I did."

"Not even in school?"

Rockwell let out a derisive laugh. "Sir, Jews didn't come to my school. If they had, me and my mates would have beaten them to a bloody pulp."

"Are you aware that I am a practicing Jew?"

"No, sir." The sergeant's eyes widened with sudden recognition of where this might be going.

"I am sorry your family suffered, and it sounds as though your father was a good man. But it is not right to blame others for what some men do." Josh decided to make his reasoning personal. "On this team, there will be Major Mogen and me. Both of us would have to trust you with our lives. Based on what you just said, I would be worried that you might allow one or both of us to get killed. And in doing so, your actions would jeopardize a mission, along with the lives of other members of this unit. That is a risk I will not take and this unit cannot afford."

"Sir, I don't think that I would allow that to happen."

"Sergeant Rockwell, while I would like to believe you, I am not willing to take that chance."

Josh saw a flicker of reaction on the man's face.

"Wait here." His tone meant he didn't have to add the words, "That's an order."

Ten minutes later, Josh returned with Colour Sergeant Calhoun. The tall, lean career soldier walked into the room and gave a cold glance at his fellow SAS trooper before he dialed a phone number. It took only a few words to get through to the Special Air Service's administrative officer.

"Major Ralston, Calhoun here, and with me is Sergeant Rockwell and Lieutenant Haman of the U.S. Navy, who is the number one in the 66th Joint Observation Group. Lieutenant Haman would like a word with you, sir...." Calhoun pushed the button to activate the speaker phone. "Sir, would you please tell Major Ralston what you just told me."

Josh summarized the earlier conversation, then turned to the SAS NCO. "Sergeant Rockwell, is that an accurate account of what you told me?"

"Yes, sir, it is."

Josh looked at Rockwell's grim face and wasn't sure if he saw defiance or hatred, or both.

"I am sorry to hear this," Ralston said over the line. "And I am surprised, because Sergeant Rockwell has an excellent record as a member of the regiment." That was all Ralston offered.

"Major, I am not questioning his record or his qualities as a soldier," Josh was restraining his anger. "What I am telling you is that members of this unit cannot trust him with our lives. Therefore, he can no longer be a member of this team. To his credit, he was honest and I respect that."

"I understand. I wish to apologize on behalf of Her Majesty's government and the Special Air Service Regiment for Sergeant Rockwell's remarks. I can assure you that they are not representative of the Royal Army, the regiment, or Her Majesty's forces."

"Apology accepted." Josh waited a second before continuing. "I do have a request. You know how sensitive our mission is, so we need to find a way to ensure Sergeant Rockwell is not able to compromise it in any way."

"Understood." Major Ralston's voice was now grim. "It will take me a few days to find a replacement. In the meantime, I will send someone to pick him up. Can you keep him on ice until my men get there?"

Sergeant Major Calhoun pointed to himself before he spoke. "Yes sir, we can do that."

When they finished the call, the sergeant major took a breath. "Sergeant Rockwell, you will be placed in solitary confinement for the duration of this mission while the regiment decides what we should do with you. Sir, what he said was unacceptable and those views will not be tolerated in any branch of Her Majesty's forces. Please accept my personal apology as well."

Josh watched as Calhoun escorted the Sergeant out of the room.

Chapter 13
Out of Control Dots

Friday, October 1st, 1976, 1105 local time, East Berlin

Grünewald's anxiety level was high. He hadn't heard from Stiglitz for over a month, and he wasn't in Geissen or Zehlendorf.

Damn you, Stiglitz! Where are you? The propaganda minister and the head of Stasi may like Red Hand and the carnage Stiglitz is creating, but they're not running the asset. He was. And he, Colonel Gunter Grünewald, had all the operational problems. Now he was waiting for a phone call from an agent detailed with tracking the young radical's movements.

When his agent called, the Stasi colonel strove to keep his irritation and anxiety out of his voice. "When was the last time you saw Stiglitz?" he demanded.

"Monday. He took a cab to the bahnhof in Geissen and bought a ticket to Berlin via Frankfurt. We didn't board the train, because he's done that many times before. We called the Berlin office and someone was supposed to meet the train and follow him."

"They did. He was not on it. Do you know if he bought a ticket to someplace else?" Grünewald was seriously worried they had lost track of their asset.

"I am sure he did not. I was in line behind him when he bought the tickets. I heard what he said."

"Then he must have got off at a stop and doubled back, or gone on further. What did you find when you went into his apartment?"

"Nothing new. As usual, there is very little in the refrigerator besides beer."

"Do you think he abandoned it?"

"No. His car was parked on the street outside."

"Thank you." Günther Grünewald placed the receiver down in the cradle. It was the second call this morning that caused a gnawing in the pit of his stomach. The first had come from a man on his staff who had gone to Stiglitz's Zehlendorf workshop. It too was lived in, but empty. "Shit," Grünewald said to no one in particular. The papers on his desk told him that Stiglitz's last series of bombs had killed a hundred more people, most of whom were Americans. Worst of all, the latest attacks were blatantly anti-Semitic. Grünewald was worried that Markus Wolf, the head of the DDR's Ministry of State Security, would offer to assist the Bundesrepublik's investigation. Wolf tolerated the inevitability of ex-Nazis in Stasi, but he did not tolerate open anti-Semitism.

Maybe Stiglitz had gone to ground for a while knowing that everyone—the West Germans, the British, the Americans—were all looking for him. *Now the Stasi is looking too. And if we are, then so are the Russians.*

He was just reaching for his phone when his administrative assistant opened the door.

"Sir, Colonel Krasnovsky called while you were on the phone. He invited you to lunch. Seeing nothing on your calendar, I accepted for you. He will be at the Gasthaus Kaiser at noon. I hope that is O.K?"

The Russian colonel was sitting in a corner booth in the back of the small restaurant when Grünewald arrived. Krasnovsky waited until the waiter had filled their glasses with mineral water and disappeared with their order before speaking. "You know, killing the dependents of American servicemen is a bit over the top," he remarked. "Moscow believes that the Americans are going to get much more involved in the investigation."

"That doesn't surprise me, but I didn't pick his targets." Grünewald regretted the words as soon as they were out of his mouth.

"Maybe you should take more of an interest in where he places his bombs."

"That would be difficult for me to do because my orders are to be a supplier, nothing more," the Stasi Colonel said curtly. He didn't add there was no practical way to control where Stiglitz placed his bombs unless Stasi officers were there to supervise and assist, which could lead to an embarrassing situation for the DDR.

"Your hands are just as dirty as his."

Grünewald ignored the comparison and accusation. "The leadership of my government likes the embarrassment he is creating for the West German government. I recruited a dammed good asset who may be too good. Stiglitz has got the West Germans looking under every rock and tree. So far, they have come up with nothing."

"That is a good thing," Krasnovsky nodded his head.

"Yes it is." Grünewald was glad that the conversation was taking a turn toward the better. He didn't like being on the defensive. He hoped that Krasnovsky didn't know that he didn't know Stiglitz's whereabouts. To his relief the food arrived, and for a few minutes there was silence as the two men gave attention to the fare.

"Do you know when his next round of attacks will be?"

"No, but his pattern is to set off a series of bombs and then go to ground for some time between a week and a month."

"So you think it will be quiet for a few weeks."

"Yes. This time, my guess is it will be for thirty days, maybe longer. He has to build more bombs and get them into West Germany. Why?"

"Moscow is getting concerned. They do not like it when people claiming to be socialists blow up women and children. It is not good for our image as champions of the working class and downtrodden."

"Do you realize that, this time, the Americans were all Jews?" Grünewald pushed a pile of sauerkraut onto the remaining piece of bratwürst before sticking his fork into the meat and stuffing it in his mouth.

"Yes, I do, and I know many of your former comrades are pleased, and many in Moscow feel the same way, but we won't go into that." The Soviet colonel chewed for a few seconds on a chunk of heavy black bread. "So I can tell Moscow that things will be quiet for about a month?"

"Yes."

"Good."

"Do you have any news about the American reaction?" Grünewald hoped he might get something from the KGB colonel.

Krasnovsky took a long swallow of his beer before responding. "So far nothing other than they are very, very mad. But you know that. The pressure is building in the American media for their president to act, but he is trapped by his own words. He has stated in news conferences that the West German law enforcement agencies are in charge of the investigation. He cannot do anything more until the West Germans ask."

Monday, October 4ᵗʰ, 1976, 2130 local time, Exeter

The rain had finished, leaving the stones and sidewalk shining in the streetlights. At the door of the synagogue, Josh and Rebekah said good night to Lev Mogen, who walked in the opposite direction toward his own car. Josh had his hand on her arm as Rebekah negotiated the slippery, uneven, wet cobblestones in high heels.

After Josh backed out of the parking place, Rebekah turned to him. "You've been awful pensive tonight. What's up?"

"I've been thinking about the way the cantor sang "Avenu Malkienu" tonight. It reminded me about a man by the name of Louis Ferman I knew when I was a kid. He survived Buchenwald because he had a wonderful voice. The guards made him sing popular songs sixteen hours a day outside their barracks. At night they would give him a song to memorize, and he had to show up the next morning and sing it or it was off to be worked to death as a slave laborer or sent to the gas chambers. He told me that after the war, when he tried to sing in night clubs or on the stage, his voice would crack because it brought back memories of Buchenwald. But, he said, he didn't have problems with his voice when he was singing prayers and Jewish songs; he told me that he thought it was God's way of telling him to become a cantor."

Josh was silent, letting the memory and vision of the frail old man settle before he continued. "Louis sang "Avenu Malkienu" with such a haunting voice you could feel the pain from his years in the camp. It was as if he was still thanking God for delivering him from the horrors, and at the same time asking Him to help him forget the memories of Buchenwald. The way he sang was beautiful and yet brought people to tears. Anyway, any time I hear "Avenu Malkienu", I think of him and my eyes water as I remember his voice. It haunts me in a good way, and tonight because of what happened in Germany on Rosh Hashanah, it just made the memories more vivid."

"What became of him?"

"I don't know. I know he made money from the U.S. military families who paid him to teach people like me, who can't sing, to at least chant well enough for our bar mitzvahs. I remember he was studying to become a psychiatrist. He coached me through my

Haftorah, and you know I can't carry a tune worth a damn. At first in the early fifties, the only synagogue we had was the U.S. military chapel, and we encouraged the few German Jews living in the Wiesbaden/Frankfurt/Mainz area to come to services. Then a synagogue in Frankfurt reopened, and I think Louis joined it."

"That's a sad but at the same time wonderful story."

"Rebekah, this thing with Red Hand brings back too many memories. I grew up around people who had tattoos on their arms who'd survived the camps."

"I did too. I heard some of their stories as a little girl and didn't understand. Israel was filled with people who survived the camps. My mother couldn't or wouldn't talk about it, but I heard about the camps from my father and others. Now, as an adult, I do understand, and the thought of another Holocaust is something I will die to prevent, whether as an Israeli or a U.S. citizen."

Josh held his wife's hand. "Me too."

Wednesday, October 6th, 1976, 0745, local time, RNAS Yeovilton

Despite being the largest room in the building, their operations center was not large enough. The table was often covered with photos and charts. In front of Marty, there were folders—one for each bombing—piled on top of a large road map of West Germany. On the wall behind him, the team had taped photos of each of the bomb sites; on another were the pictures Lev had brought of the Germans who went to Libya.

Marty looked up as Lev and Josh entered. "Welcome back, I assume both of you have atoned for your many sins!"

"I went with Josh and Rebekah to the synagogue in Exeter for Yom Kippur," Lev Mogen replied with an answering smile. "It is very nice and almost as old as the ones in Israel!"

"Pay no attention to him, Marty; it was founded in 1743, not during biblical times. Rebekah and I like the congregation and it is in a wonderful part of town. We took a walk through the old streets between services."

"Well, now it is time to get back to work." Marty was what he described as a holiday Lutheran, which meant he maybe went to church on Christmas and Easter and not any time in between. "Here's the good news: any day now we should be getting a package with our official tasking and guidance. John, for your information, Admiral Hastings will be in the U.K. on an official visit sometime soon to have a chat with his counterpart in the

Admiralty. I'm sure he'll want a briefing from us. As you all know, no messages referring to our task designation as Random Hook go out. Who knows who came up with that designation, but it is classified Top Secret, Sensitive Compartmented Information, Code Word Blazer."

Marty pointed at two smiling men in Royal Army fatigues who were standing in the back of the room. "Josh, go say hello to Sergeants William Bentley and Charles Goodson. Colour Sergeant Calhoun got Major Ralston to assign them to us, so we got two very good men. You should remember them from your trip to Novaya Zemlaya earlier in the year."

"I do." Josh gave each one a hug as they shook hands. "Welcome, it is good to have you with us."

"We're happy to be with you, sir." Bentley spoke for the two. "The colour sergeant was, I am told, very persuasive when he talked to Major Ralston."

"O.K., now that everyone has been introduced, listen up!" Marty yelled to get everyone one's attention. "We have gotten permission from our respective bosses to look unmilitary. That means starting today we can let our hair grow, have beards—as long as they don't look too ratty—and wear civilian clothes at all times. The Americans on the team will have to go shopping, because we need to wear clothes that don't scream American. As long as we don't get extravagant, we'll get reimbursed for every dollar or pound. Also, Rebekah and Gwen have volunteered to take us shopping this coming weekend in London and act as the fashion police."

Marty waited until the groans and chuckles subsided. "Once we're ready, I want us to visit all the bomb sites. Here's the list; I've grouped them by city. Last item: Senior Chief Jenkins, Colour Sergeant Calhoun, and Petty Officer Van der Jagt will work on getting us, as our hosts would say, kitted out with weapons and anything else they think we'll need. Understood?"

Heads nodded and a few "Aye, aye"s gave Marty the answer he needed. Next he pointed to the folders on the table in front of him. "We've got all the police reports, so we need to walk around and look for things that the police missed and figure out why each location was targeted."

"There has to be a pattern of some sort," Josh said he looked at the list of cities, many of which he was familiar with from the years his U.S. Air Force father had been stationed in Germany.

"One would think that the West German police are doing the same thing," John said. "May I can make a suggestion that may save us time?"

"Go." Marty put a folder back down on the map.

"We need the ability to go when and where we want in Europe without having to worry about public transportation. My father has a Piper Navajo that he is planning to sell, but I think he would be happy to loan it to us, and it can carry six in a modicum of comfort plus some baggage. We could fly from here to anywhere in Europe. I can get Josh checked out in it in a jiffy, which means we'll have two pilots, him and myself, who can fly it."

This caught Josh by surprise. He slewed around to look at John and said, "I'd be O.K. with that, but I want to make sure your father is compensated in full for use of the plane and any related expenses that are incurred. No freebies. Jenkins and Calhoun will figure out how to get him paid."

"Agreed. I'll get a rate per hour from my father and it'll be that plus any gas, maintenance and landing fees."

"Good." Marty went back to the task at hand. "Let's spend the rest of the week planning each site visit." Marty turned to Lev, "When do you think the next package will be arriving from Israel?"

"Tomorrow morning by courier."

The Same Day, 1848 local time, Hannover

Anna Liese Stiglitz stuck her head in the crowded living room, where family and friends were gathered, and announced, "Dinner is ready."

Helmut Stiglitz was the first to rise so he could lead the way and take his seat at the head of the table. The others filed in and took the same places they occupied each time they were together. It was Anna Liese's dinner table, and everyone knew where she wanted them to sit.

Helmut noticed an empty place. "Where's Dieter?"

"I don't know," his wife answered. "I tried to call him several times, but I got no answer."

"Well, we will proceed with this celebration without him." Helmut held up his wine glass. "To our new Bundestag member, Erik Stiglitz."

Thursday, October 7th, 1976, 1245 local time, RNAS Yeovilton

Marty waited until the others had left the table at the Yeovilton's officer's mess and leaned toward his friend. "Josh, you need to level with me about something."

"OK." The look on Marty's face said he had something serious on his mind.

"I see how this Red Hand thing is eating at you. There's an edge to you that I have never seen before. On one hand, I like it because it keeps you focused and driven. On the other, it scares the hell out of me."

"In what way?"

"Josh, I know you, I know both your and Rebekah's families lost relatives in the concentration camps, and I know what happened to your families during the war. I am sure that these attacks are bringing back very painful memories and you are thinking that this may be the beginning of Holocaust part two."

"We're not to Holocaust levels, but Marty, I know where you are going. I can't speak for Lev, but he is an Israeli and every day for them is a battle for survival that they cannot lose. Rebekah is a sabra, and she thinks that way too. So, yes, Red Hand makes me very angry. It is eating at me because it only took thirty-one years for Germans to start killing Jews again after hundreds of thousands died putting Hitler and his minions out of business. By the time World War II ended, more than six million Jews and Lord only knows how many others were murdered by the Nazis." Josh stopped as images of gaunt camp survivors came into mind. "Humor me for a minute or two while I tell you a quick story about a guy by the name of Louis Ferman."

"OK, go for it."

By the time Josh finished, tears were standing in his eyes. "Marty, I am not going to say that you don't understand, but you've never known or had to live with a camp survivor, because where you grew up there weren't many around. But Rebekah and I did. Our congregations were filled with members trying to rebuild their bodies and their lives. It affects me more as an adult than it did as a child because now I understand. I _cannot_ forget, nor _will_ I forget. So, the bottom line is, if I can contribute in one small way to stopping Red Hand, then I will do it." Josh stopped short of saying anything more.

"We joke all the time about not wanting to watch the other be put in his grave," Marty looked into his friend's eyes. "But this is serious. Josh, you have got to promise me that you and Lev will not go off on some misguided solo mission to get one of these guys and put the rest of us at risk. We have to stay covert, and we cannot call attention to ourselves by being cowboys. You've got to stay on the reservation."

Josh took a deep breath. "Don't worry, I will. It may be hard at times, but I promise, I won't go off and do something stupid; because neither Rebekah nor you would ever forgive me."

Marty wanted to hug his friend. Instead he leaned back and said, "Great. I knew you would, but I wanted to get it out in the open. It does hurt me too, and I am sure it does the others. Just so you know, I'm betting that we'll get our chance to take these bastards out, and when we do, you and Lev are going to be front and center. But we have to do it *together*." Marty tossed the fork he was toying with on the table. "And this way, I won't have to have a conversation with Rebekah that starts with, 'I'm so, so sorry....'"

"Good, because I don't want that to happen either!"

Saturday, October 9th, 1976, 1015 local time, Yeovilton

Marty didn't demand the team work seven days a week, but they began showing up on Saturday mornings, which often dragged into the afternoon or evening before they left. Marty knew that they'd burn out if they pushed the pace for months, so as a compromise he mandated that Sundays and Saturday afternoons were non-working times, except for the individual who acted as a unit duty officer. That person spent the night, brought a lunch, and slept on a cot in one of the empty offices upstairs. This morning, Marty, Josh, John, and Lev were still at work, mugs of coffee and tea to hand as they perused maps, files, and newspapers. Marty kept rubbing his jaw where the new beard itched.

Josh tossed a police report on the table. "Marty, this may be obvious, so I want to lay out the hypothesis and then we can decide whether or not it merits pursuing."

Marty looked up from the newspaper article on Red Hand that he was reading. "Go for it."

"There's a pattern and there's not a pattern. Here's what I am thinking. We know that two of the bombings targeted synagogues, and there were three bombs that seemed to target a Jewish-owned department store, Hertie's. There may be others that targeted Jews, but we know those for a fact. Then there are the others, which appear to be more random. We don't have the smarts to figure out if there is a pattern in the randomness. So my suggestion is, let's start from the other direction. Let's answer the question, why Hertie's? Why not other well known German firms? I think if we do that, we may learn more about the rationale Red Hand uses to pick its targets."

Marty looked around the room. "Lev, John. What do you think?"

John was sitting on the edge of one of the tables looking at results of one of the bombings. "It's bloody well better than trying to put together a jig-saw puzzle when you don't even know what the picture is, much less what the pieces look like."

Lev nodded.

Marty pointed his pen at Josh and Lev. "Good. You two are our resident experts. Get started."

The Same Day, 1938 local time, Schloss von Thiessen

Von Theissen rested both hands on the back of the chair at the head of the table while he waited until each of his guests stood by a chair. Sturmer had selected the blue and white Hutschenreuther china made in the 1870s to give the table a cheerful look. Next to the sterling silver utensils, light from the antique chandelier sparkled off the lead crystal champagne flutes, wine, and water glasses, giving the room a light-hearted atmosphere worthy of a celebration. Sturmer was holding an iced bottle of champagne as if he were holding a rifle, vertically in front of his body.

Von Theissen nodded, and Sturmer went around the table filling each champagne glass to the same level before resuming his station by the door to the pantry and kitchen, where a sterling silver cooler held a second bottle in readiness.

"Gentlemen, a toast." Von Theissen picked up his glass. "To fallen comrades."

In unison the six men around the table, each one a veteran of World War II, repeated the three words and drank as they remembered those who had not come home.

"To The New German Party and its future success." Von Theissen emptied his glass as a signal to all the rest to finish theirs. The slender crystal glasses had been in his family for generations. Made in Hungary, they had been given to his family by the Emperor of the Austro-Hungarian Empire in the late 1800s for setting up a factory near Budapest.

"The New German Party." Glasses were set down and refilled.

"To our ability to restore Germany to her rightful place in Europe and the world."

"A powerful Germany." Half a glass was finished.

"To our leadership."

"Leadership."

"To the man who tried before and failed because he was betrayed." Von Theissen straightened his arm so with his elbow locked, his glass raised to just above his shoulder, and clicked his heels as he came to attention.

The others did the same before they spoke together. "To our former leader." It was a Nazi salute without the Heil Hitler. None of the men used the words they would have preferred saying, knowing that the salute alone was enough to earn a hefty fine and even jail time.

"To the Fourth Reich."

"Fourth Reich." Another glass was drained and wine bottles were passed around.

"Let us eat." Von Theissen pulled the chair back and didn't sit until all of his guests were pulling their chairs toward the table. By the time he sat down, Sturmer was serving the first course.

Sunday, October 10th, 1448 Local time, Dinkelsbühl

The appearance of a new letter in von Ritter's post office box brought a crease to his brows. Six kills and six wins made it obvious that his employers were targeting districts where, if the favored candidate was eliminated, it increased the odds or even guaranteed that the well-funded New German Party candidate would win.

So what did that make him? A loose end!

Von Ritter drove south along Highway 7 towards Ulm looking for a pay phone to call the number. Each time the number changed, along with the password Just outside the Bavarian city that was about midway between Stuttgart and Munich, he dropped enough one Deutschmark coins in the slot to more than pay for five minutes.

"Allo."

"Twin bolts."

"Ahhh, you received our note."

"Yes." The fewer words the better; and if anyone was taping the call, he wanted to be off in less than a minute.

"Your mission is over, at least for now. We are grateful for your work because it was discrete and did not bring any unnecessary attention. We may have more work for you, so keep this post office box and check it at least once a week. We will send your termination bonus. "

Yeah, for six murders and one fire bombing. No extra casualties. "Do you have the payment ready?"

"Yes. Do you want me to mail it? It will be packaged like the others."

Von Ritter didn't want the money in the Bundespost system. What happened if it split open? Too many potential questions, too much risk. No, hand delivered is better. "No, I will call you with instructions to deliver it by hand to a place in Wiesbaden."

"When?"

"How about late in the afternoon tomorrow, say at three o'clock?"

"That will be fine."

"I will call you just after noon with an address."

Monday, October 11th, 1976, 0725 local time, Wiesbaden

Grenfel was sitting in the Hauptpolizeidirektor's office in the Bundeskriminalamt's headquarters to give his boss an update so he would have the latest information when he met with the Minister of Justice.

"Heinrich, give me something good to tell the minister after the Jewish Holiday bombings. The Bundesrepublik needs to show progress." It was a demand rather than a request.

"Herr Hauptpolizeidirektor, I have a question before I begin."

Starkeholz held out his cup of coffee to signal Grenfel to speak.

Grenfel felt his chest tighten as he began to speak. "What if we looked at the bombings from a religious angle?"

"You mean that Red Hand is targeting Jews?"

"Yes sir."

"The minister has made it very clear in his statements to the press that Germans are being killed. He doesn't care if they are Aryan, Jews, or men from Mars. They are all, emphasize *all*, Germans or citizens from Allied nations. So, no, don't take that tack."

"Yes sir." Grenfel waited. Starkeholz sighed.

"What about the neo-Nazis? Several of the newspapers are blaming them."

"Herr Hauptpolizeidirektor, they are bullies and thugs. In many ways, they are similar to Hitler's Brown Shirts and are criminals looking for a cause. While much of what they do. extortion, drugs and the like, is illegal , our investigators have found no evidence of Red Hand and the Neo-Nazis working together. Not like the Munich Olympics shootings when they helped the Palestinians."

Starkeholz made a note on his pad. "What about Muslims? They are known for terrorism, and Lord knows there are enough of them in this country. Most speak German pretty well."

"They don't fit the description we have. Our hypothesis is that the person who has been buying wrecked cars is a native German. We don't know if he is a member of Red Hand, a supporter, or just a contractor. While we cannot rule out a possible Muslim influence, we do not have any evidence of their involvement. It is possible that the bomber is a gastarbeiter, but not likely, because he would have a foreign accent that was noticeable. So far, every piece of hard evidence suggests that the Red Hand bomber or bombers are native Germans based in either the DDR or the Bundesrepublik."

"Are you suggesting that we contact the Stasi and ask for their help?"

"No, not at all. Before we call the DDR we need to have, as the Americans say, the smoking gun, indicating that they are involved in some way. We're far from that."

The trend of the discussion was beginning to interest Starkeholz. "What kind of involvement do you think the DDR may have?"

"We believe Red Hand is getting their Czech made Semtex into the country from either East Germany or Austria. The ball bearings are all very worn and we are pretty sure they were taken from parts that were being discarded from Soviet vehicles made in Eastern Europe or the Soviet Union. The Americans say the metallurgy suggests that they are either East German or Czech."

Grenfel paused to let Starkeholz absorb what he said before he continued with the next item on his list. "If we assume the bombs are being made elsewhere, we need to find out how they are getting into the Bundesrepublik. The easiest borders for a German in a car to cross would be from the DDR or Austria. So, we have stepped up surveillance at all those border crossings."

"How do you determine whether or not the person is driving a car packed with Semtex and ball bearings?" Starkeholz was asking the question and thinking out loud.

"A dog trained to find explosives is the surest way. We would need several dogs at every crossing. We don't have enough dogs, and it would take months to train them. Checking each car is much too cumbersome. We could use outside help."

"Whose?" Starkeholz hoped this might change the nature of an unpleasant discussion.

"Sir, we could ask the Israelis for some intelligence. They may know what Muslim terrorist groups have cells in Europe, how they operate, and who provides them support. That would tell us where to look."

Starkeholz leaned back in amazement as he considered this novel suggestion.

Tuesday, October 12th, 1976, 1530 Local time, Wiesbaden

As in the past, the payments were given to von Ritter in a public place—where members of the team could watch for potential danger. None of them trusted their employer.

This time the meeting was at an outdoor café where he could sit outside and watch the people come from all directions while he enjoyed the bakery's specialty: schlagzahnekuchen—a whipped cream cake topped with fresh fruit. As he ate, taking his time and savoring each bite, von Ritter considered the situation. This wasn't a normal mercenary contract in which the government paid you for risking your life, and at the end, if you survived, you received a bonus and lived happily ever after. *We are loose ends. These bastards would kill their own mothers and children if they thought it would advance their cause. So what will they try? It has to be something that will take us all out, because so long as one of us is alive there is a risk that someone will talk. And it won't be another team sent to take us out; that would simply be exchanging one loose end for another. No, it has to be something they can do themselves that doesn't lead back to them. Do they know who we are? If so, we are all walking dead men. If not...* Von Ritter mentally reviewed all his communications with their employer. He had done everything in his power to keep the identities of his team members secret. Had it been enough?

Hofschlanger, the lookout, had arrived a half hour before von Ritter. He was seated at a different table, feigning reading a book as he sipped his coffee, when a man von Ritter judged to be in early sixties, stopped at the front of the café and looked around. It was obvious to von Ritter that the man was trying to match a face with a photograph or a description. He waved with evident relief when he spotted von Ritter, who waved back. Before the man arrived at the table, the paratrooper stood up and pulled back a chair.

"Herr Oberst von Ritter?"

"Yes, that is me." Ritter held out his hand, which the other man pumped vigorously twice. *Why are you wearing gloves? It is fifteen degrees Celsius.*

"And you are?"

"Brunner. Alois Brunner."

"Herr Brunner, may I order you some coffee or interest you in a piece of cake? The schlagzahnerkuchen with strawberries is quite good."

"No thank you. I have a train to catch. This will take only a minute." Brunner sat on the edge his chair. "This is for you." He used just his forefinger to push the thick envelope across the glass table top.

"Thank you." *Brunner, why are you so nervous? My guess is that you've never worked in the field, and you're scared. Why? Hofschlanger, you better get pictures.*

Brunner started to get up, but von Ritter held up his hand as a signal to sit back down and used his pocket knife to slit the end of the envelope so he could peer inside. There were four packages; two months' salary for each man. "Everything is here?"

"Yes, as per our contract." Brunner got up.

Why was he in such a hurry? Von Ritter ran a finger along the edges of the envelope. No wires.

"*In ordnung.*" Von Ritter used the shortened version of the expression 'alles ist in ordnung'—everything is in order—to give Brunner a sense of security. "It was a pleasure doing business with you." Von Ritter held out his hand; Brunner shook it and then hurried down the street. Hofschlanger, who'd already paid his bill, rose from his seat and followed.

Two hours later, von Ritter was standing with the other three around a makeshift workbench at one end of an empty warehouse in Erbenheim, a suburb of Wiesbaden. Hofschlanger was the last to arrive; he had followed Brunner until the fellow got on a train to Munchen.

On the table stood a line of small bottles with names von Ritter last saw in high school chemistry and could not pronounce. A rack with two rows of test tubes stood next to the bottles. In the center of the workbench, under a fluorescent lamp, the envelope lay as the center of attention.

Goetz looked at his three comrades. "Gentleman, before we begin, I suggest you roll down your sleeves, pull on the long rubber gloves, cover up any bare skin, and don your gas masks. I have no idea what we will find, but if it is dangerous, I want us protected. First, I will make sure there is no bomb in each smaller envelope. Then, we'll check for other stuff."

Before they had come to this warehouse, which was owned by his sister and used to repair and restore antiques, von Ritter had asked Goetz if he knew how to detect poisonous chemicals, and the former legionnaire had said yes. Part of his explosive ordnance training had been to combine readily available supplies from drug, hardware, or food stores to test and neutralize the most common chemical weapons like sarin, VX, and mustard gas. It was something the Legion practiced all the time.

Their first step was to weigh the envelope to compare the amount of currency they were supposed to contain to a stack of bills that von Ritter brought along to use as a control. The good news was that the masses were within fifty grams, and the logical explanation for the difference was the envelope itself.

The ex-legionnaire eased all four packages out of the large cocoa brown envelope so they were in a ragged row. One, with von Ritter's name, was slightly thicker than the others. Goetz used his forefinger to gently rub the top and sides of each envelope, feeling for a wire or anything irregular before turning them over and repeating the process.

"No wires. I am going to slit Herr Oberst's envelop open first so I can peel back the top and see what is inside." With the steadiness of a surgeon, Goetz dragged an X-acto knife down the paper just outside the contents. After repeating the process on the other side, he made a cut at one end and, with a pair of tweezers, opened the envelope like a can, folding the top back so that it would not plop back down on the blue and green hundred-mark bills sealed in heavy, clear plastic.

Goetz used the sleeve on his forearm to wipe the sweat off his brow and repeated the process to extract the money. "*Ist gut*, there are no bombs that we can see, unless they hollowed out the center of each stack, which would be very hard to do. The black light, please."

Von Ritter placed a full soda can on the flap of plastic, then turned on the flashlight and handed it to Goetz.

"Thank you, Herr Oberst." Goetz shone the light on the stack from several different directions and then switched lens filters. After a few seconds, he muttered, "Hmmm."

"What does that mean?" Von Ritter spoke for the other two men at the table.

"It means I think someone tinkered with our bonus. There is some kind of chemical film on the top bill. I don't know if it's a residue from the mint, as these are brand new bills, or if someone sprayed them with a chemical. They could also be counterfeit, so I am going to dab some chemicals on the top bill. Oh, by the way, if they are counterfeit, it will piss me off more than if they tried to kill us with a bomb or chemicals!"

"I agree." Von Ritter took hold of the light. "I do not like being cheated. If they are fakes, we will have to decide whether or not we want to collect our bonus or write it off. I'm in favor of collecting, and I will start with Herr Brunner." Von Ritter looked at his three compatriots. All nodded in agreement.

The three men stood back from the table while Goetz measured and mixed chemicals together into two test tubes, each with about four centimeters of liquid. He immersed a long cotton swab at the end of a ten-centimeter stick into one tube, and then dragged it across the blue image of Clara Schumann on the top one hundred Deutschmark bill before he stuck it into the second test tube. The clear liquid turned a brick red. He peeled back the top bill and tested the second and then the third. All generated the same result.

"That's not a printer's chemical. It is some kind of poison. My guess it is designed to be absorbed by the skin and kill us quickly after we touch the money. We now have a choice. I can spend the next half an hour trying to figure out what type of poison it is, or I can work on a way to neutralize it, which will take about ten minutes."

Von Ritter spoke without waiting to hear from any of the men. "Save me two bills out of each envelope, which I will seal in plastic bags. Then figure out how to neutralize the chemical on all the bills, not just the ones on the top. "

"I agree." Hofshlanger made it two votes for neutralizing. Zweibel nodded assent.

"Good." Goetz looked at his comrades. "That's what I would do as well. I think simple household cleaners like bleach or ammonia will do the trick."

The legionnaire took six more samples from the bill and dissolved them in distilled water, which he then poured carefully into test tubes. He filled a plastic lab syringe with household bleach, a second with ammonia, and a third with vinegar. Each tube had been marked with a B, A, or V; he would have two test samples for each reactant. He held each vial as he dropped three large drops and then swirled them before he put them back in the rack. By the time he'd finished, the ones labeled "B" were a bright shade of blue.

"Excellent. My guess is the poison is some form of sarin, and if we wash these bills in a mixture of forty liters of water, two hundred and fifty milliliters of bleach, and the same amount of a dishwashing soap that has a mild degreaser, we should be able to get rid of all the poison. Then we wash the bills in fresh soapy water and we rinse them twice in fresh water. Before we start the first fresh water rinse, I'll test the them again. And, to make sure we are safe, I will test with another set of chemicals. If they're O.K, then it is just a matter of drying the bills. If not, we will repeat the process with ammonia and soap and water, and then vinegar and soap and water. Clear?"

"Excellent. There is a faucet and a large sink in the back wall, along with a floor drain. We can do the washing there. Hofschlanger, you and Zweibel go buy us four large buckets and some cloth bags that have holes in them, like we used to wash our uniforms in. Goetz will give you a list of what we need."

"Yes, sir."

When they came back an hour and a half later, it took two trips to carry the clothes lines, packages of clothespins, four twenty-five liter buckets, four hair dryers, four fifteen-meter extension cords, four five-liter bottles of bleach, an ammonia based cleaner, dishwashing soap, and four drawstring bags.

"Before we get to work, I have a present for everyone." Von Ritter pulled out his briefcase and opened it. "We didn't use all our expense money, so I divided the balance by four, and each share is ten thousand marks."

Von Ritter tossed the packages out on the table. No one touched them. Hofschlanger, Goetz, and Zweibel just looked at him. "Ahh, I understand." He pulled off the rubber gloves he was wearing and slit open each package, undid the rubber bands and rubbed his palms over many of the bills. "There's nothing on these, trust me. If you wish, we can wash them as well."

The contaminated bills from the first envelope of their bonus went into the bucket, and Goetz swirled the liquid without splashing. After the bills soaked for five minutes, the liquid was dumped into the sink and fresh water with more soap was poured in. The process was repeated three times, after which the water coming out of the bucket was no longer colored, but clear. To make sure, the legionnaire filled it a fifth time and tested it again. The test was negative.

"Herr Oberst, I think we can start drying the bills."

"Agreed." By then, Hofschlanger and Zweibel had four clothes lines strung around the warehouse. Von Ritter turned around to see their work. "This brings a whole new meaning to the term money laundering."

It was well after midnight before they finished. "Dump all the liquids down the sink and I'll dispose of what is left. You gentlemen need to take your bonuses and disappear," von Ritter told his companions.

"That is what we plan to do, Herr Oberst," Hofschlanger said. "We three have given the matter much thought, and we had come to a decision, even before this business of the termination bonus. We are going to South Africa to join their Special Forces Brigade. They are looking for people with our experience, and it will be a fresh start for us. They'll even take an old man like me. The one advantage my age confers is that, assuming I make it through training and qualify, they will make me a provisional Warrant Officer Second Class. Goetz and Zweibel will become provisional staff sergeants, and we will all have a year to prove ourselves in the field. Now that this contract is concluded, we will be departing to spend the rest of the year in Cape Town, getting ready. It has been a while since we have been through basic training!"

"Excellent. I know you will do well. Good luck to all of you. Here is an address you can use to leave a message for me. There is a phone number on it as well." Von Ritter gave Hofschlanger a card that had his sister's home address and phone number.

"Herr Oberst, what are you going to do?"

"First, I will dispose of all this material. Then, I plan to take care of the men who sent us this poisoned money in such a way that we are never charged with any crime."

"How will you do this?"

"I will not tell you, but I have been planning this for weeks. When you get to South Africa and are settled, I want each of you to send me a letter with an address. When I finish, I will mail a letter back with a statement in the body of the letter that says, 'all our affairs here in Germany are in order.' If you don't see that phrase, then you will know I failed. If no letter comes, I died trying."

The men all shook hands. "Herr Oberst, it has been an honor. Good luck to you."

"And to you as well."

Wednesday, October 13th, 1976, 0946 local time, Nörvenich

It was one of the larger briefing rooms at the airbase twenty-five kilometers southwest of Cologne. As Brigadier General Werfel strode through the door, his aide, standing just inside, called out "Achtung!" The word brought almost seventy pilots to their feet in unison. A smiling Albert von Theissen followed Werfel and stood a meter to the side and behind the Air Division commander.

"Good morning." Werfel looked around the room. "I thought you would enjoy talking to one of my former squadron mates from the war, who besides his fifty-three confirmed kills, was in charge of the Luftwaffe's program to fly American and British fighter aircraft so we could develop tactics to defeat them. As you know, we do the same today, but I think you will find Herr Oberst von Theissen's experience to be both interesting and still very relevant. You are free to ask him questions about his experience. It is my pleasure to present Baron Albert von Theissen."

A hand shot up and the general pointed to the young captain. "Herr Baron, of the airplanes you flew—German, British, American—which one did you like the best and which one did you like the least?"

"First, before I answer, I want to thank you for your time. It is an honor to meet the pilots of the Boelke and Steinhoff Jageschweders. The best airplane—that's easy—the Spitfire. I flew several different versions, and all were a delight. You just thought about turning and it would. The Me-109 was the worst. When we built it, it was a world beater, but it was tricky to land—we lost more of these planes in landing accidents than in combat, and it was cramped and hard to see out of the cockpit, which made it hard to see your enemy."

"What about the American fighters?"

"In a turning dogfight, the Mustang was the best. The P-47 Thunderbolt was a monster. It couldn't turn with any of our fighters, but if one ever got behind you, its eight fifty-caliber machine guns would tear your plane apart, and it was very difficult to shoot down. And you could never dive away from one. You're only defense was to try to turn away and get your opponent to overshoot."

"Did you fly the Lightning?"

"I did. It was a good airplane that could fly a long way. It had a wheel instead of stick, and at first I didn't think I would like the wheel, but after a few minutes in the air it didn't matter."

"What about the American pilots? Were they good, or was it their machines that gave them the advantage?"

"After 1944, their planes were better than ours. By then, the American and British pilots were also better trained because they got three hundred or more hours of training before they were assigned to a combat squadron. The war was eating away at our experienced pilots and we didn't have the time or the fuel to train new pilots as much as we wanted, so they would be sent to frontline units with as few as a hundred hours—or even less."

Werfel let the questioning go for two hours before he called time so that Albert and he could make it to the club before it stopped serving lunch. His aide had to call the club twice to let them know the general and his guest would be delayed.

Werfel waited to speak until their waiter cleared the corner table in the dining room of the officer's club and set down two cups of strong black coffee for the general and his guest. "So, Albert, what do you think?"

"Ah, I am impressed. It brings back many pleasant memories. I cannot thank you enough for the tour and the meeting with the pilots. Naming wings after our great aces is an excellent way to honor them. Steinhoff and I met many times during the war, and we spent many a night drinking and talking about the best way to beat a Mustang or Spitfire."

"I am glad you liked it. They are always pestering me to talk about the old days. They are much more interested in what I had to overcome than what they themselves now face. You know, they are far better trained than we were. I wouldn't tell them this, but they are also better pilots than our generation."

"How so?" Von Theissen was taken aback.

"They are better educated. All my pilots speak English as well as German. Most speak a third or fourth language. We have the luxury of using bases in the United States with access to ranges that are not available in Germany to provide very realistic training. We also take advantage of the knowledge that the U.S. has of the Soviets' aircraft and their tactics. When you and I flew our first combat missions, we had no idea of what we were facing. It was go, take off, if you encounter an enemy, maneuver to shoot him down. If you were lucky, you had a flight leader who had survived a few dogfights and had some wisdom to pass on. These young men start learning tactics during training, and they fly in realistic, unscripted exercises that are as close to actual combat as we can make them."

"Do you think they will fight with the same dedication that we did?"

"I do. But their motivation is different. There is no Gestapo holding a gun to their heads, nor are they worried about members of their families being arrested on the whim of some party hack. They have grown up in a democracy and like it. They will fight to preserve the Bundesrepublik because it is much better than what is on the other side of the wall, where a lot of them have relatives who want out. Every day we fly, we are reminded of the evil that is beyond that wall. Not much has changed in the Soviet Union since 1945, other than it is now a global power."

"So the Luftwaffe is apolitical."

"The whole Bundeswehr is. I have no idea of the party affiliation of any of the pilots or the men in my command. Do I talk politics with other generals and colonels? Of course we do, we just had a national election and the Christian Democrats retained a majority. The point is that the civilians are in charge and we report to them."

"So if Germany, through NATO, was about to be forced into a war by the Americans or British, would the military follow without question?"

"No, we wouldn't let our politicians lead us blindly into another war. We're part of the NATO command structure, so they could not drag us into a war unless one of the member nations was attacked. NATO is a ***defensive*** alliance. If you remember history, Germany's last two strong national leaders who had absolute power—the Kaiser and Hitler—started wars that we could not win. Those days are long gone, thank God." Werfel stopped to sip his coffee. "Why do you ask?"

"My party—the New German Party—stands for an independent, strong Germany that is not beholden to the

Americans or the Russians. While we understand we may not be equal, we don't want to be treated as second-class citizens either."

"Or a second-rate power?"

"Yes, that too."

Werfel clasped his hands and rested them on the edge of the table. "Albert, the days of Germany being the dominant European military and economic power are gone. We were never a global power. Today there are two super powers in the world, the Americans and the Russians. Everyone else, including us, is second or third. Our economy is one of the strongest in the world, and like the Americans, that is the core of our strength, but we cannot compete with them."

"So you have given up on unification and the benefits that could bring?"

"No, I haven't; and I don't think Germans on either side of the wall have given up on re-unification. It will happen if, and only if, Moscow lets it happen. It may happen in our lifetimes, but I wouldn't hold my breath."

"I think we can force the unification issue, if we have the will to do so and take the necessary steps."

"Good luck, Albert. To do that, you'll need the support of the Americans and British and even the French."

"That is what the New German Party intends to do. We came from nowhere and are now the fourth largest party in the Bundestag. This gives us credibility. In four years, we will win enough seats to demand a cabinet post."

"Albert, getting eleven seats in your first try is very impressive. My advice to you is stay within the boundaries of being representatives of the people. If your message is popular, you will gain more seats and more political power. Don't try a putsch, because you will fail just as Hitler did. The people won't tolerate it."

"Are you sure about that?"

Werfel didn't respond, because he saw the reaction in von Theissen's eyes that meant his words had struck a sensitive chord. *The bastards leading The New German Party are thinking putsch.* Instead he refreshed his cup of coffee.

"Herman, I know you have to go. One last question." Von Theissen leaned across the table. "Are you going to support us?"

Werfel didn't hesitate. "Albert, we spent a lot of good times together in good and sometimes in miserable conditions, but we do not share the same political views. So the short answer is no, I will not"

"Why? And I promise, I won't ask you again."

"I don't think your platform is supportable, and in many ways it scares me. I would bet money that the New German Party's leadership wants to create a Fourth Reich. Despite our republic's faults and mistakes, it is the best thing that has ever happened to Germany." *And I will die to preserve it.*

"I see." Von Theissen folded his napkin into a precise rectangle and put it on the table. "I had better get going. You have work to do. Again, thank you for the tour and the chance to meet your pilots. It was wonderful."

Saturday, October 16th, 1976, 0920 local time, Leeds

After a week of steady rain, there was finally enough sun to make a nice day. The puffy white clouds that dotted the blue sky like cotton balls were a welcome relief from the lead-gray skies. The glistening water on the slate path pointed like an arrow to the barn that was less than a hundred yards from the manor house. The home of the Duke of Leeds was about twenty miles northwest of the town with the same name in West Yorkshire England.

Josh was holding his three-month-old daughter and watching his wife chase their son over the lush green grass in front of the barn. Seven months pregnant, Gwen used her hand for support as she sat next to her friend's husband. "John should have the horses saddled in a few minutes."

Josh looked up. "It's a wonderful day for a ride. I'm sorry you can't come along."

"My riding days are over until I have the baby, besides, it will give me some time with Sara." Gwen watched the giggling Sasha, who kept twisting around to look for his mother. "I know this is a bit forward, but between the two of you, you've endured enough tragedy to fill several lifetimes. I don't know how you survived as well as you did. It had to be tough."

"Having a family helps. Having children... reminds you to have hope." Josh looked down at his daughter cradled in his arms. "Sara should go to sleep in a few minutes; thanks for offering to watch her." Josh handed Sara over and watched, smiling a little, as Gwen settled the baby over her own bulging middle.

"Friends help too, and John and I have become very good friends. Both of us are so grateful for your hospitality and friendship. I know Rebekah loves England. It was as if she were born and raised here."

Gwen smiled. "You know, if I didn't have proof otherwise, I'd think that John and you were brothers. In many ways, the two of you are closer than his two real bothers."

Josh saw John wave from the barn. "I feel the same way about him. The two of us are both warriors, we love what we do and love our respective navies, warts and all. We have fun together, but we also know we're involved in a very serious business, one in which, if you don't keep your wits about you, people you care about will get hurt, and you could die."

"Oh, I know. For generations, members of my family have been going off to do and to die for God, King or Queen, and country. Most have come back, but some haven't. What both of us like is your whole approach to life. It's infectious. John loves working with you, and now Marty." Gwen paused to delicately stroke Sara's cheek. "Are you and John still planning on leaving tomorrow afternoon in the Navajo?"

"Yup. We figure that if we stooge around for three or four hours and let me practice maneuvers while you drive home, we'll arrive back at Dunkeswell airport about the same time you two reach Yeovil. Rebekah said she'd drive out and get us."

"Sounds straightforward."

"It is, assuming I don't, as he says, blot my copybook."

Gwen laughed. "I doubt you'll do that."

Josh smiled and changed the subject. "Are you going to come trap shooting later with the rest of this?"

"Oh yes, I would not miss that for the world. Rebekah told me she's never fired a shotgun before, but I predict she will do very well. Underneath that sweet exterior is a pretty tough competitor."

Josh laughed. "Yeah, she's got a room full of trophies from karate meets, so watch out. Anyway, John's dad said he would teach her how to shoot a shotgun, so I don't have too."

"Well, I'll join you after you all enjoy time with the horses."

By the time the four of them got to the meadow behind the manor house, Tom Osborne had three shotguns leaning up against a small table, upon which were two stacks of boxes with the distinctive Winchester logo. There were also four chairs, one of which was occupied by John's mother, Lady Kate, who stood up as the two couples approached. John walked over and kissed his mother on the cheek.

"Lovely day for a bit of shooting," Tom Osborne observed. He was dressed comfortably in worn jeans and a faded shirt. "Josh, I want you to know that Rebekah has been peppering me with questions all morning about shooting trap. I think you may have a serious shooter and competitor."

Josh laughed and shook his head ruefully. "Of that, I have no doubt."

Tom handed one of the three shotguns to Rebekah, who took it as if she had been shooting all her life. "Ladies and gentlemen, these are all Browning A-5s. One is a pre-war model, and all were built in Belgium. The A-5, patented back in 1898, is one of John Browning's most famous designs, and was the first semi-automatic shotgun. The story goes, Browning was waiting in the lobby to present it to the president of Remington when the man died of a heart attack. So Browning then offered the A-5 to Fabrique Nationale in Belgium, since they were already producing some of his designs. These are not originals—if they were, they'd be extremely valuable. But they are still very well made."

"I didn't know all that." Josh was impressed.

"On either side of us, I have a couple of machines loaded to toss out clays. We'll load with two rounds, and in the beginning, we'll only launch one target at a time. If you get good at it, we'll make it more interesting and use two targets in rapid succession."

Tom pointed at the chairs. "Why don't you have a seat while Rebekah and I have a little practice? The ladies are going to use the two and a half inch shells, which have a bit less recoil. I've got three inch ones for the chaps."

All of them took turns shooting; then, after about an hour, Rebekah handed one of the shotguns to Josh. "I'm ready," she said, with a challenging smile.

Josh gave his wife a quizzical look. "For what?"

"I've heard that you and Marty often have bets when you shoot, so we'll do the same. Winner gets his or her choice of a present. We'll put a limit of twenty-five quid on the prize."

"You're serious?"

"Serious as a heart attack. Pressure is on, my love."

Josh turned to his friend, who gave him a palms out sign. "I didn't say anything. I'll sit over here by Gwen and watch this. It should be fun."

"Ladies first." Josh bowed. "One clay pigeon or two?"

"Let's start with one. Ten clays each, and the fewest rounds expended wins. If it is tied, then we'll go to two, and fewest rounds to get ten hits wins."

John nodded. "Fair enough."

"Oh, the price goes to fifty if I think you are letting me win!"

John laughed out loud. "Ohhhhhhhh, that's bloody nasty!"

Josh turned to his friend. "You see what I live with."

"That will cost you." Rebekah loaded two shells into the base of the shotgun and pulled the cocking lever to chamber around. "Pay attention; and you know, I have been wanting a Shetland wool sweater. Gwen and I saw one at Marks and Spencer the last time we were in London."

Rebekah raised the nine pound weapon to her shoulder, pulled it in tight and shifted her weight to her front foot before she turned to Tom Osborne, where he stood off to the side with the control that tossed the clays in the air. "Pull."

A clanking noise was followed by a circular disk crossing from left to right at about fifty feet off the ground and twenty or so yards ahead. Rebekah tracked it for a second and squeezed the trigger. Chunks of clay flew off the disk, which wobbled as it fell to the earth.

"One shot, one clay. Your turn."

Josh stepped forward, after making sure the shotgun had a round in the chamber. "Pull."

He tracked it for less time and pulled the trigger. The clay exploded under the impact of the birdshot.

"You're turn, hot shot."

Nine turns later the score was even. Each had hit nine clays and fired ten shells.

"This is fun." Rebekah lowered her voice. "It turns me on."

"Ohhhhhh. Does that mean I am going to get lucky tonight?"

"Maybe." Rebekah turned to Tom. "I need more of a challenge. How about we go to two birds?"

"Good oh. This is more fun that watching Manchester City play Manchester United!" Tom picked up the other cable that controlled the second catapult. "I'll launch the first one, count one thousand one, one thousand two, and launch the second one. The plugs are out of the shotguns so you can load four shells into each."

Rebekah stepped to the line. As she settled the Browning A5 against her shoulder, she felt the extended recoil pad mounted on the butt of the gun compress. "Pull." Four seconds apart, two clay pigeons tumbled to the earth. She'd fired two shells.

"Heat's on, love."

Josh smiled at his wife's comment. "Pull." He fired twice and got two hits; on the second one, only a small chunk flew off the clay disk.

"Feeling the pressure?" Rebekah's eyes sparkled as she downed two more clays with two rounds.

Josh was getting grim; this was, he realized, a no-win situation for him. If he lost, he'd never hear the end of it. John would tell Marty and the whole team, and every time they'd go to the range, he would hear that he was beaten by a woman. But if he won, he'll be kidded that he took advantage of a woman. The best result would be a tie, but knowing Rebekah, she won't accept that.

The pile of expended shells at their feet was growing. Josh pushed them aside so they were not underfoot. "Rebekah, how about we call it a tie? We can't use up all of Tom's clays or his shells."

Tom didn't let Rebekah answer. "Oh, not to worry, mate. I've got another crate of clays and the box under the table is full of shells. We can keep going all day. Two generations of Osborne's are enjoying a trap shooting version of family feud with two ruddy colonials. Brilliant. It is great theater. Just do me a favor, don't turn the guns on each other because we don't need a modern scene from Romeo and Juliet. It would be bloody awful, not to say dreadfully messy. And, what would we tell your Navy? So, carry on! This will make wonderful dinner conversation tonight!"

"Let's go another round," Rebekah said. "Two clays fired together so they cross. I'm enjoying watching you sweat!"

Josh made a face and stuck out his tongue.

"First one to miss one of the clays loses. How about that?"

"Done."

"Pull." Rebekah fired four shells.

Josh shouldered the shotgun. "Pull." He used three out of the four to down his two.

"Hmm," he said, "if we'd stuck with the old rules, I'd have just won."

Rebekah pulled Josh's head down to hers and kissed him deeply. After they pulled apart, Josh protested. "That's not fair!"

"All is fair in love and war." Rebekah lifted the shotgun. She knew her shoulder was going to be black and blue for days and she was ready to quit, but she didn't want to let on. "Pull."

Rebekah tracked first the clay from the left until she sensed they were about to cross and squeezed the trigger. Both fell apart. "One round, two kills. Beat that, my love."

Josh raised his hands over his head. "No way. I surrender!"

"Are you giving up?"

"I am. I didn't realize I was married to Annie Oakley."

Sunday, October 17th, 1976, 1530 local time, RNAS Leeds Bradford Airport

The Osborne's gleaming white twin engine Navajo C/R had red and blue stripes down the side. It had been pulled out of the hangar and parked in front of the fixed base operator by the time Josh and John arrived. While John signed a chit for the fuel, Josh walked around the cabin class airplane that had a maximum take-off weight of 6,200 pounds.

The C/R stood for counter rotating, which meant that the two engines turned inward in opposite directions to minimize the torque effect.

The air-stair cabin door was already down and he walked, bent over, past the four facing seats in the cabin and flipped the two battery switches in the overhead to the on position. As some of the instruments came to life, he waited until the fuel gages settled down and showed that the tanks were full before he rotated the rocker switches to the off position. Once the preflight was finished, Josh climbed into the cockpit and began familiarizing himself with the layout.

This wasn't the first time Josh had flown a piston engine twin. After his first tour in Vietnam, Josh used part of his GI Bill to pay for a multi-engine and an Air Transport Pilot rating, known by its letters, ATP. He had almost eighteen hundred total Navy hours, plus the hundred he'd flown before joining the Navy, so he was above the minimum number of hours needed to qualify. By the time he finished, he had almost thirty hours in the 1970 Aztec D the flight school was using for multi-engine training.

Once he had the ATP, he'd asked a reservist who was flying as a RAG instructor and who was also an FAA examiner to give him his NATOPS check and sign off on a type rating for the SK-61, which was the commercial version of the H-3. Josh also built multi-engine time in the Aztec flying airplane that was used for charters, and for carrying checks to San Francisco's Federal Reserve Bank for processing. By the time he left for his second tour in Vietnam, Josh had almost three hundred hours in the Aztec. His plan at the time had been to get on with one of the airlines when his Navy commitment was up. In an odd way, this felt like coming home.

As Josh reacquainted himself with the controls, John settled in beside him, and soon they were cleared for departure.

After they had climbed to eight thousand feet in a designated practice area, Josh rolled the Navajo into a series of left and right turns, first holding the airplane in a ten degree bank while he maintained his altitude, plus or minus twenty feet. The next series was for ninety degrees of turns to the left and then to the right, before he rolled into one that he held at a steady twenty degrees angle of bank for two circles, first one to the left and then one to the right. These were followed with two more circles at thirty degrees, after which Josh eased off the power. As the twin slowed, he dropped the first notch of flaps, then the gear followed by full flaps. John noticed that the altimeter moved less than forty feet up or down as Josh trimmed the Navajo to fly at ninety knots in the landing configuration.

"Pretty tidy flying." John had expected Josh to be smooth and precise after flying with him in a helicopter, but as he watched Josh's eyes dart from instrument to instrument and the use of trim to minimize control pressures, he was still surprised at how good Josh was the first time he flew this airplane.

"Mind if we do some stalls?"

"No, but the book says once the stall warning horn comes on steadily, we have to recover. We're not supposed to let it fall off into a spin."

"Not a problem." Josh held back pressure to slow the Navajo and let it balloon in altitude. The stall warning horn beeped, and the airplane started to shudder. "Buffet at sixty knots. Holding to fifty and it is starting to fall off on the left wing." As he was shouting over the blaring stall warning horn, Josh lowered the nose and, in quick succession, flipped the landing gear handle to the up position, followed by the flap lever. As they were coming up, he added power and the twin began to accelerate back to its cruising speed of two hundred and twenty knots.

"How about we go to Dunkeswell and do some touch and goes, shoot a couple of instrument approaches and then call it a day?"

"Sounds like a good idea!"

Two hours and thirty minutes later, Josh kept the Navajo in a left crab to compensate for a fifteen knot crosswind on what they agreed was the final landing of the flight.

"Josh, how about trying to grease it on, rather than plunk it down smartly on the runway?"

"You mean you don't like my Navy landings?"

"Oh, they are quite good, on the centerline and on the numbers, but a bit firm on the touchdown. They're more like arrivals than landings. It's hard on the equipment, and we have a longer runway than a carrier deck, so we don't have to land on the first two hundred feet. As soon as you feel we are in ground effect, squeeze off some power and think flare and it will settle on the runway. Oh yes, the civilian check pilots like pilots who make gentle landings, and unless they flew in the Navy, they have no idea of what it is like to land on a deck that is pitching and rolling."

"I'll try it your way..."

"Just remember, paying customers don't like having their fillings rattled!"

Josh was quiet for a few minutes while he kept the Navajo in at a ten degree left crab on the extended centerline. As the airplane crossed the threshold of the 3,176 foot long runway, he pushed on the right rudder pedal and added left aileron to align the plane's nose straight down the runway.

About fifteen feet off the runway, Josh barely moved the yoke aft, and as the Navajo settled, he squeezed off power on both throttles. When the upwind main mount kissed the asphalt, he neutralized the ailerons, and the other main mount touched down with a squeak.

John grinned with satisfaction. "Bloody good. Now you can call yourself a pilot."

Chapter 14
Find and Neutralize

Monday, October 18th, 1976, 0830 local time, RNAS Yeovilton

Marty walked into the unit's operations center and started passing out letter-sized envelopes. "Well, gentlemen, Lev will be here in a few minutes with some new intel. But first, our official orders have arrived, along with a very interesting document for each of us."

Josh took the sealed envelope. "My official orders?"

"Yup. After you read them, I suggest you find a very safe place to keep them."

After giving Marty a quizzical look, Josh slit open the envelope and unfolded the one page letter. The orders, signed in blue ink by the Chief of Naval Operations himself, stated that Lieutenant Joshua Jonathan Haman was, *"As the executive officer of the 66th Joint Observation Group, to find members of the Red Hand organization and any of their affiliates, then neutralize and render them harmless to the United States and its allies."*

No rules of engagement, no restrictions. It looked like a blank check—or maybe a length of rope. "Marty... does this mean we are sheep dipped?"

"Nope."

"Why not?"

"Because when you are sheep dipped, you don't know your employer. Your contact gives you tasking and targets and provides access to stuff like money, safe houses and weapons. But if anything goes wrong, you are definitely the fall guy. In this case, my friend, we know who our boss is, and he has made it very, very clear as to what our mission is."

"OK, what's this?" Josh picked up a small laminated document. On one side it had two phone numbers and what he recognized as an accounting code. He turned the card over and read:

The President of the United States directs the reader of this card to immediately provide whatever personnel, financial and/or material support requested by the bearer of the card, Lieutenant Joshua Haman, United States Navy, without question or hesitation.

Underneath it there was the personal signature of the President of the United States, a date and a three digit number. "Wow, this is powerful." Josh held the card as if it were a winning lottery ticket.

Marty was putting his in his wallet. "Senior Chief Jenkins, Van der Jagt, and I have similar cards, and ones from the prime minister came for John, Sergeant Major Calhoun, and Sergeants Goodson, Bentley, and Thorne. Each has a unique number under the signature. There are not many of these around. Anybody employed by the U.S. or British government who doesn't help is going to be in a world of hurt."

"That's not all the goodies we got!" Senior Chief Jenkins unwrapped a small stack of green American Express credit cards. "Each of us gets one, so you better get receipts. We've also got a bundle of cash—pounds and dollars—that we are going to count to verify the amount and then put in a separate safe."

"One last piece of info." Marty looked around the room. "There was a note in the package that said Vice Admiral Hastings will be here on the ninth of November."

Tuesday, October 19th, 1976, 1646 local time, Ludwigshafen

The two German Landespolizei with Rheinland-Palatinate patches on their left sleeve, designating the West German state in which they worked, were walking down the street when they noticed a VW pulling into in a no parking zone in front of the Hertie's store. The clear area, about a hundred meters wide, was a new preventative measure by the mayor to protect the large general merchandise stores in the downtown area.

As the driver started to walk away, the senior of the Landespolizei yelled out, "Halt! you can't park there."

The man turned, and when he saw the two policemen, started running down the street. Instincts took over; the two policemen took off after him.

The younger policeman turned the corner, only to duck back as two shots sent shards of concrete flying off the building. The older one stopped and spoke into his radio as he drew his nine millimeter Walther P-38.

Edging around the corner, the younger man caught a glimpse of the fugitive fleeing down the street, pistol in hand. He beckoned to his partner and picked up the chase, yelling, "Halt, polizei!"

The man turned and two more shots rang out, sending the younger policeman into a sprawling dive behind a car. The older man, a Wehrmacht veteran of World War II, rested his elbows on the hood of a car, aimed and squeezed off two shots. The first one hit the man just above his belly button and the second shattered his shoulder.

By the time the two policeman reached the fugitive, he was lying in a growing pool of blood and his eyes were glassy. Two fingers on his neck confirmed that the man no longer had a pulse. There was no need to kick the man's pistol away from his body. Instead, the older man used his pen to pick up the weapon via the trigger guard and examined the pistol, a P-38. By the stampings and serial number, he knew the gun was made after World War II and probably stolen from a police armory.

While the younger police officer stayed by the body waiting for the ambulance to arrive, the older officer retraced their steps. As he turned the corner, the illegally parked VW exploded in a fireball. The force of the explosion and six ball bearings knocked the former Wehrmacht Feldwebel, who had survived the battles in the hedge groves of Normandy, backwards and slammed him into a parked car.

Grenfel was reading one of many interviews when the call came in. He ran through the hallways and down to the helipad. A police helicopter flew him to a parking lot outside Mainz. He hurried over to a waiting police car that already had its lights flashing; it started moving before he got his seat belt buckled.

While the car was weaving in and out of traffic on its way to an apartment complex, Grenfel pulled out his Walther PPK and eased the slide back to make sure there was a round in the chamber. Then he checked to make sure that two magazines were in the pouches of his shoulder holster, and two more were in one of the pockets of his sport coat. The car pulled into a ring of small vans, all with the green and white stripes and shields of the Landespolizei. An officer with three silver stars on his epaulets, the Hauptpolizeikommisarin, or captain, jogged over to Grenfel, came to attention and saluted. Grenfel glanced at his name tag.

"Hauptman Heligmann, what do we have?"

"Herr Polizeioberrat Grenfel, we have determined that the address on his identify card and driver's license is false. However, when we searched the body, we found a letter with the address of an apartment about a half a kilometer from here. We already have men in the area watching it. The warrant for a search arrived a few minutes ago. It authorizes us to kick the door in if there is no one home. We have men who can pick the lock if you prefer."

"Excellent, let's go."

Grefel stood about ten feet down the hall, away from the three-man rows on either side of the door. The captain nodded to the two men with a small battering ram.

It took one blow for the door to slam open against its stop, and less than ten seconds for the six men to determine that the apartment was empty. By the time they secured the one bedroom apartment, which reeked of cigarette smoke, a small crowd had gathered outside the entrance.

"Herr Polizeioberrat, please come here." Grenfel recognized the voice of the police captain and found him in the small bedroom. "We found these!" The captain, wearing white cotton gloves, held up two plastic bags and pointed to a hole in the wall in the back side of the closet.

Grenfel could see the first bag held passports, other documents, and a wad of British pounds held together with two rubber bands. The second bag held German marks, Swiss francs, and U.S. dollars. The forensic team spread a sterilized cloth on top of the kitchen table and stepped back while the bags were photographed and then dumped out on the table, one at a time.

Wednesday, October 20th, 1976, 1520 local time, Bonn

The main entrance to the Justice Ministry headquarters was blocked by a half-dozen uniformed Landespolizei, who forced the throng of reporters assembled for the press conference to stand on the outside steps. Some waited quietly, while others talked shop with their counterparts from other news outlets.

When the doors were opened, precisely ten minutes before the press conference was to start, the policeman checked each person's identification against a list. Inside, a grim looking Reinhard Jurgend stood behind a battery of microphones and three rows of chairs, which was just enough for the invitees. Policemen took up positions at each of the doors.

Friedrich Starkeholz was the only other person in the front of the room. Late afternoon was an odd time for a German official to hold a press conference, but the time was chosen to accommodate two audiences, this German one and the one six hours behind, located in Washington, D.C.

Jurgend looked at his notes for a few seconds and then at his Rolex as reporters took their seats. At thirty minutes past the hour he nodded, and when the red light on top of a camera aimed at him came on, he began to speak.

"On behalf of the President of the Bundesrepublik and the German people, I would like to thank you all for coming this afternoon. Before Herr Hauptpolizeidirektor Starkeholz, from the Bundeskriminalamt and I answer questions, I have a few comments to make."

Jurgend, the former trial lawyer, was about to speak to the jury, his fellow West Germans. "It saddens me that since the Red Hand bombings in the Bundesrepublik began, hundreds of law abiding Americans, Englishmen, and Germans of all ethnic groups and religions have been killed or injured. These murders, and that is what they are, will not be tolerated by this government. I want to make this clear: we are determined to hunt down and destroy Red Hand by the legal means at our disposal."

Jurgend paused and surveyed his audience, many of whom were holding hand-held tape recorders. "I want to put Red Hand on notice. No matter how many of us you kill, you will not succeed in changing our society, or our government, or our policies. We will not abandon the democratic principles on which this nation was founded. With each bomb that goes off, our resolve increases, along with our determination to end the bombings. Red Hand has not chosen the ballet box to push their ideas. Instead, they have declared war on Germany, the United States, and the United Kingdom. That was a mistake. They have picked the wrong countries to take on, and this is a war they cannot win. I know my fellow citizens are impatient and want us to find these madmen as fast as possible, but we will not sacrifice the freedoms we enjoy or violate our laws to take shortcuts for the sake of expediency."

Jurgend stopped for a few seconds to let the journalists with pens and pads to catch up with their note-taking. Then he decided to deviate from his notes. "Some commentators have speculated that we were considering imposing martial law. They are wrong. It has never been under consideration by my office or this government." He jabbed at one of the microphones with his forefinger to emphasize his point. "In fact, the one time it was suggested as an agenda item, the individual was told by me that neither the president nor I consider martial law as an option under any circumstances. Those of you who claimed sources suggested that it was under active consideration need to check them again, because they were wrong."

The justice minister paused to give the reporters time to take pictures so flashes and clickings wouldn't interfere with what he was about to say. He jabbed the air with his thumb and forefinger together and leaned forward to emphasize his words. "I want to state in unequivocal terms that neither this government nor those of our allies whose citizens have been killed and maimed will negotiate with Red Hand. With regard to those bombings that happened on German soil, the Bundeskriminanamt is leading, and will continue to lead, the effort to stop Red Hand. We are making progress, though all of us will admit, not as fast as we would like. However, we are making sure that as we gather evidence, it will be admissible in court. Our friends and allies have been very helpful and respectful of our desire to lead the hunt for these criminals, even though they could, via the Status for Forces Agreement, take over the investigation."

Jurgend paused again to let the significance of that sink in. "I hope this makes the German government's position clear to everyone in this room, and puts to an end any speculation that there are any secret negotiations with Red Hand to change government policies, or to declare martial law. There are no negotiations going on now, there have never been any, and there will be none."

Jurgend nodded his head to emphasize his words. "Now, I would like to spend a few minutes updating you on the investigation. There has been speculation in the media that the Neo-Nazis are behind Red Hand. We do not believe that to be true. Experts have suggested that former members of the National Socialist Party may be behind Red Hand. We have not seen evidence that suggests this; however, we have not ruled them out either. If any members of that regime are arrested in conjunction with Red Hand, we will, based on the charges under

Bundesrepublik law, also determine which statutes from the Nuremburg war crimes tribunals will apply, if any."

With that point made, he was ready to change subjects. "Here is what we do know. We know Red Hand is being supported by organizations that have a history of sponsoring terrorists. At this time, we cannot reveal who these are, but we know they are providing money, documents, explosives, and sanctuary to Red Hand."

Jurgend looked around the room. "Yesterday, as many of you know, there was a bombing and a shoot-out in Ludgwigshafen. There were no deaths caused by the bomb, and only a few were injured, including a Landespolizei officer. In the gun fight, however, a Syrian national, who we believe set off the car bomb, was killed."

Jurgend looked at Starkeholz; both of them knew they were about to get a storm of questions.

"Next to me is Herr Hauptpolizeidirektor Friedrich Starkeholz of the Bundeskiriminalamt, who is responsible for the investigation. At this time we will take a few questions, but let me remind you that we are limited in what we can say."

Jurgent pointed to a reporter in the third row who was the first to raise his hand. "Question?"

"Herr minister, is this man a member of Red Hand?"

Starkeholz stepped forward. This was his department. "We are not sure yet, but we believe so. Everything about the car bomb says Red Hand. We think the police officers caught him in the process of setting the timer."

"How do you know he is Syrian?" a reporter shouted out without waiting to be recognized.

"Please wait until you are recognized, but to answer the man's question, we have his passport, and the Syrians have told us it is a valid passport. He had three more—one from Germany, one from Lebanon, and one from Turkey. We are investigating whether or not they are forgeries." The policeman pointed to a man in the back row who had his hand raised.

"Herr Starkeholz, do you have any other suspects?"

"There are several persons we are interested in, but no arrests have been made."

Starkeholz surveyed the forest of hands and pointed at a woman.

"Herr Jurgend, it has been reported that the country is considering imposing martial law or a curfew. Is that under consideration?"

"No!" Jurgend's answer had the ring of finality, and he tried to contain his irritation at the question. "I thought I made that clear when I said martial law was not under consideration. A curfew is a step toward martial law. Restricting travel would disrupt the economy, which is what Red Hand wants."

"Herr minister, may I ask why not?"

"We don't think it will help the investigation. Next question."

"Herr Hauptpolizeidirektor, how long do you think it will be before arrests are made?" This reporter was in the front row.

"That is difficult to say." Starkeholz chose his words with care while doing his best to hide how uncomfortable it was to be quizzed by the press. "I do not want to set a timetable."

"Can either one of you say who the other countries or organizations are assisting Red Hand?"

"No. We will add nothing to what has already been reported." The words came out of Starkeholz's mouth before he could ask the minister for permission to answer the question.

'Will Germany consider the death penalty for members of Red Hand?" This reporter spoke in American-accented English.

Starkeholz stepped back to let the justice minister handle this question; it was one he had raised in a staff meeting several months ago.

"The death penalty can only be authorized by the Bundestag on a case by case basis. Prosecutors will be expected to ask for sentences without parole if members of Red Hand are convicted. One of the reasons why I mentioned the possible use of the Nuremburg statues is that they allow the death penalty for war crimes and crimes against of humanity. Under those laws, we do not have to go to the Bundestag."

"Do you consider members of Red Hand to be war criminals?" This question was asked in German.

Jurgend was smiling when he leaned forward to the forest of microphones in front of the two men. "Criminals, yes. War criminals? The possibility that we may try them under the Nuremberg laws is an option we are considering, given the weapons used and the number of civilians who have been killed or injured."

Sensing the allotted half hour was almost up, Jurgend glanced at his watch and held up his hand. "Thank you for coming ladies and gentlemen. Good afternoon."

Chapter 15
Odessa Still Lives

Photos were taped onto the maps that were tacked on the walls of the operations center. On the large wooden conference table was a map with all the bombings plotted under a sheet of Plexiglas. In the corner, two fireproof filing cabinets with combination locks had a file for each bombing, and now a file for each name of the six Germans—Hermann Berger, Wilhelm Gestner, Anna Schlemmer, Ludwig Kammer, Karina von Berg, Gerhard Wolff—that had entered Libya. Josh sipped hot chocolate as he roamed, reviewing maps and photos.

"We've been looking at the same stuff everyone else has, and it all leads us to the same place called nowhere. We know these six arrived in Libya and were driven to a Fatah training camp in the desert, but that doesn't make them members of Red Hand." The frustration evident in his voice caught everyone's attention.

"So, what's your point?" Marty prodded. If Josh was starting down a thought process, it might be worth pursuing.

"So, I think we need to find answers to three questions.... First question: a statistically significant number of the twenty-three bombings we know about have damaged Stern's or Hertie's stores, why? Second question: is it just a coincidence that The New German Party has formed in the same timeframe as the Red Hand bombings, or is there a connection? What do they have in common, if anything? Third question: do any of the members of the SS who are still alive have the wherewithal to either start a political party or support a terrorist organization?"

Marty blew out a heavy breath. "Osborne, Jenkins, Calhoun, will you get started on three new files and see what your sources can provide?" John was about to reply when Josh interrupted.

"Wait, there's someone who already knows the answer to question three, and he could probably shed some light on question one as well."

"Who's that?"

"Simon Weisenthal, the Nazi hunter. I think we should go pay him a visit and see what he knows."

Friday, October 22nd, 1976, 1304 local time, Wiesbaden

On the rare occasions when he did not eat at the facility's cafeteria but went out to lunch, Grenfel returned to the Bundeskriminalamt office as close to thirteen hundred as he could. Waiting on his desk today was a thick manila envelope. According to a note from the mail room taped on the front, the package was hand delivered; it had been x-rayed to see if there were a bomb inside and then checked for fingerprints. No prints were found.

After staring at the package for a few minutes, Grenfel pulled on a pair of white cotton gloves from a plastic bag in one of his desk drawers. He slit the end with a single edge razor blade and found inside another sealed envelope. Again making sure to touch only the edges, he used the sharp blade to open one end and dump out the contents. In front of him were a number of eight-inch by ten-inch black and white photos and a type written note.

10/20/1976
Herr Grenfel,

I suggest you look into the passports and travel activities of the following six German citizens:
1. Wilhelm Gestner
2. Gerhard Wolff
3. Ludwig Kammer
4. Reinhard Dorf
5. Anna Schlemmer
6. Karina von Berg

They all arrived in Tripoli, Libya in late September via ship and were driven to a Fatah training camp where they are now staying.

An interested third party.

There was no signature, but clipped to the note were two photographs of each individual's face, with their name taped in the upper right hand corner and then again on the back. The degree of organization and the wording of the note sent off alarms in Grenfel's mind. This looked like the work of military intelligence or of a police officer!

Grenfel was careful to hold the edges of each photograph with his fingers as he laid them out on his desk. Three other photographs at the bottom of the stack had captured enough of the surroundings to show they were walking along a dock and passing a ship named *Corinthian*. Each photo had a date in late September of this year. One photograph showed two of the individuals, one showed three, and the third just one. After studying each photo with a magnifying glass, Grenfel dialed a phone number from memory.

Monday, October 25th, 1976, 1227 local time, Bonn

Starkeholz was walking to his car in the underground parking lot near the Ministry of Justice building. He was about ten empty reserved spots from where his car was parked when a loud voice, made hollow by the empty concrete structure, boomed out from behind him. "Herr Hauptpolizeidirektor Starkeholz!" He knew a command when he heard one and it stopped him in his tracks.

"Please do not turn around, because if you do, I will disappear. I am sorry to interrupt you, but I thought you might be interested the activities of some former Nazis who influenced this past election."

"How did you know who I was?"

"I saw you on TV during the news conference."

"Are you going to shoot me?"

"I hope not."

"Good. I wouldn't like that." Starkeholz put his briefcase down on the concrete and kept his hands well away from his sides. "Will you tell me your name?"

"*Who* I am is not important at this time. *What* I have to say is." Von Ritter opened the clasp of an envelope he was carrying. "I have first-hand evidence that the New Germany Party had candidates in at least six districts assassinated in order to improve the chances that their candidate was elected. Here is some of the information I have. It is enough for the Justice Ministry to consider declaring the election results invalid and holding new elections in those districts. Please do not be alarmed; I am approaching you." Von Ritter slid the pages halfway out of the envelope to make them easy to see and tapped the envelope against Starkeholz's hand for him to take it.

Starkeholz did so, without turning his head, and flipped through the pages. "You've blacked out the names and places in the report. This is of no use to me." He held out the papers, behind and to the side, to return them.

"Keep it. I suggest you study it when you get back to your office. Know that I have the originals, with all the names, dates, and details of what was done, plus photographs that will help you get convictions. Also, I can give you details about how these bastards tried to kill me."

"Did you say Nazis tried to kill you? Why would they want to do that? Why didn't you come to the police?"

"It is a long story, which I will tell if you want to talk more."

The mystery man's voice was confident, commanding, and displayed no fear. Starkeholz kept his hands out to his sides. "What do you want for this information?"

"I want immunity from prosecution for myself and the three others who were hired to do the dirty work. No immunity and no pardon, no further discussions. That is not negotiable."

"I can't do that. Last time I checked, murder was illegal in this country." He started to add, *Come to my office and we can talk,* but he was sure the man wouldn't. This was the cautious first step in what could only be very delicate negotiations.

"I know that. But so is conspiring to overthrow the government. If you are a former Nazi and you want to return the country to National Socialist ideology, you will wind up in jail for a very long time if you try a putsch and fail." Von Ritter paused. "I will call you tomorrow afternoon at 1530. There are men who want to create a Fourth Reich. You can either have their leaders' heads on a platter, or I disappear along with my information. Have a good day."

Starkeholz turned around, but no one was there. He didn't feel threatened by the man, just disturbed by what he said. When he got into his car he read, and his insides churned as he read what he had been given. If he didn't know better, Hitler and his Brown Shirts had returned. And then he wondered if this was in any way related to Red Hand.

As soon as Starkeholz got back to his office, he cleared off the work table behind his desk and spent hours going through his files on former Nazis, trying to link the faces and names to the data he had. None of these men were his friends or from his unit. That, at least, was a relief.

Should I call some of my close friends to see what they know? If I did, what is the risk of them tipping off the conspirators? It is better that I keep this a police matter? Once I made a personal call, it would be difficult to keep it secret.

The next day, after a sleepless night, Starkeholz told his administrative assistant to hold all his calls until 1530, when he would be expecting a call that would need to be traced. He headed down to the agency's archives and took notes on former Nazis and their current whereabouts and activities. Nothing stood out. He hoped the secretive man would call as promised.

Tuesday, October 26th, 1976, 1530 local time, Bonn

Starkeholz was going back and forth between the five files that were in a row on the front of his desk, making notes on a pad next to the sheets given to him by the mystery man. He was trying to find a link between the men in the files when the ringing phone interrupted his analysis.

"Herr Hauptpolizeidirektor, there is a man on the phone. He says the two of you met yesterday in the parking lot of the Justice Ministry and he gave you an envelope. Is this the call you are waiting for?"

Starkeholz looked at his watch and noted the time on a pad. "Yes, please put him through at once and start the trace." He reached over the papers and picked up the receiver.

"Starkeholz."

"Herr Starkeholz, are you interested in what I gave you yesterday?"

"Yes. Thank you for calling." He was surprised that he felt relieved.

"Good. Have you begun to arrange for immunity for the four of us?"

"Not yet. It takes time to do that, and it will have to be approved by Herr Jurgend and possibly others, but I will start after this call."

"I will not provide any more evidence until this is settled."

Starkeholz looked at his watch. "I wanted to talk to you for a few minutes. Is that possible?"

"Herr Starkeholz, if you think you can trace this call, allow me to save you the trouble. I am on a pay phone at a gas station. So don't bother. If I even think that you are going to try to arrest me, then I disappear and you get nothing. I suggest that you and Herr Jurgend have that conversation sooner than later. Time is not on your side for a lot of reasons. One of which is that I plan to disappear if we cannot reach an agreement. Do I make myself clear?"

"Yes, yes you do."

"Good. I paid for five minutes. We have used two. What do you want to know?"

"What other information do you have, I mean, in addition to details on these six assassinations?"

"Let me give you the list. One, I have information on the two hits we turned down. Two, I have several tainted one hundred mark bills that were sprayed with some kind of nerve agent that was used to try to kill us when we were paid off. Three, I have the name and address of the man who hired us. Four, I have the names, addresses, and photos of the men who delivered the money to me. Five, in my files, I have the original material that they sent us to identify the victims. We took great care not to get our finger prints on the documents before we made copies for our own use. Six, I kept a detailed diary of each operation which I will turn over to you. Is that enough? We're running out of time on this call."

"Yes, that is quite impressive." Starkeholz wanted to get a snippet of information on the caller and his men. "Can you tell me about your background and that of your men?"

"So you can start digging? Nice try, but no. The others are already out of the country with proper, legal paperwork and are restarting their lives. For them, whether or not they receive pardons is a detail which, if resolved in their favor, will give them peace of mind. For me, it is an opportunity to pay back some men for trying to kill us to cover their tracks. We did what we were hired to do. It was wrong, but it cannot be undone and I will have to live with that. I will call you tomorrow at this time and maybe, after you assure me that the pardons will be given, we can work out a timetable. Is three-thirty a good time?"

"Yes, it is."

"Excellent. Do not try to trace the call and put an observer in place, because I will at another pay phone." There was a click, and the line went dead.

Starkeholz spent much of Tuesday working on what was most important to the caller. It took a great deal of time, and he had to justify his requests and push his authority to its limits more than once. As each week passed with no break, no results, Starkeholz could feel his authority eroding; orders were obeyed, but fewer men met his eyes. By Wednesday afternoon he was annoyed and frustrated, and kept looking at his watch. He was stirring his coffee when the phone rang. It was 1530 on the dot.

"Starkeholz."

"Good afternoon, Herr Hauptpolizeidirektor. Do you have time for a chat?"

"I do. Let me get right to the point. After much discussion, Herr Juegend has agreed to a pardon for you and your men with two caveats. One is that if you do not provide adequate information to justify your claims, you will be prosecuted using the material you provided as evidence. Two, if you provide false information you will be prosecuted. Do you agree?"

"I do. I have two provisos of my own. Some of what I have was given by men who are supporting The New German Party. I cannot be responsible for the accuracy of that information. I can only be responsible for the information that we collected and used. The second condition is this. Once my identity is known, I expect to come under investigation; that is understood. I have a collection of what one could call ... historic infantry weapons, many of which I will be happy to turn over to the government. There are some, however, I wish to keep."

Starkeholz was momentarily diverted, and intrigued. *We all had our favorites, yes. What were yours?* "That may be difficult. What are they?"

"My personal weapons from the war. I still have them and they are quite valuable, for they are in excellent condition. I would like to keep them and will provide a list, photos and serial numbers as part of the paperwork that I send to you. That should make them legal for me to own, and in the proper venue, to shoot."

"I think the minister will agree to that." Starkeholz paused. Would the man answer his next, all-important question? "What names should I put on these documents of pardon?"

"I will do that myself after I receive them in a law office of my choosing; the lawyers will, as part of the process, attest to the veracity of the names and the individuals. I have the powers of attorney from the three men that allow me to do this."

"I will have to check with the minister, but that sounds reasonable."

"When will you have the papers ready?"

"Tomorrow morning. I will pick them up myself and I should be back here by eleven."

"Excellent. At one p.m. I will call you with an address in Metz, France, where you will have someone deliver the documents. You will tell me the name of the courier, and he will be expected to show identification. Please do not try any tricks, because I will be nearby, but not in the building. If I detect surveillance, the deal is off. If all goes well, I will take the documents to an attorney's office. When I have them completed I will call to set up our first meeting on Friday. Is that agreeable?"

"Yes, it is. We have a team investigating former Nazis; they will be very interested in what you have to say."

"I would prefer that you and I talked for an hour or so first and then meet with your team. There are some things that need to be said in private."

"I see." Starkeholz sipped his coffee. "Is there anything else we need to discuss?"

"One minor point on logistics. The material is in a box that I will not allow out of my sight. I presume you will want the dogs to sniff it, which is fine, but I do not want to walk into the front door of your headquarters building carrying a big box. Too many questions will be asked."

"You are right. Everyone is very jumpy about potential bombs. So when you arrive at the gate, they will call my office. I will have a reserved spot for you in the restricted area in the back of the building labeled Starkeholz guest. I will send a couple of my men and they will carry the material to my office. When we finish our talk, I will have them take the information to a secure conference room that will be locked at all times and begin the process of cataloguing it. We will make safety copies as we do. Is that agreeable?"

"Perfectly. Any other questions?"

"No, Herr Starkeholz, I think we have covered everything."

"I am looking forward to meeting you. It should be interesting."

Thursday, October 28th, 1976, 1309 local time, Libya

A warm breeze with faint sea smells from the Mediterranean thirty kilometers to the north was flowing through the open flaps at each end of the tent. It wasn't strong enough to blow sand around, but anyone who spent time in the desert knows that sand, breeze or no breeze, gets in everything. Mohammed wiped off tiny grains of sand from the bits of fruit left on the plate before he popped them in his mouth. He chewed, swallowed, then asked his companion, "When do you think you will be ready to go back?"

"A few more weeks." Dieter tore a piece of flat bread in half to dip into hummus. "I want to think through how we are going to use your people."

"I thought that was all settled."

Dieter took a long drink of water. "Maybe in your mind, but not in mine."

"Why the change?"

"We need several safe houses in Germany, and a safe place to hide beyond the reach of the Americans and the Bundeskriminalamt. So it has to be someplace we can get to in just a few hours without arousing any suspicions."

"You can always come here via a direct or a connecting flight. Your visas and our contacts in the Libyan government will make sure that you do not have trouble with customs and immigration. If you need them, we can get you Libyan passports and papers that say you are a Libyan citizen."

"Good. Let's plan on that, but we have to assume that the airports in Europe will be watched. So we have to use transport that does not have as much surveillance. I was thinking of a ferry to Sweden then flying here, or we could take a second ferry to the DDR and fly from there. Tramp cargo ships are another option."

"Either may work. So, where does that leave us?"

"East Germany. However, I don't trust the Stasi. They can keep us locked up in their country or make us disappear. We want to avoid attracting their attention, and since I am known to them, I must not be associated with your people. I can bring the Germans to Zehlendorf, but your people will have to hide amongst the Muslim *gastarbeiter*. Getting them out, if it gets too hot, will be a problem."

"That is a risk you have to take in this business."

"Agreed. That is why I am paranoid about who I let into Red Hand."

"So how are you going to maintain each cell's integrity?"

Dieter ripped another piece of pita bread in half and then in quarters before he used one of the wedges to scoop up a blob of hummus. "My plan is to have two, maybe three Germans and three or four members of Fatah in each cell. I will be the only one who contacts the cell leaders, and they will know how to contact their members. The less you know about how we will operate, the better for you and the safer for us."

He shoved more pita bread and hummus into his mouth. "The more I think about it, the more I like the idea of using Zehlendorf as a safe base. We enter West Germany, conduct an operation, go to a safe house in West Germany, then go to East Germany or fly here. Or, if we have to, go through Algeria or Morocco or Egypt. Your people can disappear into the *gastarbeiter* community or do the same. I can get my Stasi contact to support our movements. He has been bugging me to recruit more people, so I will tell him that I have and that we need documents to get in and out of East Germany at any time, without questions. He'll provide the necessary papers. You and I will communicate as before."

"What about supplies?"

"Let us work that out when we have a shop in West Germany. For now I get what I need from the East Germans, but I want to set up a workshop in West Germany so we don't have to drive the cars through the border. As pressure mounts to find Red Hand, inspections will become more thorough, and inspectors will be told what to look for. The new shop's location will have to be well vetted and its ownership not traceable to me."

Friday, October 29th, 1976, 0830 local time, Wiesbaden

The sun was out and von Ritter could see the hills of the Taunus Mountains in the distance as he drove to the concrete and glass Bundeskriminalamt headquarters outside Wiesbaden. Starkeholz was waiting for him in the reserved parking lot as he pulled his Mercedes 220 diesel in place and got out.

"Herr Starkeholz, I am Klaus von Ritter."

The two men shook hands. "It is much nicer meeting you face to face."

"I agree. I apologize for being so secretive, but under the circumstances, it was necessary for my own safety as well as that of my men. Their safety is still is my concern."

"I have taken some precautions of my own," Starkeholz said. He sensed von Ritter had experience taking care of himself. "A code name—Gray Wolf—will be used instead of your real name in all official documents. Just the minister, our administrative assistants, you, and I know these documents exist. I will have them couriered to our archives in sealed envelopes later today. The minister will be told when we are ready to bring cases to him for indictment and arrest warrants."

"Are you worried about being penetrated by Germans who are still Nazis and who want to return to power?"

"Yes, it was a big concern when I got back into police work after the war, and it still is. There are many Nazi sympathizers in the government; we are rooting them out one by one. Even after our generation dies out, it will be a concern. You wouldn't believe what I had to go through because I was assigned to an SS Panzer Grenadier unit during the war, even though I wasn't a party member. We have a new generation of police officers who look at Nazis as criminals, and when they find one who has committed a crime, they are like sharks who smell blood in the water."

The two men stood side by side for a long moment, and then von Ritter opened the trunk of the car to reveal a large box. "Understand," I have kept copies of everything. I have also left directions for the copies to come to light in ways that would be most embarrassing for Der Vaterland if the pardons issued are not honored. This is a necessary precaution on my part." When Starkeholz bowed his head ironically, Von Ritter continued. "You may call your officers over now, and I will wait in the car. The fewer of your men who see my face, the better."

Starkeholz signaled to two officers waiting by the entrance who walked up to the car, lifted the heavy box out of the trunk, and put it on a hand cart. While one pushed the two-wheeled dolly along, the other acted as a lookout. As they passed through the door, von Ritter rejoined the Hauptpolizeidirektor.

Starkeholz was about to lead the way to his office when a question occurred to him and he stopped. "Herr von Ritter, I have to ask before go inside, are you armed?"

"No."

"Is there a firearm in the car?"

"Yes, two pistols. There is a P-38 that I have had since 1938 and carried throughout the war. It is in a special holster next to the driver's seat with several spare magazines. There is also a pre-war Walther PPK in the glove box."

"We'll leave them there." Starkeholz turned and crossed the parking lot, von Ritter following with his hat drawn low over his face.

Inside the modern building, whose green window tint reminded the viewer of the forest green color of the Landespolizei uniform, Starkeholz and the two officers showed their badges to the officer at the reception desk, who handed a badge to von Ritter. It had had a large red B in the middle for *besucher* (visitor) along with a three digit number. Von Ritter clipped it on.

Nothing was said until the two officers deposited the cardboard box just inside the door of Starkeholz's office.

Von Ritter held up a sealed envelope with four 100 Deutschmark bills.

"Ah, yes." Starkeholz took the plastic bag from Von Ritter and turned to the officers. "Take these down to the lab and have them analyzed. It seems there is some kind of poison on them, possibly sarin, so tell them to be extremely careful and tell me as soon as possible the name of the substance."

At a look from the elder, the younger man reluctantly used his thumb and forefinger to take hold of the corner of the bag. "Yes sir." The two men nodded and left, closing the door.

"Herr von Ritter, are you sure it is sarin?"

"I am fairly sure. One of my men tested the bills. Skin absorbs sarin on contact, and whoever sprayed it on assumed we wouldn't live to spend it. Our deaths would have cleared up a loose end. I wonder how they planned to contain the poison afterward. Or perhaps they did not care. What tipped me off was the man who gave me the package was very nervous and was wearing gloves on a warm day. That made me suspicious, so we checked the bills."

"It pays to be paranoid some times, especially in combat situations."

Von Ritter chuckled. "Yes it does."

"Coffee?"

"Bitte schön."

Starkeholz poured two mugs and then slid the tray with milk and sugar across the desk top. "So, Herr von Ritter, what unit were you in?"

"During or after the war?"

"During. We'll get to the after later."

"First Parachute Regiment." Von Ritter said it in a matter-of-fact manner, but he was proud that he had been a member of one of the Werhrmacht's most elite units that didn't have an SS designation. "I made drops into Holland, Norway, France, and Crete, and then fought in Italy until we surrendered to the British in the mountains north of Verona, Italy."

"You were an officer?"

"Yes, I finished as a lieutenant colonel and battalion commander with about two hundred men in my command. That was all that was left. When we surrendered, we were almost out of food and ammunition and had lost all hope. We were sure we were all going to die, that it was just a question of in which battle. It took a while for me to accept the fact that I survived."

"I also. My war ended at Falaise, when I surrendered what was left of a Panzer Grenadier Regiment and became a guest of the Americans, who sent me to a camp in Texas." Starkeholz enjoyed the aroma before he took a sip of his coffee as a way to facilitate a change in the subject.

"So, do you have the paperwork?"

"I do, Herr Direktor." Von Ritter reached down an unbuckled the brown leather briefcase and opened the flap. He laid out four envelopes on the cleared desk in a neat row. "They are all the same. Each contains the pardon with the individuals name on it, the document attesting that the names are real. Attached are copies of their birth certificates, discharge certificates, as well as their passports they used to exit the country. These can go into the Justice Ministry's files."

"I assume that these will check out?"

"They will."

"*Alles ist in ordnung.*" Starkeholz noticed that the man in front of him appeared relaxed and confident, not at all apprehensive. "Do you think you need protection? We can arrange for you to stay at a guarded safe house?"

"For the moment, no."

"We would prefer if we had you in a safe place."

Von Ritter shook his head. "My former employers think I am dead. I'd prefer to keep it that way. Are you worried about leaks?"

"I always am. Between the Stasi and some of our former so-called comrades in arms, this government is like good

Emmenthaler cheese. I don't think we have a problem in this department, but you never know."

"Then I will arrive here at different times in different rented cars. I prefer to hide in plain sight. If I detect surveillance, I'll let you know and I can move into a safe house."

"Very well. After you and I have our conversation, I will turn you over to the two members of my team who will handle the debriefing. I assume you are prepared to answer any of their questions."

"I am, as long as they are relevant to my actions over the past six months, yes. My life's history until then is not relevant. After the war I was a mercenary; I will share what is necessary, but there are some things that I did in those years that have nothing to do with our agreement. Then, I joined the Bundeswehr to help create a parachute unit and retired as a colonel a few years ago. I can assure you that if I have to appear in court as a witness, there will be no surprises that will affect my credibility."

Starkeholz was impressed by the man's composure. He knew what he was doing and the risk he was taking. "Good, let us begin. Just so you know, we will have to check everything you tell us to make sure that it is accurate. It could be months before we make an arrest. If there is a conspiracy against the government, it will take time to ferret it out."

"There is and they are moving faster than you think. These people have decided that now is a good time to return to National Socialism. They talk about creating a Fourth Reich in the very near future. Both of us have had enough of their idea of government to last a lifetime. I understand whatever you find as evidence will have to stand up in court."

"If it gets that far."

Von Ritter wondered whether Starkeholz didn't believe the men involved would make it to trial, or thought the information wasn't good enough to pursue, or that the government would choose to wait and watch or worse, do nothing at all. But then, he has his pardon and immunity from prosecution, so it was the justice minister's call, not his. Von Ritter thought silence was the best answer as he sat back in the cushioned chair.

Starkeholz pulled a pad in front of him with some notes and lots of empty pages. "So, Herr von Ritter, I have some questions for you, but where would you like to start?"

"With the people who hired me."

Monday, November 1st, 0733 local time, Wiesbaden

"Good morning, Grenfel, what do you have for me today? It had better be good." Starkeholz was dreading his next meeting with the Justice Minister. He was expecting to be replaced or fired any day.

"I do have good news. You know that note we got about six German citizens arriving in Libya via several steamers?"

"Yes, you said you were going to check out their names. What did you find?" Starkeholz was in no mood to allow Grenfel to 'build his case.'

"Lots of discrepancies. Some minor, like the wrong apartment number; some major, as in the address doesn't exist. Our conclusion is that while all six passports are genuine, the applications are bogus."

"So are they forgeries?"

"No. They are valid passports issued to names with fictitious backgrounds."

"What shall I tell the minister?"

"I would tell him just what I told you. We have six Germans, each with a passport issued based on fake data, who entered Libya, a known sanctuary for terrorists."

"Grenfel, I need something more, Goddammit," Starkeholz slapped his hand on his desk, "or you and I will soon be looking for another job."

"Sir, that's where we are today, it is more than we had a week ago and it is the truth." Grenfel tried not to be defensive.

"The minister wants progress, and if we don't give him some soon, we'll lose control and the Americans will be in charge."

"The fact we know that the passports are fakes is progress. If they are used again, we will know about it."

"Do you still want to release the photos?"

The younger man leaned forward in his chair. "Yes, Herr Hauptpolizeidirektor, I do."

Starkeholz debated with himself; in his heart, he agreed with Grenfel. "I will make the recommendation to the minister. In any case, continue to use them to help in the investigation."

Tuesday, November 2nd, 1028 local time, Zehlendorf

Grünewald pressed down the horn button of the three year old, unmarked Volkswagen he had requisitioned from the motor pool.

This was his third visit to, and inspection of Stiglitz's compound, and may have to be his last. As Red Hand's activities drew ever more international attention, he must not in any way call attention to his own involvement.

The heavy wooden door began to move and Grünewald was surprised to see a woman's head appeared in the widening gap. A few seconds later, an attractive young blonde wearing tight jeans and a brick-red down vest held the door open.

Grünewald entered, and noticed with approval six chassis lined against the opposite wall that were in various stages of assembly and disassembly. Dieter wiped his hands before stuffing the greasy rag in his back pocket and holding out his hand. "Welcome to Red Hand's headquarters. Come inside and I will introduce you to our new members." The blonde walked ahead of them to a door at the far end of the warehouse and passed through.

"First, a word with you alone," Grünewald said as he shook and then held Stiglitz's hand to emphasize the importance of his request.

"Let me give you a tour of the workshop and we can talk." Dieter proceeded to pace the room slowly, forcing Grünewald to follow his lead. Grünewald's mouth compressed with displeasure. He recognized that the young man was deliberately taking control of the interview *he* was here to conduct. It was past time to remind the boy who was really in charge.

"Who checked these people out?" he demanded. "I issued visas for the DDR on your assurances that they were O.K."

"I did. I have known them for over a year and have been planning to bring them into Red Hand when the time was right, which is now."

"Where did you find them?" After eyeing the assorted chassis Grünewald wheeled to continue the interrogation face to face.

"Through contacts I made at school, in either Marburg or Heidelberg," Dieter replied easily. "Trusted friends led me to like-minded people. These six didn't find out about Red Hand until last month when we were together for the first time in Morocco. They thought they were being recruited by Abu Nidal." Dieter didn't mention that he had dated Giselle at the University of Heidelberg.

"What name and passport did you travel under?" Grünewald wondered if Stigliz had been naïve enough to use his West German passport.

"My West German one to get in and out of the Bundesrepublik. My DDR one to come here." He just didn't tell Grünewald which one of his two West German passports he'd used.

"Let's go meet your friends." Grünewald decided he would confront Dieter again when he knew more. *This is the last time the kid is going to put me on the spot. I don't like being played.*

Six hours after Grünewald left, Giselle laid her bare legs across her boyfriend's lap. She was naked, leaning against a pillow propped against the stone wall which was cold to the touch, even though it was toasty warm in the bedroom.

Dieter handed her a bottle of cold local beer—one of the few things he thought was good and cheap in the DDR. That and potatoes.

"Colonel Grünewald seems to be very nice. Very formal and menacing, but nice." Giselle popped open the bottle and took a sip.

"He's Stasi and an ex-SS officer. What do you expect?"

"I don't know. He's the first Stasi officer I've ever met."

"He reports to the director, so he is pretty high up in their organization."

Giselle shifted position.

"Does your father know you are doing all this?"

"No."

"Why not?"

"Because he would try to control me. He would want to give directions and make all the important decisions. This is something that I am doing on my own. If it helps him, great, but Red Hand is *my* invention: my terrorist group and my movement."

"Don't you think Red Hand could help his friends and their political aspirations?"

"I already do, indirectly. But I want to be independent as long as I can."

"Hmmmmm." Giselle reacted to her lover's fingers touch on her upper thigh as she ran hers fingers through Dieter's hair. "What about your mother?"

"She ... would be appalled. I once heard her tell my father when they were arguing about his desire for a Fourth Reich that she could replace a husband any time, but sons are impossible to replace. My mother doesn't want to see another war in her lifetime. Why did *you* come with me?" Dieter changed the subject;

he didn't want to talk about his family. "This could end with us both being killed, or in prison for a very long time." His hands wandered some more, and Giselle sighed.

"I love you. And I believe in your vision. People will remember us for what we do. It gives our life purpose. And I don't like having the Americans, the British, and the French telling us what to do any more than you do." She bent down and kissed Dieter's head, and then there was no more talking.

Friday, November 5th, 1976, 0710 local time, Nörvenich

Of all the planes he has flown, Werfel liked the F-104G the least. Every time he flew it, he thought it was trying to kill him. His favorite was the Focke-Wulf FW-190, which he had flown from the time it was introduced in 1941 until early 1945. With one hundred and fifty kills, Werfel was one of the few pilots chosen to fly the first jet fighter, the ME-262. Six years after the war ended, he had been invited to help create the new Luftwaffe.

The dull gray VW Type 81, used by the Luftwaffe as a light utility vehicle, stopped at the eleventh F-104G in the line of twenty-four aircraft. Werfel lifted his parachute out of the back seat and handed it to the driver, a young airman named Baumann, who hauled the olive drab back-pack parachute up the ladder along with the brigadier general's helmet and navigation bag. Once he was satisfied with their placement, he returned to the ground and followed a step behind the general as he walked around the jet.

When he finished his inspection, Werfel nodded, climbed up the ladder, and stepped down into the cockpit.

Baumann followed him up and helped with the straps, then handed Werfel his helmet with an oxygen mask clipped on one side. Werfel checked to make sure it was plugged into the console and left the mask hanging loose. Before removing the ladder, Baumann showed Werfel the ejection seat safety pins. Then Baumann, who had been in the post-war Luftwaffe thirteen months, manned the large fire extinguisher as Werfel went through the pre-start checklist.

Werfel looked at his watch and noted that it was 0725. After twirling his right forefinger where Baumann could see it, Werfel engaged the starter; when the rpm rose to about 20%, he moved the throttle forward and used the brakes to keep the jet in position as he felt the J-79 generate thrust. With all the gauges showing normal indications, Werfel looked down the flight line to see if the other F-104G's canopy was closed. It was, and he caused his own to come down and seal him in. When it was locked in place his headphones crackled.

"Hunter Two Four Zero Three is up and ready."

Werfel acknowledged with two clicks of the UHF radio and keyed the mike. "Nörvenich ground, Hunter Two Five Three Eight and Two Four Zero Three, flight of two, ready for taxi and take-off, sortie numbers eleven-five-zero-one and eleven-five-zero-two."

"Hunter Two Five Three Eight and Two Four Zero Three, this is Nörvenich ground, we copy sortie numbers and you are cleared to taxi. Contact the tower on three-one-eight point six when ready for take-off."

Werfel held the brakes as he gave the balled fist, thumbs out gesture to signal Baumann to pull the chocks and the safety pins. As he eased out of his spot in line, Werfel saw the other Starfighter nose out on the taxi way.

Werfel kept his speed down as he used the nose wheel steering to stay on the left side of the taxiway centerline so his wingman in Two Four Zero Three could catch up and follow in a right echelon. At the end of the runway, Werfel went through the take-off checklist. He knew it by heart, but years of cockpit discipline insisted that he touch each item on the list to make sure it was in the right position and then speak it out loud to confirm what his hands and eyes were telling him.

Werfel looked to his right and saw the thumbs-up from his wingman. "Nörvenich tower, Hunter Two Five Three Eight, flight of two, ready for take-off."

After he read back his take off and initial climb clearance, Werfel led the two F-104Gs out on the runway and stopped on the left side of the white centerline stripe. He twirled his right hand around his head, got an acknowledging nod from his wingman, then pushed the throttle up to the detent. Again he checked the gauges, as he kept the straining F-104G in place by standing on the brakes. Knowing his wingman was watching, Werfel moved his head forward, once, twice, and on the third time moved the throttle an eighth of an inch to the left and pushed it forward until it stopped. Feeling the thump of the afterburner lighting off and hearing a definite rise in engine noise, he again checked the gauges and warning lights. Seeing nothing wrong, he tightened the friction knob on the throttle to keep it from creeping back and released the brakes. The F-104G, loaded to its maximum take-off weight of just over twenty-nine thousand pounds, shot forward pushed by fifteen thousand, six hundred pounds of thrust.

Forty knots. Werfel's mind was already ahead of the accelerating jet. Disengage nose wheel steering, check the rudders for control. Keep it straight down his side of the runway. Eighty knots, one hundred knots, one-twenty, one-fifty knots—*rotate*! Werfel eased back on the stick and the nose of the F-104G rose off the concrete and rolled down the runway for another thousand feet before the main wheels left the ground at just over one hundred and ninety knots indicated airspeed.

His hand pulled the lever that looked like a wheel out and up. Three faint thumps and the indicators on the instrument panel said that at two hundred knots and accelerating the wheels were in their wells. Werfel thought that the F-104G was living proof that if you got anything going fast enough, it would fly. At two hundred and twenty knots, he raised the flaps, using the lever on the left side of the console that looked like a wing, and then pushed on the throttle to make sure it had not slid out of the afterburner descent.

BANG! The plane shuddered and started slowing as warning lights came on all over the cockpit. The engine RPM gauge was unwinding, engine oil pressure was plummeting, and the airspeed indicator was passing one hundred and eighty knots headed toward zero. The airplane started rolling left despite his moving the stick to the right—there was no hydraulic pressure in either of the two flight control systems.

"Three Eight, eject, eject, *EJECT NOW*!!! General, the whole back end of your airplane is on fire!"

The airplane was still well above the minimum ejection speed of one hundred knots. As the dying jet performed an uncontrolled bank to the left, Werfel shoved his head back into the notch in the headrest and squeezed the triggers on the sides of the seat. He'd bailed out of many planes during World War II, but this was his first ejection.

As he shot upward in the rocket-powered seat, a searing hot flash of red and orange sent him tumbling, before the gyro in the ejection re-directed him upward. Werfel saw the blue sky and smelled burning nylon and hoped his straps would hold when the parachute opened.

Just after he heard the soft pop of the drogue deploying, Werfel felt the ejection seat fall away. As he tumbled through the sky, he felt a familiar jerk as the parachute opened. The World

War II ace was calmly pulling off his oxygen mask when he slammed into the ground.

Nineteen year old Viktor Baumann sat alone in a small office off the flight line where he had been brought right after the crash. After being given a bottle of water, he was ordered not to leave and the door was closed.

The room was as cold as it was bare. He'd looked out the window several times at the pall of dark black smoke, which slowly dissipated. One by one the ambulances drove away, leaving a solitary fire truck to stand watch on what he hoped was not a funeral pyre for one of Germany's greatest pilots.

A glance at his watch told him that it was just over two hours since he'd seen the general's jet burst into flames. Baumann was lost in thought when the door swung open and two men entered. He recognized the Luftwaffe officer as the chief of maintenance for Jageschweder 31; the second man, a civilian, seated himself at the desk, showed him a badge with the emblem of the Bundeskriminalamt, and took out a small notebook.

"Hauptgefreiter Baumann, You were the plane captain for the F-104 Herr General Werfel flew today, is that correct?" The inspector didn't bother to introduce himself.

"Yes, sir." He turned to the Luftwaffe officer. "Why is a police inspector asking me questions? I didn't do anything wrong." As soon as he'd seen the F-104 explode and the general eject through the fireball, however, he'd known he would be questioned. No one had told him whether Werfel lived or died.

"Hauptgefreiter Baumann, answer the question," the Luftwaffe major ordered.

"Baumann, we hope you didn't do anything wrong." The inspector went back to his questions. "Did you conduct a pre-flight inspection of the F-104 before General Werfel took off?"

"Yes, sir, I did. I followed the check list and noted in the aircraft logs that some steel cord was showing on the right main mount but was within limits. Both the general and I thought it might need replacing after this flight. I took fuel samples and everything was in order. Then I opened all the panels I am supposed to check and found nothing out of the ordinary. I did my job as I am supposed to."

"You found nothing unusual."

"No sir. Like what?"

"An explosive device."

Baumann's stunned reaction startled the inspector. "A bomb? *Gott in himmel*! Not on my plane! I would never do anything to hurt General Werfel. My father was a mechanic on his staffel during the war and is proud that I am a Hauptgesfreiter in the Boelcke Jagbombergeschweder. He would kill me if I let anything bad happen to Herr General Werfel!"

"No one gave you anything to put on the plane?"

"No!" Baumann screamed with tears running down his cheeks. "*No, NO*!!! I would never let anyone do that to my plane or put anything on it that would cause it to crash. I would have stopped them or died trying. I would never, *never* let anyone harm Herr General Werfel."

The inspector sat back and closed his notebook. His training told him that the outburst and tears were spontaneous. An explosive device had been placed on the F-104. The question now was, by whom? "Thank you, Hauptgefrieter Baumann. I have no other questions."

Sunday, November 7th, 1976, 1920 local time, Yeovil

The driving rain from a storm over the Irish Sea was pelting the small cottage that Josh and Rebekah called home. Outside it was five degrees Celsius. It was not just cold; the air had a damp, bone-chilling rawness to it. Josh held up a bottle of scotch. "John, Lev, how about a taste?"

"Is it decent scotch?"

"You should know, you bought it for me!"

"Then I'll have a few fingers, neat. One wouldn't want to dilute the taste of a fine whiskey, would one?"

Josh looked at the Israeli. "Lev, you've been awful pensive this evening. What's up?"

Lev looked around to make sure that neither Gwen nor Rebekah were in earshot. "I talked to our folks in the embassy this morning. They are finished with the analysis of your father-in-law's letters and have returned them to your storage facility."

"What did they tell you?"

"Nothing, it was an open line. but I think we have another problem."

"Which is?" Josh was quick with the question.

"Let's assume for the moment that the Vishinski brothers arrive in Austria on schedule. Where do we take them? They can only remain in Austria for forty-eight hours on their visas. We'll need more time than that to determine if they are really Artur's brothers."

"You're assuming that they are impostors?" Josh was spring-loaded to the impostor theory.

"No, I want to get them to a quiet place off the beaten path that the KGB or Stasi or any of the other Warsaw Pact nations don't know about. It has to be remote, easy to protect, and it has to accommodate a lot of people so we can talk to them for at least a week or so. By then, we'll know if what they are carrying is good information and if they are who they say they are, or if they are agents. If they're agents, then we deliver them to the nearest Soviet embassy so they can be sent home."

"Tell me, how many people?" John leaned forward and asked, his drink dangling forgotten in his hand.

"At least twenty, and that doesn't include the security detail."

John sat up straighter and seemed to expand with satisfaction. He smiled at Lev and nodded. "I have the perfect spot. My father has a house on the island of Islay off the west coast of Scotland. It is like the Stewart House. I'll check with him, but if I remember, it has enough bedrooms to house at least twenty. Some unlucky sods like the security people will have to sleep in bunk beds. When I was growing up we'd have several families over at a time, and the kids stayed in the four rooms in the basement that have four bunks in each."

"How do we get them there? Her Majesty's customs may want to have a say in the matter?" Lev was already thinking about logistics.

"Not to worry." John was grinning now, thinking how much his father liked this kind of cloak and dagger stuff. "We can fly them in my father's company planes and my father will have a word with the customs people at the airport. The rest of the welcoming party flies commercial, and we can have some of the people waiting at the lodge when they arrive. It shouldn't be a bother."

"How far is the airport from the lodge by car?"

"That's a bit dodgier. About an hour over narrow, winding twisting Scottish roads, I'm afraid."

"John, can you ask your dad if we can check it out?"

"Sure, we can go up there anytime we want in the Navajo." John turned to Josh to see what he thought of the plan that was taking shape.

"OK, guys, here is what I suggest we do." Josh put down his empty glass on the coffee table. "Admiral Hastings will be here later in the week for a briefing. I will talk to him after I talk to Marty. Hastings will give us some guidance. He's pretty open minded, but the key is that we have to wait until they cross the border into Austria before we can do anything. We have absolutely no jurisdiction until then, and showing any interest in our émigrés before they arrive could tip our hand. Especially if the leak is anywhere in the chain of command that would deal with the matter."

"Certainly that holds true for your side," Lev replied seriously. "It is expected that we will be investigating, and we will continue to do so."

The Same Day, 1946 local time, Bonn

Behind them, rain beat on a window that during the day illuminated the landing in the old apartment building that had managed to survive the war intact. It didn't have an elevator, and its small lobby was open to the public so that anyone could enter and walk up the stairs. The glare from the street lights six stories below was dimmed by the water streaming across the glass. Their wet, shiny black vinyl raincoats looked slate gray and their hats sagged, soaked with rain. They arranged themselves on each side of the door with weapons drawn, ready to burst into the apartment.

It was a risk to knock, but Grenfel had decided, after speaking to the man's supervisor, that the Palestinian probably wasn't violent; still, you never knew, which is why he was not standing in the center of the door frame. He rapped on the door twice.

"Who is it?"

"Herr Grenfel from the Bundeskriminalamt. Please open the door, it is important that we talk."

Grenfel decided he would give the man thirty seconds before signaling one of the policemen to kick open the door. He was about halfway through his mental countdown when he heard the latch being withdrawn and watched as the door knob turned. As soon as the door cracked open, he pushed on it and held his badge in front of the man's face. "Polizeioberrat Grenfel from the Bundeskriminalamt."

There was no resistance. The man took several steps back, allowing Grenfel to enter. "Am I under arrest?"

"Not yet. We want to talk to you and can do it either here or at my office." Grenfel extended a heavy piece of blue paper, folded in thirds, with the logo of the Justice Ministry on the cover. "And we have a warrant to search your apartment."

The man closed his eyes for a moment and sagged as he reached out for the arm of his couch. Finding it, he collapsed onto the cushion and took a deep breath.

Monday, November 8th, 0730 local time, Wiesbaden

Grenfel was waiting by his boss's door in the Bundeskriminalamt's office building like an excited puppy when Starkeholz arrived and unlocked the door. He was barely able to contain himself as the two men passed inside and the door closed behind them.

"Good morning, Herr Starkeholz. Last night, we made our first arrest and have our first major break in the case."

"Excellent." Starkeholz allowed himself a smile as he sat down behind his desk, holding his coffee aloft, careful not to spill it. He didn't want to say, *it's about time.* "That **IS** significant!"

"Yes sir." Grenfel took a gulp of his own coffee. "We are holding a man who processed all of the passports in question, including the one the Syrian had. His papers say he is a Yugoslav who came into the country as a *gastarbeiter.* His personnel file says he was injured on the job and the German government gave him work approving work permits for *gastarbeiter,* on the assumption he knew Yugoslavia and could help evaluate the applications. After two years, he moved into passport and entry visa processing."

Grenfel lowered his voice. "But... his background is what our friends in the intelligence community call a very well-constructed legend."

"A what?"

"A legend. A fictitious background created for agents sent to spy on a foreign government."

"You mean what us old police officers would call a cover?"

"Yes sir." They both smiled. "In short, nothing in his background file checks out. We pointed this out to him and he is cooperating with us."

Starkeholz knew there was more by his subordinate's excitement. "What do you make of this?"

"It is a step in the right direction. His information may lead to the identity of the people in the pictures and help us solve the mystery of who is helping Red Hand. Fatah could be providing plastic explosives and money. It might explain the Jewish targets, and could mean that Fatah is planning another attack like the one during the Munich Olympics. Neo-Nazis helped facilitate that one, and it killed eleven Israeli athletes. We botched the take-down. This time Fatah may want Germans pulling the triggers."

Starkeholz didn't say anything; he remembered the soul-searching within the German law enforcement community that followed the massacre. It led to creating the ST Division, and to recruiting and training the GSG-9 hostage rescue team, which would be operational next year.

"It also explains how the members of Red Hand may have gotten to Libya."

"Yes it would. It also seems to rule out our friends to the East."

"I wouldn't go that far, Herr Hauptpolizeidirektor."

"Why?"

Grenfel wiped the condensation off the bottom of his mug before he set it down on the corner of his boss's desk. He knew he would have to be careful as he chose his next few words. "I would not put it past the Stasi and their Russian friends to marry the two up. Red Hand is a propaganda coup for the DDR and a nightmare for the Bundesrepublik. Let's face it: it took just thirty-one years for the Germans to start killing Jews again, in a time and in places that embarrass us deeply. Indirect interference and misdirection is very typical of our friends to the East. So if I were a betting man, I would bet on the Stasi supporting Red Hand."

"You don't have to feel guilty about Hitler and the Holocaust. He was a madman."

Grenfel thought that was an interesting comment, coming from a decorated SS officer; he decided not to respond. "Herr Hauptpolizeidirektor, I have a request."

"And that is?" Starkeholz wasn't surprised that Grenfel wanted something.

"I would not recommend that you share my information about the Palestinian we are holding with the minister for seventy-two hours, which is the maximum before we have to charge him. Then we will ask the minister to allow us to hold him in solitary confinement. He is at a secret location for protection. We should make some more arrests very soon based on the information he is giving us."

Starkeholz looked at his subordinate for several seconds. "Agreed."

Chapter 16
Flag Briefing

Vice Admiral Hastings was standing in the middle of their operations center, looking at the maps as well as the piles of classified material scattered on the table. He spent a couple of minutes studying each of the photos taped to the wall, after which, he turned to the group.

"So what's on the agenda for today? I just paid my respects to the Commodore, so the official reason I am here has been completed."

As the officer-in-charge of the 66th Joint Observation Group, it was Marty's job to respond.

"Sir, after formal introductions to the team members you've not yet met, you're having lunch with Colour Sergeant Calhoun, Senior Chief Jenkins, Petty Officer First Class Van der Jagt and Sergeants Bentley and Goodson at a local eatery. You can change in to civilian clothes here. When you come back, we'll brief you on what we know and what we plan to do. Then the Admiral and Mrs. Hastings are having dinner with the future Duke and Duchess of Leeds; commoners Lieutenant and Mrs. Haman, Lieutenant Marty Cabot and Major Lev Mogen of the Israeli Defense Forces in attendance."

"Outstanding." Hastings chuckled at the reference to the commoners. "What about my aide, Lieutenant Hodges?"

"Sir, he is welcome to join us for dinner. History suggests that right now he is escorting the Admiral's wife and acting as a pack animal. Your wife forwarded her shopping list before you got here, so Gwen—that's John's wife—and Rebekah had plenty of time to prepare Jeanie's shopping itinerary in London."

"It sounds like it's going to be expensive."

"I expect it will be, sir."

Lev was just putting coasters on the corners of a map of the northern half of Libya when Vice Admiral Hastings walked into the room an hour a half later. The Israeli tossed a dozen new photographs on the table and pointed to one of the squares that had been drawn on the map. "Sir, these were just delivered to me last night. We think the Fatah training base Red Hand visited is here." He drew an imaginary circle around one of the squares about twenty-eight miles west south west of Tripoli.

"When were these taken?" The admiral asked.

"About two weeks ago, when a delivery of fresh food was made to the camp, sir." Lev picked up one of the eight inch by ten inch pictures. "Three—von Berg, Schlemmer, and Gestner—were identified. The note also said they refer to Gestner as *the mechanic.*"

"Hmmm, that could be our bomber" Admiral Hastings said.

"Sir, it is a possibility," Lev said.

"OK, let's start at the beginning." Admiral Hastings sat in the chair that had been prepared for him alongside the table so that he could see the charts on the walls as well as the screen set up at the end of the room. "But before you begin, let me give you an update of the political lay of the land. As you know, the president knows we have a group developing options in case the law enforcement agencies can't stop Red Hand. Besides me, there are just eight people in the U.S. and six here in the U.K. who know about this organization. Neither SACEUR nor anyone in the German government knows this team exists. We plan to keep it that way. Off the record, SACEUR *asked* the chairman to create a separate intelligence group to find Red Hand and develop options. But he has not followed up on the request; I am guessing he wants plausible deniability."

Hastings paused for a second. "Every week I brief three people, the Chief of Naval Operations, and General Cruz, who is the Joint Staff's head of operations, and the First Sea Lord here in the UK. You are to continue to gather intelligence, just don't bring attention to yourselves while you are doing it; and at this time, no direct action is authorized."

"We understand, sir." Marty stepped aside. "Lev..."

"Thank you. Admiral, "I want to thank the U.S. government for allowing my country to participate, and for me to be a team member."

"Major Mogen, you are here because General Cruz and I believe Israel can help. The fact that two of this merry band of thieves welcomed you says a whole lot more about you and than any resume or recommendation a general could make."

"Thank you, sir." Lev paused for a few seconds to create a natural break before resuming. "The Fatah training camp where the Germans were seen is known for training bomb makers. Whether or not they were learning new skills or practicing existing ones, we're not sure. The camp also has extensive small arms training facilities, so we must assume they were being taught how to use rifles, pistols, and light machine guns.

Lev nodded to the senior SAS sergeant, who replaced the satellite picture with one showing three individuals walking down a dock. "We've confirmed that all six came by ship from Genoa to Tripoli on two different tramp steamers. Passage was paid for in cash. We had a man in position to take these and other photographs as they walked down the docks, and then again as they boarded a truck. We didn't find out which camp they were at until another asset reported seeing them and took pictures. As a driver, he is not allowed to do anything other than back the truck into an unloading area, go to a bathroom by the supply tent, and leave. The convoys are escorted by two cars with armed guards, and unloading is done by the camp members. If drivers are caught taking pictures, they would be tortured and shot."

"Next slide." Lev waited until the photograph appeared. "This picture was taken at the airport in Marrakech, Morocco, less than two weeks ago. We have others, but our agent watched as Bischoff and Gestner boarded a flight to Cologne, Dortman and Berger went to Frankfurt, and Finchafen and Holz to Munich. There is a remote possibility that we may get copies of the passports they used on their Moroccan arrival cards in a few days."

Admiral Hastings asked the obvious question. "What do they have in common?"

"Sir, that is a great question, and Lieutenant Haman has a theory he would like to share with you. But before he takes over, I would like to share some more facts."

Admiral Hastings nodded.

"We know that Ahmed ibn Khaldun stayed at this camp for several days and it is the only camp Khaldun visited. Ibn Khaldun is the head of Fatah's group that funds and supports terrorist activities. He was accompanied by this man, whose name we do not know, but we believe he is some kind of arms dealer. Mossad is working to identify him, his sources of weapons, and where he stores them or sends them. Right after the Germans arrived, six Palestinians, two of whom were on our watch list, arrived. We don't think Khaldun would have risked traveling to Libya unless he was to meet someone important."

The pause was Calhoun's cue to change slides and show a photo of a solitary person walking along the dock. "We think ibn Khaldun was there to meet this man, Wilhelm Gestner, whose code name is *the mechanic*. All of us would bet money that Gestner is one of the leaders of Red Hand, if not the leader, and maybe the bomb maker."

"But do you have proof?"

"No sir, not yet, but we're getting there."

"Excellent... That's what we want you to do. Get proof."

Josh replaced Lev at the front of the room. "Sir, what I am about to share is a bit out of the box, so please humor me, because it will shed some light on who we think these people are and who is supporting them."

"Lieutenant Haman, I would have been surprised if this group didn't have an idea by now. And knowing you as I do, I know your mind works in mysterious ways." Admiral Hastings paused for a second to let the laughter subside. "Go on, I'm all ears."

"As of today, there have been twenty-seven bombings in Germany, plus four in the U.K. Three of the ones in the U.K. killed senior executives of major U.S. companies, who happened to be Jewish. Two in Germany were near British Army bases. Three of the bombings in Germany targeted synagogues—one was a temple in Frankfurt and the most recent ones at the chapels of the army bases in Frankfurt and Ludwigshafen on Rosh Hashonah, the Jewish New Year."

The Colour Sergeant put another slide on the projector. "Of the twenty-two remaining bombings in Germany, twelve damaged either a Hertie's department store or a Stern's jewelry shop. For the record, in 1947 both chains were given back to surviving members of the families who owned the businesses in 1933 when they were seized by the Nazis. They were also given cash and other support as part of the reparation program to help them restart businesses."

Josh waited while the Colour Sergeant changed slides. "Here's where it starts to get make us feel we are on to something. We started looking Hertie's and Stern's main competitors and the list is very short. Then we looked at former Nazis who are either owners or senior executives at their competitors and the list got even shorter. Then, Major Mogen and I met with Simon Wiesenthal and a member of Mogen's staff to learn more about reparations to families who were victims of the Holocaust. Mr. Wiesenthal has devoted his life to hunting those responsible for the Holocaust and helping those who survived the camps find out what happened to their relatives.

"We asked three questions about each man on the short list." Josh waited until the slide was changed. "First was, what former Nazis—SS or Gestapo, but also Wehrmacht and Luftwaffe—have the wherewithal to fund a terrorist campaign? The second question was, which of these officers have sons in their late twenties to mid-thirties years who fit the description the Germans have or match any of the photos we have? And the third one was, did any of them serve together in the same unit during World War II and do they know each other?"

Admiral Hastings' brow contracted, and he leaned forward. Josh continued.

"Here's where it gets interesting. The Mossad agent told us there was a gathering of members of SS units in April of this year at an estate about fifty miles west of Buenos Aires. Many who went have young sons, eighteen of whom *just ran for office on the New German Party platform,* which is, at its core, Germany for Germans and everyone else go home. When you read their campaign material, it takes you right back to the Nazi party ideology first distributed in the 1920s. If you follow some of their platform planks to a logical conclusion, one interpretation is that they want to create a Fourth Reich."

Hastings reacted as if he was just stabbed. "Are you sure about that?"

"Yes sir. Colour Sergeant, pull out the slide that compares the New German Party platform to the Nazi manifesto." Josh waited until the slide appeared on the screen. "This is based on the National Socialist Party Platform published first in 1920 and then revised and re-issued in 1933. These are the words verbatim from the first eight items, and I've italicised the ones that are also in the New German Party's official platform."

Hastings stared at the screen. The others in the room could see his head moving as he read.

The Program of the German Workers' Party is a program for our time. The leadership rejects the establishment of new aims after those set out in the Program have been achieved, for the sole purpose of making it possible for the Party to continue to exist as the result of the artificially stimulated dissatisfaction of the masses.

1. *We demand the uniting of all Germans within one Greater Germany, on the basis of the right to self-determination of nations.*

2. We demand equal rights for the German people (Volk) with respect to other

nations, and the annulment of the Peace Treaty of Versailles and St. Germain.

3. We demand land and soil (Colonies) to feed our People and settle our excess population.

4. *Only Nationals (Volksgenossen) can be Citizens of the State. Only persons of German blood can be Nationals, regardless of religious affiliation. No Jew can therefore be a German National.*

5. Any person who is not a Citizen will be able to live in Germany only as a guest and must be subject to legislation for Aliens.

6. Only a Citizen is entitled to decide the leadership and laws of the State. We therefore demand that only Citizens may hold public office, regardless of whether it is a national, state, or local office.

7. *We demand that the State make its duty to provide opportunities of employment first of all for its own Citizens. If it is not possible to maintain the entire population of the State, then foreign nationals (non-Citizens) are to be expelled from the Reich.*

8. *Any further immigration of non-Germans is to be prevented. We demand that all non-Germans who entered Germany after August 2, 1914, be forced to leave the Reich without delay.*

"OK, I get it," he said finally. "I think I see where this is going. Josh, what's next?"

"Colour Sergeant, the slide with the names, please?"

The sergeant major put a slide on the projector that had twelve family names on it. "Admiral, we're focusing on the first several families, since they best fit the profile."

The colour sergeant put up an annotated slide with showing a serious man in what was obvious a photo for an identity document.

"Alois Brunner. He worked in the Nazi treasury for Finance Minister Lutz Graf Schwerin von Krosig. While no proof has been found, he has been suspected of funneling Nazi money to bank accounts in both Argentina and Switzerland. He has a small accounting firm in Munich and owns a money changing business with kiosks at several airports and many train stations. One of his boys was elected to the Bundestag."

Josh waited for the next slide. "Viktor Horst. He owns one of the larger wholesale jewelry operations in Germany, as well as many retail shops that compete with Stern. He has two boys, one of whom ran for election and won. Horst, according to what we learned, was responsible for turning gold fillings into gold bars and appraising the jewelry taken from the Jews gassed at the camps. Then if he didn't think someone high in the Nazi hierarchy would like the piece, he is suspected of stripping off the precious stones and melting the metal into bullion. No one knows where the bullion was hidden. After the war, there was an investigation into how much of that gold and jewelry went into his pockets. He was not charged with war crimes, and in the chaos of the aftermath of the war, the appraisal records went missing or were destroyed. Speculation by the investigators suggested that his early store inventory was seeded with stuff he collected in the camps and funded by gold bars he sold in Switzerland."

Josh waited for the next slide. "Baron Ernst von Spee. He is a now in his sixties. The pocket battleship, the *Graf Spee*, was named for his uncle. He was one of several officers sent by Hitler to prepare the national redoubt down in Bergesgarden. He has, on several occasions, publicly denounced the current government. His family lands were seized by the Allies, but we suspect he managed to spirit away a fair amount of his family's money during the war, because he was one of the few men Hitler allowed to go back and forth to Switzerland. Von Spee has several sons and daughters. One of his sons was defeated by ten percentage points.

He is a merchant marine captain and lives very well: outside Stuttgart in a small castle and five hundred acres of land he bought after the war."

Josh looked down at his notes while the next slide was put up. It had the same format as the other two—mug shot and a summary of the reasons why he was a person of interest. "Friedrich Starkeholz. He is a former SS officer and the Bundeskriminalamt director leading the Red Hand investigation. He was captured during the battle around Falaise and was vetted numerous times by the Brits and us before he was allowed to become a police officer. He is squeaky clean as far as we can see and was never accused of any war crimes. He is under consideration even though he was not at the meeting, and neither of his sons ran for office, because he is in the best position to cover for Red Hand."

"Helmut Stiglitz. He owns one of the competitors to Hertie's and has closed eight general merchandise stores in the past five years. Stiglitz is a former senior SS officer who spent most of the war on the Russian front and was never accused of any war crimes. He was awarded the Iron Cross with Swords and Diamonds after the battle of Kursk. He has four sons, and one, Erik, was elected to the Bundestag."

Josh stopped until the next picture popped back into focus. "Last is Oskar Zimmer. He suggested to Hitler that they form squadrons of pilots who would aim their ME-109s to crash into B-17s and then just before impact, bail out. He was also Himmler's and Bormann's personal pilot. He retired after running Templehof Airport for many years and is a widower who lives alone in West Berlin. One of his sons works for the city government as a prosecutor and the other is a pilot in the new German Luftwaffe."

"All meet your criteria. So what's next?" Admiral Hastings had been sitting intent on listening to Josh's theory.

"Sir, we want to begin surveillance on each of these guys one by one. We're betting that one of their sons is in one of these photos."

"What happens if it's a dead end?"

"We go to the next six names on the list, sir."

"And if you don't find anything after the second group of six, then what?"

"We take another look at what we have found and come up with another plan."

The Admiral sighed. "What kind of help do you need?"

Josh looked at Marty before he answered. "A dedicated intelligence analyst who can get us info from our intelligence community without someone very senior asking questions we can't answer. If he speaks German, so much the better."

"O.K., keep going. This is much more valuable than what is being passed off as analysis in D.C. I don't want to ask the CIA for help. Way too much bureaucracy, and if there is a leak I don't want to take the chance. I'll find a guy in our Navy."

Marty moved to the front of the room. "Once we find a connection, we can point the Germans in the right direction, and they'll be like bulldogs going after a rawhide chew."

Admiral Hastings laughed at the analogy. "Excellent! Let me see what I can provide. I will report that you have a hypothesis worth exploring. Maybe we'll get lucky and it'll be something he can take to the president. He is fit to be tied, because Americans are dying and the Germans can't seem to find the bastards."

Chapter 17
Connect the Dots

Thursday, November 11th, 1231 local time, East Berlin

"Do you know what today is?" The KGB officer spoke around a mouthful of dark rye bread he had used to wipe up some of the gravy on his plate. These Red Hand bombings were a break from the dull, routine meetings and reports he had to read. But Colonel Grünewald had a tiger by the tail. If the West ever found proof that the Stasi was both funding and supplying Red Hand, the firestorm would send the former tank officer to an early grave.

Krasnovsky genuinely liked the Stasi colonel as another kindred soul who didn't swallow the bullshit coming out of either of their governments' propaganda organs. Their common backgrounds as former officers made their candid lunch conversations much more enjoyable. The East German also told him the truth about Red Hand, something no one else in the KGB had.

Grünewald finished cutting a chunk of bratwurst and dipped it in grainy mustard before pushing some sauerkraut onto his fork and putting it all in his mouth. Chewing gave him time to contemplate his answer.

"I do. The Tommies call it Rememberance Day, commemorating the end of World War I. The Americans call it Veterans Day."

"Good. I wanted to see if you knew the significance of the date." Krasnovsky paused to chase his last bit with a swig of beer. It was one of the things the Germans made much better than his countrymen. "So comrade colonel, what's the latest on your boy Stiglitz?"

"Mmm, the good news is that Stiglitz is back in the DDR and he has five comrades with him."

"Ah! Any idea of what is next?"

"They are going to set up three cells, two to a cell, and recruit more people. I have two officers up there this week doing some training."

"Who vetted them?"

"Short answer is Stiglitz. He claims he did it on his own."

"Do you believe him?"

"Yes and no. Yes, because he knew them all from his days at the University of Heidelberg or the University of Marburg. We have files on all five of his friends and our information suggests they are radicals susceptible to recruitment."

"And no?"

Grünewald lifted roasted potato to his mouth as he stared at two young men having a heated, in-your-face argument at the bar. He waited until the arm-waving stopped and they went back to their beer. Reassured that there would not be a fight, the former tank company commander answered Krasnovsky's question. "No, because Dieter has no training as an investigator. So he is either very naïve, thinking that he can go on his gut instincts, or he had help. I believe he had help. The question is, who? We have our suspicions."

"And you suspect whom?" Krasnovsky tilted his head to the side, reminding Grünewald briefly of an inquisitive bird.

Grünewald answered carefully. "Arabs are at the top of the list. Your KGB is number two."

"I would bet on the Arabs. I am pretty sure that the KGB is not involved. I would have heard and told you."

"That is good to know. Unfortunately, we don't have a lot of contacts with the Arab organizations."

"We do. I will make some inquiries."

"Thank you. I will be very interested to find out what you learn."

"Me too." Krasnovsky put the last piece of bratwurst into his mouth. "Do you know where he went?"

"Morocco. He said he was on vacation."

"Why there?"

"It is a common destination for Germans. Cheap, good beaches, lots of sun."

"Do you believe him?"

"Again, yes and no. Yes, he went there. No, because I suspect there was more to the trip than drinking beer and laying on a beach."

Krasnovsky didn't say anything for a few seconds. "That's what I love about this business. We never have all the facts. We have to, as you say, connect the dots and make choices. Sometimes we make good ones, sometimes our assumptions are wrong and we make bad ones."

"There is one other interesting tidbit." Grünewald didn't want to react to Krasnovsky's comment. He knew that one major misstep, real or perceived, would mean the end of his career or worse, his life. "Stiglitz has a girl friend."

"Is that so?" Krasnovsky was surprised by the revelation.

"Yeah. Giselle Bischoff, a real head turner, with brains."

"So we can add screwing to what Stiglitz did in Morroco." Krasnovsky took a sip of his beer while he enjoyed Grünewald's smile. "This should be fun to watch. Women are more vicious terrorists than men. Do you know when they are going back into the Bundesrepublik?"

"No, but we gave them all new papers this week so they can go back and forth between the DDR and the Bundesrepublik."

"I will be watching to see the results of their work." Another sip of beer. "I do have something for you that you will find valuable. It is up to you on how you use it."

"What do you have?" Grünewald was delighted to have information coming his way.

"We have a source inside the Simon Weisenthal Center in Vienna. In a routine report, the source noted that, a few weeks ago, an American by the name of Joshua Haman and a man named Lev Mogen, along with a Brit named John Osborne visited the center. Normally, the report would have been filed in the archives, but the fact is that *Weisenthal himself* spent two hours with them. Weisenthal doesn't grant interviews to just anyone who calls, so either Haman, Osborne, and Mogen made him want to share what he knew, or someone he knew called him to say 'Talk to these men and give them what they need.' That triggered a request for research on the three men by the head of the First Chief Directorate."

Grünewald's delight vanished, replaced by a distinct chill. "What did you learn?"

"Our files show Haman has many decorations from when he flew combat search and rescue missions in Vietnam. Our Vietnamese allies could never shoot him down and called him a ghost. They claim he flew in SEAL teams that conducted raids inside North Vietnam."

"Osborne?"

"Interesting, that one is. He comes from a wealthy British family that made its money in shipping. John is the oldest of three sons and is a pilot in the Fleet Air Arm with 846 Squadron. He saw service in Northern Island, where he flew the Commando version of the British Sea King. His father was also a Royal Navy pilot in the war. John's brothers work in the family business with their father."

"So two of these guys are helicopter pilots and combat veterans?"

"Yes."

The chill worsened. "And Mogen?"

"Nothing other than his nationality, which is Israeli."

"Mogen sounds German." Grünewald spoke disinterestedly. He wondered if the Stasi colonel guessed at his discomfort.

"It could be a name changed from something else when his family arrived in their new country. We can't find anything about him."

Grünewald saw several more dots, but with lots of distance between them. He didn't believe in coincidences and made a mental note to get the names of the foreigners helping the Bundeskriminalamt. With the DDR's sources, it shouldn't be too hard. "Hmmmm, that is a very unusual group. Do you happen to know what kind of information they were given?"

"Our report said it was lists: families whose businesses were seized by the Nazis, and wealthy Nazis living in West Germany or Austria. They also wanted a list of those wanted for war crimes. The report didn't have any other details, so we don't know everything that was provided. I have been told that Moscow has asked for more information; when we get it, I am to be informed, and then you will be as well."

Grünewald resolved not to wait for this, but to start his own investigations that very afternoon.

Sunday, November 14th, 1976, 0951 local time, Schloss Theissen

Floor to ceiling windows in the suite of offices of Schloss Theissen gave the occupants and unobstructed view of the gardens, three stories below, and the Eifel Mountains. Except for the pines, the trees in the forests had shed their leaves, leaving the gardens as an isolated green island on this cloudy, late fall day.

Adolf Sturmer had served Albert von Theissen since he'd joined the Lufwaffe in early 1940 when, because he had worked in his father's restaurant, the eighteen year old had been assigned the officer's mess of Jagescheweder Two, near the Franco-German border. When von Theissen was transferred to Luftwaffe headquarters in 1943, the young man followed, officially assigned as his personal batman or servant.

He became an orphan when a bomb killed his mother, and his father, drafted into the Volksturm, died during a battle that tried to keep Patton's Third Army from crossing the Rhine. After the war, Von Theissen brought him to the schloss as his personal servant, and when the major domo died in early 1970, Sturmer became the head of the household.

He was supervising setting the table in the main dining room when the phone rang. After answering it, Sturmer ran up stairs and tapped twice on the door to the office. "Herr Baron, Gruppenführer der Waffen-SS Bruno Glockner is on the phone."

"Thank you, Sturmer." Von Theissen picked up the handset that had been laid on the small table just inside the door. "Good morning, Herr Gruppenführer, what can I do for you?"

"Herr Baron, I have something for you to look into this coming week." This learned formality was nothing new; Glockner came into the SS from a family of tailors. Even before the war, his superiors had recognized his leadership skills and rewarded his efforts. Von Theissen knew that the man was all business; he never exchanged pleasantries and he had a reputation as a no nonsense commander used to giving orders that sounded like requests. "I believe you reported that you took care of von Ritter and his team. Is that not so?"

"We left them a lethal present in the form of sarin nerve gas sprayed on their last cash payment. One touch and they would be dead in a few minutes. Brunner delivered the money as per von Ritter's instructions. We do not know when he opened it."

"Do you know where von Ritter is today?"

"No. I presume he along with his team is dead. Being killed by a poison like sarin is not something the government would publicize. We did see his obituary in a Frankfurt paper. We don't have the names or backgrounds of the other men, and we decided it was unwise to contact mortuaries or the police looking for men who died under suspicious circumstances. Why?" Von Theissen knew the SS-Gruppenführer wouldn't be asking without a purpose. It was like talking to a lawyer who never asked questions without already knowing the answer.

"I suggest you check into his whereabouts. A birdie who told me he is alive will call you to tell you what he knows. If von Ritter is still among the living, you need to take care of him."

Von Theissen heard a dial tone before he could say *Jawohl, Herr Gruppenführer.*

The Same Day, 1830 local time, Hannover

AnnaLiese Stiglitz was beaming when she opened the door, knowing that Dieter was bringing his girlfriend to their Sunday afternoon dinner. Before he could introduce the two, his mother gave his one hundred and forty centimeter tall, fifty-five kilogram blonde woman-friend a big hug. "Giselle, welcome to our home."

Dieter had warned Giselle that his mother was very traditional, a *"kinder, kuche und kirche"* woman, who'd endured the bombings of Hannover by both the RAF at night and the American Air Force by day, and made sure her boys survived. Throughout the war, she'd managed to find food when it was scarce and still bear two more children. Born in 1944, Dieter would always be her baby.

After the introductions and some general conversation, Helmut Stiglitz addressed her. "Giselle, are you related to Major Hans Bischoff?"

Dieter looked at his watch and noted that his father had waited thirty minutes before delving into what Giselle's father had done during the war. Dieter was convinced his father catalogued the potential value of humans by their wartime role.

"Yes, he is my father. Do you know him?"

"No, I just read about his accomplishments. He was one of our top aces. I believe he had over seventy kills as a night fighter pilot." Helmut looked around to make sure everyone knew that Giselle's father was a Luftwaffe ace. "Is he well?"

"I believe so. I don't see him very often. My parents are divorced." Giselle hid the still gnawing pain of that nasty, divisive divorce.

"That's too bad. From what I understand, Major Bischoff was an excellent leader."

"I wouldn't know about that, Herr Stiglitz. My dad doesn't talk about the war. It is, as he says, in the past. He is proud of what he did, but he wants to focus on the future, training pilots in the new German Luftwaffe." Giselle hoped that ended the discussion about her father. Hans Bischoff wanted to see the Bundesrepublik flourish, whereas she shared her mother's view that it needed a revolution to become a much more socialist country.

"I see." AnnaLiese's look in her husband's direction told him to drop the subject. He turned to their son.

"I saw an article in *Der Stern* that quoted government sources and said that neo-Nazis are not behind Red Hand. Dieter, what do you think? Are they involved?"

"Vati, I don't know."

"It was just a thought." Helmut took a long swallow of his beer. "The neo-Nazis remind me a lot of Hitler's brown shirts of the thirties, who were undisciplined thugs. It was a good thing they were placed under the SS's control." Another long swallow of his beer, and then the former SS officer looked at his youngest son. "Dieter, there is a meeting of the leadership of the New German Party on the 23rd of this month. I would like you to come, as there are some people I would like you to meet. Can you make it?"

Dieter knew a request like this was, at least in his father's mind, an order. As he took a sip of the pale Reisling wine, Dieter's mind raced through a schedule he'd worked out with the other cells. "I believe I can make it."

"Excellent." His father was satisfied. Order given and acknowledged.

"Why don't you and Giselle join us for dinner that night, and then we'll go to the meeting."

AnnaLiese saw a chance to get to know Giselle better. Who knows, she might one day be the mother to more grandchildren. "Giselle can stay here with me."

"Mother, why don't you ask Giselle?"

Giselle didn't wait for the question. "I would like that." She smiled warmly.

Monday, November 15th, 1976, 0828 local time, RNAS Yeovilton

Earlier in the morning, Lev Mogen met a courier from the Israeli embassy at the train station in Yeovil. Back in their building, he was slitting open a thick, sealed envelope with a long, slender, double-edged knife when he called out, "Marty, we need to get everyone together. I got some very useful intelligence this morning."

"What's up?" Josh had just walked into the operations center carrying a cup of coffee for Marty, tea for Lev, and hot chocolate for himself.

"The courier gave me a heads up that our Vienna office is convinced that both the Documentation Center and the Union of Councils for Soviet Jews have a leak. I don't have any details, but we heard about it from the Soviet side of the fence. That would not surprise me; the KGB's Second Directorate is always looking for information it can use against its citizens. Those who still practice Judaism—or any religion—and those who want to emigrate are prime targets."

"So we have to assume that the Soviets know we were there and what was discussed." Josh was looking over the edge of his mug as the others filed into the room.

"I think," Lev Mogen looked grim, "that we then have to assume that they are asking the question of why Josh Haman, U.S. Navy, John Osborne, Royal Navy, and Lev Mogen, Israeli, were asking for information about Nazis and the businesses they own in Germany. At least it is unlikely that they know that I work for the Mossad."

"That would be my read." Marty tossed the photo he was studying on the table.

"My guess is that, right now, KGB officers in the Soviet embassies in London and D.C. and their San Francisco consulate are gathering information on John Osborne and Josh Haman," Lev continued with his assessment. "It also means they may come up with the name of Marty Cabot, Derek Van der Jagt, and Gary Jenkins, and they may figure out that you all worked together at one time. This will arouse the curiosity of someone in the Seventh Directorate, the part of the KGB charged with gathering intelligence about foreigners. They may already have dossiers on Marty, Josh, and John, begun when you were commissioned. They create the dossiers so that if you rise in the organization and some asks who is this guy, they'll have some background info.

"Yeah, and mine has an extra word in it." Josh interrupted.

"Which is?" Lev didn't pick up on the sarcastic humor.

"Target."

Lev let the chuckles from everyone in the room die down before continuing. "We have to assume someone in the KGB is asking questions, and if they are senior enough, the name Koniev may come up. If it does, it will raise their blood pressure. The question is, how long will it take, and what conclusions will the KGB reach?"

"Who is Koniev?" John asked.

"Tell him." Marty pointed at Josh. "You captured him."

"You made it possible." Josh quickly summarized the less classified details of the mission that had lead to the KGB officer's defection. "As it turns out, the good colonel was one of the Soviet's top experts on surface-to-air missile tactics. He was in Vietnam on a two year tour, testing his ideas, and he gave our intelligence folks a brain dump on how the Soviets intended to use their SAMs in a war with us."

"Why did he defect?" John asked, fascinated.

"He was... not happy with the Soviet Union, and blamed his country for the unnecessary deaths of his wife and daughter. When he said he wanted to defect, I figured the barrel of a sub-machine gun in the back of his neck was motivation enough; but now that I know him, I believe his desire to defect was genuine. We just provided the means."

"That's not all." Marty thought he would add a key point. "We think it was at least six months before the Soviets figured out that he was alive and well and living in the U.S."

"Jolly good." John was impressed. "So we have to assume that at some time in the near future they will have their dossiers on us in one big pile."

"Yes, but the Soviets are not supermen." Lev Mogen spoke up. "They too have to connect all the dots. The KGB is much more compartmentalized than a Western intelligence agency, so it will take them much longer to figure it out. And it is an organization in which knowledge is power, and that power is used for political and personal advantage as much as it is for the benefit of the country. Sharing information is not one of the KGB's strong points. There's one more thing. We also have to assume that the Soviets may have put together the fact that Vishinski is Josh's late wife's maiden name. If they connect that name to Josh's military career, and to

Koniev, they may revoke Artur Vishinskis brothers's exit visas. It is unlikely, but possible."

"They'd have to act pretty fast. We are leaving for Vienna a week from today, and the Vishinskis arrive on Wednesday."

"That's why," Lev tapped the documents that just arrived with the hilt of his knife, "I hope time is on our side."

"May I make a suggestion or two?" John leaned forward over the table.

"We're all ears," Marty said, gesturing for John to continue.

"First, I think we all agree that we need to get the Vishnskis out of Vienna as fast as possible."

"Agreed." Josh and Marty spoke almost as one.

"Now, we expect eight of them—four adults and four children, ranging from ten to seventeen." John wanted to summarize the logistics plan. "Once they get off the train, Josh, Lev, the Colour Sergeant, and one of his mates meet them, and we drive them right to the general aviation terminal at Vienna's international airport. There, my dad will be waiting in his new Hawker, and I will be there with the Cheyenne; we put one family on each plane and fly them to the hunting lodge. Lord knows, the place has plenty of room. There, we can start the debrief and protect them until we decide whether they are real or not."

Marty took over as the unit leader. "Admiral Hastings said to just let him know and he will call the First Sea Lord; U.K. customs and immigration won't be a problem as long as we let them know what we decide to do so they can get their paper work in order. It will be an unofficial official request. Lev, do we know what kind of documentation the Vishinskis will have when they arrive in Vienna?"

"Yes, Marty, we do. They should have valid emigration papers from the Soviet Union, which means they will have passports as well as visas to enter Austria. The Austrian customs officials get on the train in Brataslava, Czechoslovakia, and stamp documents, so when they get off the train, they can go where they want. We can have the U.K. customs people board the planes and stamp their passports before they get off. If not, as you said, we can take care of the paperwork later!"

"I have a better idea." Lev Mogen spoke up. "Because they are Jews, I can have Israeli passports ready for all of them with the U.K. visitor visas already stamped in the passport. We can take the pictures with a Polaroid as soon as we get them on board and paste them into the passports on the plane. They'll also have their exit visas and Soviet identity documents we can use as back-up. If they are impostors, Her Majesty's government can revoke their U.K. entry visas and we can cancel the Israeli passports just before we give them back to the KGB"

"Brilliant. I like Lev's plan better." John waved his mug of tea.

"OK." Marty moved on to the next question. "Assuming they are the real deal, how do we get them to the U.S. or to Israel?"

"That's simple." Senior Chief Jenkins was making some notes on a pad. "Once we have some idea of what they are bringing out, and assuming it is valuable, we ask Admiral Hastings to task a Special Air Mission airplane to take them wherever we want. My guess is that either the D.I.A. or CIA will want to get their hands on whatever they have pretty damn fast. Give the Colour Sergeant and me a couple of hours and we'll have a plan. This is a simple snatch. What we have to do is figure out how to keep the Soviets out of the game."

"Do you know what is so important?" Marty asked the question that all of them have been asking; so far, no one has an answer.

"No." Lev was emphatic. "Josh doesn't know and I wish I knew. But the fact that my government is willing to risk sources and do whatever else is needed to make sure they get out tells me someone has a very good idea of what they are carrying. All I can get from Tel Aviv is that Mossad analysts think it may have to do with Soviet nuclear and chemical weapons."

Jenkins whistled. "That's reason enough."

Wednesday, November 17th, 1976, 0928 local time, Karlshorst

Colonel Grünewald waited for his Soviet counterpart in the visitors' area of the dull, gray, concrete complex that was the KGB's offices in Karlshorst, a few kilometers southeast of Berlin's center. He'd already given the guard his identity papers in a tray that came out of a trap door. They were returned with a log that he signed.

The delay gave him the opportunity to study the pictures on the wall in the small lobby. Smiling down from one wall were the obligatory pictures of Lenin and Brezhnev. Grünewald assumed Stalin's picture had been removed during Nikita Khrushchev's de-stalinization campaign, after he revealed the dictator's role in the purges of the 1930's and his crimes against the Soviet people. Between them sat a large glorified color print of workers in a cornfield looking up and to the right.

A montage of black and white pictures on the opposite wall showed what this building had looked like after the Soviet Army captured Berlin caught his attention. He hadn't known that the KGB headquarters in East Germany had at one time been one of the buildings used by Abwehr, the German military intelligence organization during World War II.

"Colonel, thank you for coming."

Grünewald was surprised to see Krasnovsky standing in the opening of a heavy, steel reinforced vault-like door that he assumed could withstand hundreds of rounds of rifle fire or even a rocket propelled grenade or two. "My pleasure."

On the elevator, The KGB officer entered a six digit code into a pad before he selected the fifth floor; there he led the German down a long hall passed closed doors, each with its own cipher lock. They entered a windowless conference room. Waiting for the two officers was a short Oriental officer wearing the shoulder boards of a lieutenant colonel. Grünewald thought that if his late mother were introduced to the man, her first reaction would be to try to feed him; he looked emaciated.

"Colonel Grünewald, may I introduce you to Lieutenant Colonel Chinh Loi of the North Vietnamese People's Army."

Krasnovsky spoke in Russian, which was a signal to the German that it was the only common language amongst the three men. "Lieutenant Colonel Loi is attached to their embassy in Moscow while he attends one of the KGB's schools. As part of that training, he is working in our military counter-intelligence and armed forces political surveillance. It was there that he heard that you were looking for information about two American Navy officers, and someone in Moscow thought you two should meet. Colonel Loi has some first-hand experience with the two Americans you have been asking about." Krasnovsky paused. "Colonel Loi..."

"Yes, thank you. Colonel Grünewald, it is nice to meet you." The Vietnamese officer placed his fingers on the top of the table and his thumbs along the edge of a folder. "You are interested in two officers. Cabot is a Navy commando and Haman is a Navy helicopter pilot." Loi used the tips of his forefingers to push the folder across the table. "I asked Hanoi to send these pictures of Lieutenant Haman and his friend Lieutenant Cabot; they were taken in 1972."

"Where were the Americans when the photographs were taken?"

"At a base called Tan San Nhut. It was an American Air Force base near Ho Chi Minh City at the time."

"What do you know about them?"

"Not much, other than they are very good at what they do."

Grünewald studied each of the eight photos. "Thank you. Should either enter the DDR, these will help identify them. If we think they are about to commit a crime, then we will arrest them."

"Colonel Krasnovsky, may I ask a question?" Loi leaned forward, intensity flashing in his eyes.

"Go ahead," the officer replied.

Do you know where the Americans Cabot and Haman are today?"

"I don't know. But if they are in West Germany, Grünewald here will find them without much effort. Why?"

"My country would be very grateful if they were eliminated."

Krasnovsky looked at the young Vietnamese officer. "Your country, or you?"

Loi didn't answer immediately, which told Krasnovsky the answer. "Colonel, may I give you some advice?"

"Yes, comrade colonel, please."

"The war against the Americans in your country is over. You can't keep fighting it, but you can learn its lessons while you mourn and honor your fallen comrades." Krasnovsky reflected for a few seconds. "Thirty-one years ago, if Colonel Grünewald and I had met, we would have done our best to kill each other. Now, we are friends and our countries are allies. The world is a strange place."

"Cabot and Haman are enemies of my country." Loi stared coldly at the Russian, not wanting to give up.

"I would change the word 'are' to 'were.' A treaty was signed, and your countries are no longer at war. As a soldier, you will be given other battles to fight." Krasnovsky could see the defiance in Loi's eyes. He was trying not to give away his thoughts, but Krasnovsky believed he knew what the man was thinking. "When the war is over, it is over. We don't go on personal vendettas. And if you are thinking about sanctioning an assassination of either one or both of those officers on your own, don't do it. It will ruin your career."

"My career does not matter."

"Revenge is not a valid reason for killing these officers. If they were attacking your country or mine, then killing them would be our job. Neither Colonel Grünewald nor his government is going to create an international incident unless they have very good reason to do so. Beyond that, you should be grateful that you could provide some help."

Sunday, November 21st, 1976, 0804 local time, Geissen

The jangling of the phone woke Dieter. Untangling himself from Giselle, he picked up the handset. "Allo."

"Good morning, it is your father."

His father's command voice caused him to sit up and the sudden motion woke his lover. "Good morning, vati."

"I hope I did not wake you."

"You didn't." Dieter thought his father was enjoying the fact that he was sure he woke up his youngest son and was wondering if Giselle were in the bed with him.

"I wanted to remind you about the meeting on the 23rd. I'd like you to be at the apartment by four. We can talk before going to the party office. I want to get there early so you can meet several party leaders."

"OK. I can do that."

"Also, you and I are going to Argentina next month. It won't cost you a cent, but you will find the trip worthwhile. We'll leave Friday night and be gone a week. Make sure your passport is current."

It would be very, very difficult for him to turn his father down. Dieter knew an order when he heard one. He thought wryly of his several passports. "It is. What are the dates?"

"We leave Friday, the third of December, and will be back the following Sunday, the eleventh. All the visa paperwork will be ready for your signature on Tuesday, then it will be hand-carried through the process at the Argentine embassy in Bonn. By the way, the weather is nice in Buenos Aires this time of the year."

After receiving appropriate sounds of acquiescence from his youngest son, Stiglitz abruptly rang off.

Tuesday, November 23rd, 1976, 0746 Local time, Vienna

Josh had found a bakery on their walk back from dinner the night before. The warmth from the ovens surrounded him as soon as he walked into the store, and he savored the smell, salivating in anticipation of tasting the freshly baked bread. The aroma brought him back to his childhood when his mother would send him down to the local bakery to get rolls for breakfast and bread for the day. The family joke was that he had to buy eight if his mother wanted six to arrive home.

In the center of the store, between the cases on three sides, was a small table with a kilo brick of soft butter and a knife for the bakery's customers to smear butter onto fresh rolls cut into chunks. Josh stepped outside as he ripped one of his favorite *mun Brötchen* poppy seed rolls in half and stuffed it into his mouth.

He was looking down the street when two men stepped in front of him and blocked his path.

"Good morning Lieutenant Haman." The man in front spoke English and held up a KGB badge; the other stood at his side.

"Go fuck off. I'm an American citizen." Josh shoved his right hand into his jacket pocket and pressed the bag of rolls against his chest.

"We know who you are. We thought you would like to know that KGB is very interested in why you are in Vienna."

"I'm glad the KGB has time to worry about a mere U.S. Navy lieutenant. That means you'll miss the important stuff, and in a war we will kick your ass. Now get the fuck out of my way."

"Not so fast, Lieutenant Haman. You know, we can kill you any time we want."

"I don't think so." Josh shoved the barrel of his .45 hard against the front his ski jacket pocket and spoke Russian in a hoarse whisper. He could smell the pungent aroma of stale tobacco smoke as the Russian spread his hands wide and took an involuntary step back. "Either move away from me, or I start yelling for the police and have you arrested for assault." Josh waited a second. "Or maybe I will blow a hole in you so large you will be able to watch your guts come out as you fall. So I suggest that you go back into the hole you crawled out from. And if you or one of your fellow agents ever come near me or anyone in my family, I will kill every KGB agent I can find. It will become my personal vendetta. So go find someone else to bully. *Do you understand?*"

The Russian nodded.

"Good. Don't let me see you ever again."

Josh watched them turn and walk away. He stepped down into the street and saw Lev standing on the steps of the store next door carrying two net bags, one with bottled water and juices, the other with sliced meats wrapped in paper. "What was that all about?" Lev asked quietly.

"The KGB wanted to remind me that they know who I am and can kill me at any time. I wanted to let them know I was armed and would defend myself." Josh looked at the remains of the roll in his hand. He had lost his appetite. "The sad part is that what they said is true. If I had been in bed with Natalie, I wouldn't be here. If they want to take me out, I probably won't be able to stop it. But if they miss, I will declare war on them and kill every KGB son-of-a-bitch I can find. It'll be ugly, but the kill ratio will be in my favor before I am dead."

"Josh, the KGB have to know you were married to Artur Vishinski's daughter. Do you think there were just sending a message or up to some kind of mischief?"

"I wish I knew."

Lev put his hand on Josh't shoulder. "I expected some kind of trouble. Our embassy and the council representative told me that the local KGB officers like to threaten relatives of émigrés just before they come out, as a not so subtle reminder of their power inside and outside the Soviet Union."

Josh took a deep breath. "Look, the KGB scares the shit out of me, but what can you do? I can't let them get to me." The desire for the tasty roll reasserted itself and he resumed his attack on the *mun Brötchen* as they walked down the street.

Lev waited until they were about halfway back to the Hotel Furstenhof before he turned to his friend. "Tonight, we're going to give the KGB a black eye," he said.

"How so?" Josh could see the entrance to the seventy year old hotel, across the street from Vienna's main train station.

"Tonight, agents will pick up the men we think are the spies at the Documentation Center and the Union of Councils of Soviet Jews. We're pretty sure they are both KGB and it might get messy. We want to learn what they have been passing on to Moscow over the years, but also what they sent on the Vishinkis and you."

"What do you mean by messy?"

"They may not be cooperative, and then we have to decide how long we keep them before giving them back to their masters. To the Austrians, the agencies are private organizations, so the Austrians can't arrest them for spying. At best, they might be sent back to the Soviet Union because they were here illegally. So this is going to be a Mossad operation; that way the U.S. and U.K. won't be embarrassed if something goes wrong. I'll be back in time to meet the train, and later I'll brief Marty. What he doesn't know in advance, he doesn't have to report."

"What about what *I* know?" Josh asked in a voice muffled by *mun Brötchen*.

"After what I just saw, I thought knowing what is about to happen might prevent you from getting a premature start on that kill ratio."

Wednesday, November 24th, 1445 local time, Vienna

It was minus two Celsius outside the station and not any warmer on the open platform. The open ends created a venturi that increased the wind chill by a few knots. The breeze was most noticeable where it swirled around the floor-to-ceiling stanchions. Josh was glad he'd decided to wear a ski parka and a pair of boots with crepe soles to keep the cold of the concrete from seeping into his feet.

For the umpteenth time, Josh glanced down the track. He could see several customs and immigration officers gathering in the middle of the platform waiting for the Budapest-Vienna express. Their very warm and waterproof forest-green woolen loden overcoats were buttoned against the cold, and the round black hats with silver striping were placed on their heads in the prescribed manner. *Alles ist in ordnung....*

"Good afternoon."

Lev's distinctive voice interrupted his silent prayer that his late father-in-law's brothers and their families were on the train.

"Good afternoon. The train must be on time because the customs officers are here." He turned to face the Israeli. "How'd it go last night?"

"The leak is plugged. The Soviets planted a young KGB captain at the Union of Councils of Soviet Jews and a KGB major at the Documentation Center on deep cover assignments. We gave them a choice, defect and talk or go home and face the music. They are in a safe house for the initial debriefing, then we'll fly them to Israel where the CIA will have access to them. The sad news is that their families will be held hostage back in the Soviet Union. This is an ugly business sometimes. The KGB deliberately recruits men with families to have leverage over them and prevent spontaneous defections."

Lev pointed in the direction of a small crowd gathering on the platform. "That man with the gray leather coat and hat is from the council. He let me know that Dov and Sol and their families were on the train and their passports and visas are all in order."

"Good."

"He told me that each person will be carrying one medium sized suitcase—that's all that is allowed by the Soviets—and reminded me that they have forty-eight hours to leave Austria."

Josh looked around when he heard the excited voice of a young boy shouting the German equivalent of "Train... Train!!! Train!!!"

From his position on the far side of the platform next to a collection of luggage carts, Josh could see down the line of the green passenger cars with black trim. He watched the man from the Union of Councils of Soviet Jews separate himself and hold up his palm as if to signal to the group: stay here. Head high, he strode down the platform to the last two cars, where two immigration officers were waiting by the door of one of the cars. Once there, he pulled out a folded sheet from his breast pocket and opened it.

Josh could see passengers stopping first in front of the Austrian customs officers and showing documents before they were allowed to continue. A few, businessmen in dress coats carrying briefcases and hand luggage, headed toward the exit, knowing where they were going and what they wanted to do.

The press thinned as families ran toward each other, gathering in a dance of kisses, hugs, and arm waving. One group, their clothes shabbier than those worn by the well-dressed businessmen, hesitated, not sure of what to do or where to go. Eventually they gravitated toward the Austrian customs official, whose outstretched hand signaled, without saying a word, *Please show me your documents*. Apparently satisfied, the Austrian official spoke to the man from the council, who nodded and pointed toward the group of them on the platform.

The two families started walking in their direction, and Josh suddenly saw certain resemblances to the man who had been, all too briefly, his father-in-law.—*The Vishinskis!* Josh felt a slight nudge in his back, which he was sure came from Lev, and started toward them, not knowing what to say or expect.

The older, taller man stopped, looked at him for a few seconds, cocked his head and said in accented English, "You are Joshua Haman, no?"

"Da, I am." Josh responded in Russian.

"I am Dov Vishinski." The words were followed by a bear hug and kisses on both Josh's cheeks in a traditional Russian greeting that made Josh very uncomfortable. "I am happy to meet you. Our families are free at last."

Wednesday, November 24th, 1976, 0627 local time, Wiesbaden

The radio phone in his government issue Opel Commodore jangled.

"Starkeholz."

"Good morning, Herr Starkeholz. Von Ritter here. I need you to send a couple of your men to my hotel here in Wiesbaden. Make sure they have handcuffs with them. It seems there were two gentlemen inquiring about me. One will need a trip to the hospital after he is arrested and you have a conversation with him."

"What happened?"

"I noticed their interest in me when I went out for my morning jog. Their manner raised my suspicions. When they didn't follow, I ducked back into the hotel and caught them as they entered my room without either the manager's approval or my own. So their crime is breaking and entering. One of them was unhappy that I showed up and he is lying on the floor right now. Even after a hospital stay, he will be unable to raise one of his arms for a while and will limp for the rest of his life. Other than that, I am sure he will live. The other gentleman involved in the scuffle is sitting in a chair with his arms tied behind his back. He is a bit bruised and will find it difficult to talk because his jaw is broken. He can answer questions by nodding."

"Do you know them?"

"No. When you get here, they will take us to their car and you can inspect it. I found it curious that they did not have any identification."

Starkeholz knew where von Ritter was staying. "I will be there in less than ten minutes with some help." He made a quick u-turn and headed to the hotel a few blocks away. *Von Ritter*, he mused, *is a very dangerous man. One I prefer to keep on my side.*

Chapter 18
Training Ground

Thursday, November 25th, 1976, 0823 local time, Leeds

Unlike Stewart House, which sat on a barren hilltop and gave the viewer a commanding view of the countryside from any window, the Osborne hunting lodge was in a valley surrounded by two hundred year old oak trees that had survived the demands of the Royal Navy of the prior century for wooden hulls. A small river flowed passed in front of the grey stone mansion; a large pond formed by a small dam was full of trout. The three story building, whose corner stone dated it to 1878, had a dozen bedrooms, two living rooms, a dining room that could easily seat thirty, and two sitting rooms, which was where the debriefings were being held.

The smaller of the two living rooms had several large coffee tables; Josh and Marty were using them to sort through a pile of photographs they had taken of the bomb sites when Lev walked in.

"Josh, do you remember writing a letter to either Dov or Sol telling them of Artur's murder?"

Josh took a deep breath. "Lev, to be honest, I don't. If I did, it was in that time I call the great fog. I didn't know what I was doing and was barely functional. I could have, I just don't remember." Another breath as he tried to access memory banks that were still locked in his subconscious. "Why?"

Lev opened the folder that he was carrying. On it was the flimsy, light blue airmail stationary that you could buy at post offices around the world. Its primary benefit was that it had four panels on which you could write and weighed less than an ounce. "Did you send this to Dov Vishinski?" He handed Josh the letter, hand-written in Cyrillic script.

This time Josh didn't hesitate. "That's not my handwriting," he said flatly. "I'd have printed it or used a typewriter. My Russian is good, but not that good."

"I didn't think it was your handwriting."

"No, it's definitely not. Whoaaaa! Lev, what's going on?"

"We're not sure yet. What date were Natalie and her parents murdered?"

"August 11th, 1973."

"How long did you sit shivah?" Lev turned to the SEAL. "Marty, that's the Jewish mourning period after the dead are buried. Traditionally, it is a week, but it can be shorter or longer."

"A week. I remember my parents coming out for a few days. But I got back two days after the funeral, which was on the thirteenth."

"What did you do?"

"Besides cry my heart out? I don't remember much. I remember a meeting with the FBI Again, why?"

"This is the letter that Dov Vishinski received, supposedly from you, that told them of their brother's death. Look at the date."

"Shit, Lev, this is dated August twentieth. Ask Marty; I was in no shape to write a letter like this seven days after I saw her grave."

Marty didn't say anything but nodded.

"Now, read it."

Josh scanned the letter. He looked up, anger and grief at war in his face. "This is all wrong. It says my father- and mother-in-law died. It doesn't say they were murdered, and I would have told the truth. And it doesn't even mention Natalie!"

"So Lev, do we have impostors on our hands?" Marty broke in.

"Not necessarily. But the person who wrote this letter knew your in-laws were dead, and wanted the brothers to know." Lev took and closed the folder. "What is bothering me more is that someone told them to expect a debrief. Was it their friends who gave them the data to smuggle out, or the KGB?"

"Lev, how'd they get any data out? I thought they were searched by the KGB before they got on the train, and then before they crossed the border."

"They brought out a packet of personal papers that go back several years, including the photos that helped them recognize you. The KGB officer who searched them before they crossed the border probably thought that since they got through the boarding censors, it was O.K. to let them leave the country with them. Again, does that mean they were lucky, or that they were supposed to get through with planted information?"

"What kind of information did they bring out?"

"Patience, my friend, patience. I've only had two sessions with them since they got here. The notebooks they brought with them need translating into English."

"Translation of what?" Josh was in no mood to be patient.

"They brought out two sets of data hidden in notebooks written in Yiddish. To anyone looking at them, even one who spoke Yiddish or Hebrew, they would appear to be the work scholars studying the Talmud, something that is not interesting to the KGB. Sol claims he has most, if not all, the formulas and descriptions of the manufacturing processes for the primary Soviet's chemical and biological weapons. His data includes the factory names and locations."

The Israeli helped himself to a cup of tea and buttered a toasted muffin that was now cold. "Dov says his notebooks have the location of the main Soviet nuclear weapons plants, the mix of radioactive materials used in their bombs and ship nuclear power plants, and some data on the reactors. If either or both is accurate, it will be, as you Americans say, an intelligence bonanza."

No one said anything for about thirty seconds before Josh broke the silence. "Two questions, Lev. How did they get the information? How did they conceal it?"

"The first answer is easy and the second is more complicated." Lev stopped to butter a second muffin. "They say the information was passed to them either in conversations or by hand on scraps of paper by trusted friends of Sakharov. The second is what made getting them out of the Soviet Union alive so important. What they did is write everything in Yiddish with the sensitive information in a word substitution code only they knew. It is based on two prayers that have all the letters in the alphabet. Then they imbedded the information into their analysis of each passage. Even if the KGB read the notebooks, the translation would have appeared to be scholarly unless they had the key to the substitution code. Without the code, the notebooks are indecipherable—and useless. "

Lev paused to see if there any questions before continuing. "For locations they plotted the distance to each factory or facility using a Talmudic measurement of distance called a Parasang."

Lev chewed while his audience digested what he just said. "Now the hard part will be debriefing them, translating and decoding the information, getting it organized, and filling in the gaps with their answers to the debriefer's questions. They spent most of the past two years collecting and memorizing as much of the data as they could, just in case the notebooks were indeed confiscated. Dov said when they began the trip, they were searched and questioned by the KGB, asked when they had time to study the Talmud and write their notebooks. They told the KGB that they were written after they lost their jobs and applied for exit visas. The answer satisfied the KGB officers, who didn't know Hebrew or Yiddish from Swahili. Both Dov and Sol were afraid that the KGB would, as a matter of spite, confiscate the notebooks; but they gave them back—missing a few pages, which they are sure the KGB destroyed testing for invisible ink."

"For us non-biblical scholars, what is a parasang?" Marty asked.

Lev put his cup of tea down on the coffee table. He was almost finished with his doctorate in archeology, a passion he planned to pursue once he retired. "A parasang is a biblical measurement of distance based on the average distance a man could walk in a day carrying a load. It translates to about four miles or six kilometers. There are other Phoenician, Egyptian, and biblical measurements, but since they studied the Talmud as young boys, they picked the parasang. In their notebooks, Dov and Sol let one parasang equal four point zero kilometers to make the math easy."

Lev held up his hand because he knew the questions were about to start flying. "We need to get someone here who really knows the scientific stuff. When does Admiral Hastings arrive?"

Marty answered. "I spoke with Admiral Hastings late yesterday. He arrives tomorrow on a special air mission plane with a small debriefing team, and I suspect that, if the material checks out, he will fly them all to the States. He is, as we all are, concerned about possible leaks; so only a few people will know about it. If the Soviets even get a sniff of what they brought with them, they'll know its source. That could bring retribution of the worst sort on anyone who ever knew them or worked with them."

"Any chance that the data is bogus, even if they aren't?" Josh had seen enough bad intelligence to be suspicious and wasn't about to give up.

"Honest answer is, I don't think so, but I'm not an expert on any of this." Lev thought for a second. "There is always that chance, but we were able to verify that many people gave the Vishinskis information wanted to get out. The experts should be able to compare their info to what we already know and will provide more details about Soviet reactor metallurgy. If Dov and Sol are who they say they are, I don't believe they would have taken this kind of risk if they suspected they were delivering disinformation. Neither Dov nor Sol had any reason to solicit the data. Sakarov picked them because he knew they were being let out. On the other hand, there is a real risk that they are impostors. We have to find that out before we go any further."

"So Lev, Marty, what happens next, assuming this is not a hoax of, pardon the expression, biblical proportions?"

Marty chuckled. "I think that Admiral Hastings' plan will be to get them to San Diego or Israel as soon as we can find them a place to live, get their kids in schools, etc. But nothing is going to happen until we know they are the real deal."

Josh turned to Lev. "How's their English? I've only spoken to them in Russian and haven't said much to them except to tell them where we are going and why."

"They're struggling with the English terms for what is in their notebooks. We need someone here who understands both Russian and the technical terms and the technology."

"I'm not surprised. My Russian, unfortunately, will not hold up in a scientific discussion." Josh turned to his friend. "So Marty, what do you think we should do?"

"Once we decide they are valid defectors and not impostors, we ask them where they want to live. If it is the U.S., they may become full or part-time consultants to the intelligence community on Soviet nuclear reactors, as well as their chemical and biological weapons, or they may go back to teaching. Lev, what do the Israelis do?"

"Pretty much the same thing."

Lev put his hand on Josh's shoulder as a father would. "Josh, we have to talk to them one at a time to find out if they are really Artur's brothers. You're the only one who knew Artur. I'll ask the questions, you evaluate the answers. This may bring up some painful memories, so you have to control your emotions. Remember, if what they brought with them is valid, Dov and Sol took a huge risk, and everyone who gave them information also put their lives at risk. Once this gets out, and it will at some point, the witch hunt for those who helped them will go on for years, and the KGB won't think twice about torturing entire families before sending them to the Gulag or shooting them in the basement of the KGB's headquarters."

"I understand. Let's get this over with, because we may save Admiral Hastings and the U.S. government an unnecessary trip to merry old England."

The Same Day, 0838 local time, Moscow

The office of Major General Nikolai Volkova, the number two man of the KGB's First Directorate, was on one of the upper floors of a building which had been built in 1898 to house the All Russia Insurance Company. Right after the Russian Revolution it was seized by the Cheka, the Soviet Union's original secret police agency, which over the years changed names from Cheka to O.G.P.U. to N.K.V.D. to M.G.B. and finally to the KGB, but the mission stayed the same: spy on and control the people of the Soviet Union.

In the last modernization, six-centimeter-thick bullet proof glass had been installed. The two windows in his office gave him an excellent view of the square below, from which the building got its name, Lubyanka. When the sun was out, the thick glass acted like a prism, separating the light into a multi-colored rainbow on the window frame. Now he had an unobstructed view of the dark gray clouds that looked ready to dump at least ten centimeters of snow on Moscow.

In an agency in which seniority and experience was prized, he was one of the youngest men to make general in the post-World War II, post-Stalin KGB. Volkova's near photographic memory and ability to absorb and analyze details enabled him to connect dots and draw conclusions with astonishing accuracy. His reputation as a young lieutenant doing wet work for Stalin's N.K.V.D. that never backfired helped him rise through the ranks.

Now responsible for foreign espionage, Volkova continued to manage the program he'd started about ten years ago, which was to expand the number of illegals positioned in the West. Besides the main enemy, the United States, Volkova targeted four countries:

• Canada, because of its loose immigration policies and open border with the U.S.;

• Japan, because of its ability to develop and manufacture technology that the Soviet Union could use;

• South Korea, because in any global war with the U.S. both Japan and Korea would have to be knocked out early;

• and the U.K., because in any war in Europe, they would be the hardest to defeat.

The project originated from one of his assignments as a young officer, to check up on Soviet illegals set up abroad. Some needed reminding of why they were there and what needed to be done. Others had to be eliminated, a task he'd performed. Those actions established his political reliability; and unlike many of his peers, he was one of the few allowed to travel abroad without restrictions.

These missions taught him two valuable lessons. One was that repatriation of illegals to Mother Russia was simply out of the question unless it was to prevent arrest and imprisonment. Two, once an illegal was in place, if they were not productive, a cold assessment had to be made on potential risks of leaving them in place and being turned. If it was high, they had to be terminated.

It was also his experience that, sooner or later, every agent became a problem of one sort or another.

It was the topic of illegals that had occupied much of his morning since entering the building at 0700. He was looking out the window when his direct line rang.

"General Volkova."

"General, this is Major Karlov. We have some answers."

Volkova knew why Karlov was in Vienna. "Major, what are they?"

"Sir, it seems the two KGB officers were abducted, not defectors. I suspect the Israelis. We have men watching for them at every international airport in Western Europe and don't believe they have left Austria yet."

"O.K. What about the Vishinskis?"

"Sir, they left by private plane and we don't know where they landed. We went to the general aviation terminal but they were not very helpful, saying that they have to protect the privacy of their customers. A few thousand Austrian Schillings to someone in the fuel concession helped him remember seeing the Vishinskis board a Hawker business jet. He didn't fuel it so it wasn't on his log. Through Aeroflot's access to the European Air Traffic Control Agency, we were able to find out that a Hawker did leave Vienna that day for the U.K., and the British will only confirm it entered British airspace."

"Good work, major. Keep digging and keep me informed on what you find out."

"Thank you sir. There is one more thing. Our agents in Vienna positively identified the Navy lieutenant Joshua Haman. He was with another man whom we photographed, but we do not know his name. Both men met the Vishinskis at the train station and left with them."

"Did they go to England?"

"We're not sure. The Hawker only has seats for eight to ten."

"Thank you."

Volkova hung up the phone. The Vishinski brothers were becoming a problem far, far ahead of schedule. To start with, who got them U.K. visas? And who paid for the private plane? On a lined pad, he began drafting a memo that would go to the heads of the KGB.'s Second Chief Directorate—the Internal Security and Counter Intelligence; the Sixth Department—Interception and Inspection of Foreign Correspondence; and the Twelfth Department—Eavesdropping—asking them provide what they know about Sol and Dov Vishinski and their associates. After reading the files, he would determine what steps to recommend.

The Same Day, 0900 **local time,** *Scotland*

Josh tented his hands, lowered his forehead to his fingertips, and took a couple of deep breaths. He was standing in front of a door; passing through it was going to rip off the scar tissue that had formed since he lost Natalie. Josh looked up and nodded to Lev, who opened the door.

Dov Vishinski stood up. At just over six feet tall, he was both the tallest of the three brothers and the eldest. Any American might think he was frail, but Josh understood that to stand up to years of harassment by the KGB, and his native country's institutionalized anti-Semitism, took a level of mental and physical toughness that he wondered if he had.

"Josh, what is happening?" Dov asked. "Why all the questions about me, and my family? We brought intelligence gift. What is not to like?"

Lev nodded to Josh, who answered.

"Dov, we just want to make sure that you are who you say you are. If Artur, may he rest in peace, were here, he could do that in a few seconds. Unfortunately, we cannot. We have to be very careful. There is a lot at stake here. You, your family, the people who gave you the information and helped you get out, are all in danger if we get this wrong. So please be patient."

"I am understanding..." Dov put his hand out to reach for the cushion as he sat back down. "I smell KGB"

"We are not the KGB, far from it. But we also smell the KGB for different reasons." Josh sat down. "Dov, do you have any of the pictures Artur sent to you after my wedding?"

"Ahhhh. Yes. Your wife is a very pretty woman. Wait. Can you give me notebook number three and sharp knife?"

Shit, he thinks Natalie is still alive. "When did you get the photographs?"

"July, right after wedding. Dates of wedding on back of picture. We note in prayer book that has history of our families."

Lev handed Dov the requested notebook along with a small, very sharp knife. The Russian's bony fingers deftly slit open the cover and three photographs fell out and landed face down. Josh looked the man in eyes.

"When did you get the letter that you gave to Lev?" *Don't lie to me!*

"End of August, 1973. It was shock. Someday I want to say Kaddish at his grave."

Josh was sure he saw the Russian's eyes moisten.

"How did the letter come?" He didn't want to look at the pictures yet.

"Like usual. Had to go to post office, fill out and sign form because it came from outside Soviet Union. KGB officer had me open letter and then he read it before I got."

"Did you recognize the handwriting of this last letter?" Josh felt a calm peace coming over him. Maybe it was relief.

"Yes... well, no. I not sure. It read like you but not same. We thought maybe you sick when you wrote."

"In what way was it not the same?"

"No sure. But inside," Dov patted his stomach, "think maybe someone else write letter. Maybe a, how you say it, fake. KGB does things like that to make you doubt what is in letters from outside Soviet Union. With Artur, we used code and past family events to number letters."

"Did your brother think the same thing?" Josh glanced over at Lev, who's slight nod said, *continue asking questions.* The plan was that if Josh couldn't continue, or ran into a roadblock, Lev would take over.

"Da, I mean yes."

"Is Sol acting different lately?"

"What way?"

"I don't know; you are his brother."

"Last two years have been very bad. Others support us. We not see each other often. KGB all over us. So, yes, it affected me and him. We support each other. He had to leave son behind."

"Why?"

"Son is Air Force pilot. Flies latest MiG and lives in East Germany."

"Excuse us for a minute." Josh got up and left the room and Lev followed him to a room where Sol was waiting. The Russian was sitting on the couch with his arms crossed over his mid-section and bent over. When the two men entered he looked up, and Josh saw a look he'd never seen before. It was pure terror, and tears were streaming down his cheeks from bloodshot eyes.

"I so sorry." Sol bent over, sobbing. "I so sorry."

"I'll get his brother." Lev stepped out of the room. Josh sat on the coffee table in front of his father-in-law's brother and put his hands on his shoulder and began to gently massage the man's back. The muscles behind his neck were taut and hard.

When Dov entered the room, Sol sobbed. "Dov, I so sorry."

The older brother sat down and put his hand around his brother's shoulder. "About what?"

"I not as strong as you. All these years, I tried to be brave and strong, but finally, I could not take it anymore."

"Take what?"

"Pressure from KGB bastards. They told me that Avram would be court-martialed, thrown out of air force and jailed if I did not cooperate. KGB want to know if Americans asked me questions and to call them every month when we get to America. It seemed not bad, so I agreed. They not know what is in the books, but I think they suspected something, but not know what."

Dov caressed his head, then hugged his brother as the man's sobs shook his body.

"It is O.K., we will survive. We are out of Soviet Union now, will have better life. No more KGB bastards." He lifted up his chin. "What did they want you to do?"

"Call at each stop and tell who we met, what we did and what questions we were asked. They gave me a number, one for Israel and one for America, to call every month. Said it would be no cost, free. Just use my name and answer questions."

"Sol, are you sure they do not know about the notebooks?"

"Da, I am sure. I would die before I let KGB bastards know what is in them."

The older Russian looked up and the American and the Israeli. "So, we make a call? No harm?"

Josh looked at Lev, who nodded. "You tell them I met you because I am Artur's son-in-law and that my rich British friend flew you to the United Kingdom to spend a few days. We are buying you clothes and other things to help you and your family. Tell them that this is a vacation. You will leave in a week or so."

"But what if they ask me where I am?"

"You can say some place in Scotland but you do not know where."

"And then what if they ask name of owners?"

"Tell them you are with the Rothchilds."

"Who are Rothchilds?"

"They are a famous European banking family who happen to be Jewish."

"But the people who live here have different name, da?"

"Yes."

"Then we screw KGB bastards mind?"

"Yes."

"That is good, very good." Sol took a deep breath. "Then what we do?"

"You have to agree to cooperate with Lev and with the CIA. You have to tell them everything that they did to you and your family. We need to know so we can feed bad information back to the KGB."

"You are going to fuck KGB?"

"Yes. In more ways than one."

Sol brightened and smiled. "I like that."

"Will you make the call?"

"Da, I mean yes." He nodded and held out his hand. "Give me phone."

Josh squatted down in front of Sol and put his hand on his knee. "Before we do that, can you show me the pictures you brought out?"

"Da," He looked around. "I need knife."

Within seconds, five pictures of Artur and Rimma were face down on the table, each had the date it was taken, generally someplace around San Diego, written on the back in what he recognized as Artur's handwriting. The sixth fluttered to the floor, face down, and Josh could see the notes that Natalie and he had written on the back. Sol put it on the table face up, and as soon as Josh saw the image of his dead wife, he started to cry.

Thursday, November 25, 1 1147 local time, Scotland

For security reasons, they decided that a stop by a silver and blue U.S. Air Force Special Air Mission jet at the Glenegedale Airport would raise too many questions. So the VC-140 Jetstar dropped Admiral Hastings off at Mindenhall Naval Air Station outside London, and after he changed clothes, a staff car took him to Gatwick airport for a commercial flight. Three hours after he landed in England, Marty met the vice admiral at Glenegedale and drove him to the Osborne's hunting lodge.

Vice Admiral Hastings was smiling when he addressed the four officers in the sitting room. "Josh, Marty, this is a step up from the places I've seen you stay before. I'm quite impressed. Without being intrusive, the security around here is pretty tight."

"Yes sir, it is. We've got about a dozen Royal Marines patrolling the grounds in two man fire teams to keep nosy people out." Marty, as the detachment officer in charge, responded. "And, sir, as far as the accommodations go, you have to thank Mr. Tom Osborne."

"I will do that before I leave. Anyway, getting the Vishinskis here is another job well done."

"Thank you, sir." Both Marty and Josh knew that the admiral was about to shift subjects, so they waited for him to speak.

"I just spoke with the two D.I.A. experts who arrived the day earlier. They are very, very impressed, and while not a hundred per cent certain, they believe Dov and Sol did indeed bring us an intelligence bonanza. It fills in a lot of blanks. We need to find a way to thank the Israeli government for its help, and I'll take that on as an action item."

"Thank you sir. We're glad to be of assistance." Lev nodded to emphasize his words.

"I also came over for another reason." The Admiral paused to look around the sitting room, furnished with chairs and tables made in the 1700s. "The West Germans now know Fatah is involved with Red Hand. They arrested the Fatah operative who issued the passports used by the six Germans to get to Libya."

All four officers were standing in front of the admiral, and while they were not at attention in the military sense, their body language was alert and respectful.

"If you haven't heard, two more bombs went off yesterday. One was in Kaiserlauten and the other in Hannover. Sixteen Americans, six Brits and about twenty Germans were killed, and about forty more were injured." The admiral paused, sighed. "In addition to finding the bastards, you are now authorized by *both* governments to do what is needed to build a plan for direct action against Red Hand."

"Yes sir." Marty was speaking for the assembled officers. He was grim, not grinning.

Admiral Hastings looked at each officer. "Let me know when you are ready; the groundwork to get it approved has been laid, but we still need approval. At that point a decision will have to be made as to whether we let the Germans do it, or we go at it ourselves. Understood?"

"Yes sir." Marty spoke for the group.

"Good, because as soon as we leave with the Vishinskis, it is back to work for you guys."

Sunday, November 28th, 1976, 1645 local time, Mainz

Yassir was one of the agents controlled by Mohammed al Jalani, and when the Syrian didn't respond to the agreed upon set of rings and hang-ups, Mohammed decided to use the alternate way of communicating with the deep cover agent. After parking his car a few blocks away, he headed toward Yassir's building to leave a chalk mark at a place he could see from his bedroom window. It was a signal to call him.

As he got close to the dull gray concrete building, the hair on the back of Mohammed's neck stood up. Something was very wrong. He stopped. Scanning the area block, he spotted one car at each end of the street. Each had two men, which screamed stakeout.

No response plus police surveillance of Yassir's flat spelled arrest; he needed to let Fatah know. Mohammed forced himself to walk past one of the cars and headed toward the post office. Using an indirect route, he wandered through the neighborhood to make sure that no one followed him.

Forcing himself to be calm, he paid the Bundespost clerk for the first three minutes of an international call to Egypt and went to the assigned booth to wait for the operator to dial the number. The person he asked for was not there, so he left a message saying a friend has passed away and to please call him. The number he left, 46 23 11 29 09, was a simple cipher to tell the recipient to call him on the twenty-ninth of the eleventh month at nine in the morning.

Friday, December 3rd, 1976, 1423 Local Tim, East Berlin

At his desk and behind the locked door, Colonel Krasnovsky stared at three things on the center of his desk. One was a handwritten note from a friend who worked in the Seventh Directorate whom he'd known since they were at the KGB academy. It had arrived in a sealed envelope that had been slipped under his locked door. The note was clipped to the second item, which was a picture.

Beside the picture was a yellow piece of flimsy paper, the kind fed into teleprinters attached to Soviet decoding machines. He was not one of the six officers on the decoded message's distribution list, so he was wondering whether it was a warning, a mistake, or information someone wanted him to have, so he read it again.

SUBJECT: TWO MISSING KGB OFFICERS

TWO DEEP COVER PENETRATION KGB OFFICERS —CAPTAIN VASILY ORIANOV AND MAJOR EVGENY EVCHENKO—HAVE BEEN REPORTED MISSING BY THE VIENNA RESIDENT WHO SUSPECTS DEFECTION OR MURDER. ORIANOV WORKED AT THE JEWISH DOCUMENTATION CENTER WITH ACCESS TO INVESTIGATIONS OF POTENTIAL NAZI WAR CRIMINALS. EVCHENKO GAVE US INFORMATION ON WESTERN SPONSORS OF SOVIET CITIZENS OF JEWISH ORIGIN WHO APPLIED FOR EMIGRATION. THEIR DISAPPEARANCE WAS ON OR ABOUT THE SAME DAY—19 NOVEMBER—A GROUP OF SOVIET JEWS ARRIVED IN VIENNA AUSTRIA. RECOMMEND YOU REVIEW ALL CASES TO DETERMINE IF THEIR DEFECTION COULD COMPROMISE ANY OF YOUR CURRENT OPERATIONS. TAKE AND REPORT APPROPRIATE ACTION(S).

The terse note stated that the photo and the individual whose face was circled might be of interest. On the back of the photo was detailed information explaining that it had been taken by a KBG officer who routinely photographed Soviet émigrés arriving in Vienna, and that this man, an American Naval officer, had met the Vishinskis, two of the emigrating families.

Krasnovsky had learned a long time ago that nothing in the KGB happened by coincidence. Nothing about these two officers affected any of his cases. Someone—*but who?*—in Moscow wanted him to have this. *Does the KGB want Stasi to know that two of their officers have, as the message suggests, defected*? He recognized the American Naval Officer, Joshua Haman.

Krasnovsky's first thought was the KGB's paranoia about potential spies and traitors was showing. If he told Grünewald, what would he say? Logic said Haman was in Austria to meet the émigrés and help get them back to the U.S. Why complicate what was simple?

Oh fuck, there are four dots, not two!

Dot one is the visit by Haman to the Jewish Documentation Center.

Dot two is the abduction or defection of the KGB officers.

Dot three is Haman was in Vienna when the officers went missing.

Dot four is the arrival of the Vishinskis.

So, are *they connected? Would knowing this help Grünewald?*

Is he paranoid too?

Monday, December 6th, 1976, 0635 local time, RNAS Yeovilton

Spread out on the table in front of Josh were two Aerad instrument flight rule charts laid side by side. Chart 8N had the airways from Yeovilton to northern France, where it overlapped with 5S, which he used to plan the route into Munich. He was using the wheels on the E-6B circular slide ruler to check the leg flight times and fuel burn for the flight one more time. At seven hundred miles, it was close to the limit of the Navajo C/R's range under instrument flight rules. It also gave him something to do while he waited for the surveillance teams to gather. The plan was that John and he would fly the teams to their assigned cities. The team assignments were:

<u>Target—City—Team</u>
Alois Brunner—Munich—Calhoun/Bellows
Victor Horst—Nuremberg—Cabot/Bentley
Ernst Von Spee—Stuttgart—Mogen/Goodson
Friedrich Starkeholz—Bonn—TBD
Helmut Stiglitz—Hannover—Haman/Van der Jagt
Oskar Zimmer—Frankfurt—Osborne/Hatcher

Laid out on the table were distinctive yellow and black boxes of Kodak 400 ASA Tri-X black and white film, and five identical sets of motorized Nikon Fs, each with an eighty to three hundred millimeter zoom lens. In front of each camera was a folder with copies of everything the team had gathered about each family.

"Everyone needs to stop for a moment."

Lev, who was a master of understatement, was not given to issuing directives unless it was very important. "This package just arrived by a special courier who came straight from Argentina to my hotel."

Lev dumped out pictures, face shots, each one labeled with the person's last name and the time, date, and place the photograph was taken.

"These photos were taken this past Friday and Saturday at the airport in Buenos Aires." He slid a photo across the table. "This is Helmut Stiglitz and his youngest son, Dieter. So hunting him down this week is going to be a waste of time." Another picture went in a slightly different direction. "This is Viktor Horst and two of his boys, Wilhelm and Heinrich. This is Eric Dortmann and son, Gustav." Two more photos were slid into a ragged row in the middle of the big table.

"There are more photos coming, but we confirmed that *Die Kameraden* are again meeting at an estate west of Buenos Aires owned by a member of the Hitler regime who arrived in Argentina in 1944. Each attendee brought one or more of their sons or daughters. Our embassy thinks that there will be sixty to eighty of them at the gathering."

"Wait a second. Do you have any more shots of the young Stiglitz?"

"Yes." Lev started rifling through the stack of photos.

Josh pulled the photo from the dock in Libya out of his file. He laid the two pictures side by side for all to see the likeness and tapped them with his forefinger for emphasis. "I'll bet money that Dieter Stiglitz is Wilhelm Gestner."

Lev picked up two of them. "I agree. Do you?" He handed them to Marty.

Marty studied them for a few seconds. "Yes. What about the others?"

"Ludwig Kammer is a match for Gustav Dortmann." Josh began to lay out the pictures of those they referred to as the "Libyan Six." "Lev, when are they coming back?"

"We don't know," Lev responded, "but the last time they all stayed a week and came back on the Saturday and Sunday Lufthansa and Air France flights. I'll see what we can find out."

"This changes everything." Marty tapped the pictures on the table. "It looks like we've identified two of the Libyan Six, so rather than chasing ghosts, I want to focus on them. We need to be in position when they arrive back in Germany this coming weekend, which means that we leave on Friday a.m. By then, Mossad should have given us some info on their arriving flights, and once we have that we'll complete our plans. Meanwhile, let's find a place in the Frankfurt area to use as a command center."

The Same Day, 0735 local time, East Berlin

Colonel Grünewald could hear his phone as he struggled with the balky cipher lock that protected his office. He was late; the streetcar had been delayed by electrical problems with the overhead wires, caused by a recent snowfall. Just as he opened the door, the ringing stopped. As he put his briefcase down and sat in his chair, wondering who had called, the ringing on his personal line began again. The words 'persistent bastard' ran through his head.

"Grünewald."

"Good snowy morning to you."

Grünewald recognized Krasnovsky's voice. "The weather should make you happy. It is like a Russian winter."

"You should know; *we* knew how to dress and fight in one. *You* didn't." Krasnovsky took great pleasure in reminding Grünewald that the Wehrmacht had been unprepared to fight a war in the Russian winter.

"I try to forget." Grünewald was not in the mood to discuss either the weather or the three miserable winters he spent on the Russian front. "What's on your mind?"

"Dots. I got two more and need your help connecting them."

Grünewald chuckled; both were fond of using the term when they were trying to analyze a piece of intelligence and figure out what it meant.

"Lunch?" Krasnovsky offered to the silence on the other end of the line.

"Sure, but not Gasthous Koenig. I am tired of their food."

"Then join me at a place run by a good Italian communist. It is the Trattoria Tagliatti, on the corner of Karl Marx Allee and Friedenstrasse. I'll get us a table for noon."

"I'll find it." Grünewald hung up.

He had a problem. Yesterday he'd read a report from the Stasi officer at their embassy in Buenos Aires that the elder Stiglitz and some of Die Kameraden he'd served with were in Argentina again. *What does it mean? And why did young Stiglitz go with his father?*

Stiglitz had said that when he got back, he needed to find a place for a bomb factory in West Germany. Cars and trucks were being stopped and searched at the border, and their drivers questioned. Moving cars packed with explosives was no longer worth the risk.

How do I control this monster without it eating me professionally?

The East German used the kilometer-long walk through the snow to think about the probable discussions he would have during his lunch with Krasnovsky. He had begun to trust the Russian officer and hoped that it hadn't been misplaced. If it was, it would be a painful trip on the way to the grave.

Krasnovsky was waiting at a table in the back, presiding over a pot of coffee and cups. "Lovely Russian weather!"

Grünewald grimaced and settled in his chair, after shaking the snow off his gray uniform overcoat and hanging it on a nearby peg.

Krasnovsky didn't wait to open the "official" conversation. "I hear your friends on the other side of the wall still can't identify or find Stiglitz."

"Your information is correct. I think, however, that the Americans' patience is running out. Our sources tell us there have already been several tense, angry exchanges between the American and the West German presidents, which no doubt is good news to the Kremlin."

"What about the Jewish issue?" Krasnovsky knew the West German press was beginning to take notice.

"The West German government is taking great care not to call attention to the numbers of dead Jews, but several German newspaper columnists are already saying that this is another version of the Holocaust." Grünewald paused. "It is a public relations nightmare for the West German government. Helmut Stiglitz's anti-Semitism has rubbed off on his son."

Krasnovsky pulled out the official message given to him, along with the note from his friend and the photo. "What do you make of this?"

Grünewald wondered why he was being shown a classified KGB message that mentioned the possible defection of two KGB officers. *How does this relate to Stiglitz?* "The one connection I can see was that an American officer—Haman—and a British officer—Osborne—paid a visit to the Documentation Center. Maybe it is a coincidence and maybe not. They are pilots, not intelligence officers. I don't see any connection between Stiglitz and Haman. And I don't have a clue as to who the mysterious gentleman next to Haman is."

"Moscow suspects the defections and Haman's visit to the documentation center are somehow connected. Also, he would have friends who could help him make his first wife's uncles disappear. I am not paranoid like Moscow, but I also tend not to believe in coincidences."

"Neither do I." Grünewald stirred the coffee and dropped another lump of Cuban sugar into the cup. "You've told me on several occasions that the KGB would know if there were any counter-intelligence operations against Red Hand. You might want to have them query their sources again. Maybe there's a rogue element, or one of their services is doing something off the books. Both the Royal and American navies are known for doing that kind of stuff."

Chapter 19
Arrivals

Tuesday, December 7th, 1976, 0745 local time, RNAS Yeovilton

Josh picked up the ringing phone, and after saying his last name listened for a few minutes. He broke into a grin. "Congratulations! Well done. We're expecting cigars and a few celebratory rounds on your shilling."

He turned to the room spoke with joyful formality. "Attention on deck. I have an important announcement. Lieutenant John Osborne of the Royal Navy will not be in for the next few days. He has acquired some new, unfamiliar collateral duties, for which I can attest from personal experience that he is not trained to handle but will get better at with practice. Ian Charles Osborne, seven pounds, ten ounces and twenty inches long, arrived safe and sound with a healthy set of lungs. All systems are go! The mother, the lovely Lady Gwen, is fine."

After the hooting and hollering died down, Josh reported. "John wants to come back to work as soon as Gwen gets home with the baby, which will be in a couple of days. He emphasized that he would be, and I quote, "most pissed," and people will die slow and painful deaths if we went off and did something fun without him."

**The same day, 0820 local time, Estancia Kreutz,
70 kilometers south west of Buenos Aires**

Dieter was trying not to pay attention to the discussion at the breakfast table as he ate the eggs and bacon whose wonderful smokiness got to his nose long before the pieces got to his mouth. He was sitting next to his father and two of his SS officer friends.

"Besides creating unrest and unhappiness with the government, Red Hand is killing Jews and destroying Jewish businesses. That is something we should support. We need to find out who is running this organization and what help they need." The speaker was a man addressed as Herr Gruppenführer, or Herr Generalleutnant, and it surprised Dieter that his father was so obsequious when the sixty-year-old SS-Gruppenführer was around.

"What kind of support could be provided?" Dieter asked. Red Hand, meaning he, needed a safe place inside West Germany. Zehlendorf was now nothing more than a house with a well-equipped workshop. There were eight car bombs in West Germany. He controlled four and the two other cells had two each. Two were stuck in Zehlendorf. He hoped his question would pierce the man's arrogance and get him to talk to the lowly youngest son of an Oberstrumbahnführer.

"I think we can give Red Hand more than just money." Bruno Glockner was wearing his Knight's Cross with the swastika resting on the knot of his tie. "We could help create a factory where more car bombs could be built. With our connections, wrecked cars, or better yet, new cars would be easy to acquire. Explosives and weapons and safe houses for the members of Red Hand could be provided as well. Why are you asking?"

Dieter steeled himself not to be intimidated by the ice blue eyes that were trying to bore into his soul. "I may know a member of Red Hand."

Dieter was unnerved by the silence. The tension could have been cut with a knife.

"Do you think Red Hand would accept our help?" Glockner asked quietly.

"I don't know, Herr Gruppenführer, but I could ask. I am not sure this person is a member of Red Hand, but I will find out."

"How soon could you contact him?"

"As soon as I get back, sir." Dieter surprised himself with the use of the word sir. "There is no guarantee I will get an answer."

"Do it. Figure out a way to make contact with Red Hand. If you need help, let me know." The old man paused for a second. "Before you leave, I will give you instructions on how to reach my action officer without having to worry about the police. This will also keep your father and the rest of your family out of it. Make sure you tell Red Hand that we can provide *whatever* they need— money, weapons and explosives, people, safe houses, cars—and to keep killing Jews. The more they kill, the better."

Saturday, December 11th, 1253 local time, Frankfurt

After circling in and out of the Rhein-Main airport twice, Josh found a spot at the end of the strip where cars were allowed to stop for passengers arriving on international flights. He hoped he was out of sight and mind of the Landespolizei officer hurrying along those cars he determined had parked too long.

He'd been waiting there for about five minutes when the handheld radio on the passenger seat squawked. "He's in the luggage area and heading out of the terminal." That call told Josh to get ready to pick up Van der Jagt, who was following the Stiglitzes. They would be in the first of three cars that would rotate as the tail.

The small hand held radios had come from the U.S. embassy in London. At first the embassy's security officer had been very reluctant to part with the radios used by their security teams who escorted VIPs; but after some head scratching, and an accusation the laminated cards with the presidential seal were fake, Marty had suggested the embassy security chief call the number. The person on the other end had assured the officer that if he did not provide the radios, his replacement would be handing them over a few minutes after he hung up the phone, and the security officer would be checking the wanted ads looking for his next job.

Josh was mentally reviewing the techniques from Lev's cram course on how to follow a suspect without being detected when Van der Jagt opened the car door. "The kid got into the cab that's second in line. The number on top is one hundred and fifty-four. His dad is waiting for another cab."

"I see it." Josh tossed the radio to his air crewman, who was grinning when he caught it.

As soon as Josh pulled out into traffic, Van der Jagt keyed the mike. "One is on the move and following a black Mercedes 180 diesel cab with the number one-five-four on the roof. We're heading to the airport exit now toward downtown Frankfurt."

"Two has you in sight." Josh recognized John Osborne's very proper British accent and the precise way he enunciated every word. Sergeant Bentley was driving the German-made Opel that carried them.

"Three is moving." Sergeant Goodson was driving a bright blue French-made Peugeot, and in the passenger seat Colour Sergeant Calhoun was studying a street map.

"Base copies all." That was Marty sitting in a vacant office in an unused section of Osborne Shipping's Frankfurt offices, which was on the top floor of a twenty-four story building near Frankfurt's central business district. As long as they could receive the radio calls, Marty and Lev planned to track the cars and coordinate the efforts to follow Stiglitz and Dortmann, whose Lineas Argentina flight wasn't due in for another three hours. They were hoping the tail on Stiglitz would end before Dortmann exited the terminal.

Josh, who'd grown up in Wiesbaden, was very familiar with the Frankfurt area, which is why he had the lead car. "Tell Marty that if I were a betting man, Stiglitz is headed for the Hauptbahnhof. I wonder why he didn't take the train from the airport."

Josh waited until Van Der Jagt's call was acknowledged before speaking again. "If he gets dropped off, I'm going to follow him."

"Then what, sir?"

"I go wherever the bastard goes. We've got him in sight and I am not going to lose him. You're the co-pilot, figure out what to do with the rental car."

"Boss, why do I suspect that there is some improvisation coming? Seems like I've played the co-pilot role before." Van Der Jagt was grinning from ear to ear as he spoke. He was referring to the two occasions on combat search and rescue missions when he filled in as Josh's co-pilot. The first had been an impromptu rescue mission. On the second, he'd pulled a badly wounded pilot out of the seat of an H-3 and climbed into the bloody co-pilot seat.

"Tell car two to close up. I need John to go with me."

"You're planning on following him onto the train, aren't you... sir?" The last word was spoken as an afterthought.

"Yup. When I get out, tell Lieutenant Cabot that John and I are going to follow Stiglitz on the train. We'll report via pay phone as soon as we can."

Josh looked behind him and saw the green rental Opel just behind him. When the cab entered the discharge lane at the train station, Josh flipped on the blinker and cut to the curb.

Josh jogged to catch up to Stiglitz at ticket window. As he headed to the platform, he passed John and whispered, "Buy a second class ticket to Geissen on the next train," then continued to the platform, where he bought a copy of *Der Stern* and stood one hundred feet from Stiglitz, who was sitting on a bench reading a book.

Josh was zipping up his ski jacket when John walked up.

"I talked to Marty on the phone and they'll have a rental car waiting for us at the train station in Geissen as well as a hotel room. He's sending another team in a car with our clothes to meet us at the hotel as soon as they find out where Dortmann is going. Until then, we're on our own. Marty had two pieces of advice for you. One, don't lose the guy; and two, don't do anything stupid."

John was smiling "This will be fun. It's better than changing diapers. By the way, I've got about five hundred deutschmarks. That should be enough. How much cash do you have?"

"I've got another four hundred, so we should have enough to see where he is going. After that, I have no idea what we'll do." As an afterthought, Josh added. "We'll be British and muddle through! Aren't you glad Gwen let you out of the house!?"

"The truth is that with two first-time grandmothers around, I was in the way. They told me to go out and play. So I did!" Josh's laughter was drowned out by the noise of the approaching train.

About an hour later, the two pilots were fifty feet behind Dieter on the platform in Giessen when a good looking blonde ran up to Dieter. Their kiss, while no one was timing it, lasted at least thirty seconds. Josh murmured, "Holy shit, that's Karina von Berg."

"I believe you are right."

As they exited the station about a hundred feet behind the couple, Josh saw the Colour Sergeant standing by the open door of a car and waving at them. They acknowledged and waited for the car to come toward them while keeping an eye on the young couple.

The senior SAS man tossed Josh a radio. "Sir, take this. We'll follow them; contact us on the radio after you get your rental car. I love it when there are no speed limits!"

It was a long ten minutes before the chatty clerk handed Josh the keys after asking where an American learned to speak German so well. Josh's answer that he'd spent five years in a German kinderschule and lived for the better part of fifteen years in Kronberg explaining his Bavarian accent, and triggering a spate of questions and commentary from the clerk.

"While you were passing the time of day at the rental car counter, I was doing something productive." John waved a street map of the town of Geissen at his friend. "I had a short radio conversation with the good Colour Sergeant, so I know where he is headed as he tags along behind young Herr Stiglitz and his girlfriend."

"Good for you." Josh nailed the throttle once he was out of the parking lot. Five minutes later the radio crackled.

"We have company." The Colour Sergeant's clipped accent was clear. "Meet me at the corner of Badenburger Weg and Wellesburgering."

It was a few minutes before John found the streets on the map, then another ten to get there and find a spot a hundred feet from the corner to park the car.

Colour Sergeant Calhoun walked over to where the two helicopter pilots were standing, trailed by Van der Jagt a few steps behind. "Sirs, from here, he can go either way on Wellesburgerring and we'll see him. I followed him to his apartment at number 46 Wellesburgerring, and the name on the doorbell for apartment 4C is Stiglitz. We both got a good look at the woman. Van and I are pretty sure it is von Berg."

"Good work. Anything else to report?" Josh was relieved the reconnaissance had gone so smoothly.

"We noticed that there are two cars, each with two guys who seemed very interested in Stiglitz's arrival. On the way to get us some beer"—the sergeant major held up bottles of Baba Beer, which he handed out. After the four clinked the tops, he continued —"I got a good look at one pair. I'd say they are military, not coppers."

"But whose military?" To Josh, the question was pivotal.

"Sir, that is a very good question."

"If," Josh said slowly, "our intelligence is correct and the West Germans are clueless about Stiglitz, then my gut tells me these guys are East German, here to either protect them or spy on them."

"There's one way to find out." The sergeant major grabbed the last two bottles of beer from the bag and staggered off to the nearest car. Using one, he rapped on the window, and after some discussion in which he slurred his word like a happy drunk, he handed the two bottles through the window.

On his return, the sergeant major took back his bottle from Van der Jagt. He was smiling broadly as he took a drink. "I asked for directions to the red light district. They're East German."

"How do you know that?" Josh was surprised at the conviction in the Colour Sergeant's voice.

"Because as soon as they opened their mouth, I could see their fillings, and no self-respecting West German would allow himself to have steel teeth."

Three hours later, Josh was holding the handset from the hotel phone between his head and John's so they could both hear the conversation. "So what do we have?"

"Good news is that we have positively identified three of the Libyan Six. Now we have to tie them to Red Hand." They strained to hear Marty's voice over the handset. "You've got Stiglitz and von Berg in Giessen, and Dortmann is at home with his father in Mainz. Bentley and Goodson are camped outside Dortman's apartment and are going to stay there until about eleven, then go back early in the a.m. The question is, why are the East Germans watching Stiglitz's apartment?" Marty paused for a second. "Josh, what's your plan?"

"We can't do anything about the East Germans. If they are there to monitor Stiglitz, when he moves, so will they. Since we're not going to try to take him now, that reduces the chances of a confrontation with the East Germans."

"Agreed."

"So, after this call, I'm going to pair up with John, who is watching Stiglitz and von Berg by himself until I get there. We'll stay until about midnight and make sure they're in for the night. Van der Jagt and Calhoun are going back around 0530 and will stay until about ten, when we swap. If Stiglitz and his girlfriend leave, we'll follow and see what the East Germans do." Josh paused for a second before asking the obvious. "I know we don't have much evidence, but do you think we should, as good citizens, tell the Germans police? At the very least, Stiglitz would have fun explaining traveling with a bogus passport."

"Lev and I have been talking about that off and on for hours. Right now, if the German police picked up Von Berg and Stiglitz, they don't have enough to keep them in jail without bail for more than forty-eight hours unless they confessed. If they are released, then Von Berg and Stiglitz would be spooked and go underground and we'd be back to square one. Right now, our best call is to keep following them and see what happens. If we lose them, then we can turn them in."

"Got it." After Josh hung up, he picked up his coat and told the colour sergeant, "We'll check-in from a pay phone that's about one hundred feet from where we are parked. Reception with the radios is not great, but we'll find a way to call if anything happens."

Sunday, December, 12th, 1976, 1015 local time, Geissen

Josh walked up to the car and dropped two paper bags on the seat of the blue rented Opel that John had running to warm up the interior. "Breakfast."

John rummaged through the flimsy paper bags, then looked up at Josh. "My lord, you have gone native! Look at this, butter, jams, orange juice and fresh hot poppy seed rolls. All that is missing is a proper cup of tea."

"Sorry, I couldn't find someone to brew it."

"You're forgiven." John split open a roll and began to smear apricot jam on one half and butter on the other with a plastic knife. "What about coffee?"

"Sitting on top of the roof." Josh handed the cup that was emitting small tendrils of steam through the window. "The radio reception is spotty. I see the East Germans are still here. I wonder if they slept in their cars? It should be quite a convoy if Stiglitz decides to go anywhere."

"Quite right. I wonder if the Stasi knows who we are?"

Josh stretched his lean six foot frame. "My guess is they have pictures of our ugly faces and are trying to figure out who we are and what we are doing in Giessen. They're also pissed at the Colour Sergeant who blew their cover." Abruptly he froze. "Shit, Sitglitz and von Berg are coming!"

Stiglitz and von Berg walked hand in hand toward a dirty silver BMW 1800ti that was only a few parking spaces from their car. After letting the engine run for about a minute, the young German pulled out onto Wellesburgerring and accelerated hard.

As he started to leave their parking place, Josh braked hard, expecting the East Germans to block him. Instead, they followed the silver BMW at a discrete distance, allowing Josh to move into a loose trail.

It took three tries over a scratchy radio circuit before John made contact with the Colour Sergeant. By then they were on the A45 autobahn heading south toward Frankfurt.

"Where is the East German car?" Josh had passed the East Germans and was in the right lane, letting a few cars get between while he tried to stay about a hundred yards behind Stiglitiz's BMW.

John turned around in the seat to get a better look. "Three cars back, in the middle lane."

"Let's hope they get lost!"

"Do you think Dieter knows he's being followed?"

"If he does, he doesn't seem to care, so maybe he knows who they are. If he does, then he sees them as protection. If he doesn't, then he is one dumb terrorist. I just hope he doesn't notice us!"

The silver BMW suddenly accelerated, then cut from the left across three lanes to the right to get on the on-ramp leading to the A5 autobahn, leaving blaring horns and braking cars in his wake. Josh followed, but without as much drama. Another car, one Josh referred to as "the putrid green Opel" pulled alongside, and John recognized Calhoun driving. Van der Jagt called over the radio and announced that the East Germans had missed the turn.

"Then thy're out of the picture," Josh responded. A glance at the speedometer told them they were doing a hundred and seventy kilometers an hour. Mentally, he translated it to about hundred and three m.p.h.

"Or they know where the bloody bastard is going and wanted to make it look that way."

They only pulled into the right lane when drivers behind them flashed their lights. Usually it was a Porsche or a fuel injected Mercedes 220SE doing about two hundred and twenty kilometers per hour.

At the speed they were going, it didn't take long to cover the fifty kilometers between Giessen and the interchange of the east/west autobahn north of Frankfurt and the A5. Again, Dieter waited until the last possible minute, then amid honking horns and swerving cars, he went left to right across the traffic to get onto the ramp for the A66 autobahn that headed west toward Wiesbaden. Josh stomped and then pumped the brakes to keep the car under control as he dodged a car whose surprised driver narrowly avoided hitting Dieter.

"That was dicey." Now that Josh had the car back up to one seventy, John refolded the map once so he could see route options. "Any idea where he is going?"

"Nope, but if he stays on this road, he has three choices. A66 ends in Wiesbaden or he can take the A3, which goes south toward the west side of the Rhein Main airport. Or, he can get off and go into Frankfurt proper or one of the towns along the Rhine River."

The silver BMW cruised along at one hundred and seventy kilometers an hour, slowing only when it had to, then quickly getting back up to speed. Dieter flicked on his blinker just before the exit for Highway 455 that took him over a bridge and into the industrial city of Mainz.

After weaving through the traffic at above the posted sixty kilometer speed limit, Dieter slammed on his brakes and pulled into an empty parking spot on a street of gray, six story apartment buildings. Josh went a full block past the stopped BMW and turned the corner, then pulled into an empty parking space.

Calhoun stopped at the end of the block so he could see who got in or out of the BMW. "A middle eastern bloke got in the car." Calhoun called in. "The bastard is headed back the way we came."

Josh made a quick three point U-turn and headed back. Calhoun spotted the BMW as he came into the intersection and nailed the Opel's throttle to get within a couple of cars behind the silver 1800ti. Cautiously, he got behind the car one lane to the right.

Dropping back, he radioed Josh. The two Opels stayed several cars behind the BMW which, in the Sunday traffic, was easy to do.

After several turns on the city streets, Josh was sure he knew where Stiglitz was going. "He is headed toward the Rosengarten where they can take a walk in private. I used to park there late in the evening with girl friends to make out in my dad's car."

"Ohhhhhhh! That's interesting, Josh. Did you just kiss or get lucky?"

"That's a state secret, but considering I was driving my family's Volkswagen camper bus that had a bed, you figure it out."

The lot was partly full and Germans, despite the cold, who were bundled up and out for a walk. From about two hundred meters away, John clicked away with the Nikon F.

Monday, December 13th, 0730 local time, Wiesbaden

Starkeholz turned to the waiting Grenfel as he unlocked the door to his office. "What has you so excited?"

"Herr Hauptpolizeidirektor, I think we may be on our way to another major break in the Red Hand case."

"That is very good news. What is it?"

"Sir, I don't know if you know this, but last week there was a gathering of some Nazis in Argentina. I can give you the names, if you want to know."

Starkeholz held up his hand. "Not now. Tell me the good news." He had been invited, but he had declined to go. With Red Hand setting off bombs, this was not time for a vacation.

"We had an informer in a group of about eighty Germans and about fifty were ex-SS, Gestapo or ardent followers of Hitler and the rest were sons, three of whom were elected to the Bundestag. Many of the older men are leaders of the New German Party and are in a gray area because they have not broken the law by running for political office. Our informer is a son of one of the leaders and his father demanded that he go, but he does not share his father's beliefs."

Starkeholz wondered how Grenfel knew their backgrounds. Then again, he could have read their files. Starkeholz let his mind wander to his children, who he knew wouldn't have gone. *While they are proud of what I have done since the war, they are embarrassed that I was an SS officer. They have often told me that the best thing about my wartime career was that I was cleared of any war crimes.*

Starkeholz nodded his head and didn't say anything, which was Grenfel's signal to continue.

Grenfel put his hands in his lap. "Our source was very sure that one of the young men there knew someone in Red Hand. The bad news is that he does not know the name of the person who made the comment who offered to contact Red Hand. It was something he was not supposed to hear."

Oh shit, was Starkeholz's first reaction. *Ex-Nazis, Red Hand and the New German Party is not a combination that is going to make the justice minister happy; he was surprised when they won eleven seats.*

"Can he identify the one who said he knew someone in Red Hand?"

"We are going to interview him again and show him some pictures."

"Good, so what have you done with this information?"

"Once we heard from him, we got a judge to authorize wiretaps on the sons and daughters. If we hear something suspicious, we'll bring them in for interviews."

For a moment, Starkeholz was worried that some of his good friends might be in this up to their collective necks. While he liked many of his former comrades-in-arms, he would not, nor could not, protect them if they violated the law.

"Good work. What else?" Starkeholz waved his hand as if to say, come on tell me.

"I have more news. It seems there are others who are interested in two of the other sons– Dieter Stiglitz and Gustav Dortmann."

Starkeholz leaned forward in his chair. "What do you mean by that?"

"Sir, when we sent our surveillance team to their residences, our men noticed that there were two other teams at Stiglitz's apartment in Giessen and one other at Dortmann's father's apartment in Mainz."

"Have you checked with Interpol, the Tommies, or the Americans?"

"We have, and they said no." Grenfel swallowed hard. "Herr Hauptpolizeidirektor, I would like you to ask the minister if there is another organization within our government that we do not know about following these people."

Tuesday, December 14th, 1434 local time, East Berlin

He knew the pictures just delivered to him boded no good. Grünewald placed the photos on his desk in two lines so he could examine each grainy black and white image that showed only a portion of each person's face. *Who are you, and what are you doing in Giessen? Despite the long hair and beards, your bearing says you are military. But whose?*

After careful deliberation of the pros and cons, he dialed a number.

"Good afternoon, Comrade Colonel Krasnovsky, Grünewald here."

"Good afternoon, Comrade Colonel, what can I do for you on this cold Russian winter day?" Both of them were aware that others might be listening to their private lines, so they were very careful to always make sure that they followed the proper protocol and never said anything that would come back to bite them.

"I would like to ask a favor."

"And that is?"

"Do you remember the information on the American and British helicopter pilots you gave me?"

"Yes." Krasnovsky was happy that Grünewald didn't use the word *files,* which would lead to a much broader interpretation of what was passed.

"I was wondering if you might have a recent photograph of each of them. It would be most helpful."

Krasnovsky guessed the German had a description he wanted to compare to a photo. "I will find out. It will take a week, assuming that we have any. I have that picture of Haman in Vienna that I will send over today."

"Excellent. Let me know when they come in. They will help me connect dots."

Thursday, December 16th, 0915 local time, West Berlin

Josh was studying the departure chart when the tower called, giving them their go-ahead and radio signals. John as co-pilot acknowledged "Navajo, Golf, Bravo, Tango, Oscar, Sierra, Templehof Tower, you are cleared for take-off. Contact departure on one twenty-one point six when airborne for radar vectors. Squawk three-two-three-six."

"All set in the back?" John turned around and got a thumbs-up from Calhoun and Van der Jagt.

"Back me up on the power. Looking for thirty-six inches of manifold pressure." Josh released the brakes and used the rudder pedals to make sure the Navajo was tracking straight ahead before he eased both throttles forward. A quick glance at the two needles on the manifold pressure gauge told him that neither engine exceeded thirty-six inches and the counter-rotating props offset each other's torque as the Piper twin accelerated. A gentle push on each of the rudder pedals told him the rudder was effective. When John saw eighty knots on the air speed indicator, he called out "V2" and Josh responded with the word "rotating" as he eased back on the yoke to raise the nose.

Moments later, Josh called out "positive rate" which was a reference to the fact the vertical speed indicator was showing almost a thousand feet a minute rate of climb. "Gear."

John pulled the little white wheel on the instrument panel out and flipped it up. As the big landing gear doors opened, Josh eased the nose down a few degrees to compensate for the increased drag which slowed the accelerating airplane. After the noticeable whirring sound, both men in the cockpit felt three distinct bumps before the green indicator lights went out and John reported "gear's up." Once the airplane passed one hundred and ten knots, Josh called out "flaps."

"Flaps up." By then, Josh had the Navajo C/R climbing at one hundred and twenty knots which gave them great visibility over the nose. He didn't have to look at the flap indicator because he could feel the airplane accelerate as the flaps retracted and saw the increase on the airspeed indicator.

"Templehof Departure, Navajo Golf Bravo Tango Oscar Sierra, is airborne." Josh nodded to acknowledge John's radio call.

"Navajo, Tango, Oscar, Sierra, Templehof departure. Radar contact. Climb and maintain niner thousand, heading two-seven-zero. Radar vectors through the central Berlin access corridor." The controller's accent was American.

"Roger, Templehof departure, Navajo, Golf, Tango, Oscar, Sierra, climb and maintain niner thousand, steer two-seven-zero."

When the Navajo C/R passed one thousand feet, Josh eased the throttles back to thirty-three inches and the propellers to twenty-four hundred rpm to set climb power. After sliding the mixture levers back so the fuel flow was indicating twenty gallons per hour per engine, he fiddled with the prop levers to get them in synch. The rhythmic sound in his ears confirmed he'd made the right adjustments to the propeller controls.

About ten minutes later, they were skimming the cloud deck at nine thousand feet, popping in and out of puffy cotton ball clouds that were bright white on the outside, dull grey on the inside. At seventy-five percent power, the Navajo was making just over two hundred and twenty knots. They were enjoying the view when John said, "It's getting very hot in here, I'm going to turn the heat down."

"Good idea. It *is* hot, and seems to be getting hotter."

John fiddled with the temperature control for the gas powered heater that was mounted just aft of the nose baggage compartment.

"It's still getting hotter." Josh sniffed the air. "It smells as if something's overheating, even burning."

"I agree, I'm going to shut the heater off."

John flipped the heater switch to the off position and the temperature knob to its coolest setting, yet the temperature in the cockpit continued to climb. He pulled the aircraft operating manual from a shelf in a narrow cabinet behind the pilot's seat.

"I can feel the heat through the rudder pedals," Josh called out, "and the yoke is getting so hot I can't hold it. I don't think that we shut it down. Plus the burning smell is getting stronger."

John nodded and again rotated the temperature control knob before he recycled both the heater switch and the circuit breaker.

"There is supposed to be a temperature sensor that turns the heater off if it overheats, but it doesn't seem to be working. I think we have a runaway heater."

"Agreed. We need to get it shut down or land before we get flames in the cockpit. That heater is just aft of the nose baggage compartment and just in front of our feet. Do you want to declare an emergency?"

"Not yet." John flipped through the handbook and stopped, first at the fuel system diagram, and then at the one showing the fuel lines to the heater. "There is one more way to cut the fuel flow off to the heater."

"And that is?"

"Shut down the right engine. Looking at the diagram: it shows the mechanical fuel pump for the right engine sends fuel to the heater; we can stop the flow of fuel by shutting down the engine's mechanical fuel pump. To do that, we have to shut down the engine."

"For how long?"

"I don't know! But without fuel, the heater should shut down and we should get an immediate drop in temperature—unless something in the cargo compartment is burning, which is a bigger problem. Once we shut the engine down, we need to keep it off for two to three minutes to make sure the heater has sucked all the fuel out of the line and cooled enough so it won't re-ignite. Then, if we want, we'll restart the engine. If that doesn't turn off the heater, or if we can't restart the engine, we declare an emergency and land as soon as we can in West Germany. But I'd prefer not to have to explain to the Volkspolizei and the Stasi why four scruffy looking members of the military from two NATO nations made an emergency landing in a civilian airplane at an airfield in the DDR."

"Amen to that. How about shutting the engine down for five minutes?"

"Sounds good to me." John turned around and briefed Van der Jagt and Calhoun, who were already sweating in the hot cabin, before picking up the ring of laminated checklists that the heat made soft and tacky to the touch. "O.K., engine shutdown check list."

"Ready!" Josh's voice calm. In an emergency, his emotions seemed to shut down to let his mind and reflexes deal with the crisis. Later there might be a reaction; now there was no time for fear.

They went through the items and John stopped before the last two.

"Mixture for the right engine to idle cut off." John put his hand over Josh's to make sure that they had the proper engine. A mistake at this point would be disastrous.

"Done."

"Right magnetos are off."

"Done."

"Propeller to feather."

Josh looked down again to make sure he had the right propeller control lever in his hand before pulling it all the way back, causing the propeller blades to align themselves with the wind over the wing.

"Done."

Dead foot, dead engine ran through his mind as he prepared to fly the Navajo on one engine. Turning the magnetos to the off position was the last item on the check list. No fuel and no ignition caused the three bladed prop on the right engine to come almost to a stop and then turn over at a very slow rate. As he fed in left rudder and trimmed to relieve the pressure needed to keep the airplane from yawing, he could smell the neoprene soles of his waterproof boots melting.

By now, Josh had wrapped his gloves around the scorching hot horns of the plane's yoke to keep from burning his hands, and the fungal smell of hot damp leather filled the cockpit. He could compensate with left aileron to keep the Navajo level and maintain altitude as the airplane slowed from its two hundred and twenty knot cruise speed to one hundred and eighty. Josh rolled the manual rudder, elevator, and aileron trim wheels on the console below the center of the instrument panel to minimize the control forces needed to keep the Navajo level.

Josh tried to keep from yelling, to sound matter-of-fact. "John, call Frankfurt Center now and tell them what we're dealing with! They'll notice the difference in ground speed very soon, if they haven't already."

John keyed the mike. "Frankfurt Center, Navajo Tango Oscar Sierra, we have a problem, over."

"Navajo Tango Oscar Sierra, what is the nature of your problem and are you declaring an emergency?"

"Frankfurt Center, we have a runaway heater and have shut down the right engine to cut off fuel to the heater. If the temperature in the cabin starts to drop, we'll restart the engine and continue to Egelsbach as planned. If the heater doesn't shut down, or we can't restart the right engine, we'll declare an emergency and need radar vectors to the nearest runway."

"Navajo Tango Oscar Sierra, roger. Egelsbach is about three hundred and twenty kilometers from your present position. Advise intentions, over."

"Frankfurt Center, roger and standby for our intentions in five minutes." John watched the second hand make its way around the dial and the minute hand move one click. "The temperature is going down! We have about three more minutes to go."

"Let's stay at nine thousand for as long as we can. Then we'll see if we can start the right engine. If not, we'll decide whether or not to continue to Egelsbach on one engine."

"Agreed."

Josh was concentrating on keeping the Navajo level and on their assigned heading when they felt a thump and the airplane pitched up violently and rolled to the right. Instinctively, Josh fed in a boot full of left rudder as he twisted the yoke to the left in an attempt to get the Navajo back to level flight, but the slowing and climbing Navajo, caught in the vortex, didn't respond; it kept climbing and rolling.

The airplane buffeted; the stall warning alarm beeped then buzzed continually as the airplane stalled, rolled over on its back and fell off on one wing, nose down as it entered the clouds.

"Fuck! Were in a spin to the right!" Josh had both hands on the yoke now, and could still feel searing heat through his gloves. "John, pull the power off on the left engine!"

"Done! Cloud base was about five thousand when we entered west of Berlin; no idea how low it is out here."

Josh pushed the left rudder pedal all the way to the stop, ignoring the heat coming through the firewall between the cockpit and the heater compartment. The unwinding altimeter showed they were descending past eight thousand feet. The directional gyro was spinning like a top. The vertical speed indicator was pegged at the bottom: they were falling out of the sky at more than six thousand feet per minute.

The gauges gave Josh history, and none of it mattered unless he got the Navajo out of the spin. They were less than sixty seconds away from becoming a smoking hole in the ground. *Shit, you won't find enough of the four of us to put in a large plastic bag.*

Am I sure we're spinning to the right? We were rolling right when we entered the clouds, so I'm going to guess we are spinning that way.

To get out of a spin, Josh's initial movements were instinctive. His Navy flight instructors had drilled into his head that as soon as you entered the spin, apply full opposite rudder to the direction of the spin until the rotation stops. Then, center the pedals and, at the same time, push the stick forward of neutral to get the nose down. Once the rotation stops, level the wings and apply power!

That worked well in a T-28 on a clear day, but what about in the clouds in a twin-engine airplane not designed for spins? Navy training planes had instruments designed to withstand spins and give you a clue as to what is happening, but the ones in the Navajo weren't and didn't. Josh tried not to think about the bold-faced warnings in the Navajo's pilot operating handbook that warned against spinning the airplane. *So now I am a test pilot?*

Josh forced his left leg to full extension to press the rudder pedal against the stop and pushed the yoke well forward of neutral. *If we survive, this will make a great ready room tale! It will begin with "There I was, single engine, with a runaway heater fire in the nose compartment, in a spin, in the clouds ....*

Out of the corner of his eye, he caught the directional gyro slowing. He took a chance and centered the pedals to avoid entering a spin in the other direction, ignoring the heat coming through his leather gloves as he rolled the wings level.

Scanning the instruments, he was pretty sure the attitude gyro indicated the wings were about level. The seconds ticked by and the altimeter continued to unwind, slower and slower. When they dropped out of the clouds he could see they were about five degrees nose down, in a ten degree angle of bank, with the airspeed passing one hundred and twenty knots and increasing

The directional gyro said they were headed one-eight-zero; the needle that showed their position relative to the airway was pegged to the left, indicating that they were way out of the ten mile wide airway in to East German airspace.

"Josh! We've got to get back on the airway or we'll have an unfriendly East German escort force us down in the DDR."

"Got it. We're not going to spin in, at least not yet!" Josh looked out the side window and could see the brown ground. He took a deep breath and held it as he eased the left throttle forward, applying enough power to keep the airplane level and accelerate to about one hundred and fifty knots.

"Josh, come right about thirty degrees. I'm guessing, but we should intercept the airway in about a minute at this speed." John looked across the cockpit. " I thought we were going to buy the farm back there. How you'd know which way we were spinning?"

Nodding was all Josh could do; he struggled to breathe as he maintained a death grip on the yoke and planted his feet on the floor to keep his knees from banging together.

"I didn't. It was a guess based on the fact we were rolling right and were almost inverted when we entered the clouds." A rasping, deep breath. "It is a lot cooler in here. Is the fire out?"

"Seems to be."

"That was ahelluva way to shut down a runaway heater fire. What the fuck happened? One minute we were flying along, straight and level, thinking about restarting the right engine. Then whump! The next thing I know, the airplane is in a spin in the clouds."

"The goddamn East Germans thumped us!" John replied. "As we were entering the bloody spin and upside down, I saw two olive drab MiG-21s climbing away. I'm going to tell the world. How high are you going to climb?"

"Back to five. We'll hang out here, just below the overcast. I don't want to push the left engine, which right now is at max climb power."

John bobbed his head as he reached for the mike button on the co-pilot's yoke. "Frankfurt Center, this is Navajo Golf Bravo Tango Oscar Sierra, we just got buzzed by two East German MiG-21s. They passed close enough that their wake turbulence and the concussion from their afterburners caused us to spin. We've recovered, and are now level at five thousand and getting back on the airway."

Both pilots scanned the sky; the jets were gone. With his heart rate coming down, Josh keyed the intercom. "John, we've got to get the other engine back on line. Are you ready?"

"I am." John fished around for the checklist, which had fallen to the cockpit floor. "Those bastards passed us by less than fifty feet when they thumped us. They buzz airliners and corporate jets every so often. With only one engine running we were more vulnerable, and I'll bet they knew it because they monitor the air traffic control frequencies used by planes flying through the three corridors to Berlin. It's the East German way of saying 'We're here, pay attention to us.' The West Germans will file a report, but nothing will happen until there is a mid-air collision and people die."

"What's thumping?"

"Oh, that's when a jet comes by you very close and as they pass, they go to full military power and light their afterburner. The concussion creates a shock wave that adds to the airplane's wake turbulence. It can flip you inverted, as we just found out."

"And you know about his how?"

"Oh, the Royal Air Force fighter pilots used to do this in their Jaguars and Lightnings, until one ripped the blade off a Commando and caused a crash that killed four people. The Fleet Air Arm raised a bloody shit storm that ended the careers of several pilots and their commanders."

"Navajo Tango Oscar Sierra, Frankfurt Center, maintain five thousand. We have the radar data and are filing a formal protest and flight violation. You will be contacted to file your report when you land."

"How are the guys in the back?" Josh turned around and saw two very scared passengers with the color slowly returning to their faces. Van der Jagt released his death grip on the armrest of the chair.

"Sir, please don't do that again. That tested my faith in your piloting skills more than I like."

"Amen." Josh waited until John exchanged a radio call with Frankfurt Center, which was now providing vectors to Egelsbach.

"Engine restart check list."

When John called out magnetos, Josh rotated the magnetos switch to both, waited, then engaged the starter and cracked the throttle. Within seconds, the right engine fired, belching lots of black and blue smoke. Josh eased back the mixture lever to reduce the amount of fuel the engine was getting. "Let's hope that the heater doesn't re-ignite."

"Yeah."

Later that afternoon, when Josh and John were reporting to Marty, the phone rang, and Hastings asked for Mr. Cabot. By not mentioning Marty's name or rank, Hastings was signaling that he knew this was not a secure phone. Getting a line that no one would monitor was a problem they'd discussed before, and they'd settled on using an informal code.

"Good morning, sir. I will put you on the speaker so we all can hear.... We're up, sir."

"Good. Our local friends asked the president of our company if we had any on-going work by our legal firm and overseas strategy consultants that were not coordinated with our local affiliate. He was told, if we did, it could cause a major problem and could affect our long term relationship. Our boss said no, there were no operations going on, which is true, because all you are doing is gathering information. I know it is splitting hairs, but it is the truth."

Translation: The FBI (the legal firm) and the CIA (the overseas strategy consultants) don't have anything going on at the moment and the Germans were told so, which is not a lie, it is just an incomplete answer. You guys are "researching the problem." What was unsaid, but understood, was if you fuck up and create an incident and the Germans find out, it will create a shit storm.

"Next. Our local friends are very interested in a group that had a strategy conference in Argentina and are trying to find out what they did."

Translation: The Germans are following all of their citizens who went to Argentina and have tapped their phones. You need to be careful not to appear to interfere with, or be picked up by, their surveillance, or the president is going to be asked questions for which there are no good answers.

"Last, our friends were told the executives of the company meeting in Argentina and the problem child may be working together. From what we know, they have relationships that go back a long time.

Translation: The West Germans have a source that told them that Red Hand and the New German Party may already be or trying to work together. That means they have confirmed that many of the leaders of the New German Party fought together in World War II in the SS and were ardent supporters of Hitler. Some of their sons and daughters may be members or know members of Red Hand.

"We've got it, sir." Marty knew Hastings was choosing his words with. "Do you have anything else to tell us?"

"No, other than to keep us informed on what you are doing. We'll talk later."

No one spoke after Marty hung up the phone and began adding to his notes. Before he could say anything, the phone rang again.

Marty tapped the speaker phone button. "Cabot."

"Sir, is Mr. Haman or Mr. Osborne there?" Van der Jagt's New York accent was clear on the phone.

"They're listening. What's up?"

"Good news, I looked over the Navajo, and other than some insulation that will need to be replaced, there is no damage to the airframe. There's some blistering of the anti-corrosion paint but that can be sanded down and repainted. The very, very good news is that we found the problem. It was a corroded valve that was stuck in the open position, so when you lit the heater, it kept feeding the maximum amount fuel to the heater no matter what temperature was selected. There's an airframe directive that adds another solenoid controlled shut-off valve into the system, which can only fail in the closed position and it is supposed to fix this problem. They have the parts at the German Piper distributor and they should be here in about an hour or so. I authorized the shop to make the repairs; I'll stick around until it's done and pay the bill. With any luck, I should be back in time for my shift. If anything changes, I'll let you know."

"Thanks, Van der Jagt." Josh spoke and then hung up.

"Here's my take on Admiral Hastings' call," Marty said at last. "The probability that we are onto Red Hand is getting higher and higher. We may be ahead of other interested parties, but the lead may be shrinking. However, we have to avoid any contact with the West German police, who may want to ask us a few questions if they think we are watching Stigliz/Gestner, von Berg, or Dortmann. This means we have to be extra careful and be prepared if we are..." Marty struggled for the right word. He didn't want to use the word interrogated. "... interviewed."

Josh spoke up. "We also have to assume that the East Germans know we are following at least three members of Red Hand. What we don't know is if the West Germans know or suspect that Stiglitz, von Berg, and Dortmann are members of Red Hand. We also don't know what Hastings has shared, if anything, with our own authorities. The whole point of playing our mission so close to the chest is to prevent reports or even gossip coming to the attention of a double agent. But I think that he would be holding us back, rather than encouraging us to keep going, if he suspected or knew that other agencies are as close as we are."

Marty held up his hand. "It's not ours to speculate. We keep doing what we were ordered to do until told otherwise. Therefore, we need to cover our tracks, so let's start changing rental cars and hotels every few days."

Friday, December 17th, 1976, 1422 local time, Mainz

Before leaving his apartment, Mohammed stood back from his living room window and scanned the street below. The grey skies had stopped spewing a mixture of snow and rain that mixed with the dirt on the roads turn to form a gray, black, and white slush mix. Now the sun was out, and it was supposed to get to plus five centigrade. Not noticing anything unusual, he emerged, crossed the street, and headed down the route he'd mapped out in his mind. The walk was a chance for him to think and get some needed exercise and fresh air.

Mohammed's mind was evaluating the implications of his recent conversation with Dieter when he felt a blunt object shoved up hard against his back of his rib cage. A strong hand grabbed his left arm and pulled it behind his back to prevent him from turning around.

"Come with us." The words were spoken in Arabic with what sounded like either a Jordanian or a Syrian accent.

He was pushed into the middle of the back seat of a car and a hood was pulled over his head, before his head was pushed down toward his knees. Mohammed wasn't surprised that nothing was spoken, nor did his captors try to restrain him. The blunt object, however, was kept pushed into his side.

Mohammed tried to time the ride, which he guessed lasted less than half an hour, before he was pulled out of the car and led to a metal chair that was banged into place behind him. He felt hands with a firm grip guide him down and then pulled back his arms as his elbows were lashed together. Another set of hands tied his feet to the chair's legs. The hood remained in place.

"What is your name?" It was a different voice with the same accent.

Mohammed didn't answer, which got him a sharp poke in the ribs.

"We can try this in Arabic or in German, but in the end, you will tell us what we want to know. The question is whether you survive long enough to go to prison or we turn you loose and let the world know you spilled your guts. We will make that decision, not you."

"Fuck you." Mohammed answered in Arabic.

"We can do this the hard way, or the easy way. Again, one more time, what is your name?" The man spoke in what he was sure was Palestinian accented Arabic.

"Fuck you." Within a second of him finishing the words, he felt searing pain that was so intense, he had trouble breathing. When he caught his breath, Mohammed saw stars. He gasped, "Who are you?"

"Your worst nightmare."

"Russians?"

"No."

"Germans?"

"No."

"Jews?"

"Worse."

"Israeli?"

"Worse."

Mohammed's mind began to clear. What could be worse than being captured by the Israelis? "Two Israelis?" That got a chuckle. At least they had a sense of humor.

"Mossad?"

"Fuck the Mossad."

Searing pain racked his body before blackness took over. As he was regaining his senses, he felt his body being pulled upright, so he must have fallen over. His clothes were cold and soaking wet from the water poured over him.

"OK. So you can cause me pain. So what?" Mohammed was sure that his heart had stopped for a few seconds. He'd never felt such pain, but he was pretty sure that they were not going to kill him, at least not yet. These guys knew what they were doing, and he wondered how long he could hold out before he told them what they wanted? *Allah, please take me now and spare me the pain.*

"We can keep at this as long as you want. The pain will get worse and harder for you to bear, but it won't kill you. At some point, your brain will say "enough" and then you will tell us what we want to know. Or, you can spare us the time and answer our questions. If you don't cooperate, we can always feed you to your own wolves."

"Fuck you. The Germans should have killed you all." Anything other than a shallow breath hurt and he was panting like a hot dog. More pain and more stars behind his eyelids; his arms and legs twitched and strained against his bonds as he lost control of his bladder. *What are they using?* Normal breathing brought excruciating pain and Mohammed was afraid to try a deep breath.

"What is your name?"

"Mohammed Alouf."

"Is that your real name or your cover?"

"It is my real name."

"Your passport shows you are a Turk born near the Syrian border. Is that true? You sound like a Palestinian."

Shit. Mohammed wondered how they knew about his passport, and then his pain-wracked brain realized they must have taken his keys and searched his apartment. He wondered if they'd found his hidden compartment with a half million Swiss francs, his Egyptian, Syrian, Tunisian, and Libyan passports, his Makarov pistol and ammunition. "Palestinian."

"Good. We're getting someplace."

Mohammed sensed the Arabic speaker was close to his face. He was focusing on getting oxygen into his lungs and willing his brain to make the pain go away.

"What were you and Dieter Stiglitz talking about the other day?"

"I don't know a Dieter Stiglitz."

"Maybe you know him as Wilhelm Gestner?"

"I don't know him either."

The pain paralyzed his chest and caused him to see bright strobes of light. When he awoke, he was being sprayed with cold water and he'd shit in his pants. He was sure the stream of cold water that hit him in the back and crotch was coming from a garden hose.

"Wrong answer. Just a few days ago, he picked you up in his silver BMW and took you to a park in Neufeld. Dieter, his girlfriend Karina von Berg, and you walked around for a few minutes and then he dropped you off near your apartment. So again, what did you talk about?"

"His plans. He was going to East Germany and wouldn't see me for a while."

"Where in East Germany?"

"Zehlendorf. He has a workshop there."

"Excellent." The speaker stopped for a few seconds. "What does he make there?"

Mohammed knew that if he hesitated for more than a few seconds, the pain would start again. A lie would just prolong the agony because he already suspected that they knew the answer. *Allah, please take me.* His hands and elbows were bound behind the chair and his legs spread and tied the legs. He didn't know what they were using, but *Allah be praised, what they were doing hurt.*

"Car bombs. The East Germans give him Semtex from Czechoslovakia, the ball bearings and other supplies."

"Have you ever been there?"

"No."

"Has Stiglitz described the compound to you?"

"Yes."

"Tell us what you know!"

Mohammed felt himself enjoying the sensations of the pain dissipating as he took five minutes to describe what he'd gotten from Stiglitz over the time he'd known him. The young German was very proud of the workshop and how he'd taught himself to be a mechanic.

"How long is he planning to be there?"

"I don't know. A couple weeks, maybe three. I find out he is back when he calls me from inside West Germany."

"How do you know it is Stiglitz calling?"

"By the ring pattern."

"Which is?"

"One ring, hang up, two rings, hang up, three rings, hang up. Then, I pick up on the fourth ring of the fourth call."

"Who else will be in Zehlendorf?"

"Some friends."

"Congratulations. We are getting somewhere." A pause. "Who?"

"You know one, his girlfriend. Others, maybe a half dozen." Speaking was now almost as painful as breathing.

"All Germans?"

"Yes, I think so." Mohammed didn't want to let them know that there were now four Fatah commandos living in the compound, and twelve more here in West Germany, to help support the three Red Hand cells. If they wanted to raid

Zehlendorf, let the Jews and their infidel allies find out the hard way who was there.

"How do you help him?"

Mohammed knew the next answer could incriminate him. His silence was rewarded by another jolt of pain, but by now, he'd adjusted to breathing in short gasps. *Allah, I have been faithful. Take me now and spare me this pain! Maybe they don't know the answer.*

"Answer the question."

"I'm his connection to Fatah."

"What do you do?"

"Sometimes I drive his car. He drives the bomb, parks it, and walks back to the BMW. Then he either drops me off near my apartment or I take him to a train station and drive the car back to Giessen.

"Do you help him pick his targets?"

"No, he does it himself. The targets are picked at random and I think he just likes to kill people, especially Jews. Changing the social order via revolution is just the excuse." Mohammed spit that answer out as fast as he could; he figured there was no harm in telling that truth.

The answer bought Mohammed about thirty seconds of quiet. "What else did you help him with?"

"Fatah vetted new members of Red Hand."

"How many?"

"Five."

"Is that all?"

"No."

"How many more?"

"He gave me a list of twelve." Mohammed muscles began to relax and almost feel normal. It was a good feeling.

"Where is the list?"

"I don't have it."

"Who does?"

"My control." *I can't tell them who. If he finds out that I told the Israelis, I will be killed. Does it matter? I am already dead.*

"Who is your control?"

Mohammed's lack of an answer was greeted with more pain than he could stand. *Allah, help me. I don't know how much more*

I can take. He bit his lip and tasted blood. *Was this what a heart attack felt like?*

"Who is your control?"

"Ibn Khaldun."

"As in Ahmed Ibn Khaldun?"

"Yes."

"How do you contact him?"

"By letter every week. I mailed the list of names to him and didn't keep a copy. By phone when I have to. I go to a Bundespost office to make the call through one of their operators."

"Do you have copies of the letters?"

Mohammed didn't answer.

"OK, don't answer. We found his letters to you in your safe." A pause gave him a chance to breathe and try to relax. "What number do you call?"

Shit. The numbers and addresses were all in his book in the cache, with notations. He spat out the number that would indicate he had being interrogated and hoped the Israelis called it first. Once it was called, Ibn Khaldun would know he was either captured or arrested.

"You call the number and then what happens."

"We talk. Most conversations are for just a few minutes."

"This better be a good number. If it sends a signal to your control that you have been captured, you won't like what happens. We'll check it out and be back with more questions."

Sunday, December 19th, 1426 local time, Frankfurt

The air was cold, crisp, and windy. It was, as Josh said at lunch, an ideal day to do a little window shopping on their "day off." Frankfurt wasn't the toy capital of Germany, that title went to Nuremberg, but it had some of the largest shops in the country which took great pride in their window displays during the Christmas season.

Josh led Marty and John through what was known as the Innenstadt or inner city toward Zeil Strasse to the toy stores he'd visited as a child. In the aftermath of World War II, the city fathers had decided to keep the original roads, and many buildings, including their hotel, the Steigenberger Hof, that had opened in the 1930s were rebuilt as they were prior to the war. In the daylight, they could see the frames and the strings of lights that at night bathed the sidewalks of the central business district in red, green, and white, giving the city a holiday atmosphere.

All week they'd been holed up in the office spaces they were using, only coming out to eat and go to the hotel to sleep. On those short walks to restaurants up and down Rossmarkt Strasse they didn't take the time to enjoy their surroundings, because any time spent enjoying themselves was considered as time not spent rendering Red Hand harmless.

Josh wasn't surprised by the number of people on the streets. German families loved their strolls through the area. The decorations in the shop windows gave them added incentive to walk, often arm-in-arm, and stop to admire the displays. Now it was their turn to stroll and admire. As they waited at a stoplight, Josh turned to his two comrades in arms.

"Marty, I don't know if you are familiar with Lego, but the plastic blocks were first marketed in the fifties by a company which used to make wooden toys. I still have in a box someplace a set of their wood blocks. You can build anything with them, and they keep adding new shapes. The first store we're going to stop at is known for toy buildings and doll houses."

The *spielwaren,* or toy store, was only a few hundred feet from the intersection. The first window, which was about fifteen feet wide and eight or ten tall, showed a castle made from Legos sitting on a mountain top. Artificial, but real looking snow covered the castle and the landscape, complete with rocks and trees. The label, which was in both German and English, announced it was a replica of Neuschwanstein, a castle in southwestern Bavaria ordered built by King Ludwig II in 1868.

They, along with several Germans bundled up in beige and dark green woolen loden and dark green Tyrolean hats and ear muffs, or black leather coats, stood and admired the castle before moving on to the second one, which contained a completely furnished doll house. Josh elbowed his friend. "John, you need to spend some time studying this because in a year or so, you'll be playing with them with your daughter!"

"Up yours, mate."

In the store's next four meter wide window, a fully landscaped miniature version of the Hockenheim racetrack and toy Märklin Formula 1 race cars slowly moving around the track that, like the castle, sat on an accurate portrayal of the course's landscape, complete with stands filled with people. It wasn't to scale, but the shape was right. The historic track first opened in 1932 and was used by Auto Union (now Audi) and Mercedes-Benz to test cars because Hitler forbade it to be used as a race track and directed that all major races be held at the Nurburgring. Off to the side, there was a small placard with a picture of Jim Clark, the well-liked Formula 1 champion, who had been killed at a race there in 1968.

A few blocks down, they joined a large crowd in front of a series of windows. The toy store had built a replica of the Frankfurt Bahnhof, and in each of the next four windows, moving Märklin trains, known for their incredible detail, took viewers on a tour of West Germany, starting with Schleswig-Holstein in the north and ending in snow-capped mountains of Bavaria. In each scene, the toy store had created buildings and used life-like cars, buildings, and figures.

After spending a few minutes looking at the trains moving around the tracks and all the toys moving, Marty grabbed Josh by the arm and pulled him to the side. "Look in the little village on the far right."

Josh was speechless. There was a small building that had a small Star of David in a circular window just below the roof's peak, and by the doors, two tablets with the first Hebrew letter from each of the ten commandments.

It took the three men about ten minutes per window to take in the layout and the detail. "And guys," Josh remarked, "if they still do it the way it was done when I was a kid, the entire layout goes well back into the store."

"Marty," he went on, "we need to stop at one more store. Before we head home, John and I need to buy something for our kids. It's on Töngestrasse, our way back to the hotel." The store was where Josh remembered it, and its windows were filled with stuffed animals provided by Margarete Steiff GmbH, which started making high quality stuffed animals in 1880. One stylized display had koala bears sitting on trees and black bears on their hind legs looking up a tree, another was a depiction of the famous dancing brown bears of Berne, Switzerland.

A couple of wind gusts buffeted the three along, and despite their down ski parkas, Marty was shivering and his ears were bright red. "This California boy is cold. Let's go get some coffee or hot chocolate." Marty started to walk away. Not being a father, his interest in toys and stuffed animals was considerably less than that of the other two.

"Great!" Josh pointed down the street. "There's a coffee shop on the way back to the hotel that should have stollen, what we would call a fruit cake, with a buttery sweet icing. It'll go great with a mug of hot chocolate topped with whipped cream!"

They'd were about to cross Rossmarkt Plaz and head toward the coffee shop that, despite the weather, had outside tables occupied by guests when Josh heard a familiar sound followed by a smack. Startled, he was turning in the direction of the noise and heard it again. *Zzzzzziiiiiiiiiiiiiippppppp. Smack.* This time, he could see small shards of concrete and dust coming from the second of two round holes in the wall just a few feet behind him at head height. *Sniper!!! The noise of the traffic is masking whatever sound the rifle is making.*

"Marty, John, get down, NOW!!! Sniper!" All three dove behind the same car as two more rounds hit the wall behind them. John started to pull out his Browning Hi-Power.

"John, not here." Josh made a patting motion with his hand. "There's nothing we can do at this range with a nine millimeter pistol."

"Up there, top of the building across the plaza at eleven o'clock. I saw a flash that was probably a reflection off his scope." Marty's head was barely over the trunk of the car to minimize his exposure.

Josh turned around to look at the pedestrians who, as they passed behind the three men crouching behind a car, looked at them as if they were crazy. He debated momentarily if he should warn them; if another shot was fired, he would, even though it might involve the police. While his heart tried to pound its way out of his chest, Josh peered around the front of the Mercedes, looking up. He saw a man holding a rifle stand up and look down at them, before disappearing.

When the shooter was out of sight, the three men sprinted across Kaiserstrasse to the office building. The door was locked. Josh banged on it in frustration. They tried the gate to the building's underground parking lot, but it too was locked.

After a quick conversation, the three of them agreed that trying to get on the roof would put their cover at risk. Calling the police was out of the question, so they headed back to the hotel.

It only took them a few minutes to gather the eight men in Marty's room. He looked at their grim faces.

"Guys, there's not much to tell other than someone took a couple of shots at us. Fortunately for us, it was windy, and that probably threw the shots off. We don't know who the shooter works for, but it tells me that we are closing in on Red Hand, so we're not going to expose ourselves for a few days. Instead, we're going to make them come to us."

Monday, December 20th, 0645 local time, Wiesbaden

The facts in Grenfel's notes hadn't changed since Saturday's briefing. He'd been in the office since before six and was having trouble concentrating on the reports. His eye strayed to the box his mother had given yesterday, as he was leaving, after an exchange of presents and a family *mitend essen*, which was short for a combination of *mitagessen* (lunch) and *abendessen* (dinner). He had brought it with him and put it, unopened, on the corner of his desk. He could no longer ignore the distinct smell of cinnamon.

Inside there were two smaller boxes. One had six of his favorite *schnecken*, or snail buns, that were one of his mother's specialties. She said she'd gotten the recipe from her mother, who made them every Friday so the family could them eat on the weekends when the bakeries were closed.

If he had been at home, Grenfel would heat them for a few minutes, but the first one went right into his mouth, cold. It didn't diminish the taste and he remembered the wonderful smell that filled their apartment when she made them. He sat back, savoring the memories that came with the rich buttery taste of the pastry, and walnuts mixed with the sweetness of raisins, diced apricots and brown sugar.

After finishing a second sweet roll and licking his fingers clean, he opened the second box. Dismissing the passing thought that it was too early in the morning to eat chocolate, he took a bite of the traditional *weihnacht plaetchzen,* or Christmas biscuits. His mother used the best Belgian dark chocolate and lots of butter to make the silky smooth and very rich icing that she applied liberally to the gingerbread cookies. Grenfel sat back and closed his eyes as he savored the taste and told himself that he needed to spend more time with his parents.

His father was, despite his denials, not aging well. Both of his parents brushed it off as just old age. To Grenfel, a trained investigator, something else was going on, and he made another mental note to get to the bottom of it and soon. Or, at least as soon as Red Hand was put out of business.

He wondered if the investigation was becoming an obsession. This led him to write down the two mental notes he'd just made, along with a third. *After you catch Red Hand, do something intellectually challenging that does not involve police work.*

Starkeholz wouldn't be happy that their two top suspects, Gustav Dortmann and Dieter Stiglitz, were in East Germany. What bothered him the most was that the officers watching Stiglitz's apartment were sure that there two other surveillance teams there. *Stasi? Nazis? Americans? British? Other?*

Grenfel picked up his favorite fountain pen, a Montblanc, to write questions on his yellow pad. Back in his apartment, he still had the original box, with the words "Made in Germany" embossed in small gold letters under the logo. Then he read the list, considering each one.

Do I tell Starkeholz about the Nazi connection?

Many of the people running the New German Party are his former comrades in arms and some may be friends. Is he involved? My instinct says no, because Starkeholz knows he will get fired and if convicted, lose his pension. The risk is way too high for him.

Will the Justice Department investigate the Nazis and their association with The New German Party?

Agreements with the occupying powers obligate the department to investigate the activities of former members of the SS, Gestapo, and high ranking members of the Nazi party, but will they? Will it take men away from their pursuit of Red Hand? Would it lead to a re-opening of the Nuremburg Tribunals? That would be an embarrassment that no one in the West German government wants. So, should he wait until Red Hand is put out of business? There was no statute of limitations on prosecuting ex-Nazis.

How is Red Hand linked to the New German Party?

Who is the link? What support are they providing?

Who else is interested in Stiglitz?

Was it one intelligence service with two cars, or two intelligence services? The only numbers reported were on cars with fake license plates, and we only got those because they almost caused accidents. The surveillance reports hypothesize that they could be Americans, British, Israeli, East German, former SS, or bodyguards. So who are they? I think they are Americans, because their citizens are being killed. If it is the Yanks, why haven't we been notified? Should we question them?

If so, for what reason? Sitting in a car watching someone is not a crime.

Who is sending him pictures?

The answer is linked to question number four. What do they know that I don't? How are they getting their information? What West German laws are they breaking?

Grenfel looked at his watch. It was almost 0730. Training said focus on what you know. *Stiglitz and Dortmann are in East Germany, so why did they need false passports to go to Libya for six weeks, and while there, what did they do?* He was convinced that was more than enough to pick them up for questioning when they re-entered West Germany. So he did have good news to tell Starkeholz.

The Same Day, 1006 Local time, Frankfurt

In a rented office space on the 30th floor of an office building in Frankfurt, Marty Cabot was writing the outline of the report for Admiral Hastings when Lev Mogen came into the room and walked over to the table.

Lev unfolded a roadmap, distributed by the Aral gasoline retailer for East and West Germany, and pointed to the small town east of A19 Autobahn and south of B103. "Stiglitz, von Berg, and Dortmann are at safe house outside of Zehlendorf, East Germany. It is located about seven kilometers west of the town. His workshop is in what used to be a barn that is on one side of a walled compound that also has a second building, a small, one-story farmhouse. Based on the verbal description I got, I made this sketch."

"How do you get this?" Marty looked at the Israeli; the look he got in return told him he didn't want to know the answer.

Lev answered Marty with a question of his own. "Can you get satellite pictures of a fifty mile radius around the town? We can find the compound and maybe it will tell us something."

"We can ask."

Tuesday, December 21st, 1227 local time, East Berlin

From the bar facing the windows on the thirty-seventh floor of the Hotel Stadt Berlin on Alexanderplaz you could see both East and West Berlin. The contrast between wealthy West Berlin and drab East Berlin was evident to anyone who looked out the window. Grünewald could see heavy noonday traffic on the streets of West Berlin; on this side, there were fewer cars on the road than there were in West Berlin at three a.m.

The modern, glass walled hotel had been rebuilt during the early 1960s as part of a redevelopment project in East Berlin as a place to stay for visitors from other Warsaw Pact Countries. Run by the Stasi, the Interhotel chain had thirty-eight four and five star hotels in major cities in East Germany. The few five star hotels were reserved for Westerners visiting the DDR and senior members of the government.

Grünewald had gotten to the restaurant early to make sure that some high ranking party official didn't commandeer his reserved table. When he saw Krasnovsky stop by the maître d's stand, Grünewald waved and got a raised arm in response. After the Russian got a ticket from the coat check girl, he wound his way to the table and pulled out a chair opposite his German counterpart.

"Are you going back to Odessa for Christmas leave?" Grünewald was envious that his Russian counterpart could go someplace where it was warm. The older he got, the less he liked the cold, and this winter had the makings of being much colder than normal.

"No. My wife and I are going to take the train to Prague for a few days between Christmas and New Year's. We have to be back for the office's New Year's party."

Grünewald nodded in agreement. He too had to go to a party hosted by the head of Stasi. Attendance was not optional.

"So what's new?" despite the casual tone of voice, Krasnovsky eyes revealed that he was very curious.

Grünewald didn't know what the Russian had, but information coming out of the Bundesrepublik was disturbing. "Not much other than my suspicions that the West Germans are onto young Stiglitz. He and a couple of his friends are what the Americans call persons of interest."

"So what are you going to do?"

"Right now, nothing. I told Stiglitz that he and his friends could stay in the DDR as long as he liked and we would support them."

"And his answer was?"

"'Thank you and I'll let you know.'"

"That's it?"

"Indeed. He is a hard man to read. We could prevent him from leaving, but why? If he wants to leave and get caught, that's his business. The West Germans will accuse us of protecting him, but that will surprise no one."

"You're a cynic." Krasnovsky chuckled as he sipped from his glass of hot tea. He sat back in his chair and smiled.

"Oleg, there is one other thing that you should know about."

"And that is?"

Starkeholz told Krasnovsky about the reconnaissance team's encounter. "Our Captain Schultheiss thought they were military or ex-military, and one of them spoke excellent German."

"Americans?" Krasnovsky's mind went right to the most obvious answer.

"That was my thought. But they could be Israelis, many of whom are fluent in German, for obvious reasons. After all, a lot of Jews are being killed." Grünewald pushed his plate away and wiped his mouth with the napkin. "One nagging question keeps popping into my mind, and that is, could they be part of a rogue operation?"

"By whom? The CIA? Mi6? We would know." Krasnovsky sounded sure. "Mossad, that's a different story."

"What about the American military? They have suffered the most casualties."

"Could be, but they don't get involved in this sort of stuff. They leave criminal investigations to their FBI."

"Could you find out?" Grünewald decided to press his theory. "It is possible the Americans are running their own hunt with or without the blessing of their leadership, and without telling the West Germans." *I have to know if the Americans or the West Germans are planning to arrest Stiglitz, so I can let the director know. His orders, reinforced in almost every conversation and briefing, was to let Stiglitz continue to set off bombs, and to provide a sanctuary to help members of Red Hand avoid capture.*

"Our experts on America and Britain tell us that it is not the way their democracies work. Generals who take action without permission from the civilian leadership are fired, tried, and if convicted, sent to jail for a very long time. We do not have any intelligence that suggests the Americans are running an operation to find Stiglitz."

Grünewald leaned across the table. "Are you sure? Because that is not what my lines between the dots tell me."

Krasnovsky wondered if Moscow was telling him the truth, or if they didn't know, or if they knew and didn't want to tell him. In the convoluted world of the KGB, almost any scenario was possible. "I will call Moscow and ask, as well as pass on your theory. I'll also remind them that they owe me pictures of Haman and Cabot. That will give them something to do over the Christmas holidays."

The Same Day, 2017 local time, Frankfurt

Since the shooting, they had become regulars at the two restaurants in their hotel, the Steigenberger Hof. This night they'd adjourned to the bar for an after dinner drink and then, as a group, headed across the Italian marble floor to the central bank of elevators. Colour Sergeant Calhoun darted through the closing door and pushed Josh, who had been standing next to the panel of buttons, aside.

"Sirs, we're all getting off on the second floor when the door opens. Then follow me." The commanding tone meant it was more than a request. It sounded like an order.

Alarmed, but not puzzled, Josh spoke up. "What's up, Sergeant?"

Calhoun pointed to the two U.S. Navy officers as he spoke. "There is a guy in the lobby that was very interested in you two Yanks. Call me suspicious, but he could be feeding information to the shooter from the other day. Right now, Sergeant Bentley and Petty Officer Van der Jagt are babysitting him while Major Mogen is getting one of our cars. Call me paranoid, but I insist we check each of your rooms. And, we have to do it in a way that does not draw attention to ourselves or put any of us in danger."

Josh and jack exchanged a measured look.

"Sirs," Calhoun continued, "if you don't mind, Senior Chief Jenkins and I have a plan. Lieutenant Osborne, would you please go down stairs and relieve Sergeant Bentley. Lieutenants Cabot and Haman, please walk up to the tenth floor with me."

Senior Chief Jenkins met them down the hall from where their rooms were located, pushing a cart and holding a white waiter's jacket. The chief and the three Royal Marines drew their suppressed nine millimeter Browning Hi-Power semi-automatic pistols, and Senior Chief Jenkins pointed down the hall. "I want to confirm your room numbers. Lieutenant Haman, your room is 1024 and Lieutenant Cabot, yours is 1031."

Both officers said yes.

"Good, now we know where we need to start. Sirs, I suggest you two go around the corner to where the vending and ice machines are and stay out of sight. We'll come get you if we need you."

By the time the officers got to the notch in the corridor, Calhoun had the white jacket on and the cart in front of the door of room 1024. He waited until Senior Chief Jenkins and others were in position before knocking and speaking English with a German accent. "Room service."

There was a delay before they heard a muffled voice speaking accented English. "I didn't order anything."

"We have a desert order of fruit and cheese for Herr Haman. He was very insistent that it be delivered before eight thirty tonight."

"I said I didn't order anything."

"Herr Haman, I need your signature even if you want to decline your desert order. There won't be a charge, but I can't just take it back to the kitchen. That is the hotel's policy."

Calhoun maintained gentle pressure on the door and when he felt it start to give, he shoved hard, bowling over the occupant and taking him to the floor, while Senior Chief Jenkins came in with his pistol drawn to cover him and make sure there was no one else in the room. On the floor was a silenced Makarov pistol. That was enough. The two enlisted men swiftly trussed up the man, gagging and blindfolding him.

"Sergeant Bentley, get the officers in here to cover him and let's do the other room."

An hour later, they had three men tied up and sitting in separate folding chairs in a line in the empty room of the office suite they used as an operation center. On one table, they had three Makarov pistols with detachable silencers, twelve eight round magazines, and six sets of identification, along with three envelopes aligned in a neat row.

Lev Mogen pulled up a chair, spun it around and sat down facing the three men, who were no longer blindfolded. "So, let us be very frank. We are not the West German police. In fact, we are not policemen of any sort, which means we do not have to play by any set of rules except the ones we make. We know each of you speaks German so don't play the 'I don't understand what you are saying' game." Lev picked up one of the passports and pictures.

"Based on what we have here, we suspect that you either are or were members of the Bulgarian Committee for State Security. If I am correct, that means you worked for the Seventh Department in the Sixth Directorate, which is responsible for what is known as anonymous or wet work. Am I correct?"

No one answered.

"Whether this was a sanctioned hit or not, is not the issue. What fascinates my friends and me are these pictures and the writing on the back, which, based on the smudges, is recent. Can any of you read Vietnamese?"

Silence. The men stared back at the Israeli.

"Well, one of my colleagues can."

Josh took the photo from Lev's hand, already knowing what it said, and read the words in German. "Taken outside Seventh Air Force Headquarters, Tan San Nhut Air Base, July, 14th, 1972. Left to right, Captain Mancuso, Lieutenant Haman, Lieutenant Cabot. All U.S. Navy." So, the North Vietnamese had someone inside, or at least very near the compound. For a few seconds, he flashed back to a different time and a different place on the other side of the world.

One of the men swallowed hard. Without reacting, Lev continued. "These could have come from just one country, and that is Vietnam. Someone in that country has asked you to kill three of my friends. So, who gave you these pictures and who sanctioned the hit? If you don't answer freely, we'll do this the hard way."

No answer.

"Another question. Was this sponsored by your government or is this the work of an individual? And, if so, who?"

Still no answer.

"Which one of you shot at my three friends over there?"

Silence.

"We have your car and a Dragunov SVD rifle with a high powered scope, so we are assuming you are the ones who shot at my friends the other day." Lev paused. "Whoever was the sniper, he isn't very good, because four hundred meters should not be a difficult shot with that rifle."

Lev thought he saw a reaction from the man in the middle. "O.K., one more time, all we want is the answers to those questions. Answer now or it will get very painful, very fast. It is your choice on how we interrogate you, not mine."

The three men looked at each other. Then one who had been in Marty's room spoke up. "If we tell you, what happens to us?"

Lev looked at the man. "Sorry, no deals. We're not the police. If you tell us what we want to know, all I can guarantee is that you will live to see the sun rise. That's it."

"The people who paid us will come after us for taking their money and not completing the contract."

"That is your problem, not ours. Failure in this business can be difficult." Lev paused for a few seconds. "So this was a private operation?"

"Not quite."

"What does that mean?"

"Are you going to kill or torture us?"

"Not if you tell us the truth about what we need to know." Lev's even, non-committal but authoritative tone was that of a trained interrogator. Inwardly, Josh nodded with approval.

"The man who approached us is a lieutenant colonel in the Vietnamese Army assigned to their embassy in Moscow. His last name is Loi and he is going to the KGB's intelligence school. Our friends told us that he entered Bulgaria to spend a few days with our former employer as part of his training program. He gave us those pictures when he hired us."

"How did he find you?"

"We were recommended by some friends with whom we used to work."

"So you are freelancers?"

"Yes. Most of what we do is guard drug shipments and TV and electrical appliances that are smuggled into our country. We have passports and exit visas that allow us to come and go from Bulgaria."

"Do you believe the Vietnamese government knows about this operation?"

"We don't think so."

"Why?"

"In the past, when our Committee of State Security was hired by a foreign government, we never met the person issuing the contract. We just got a package of information, some photos, and then carried out the mission. I got the feeling this is personal."

"How are you supposed to report back that you have finished your mission?"

"We are supposed to take pictures of the bodies and send him the film, or if it makes the papers, send that instead. When he gets that, we get the rest of the money. He said it was in a bank vault in Sofia. The key is being kept by a friend of his at their embassy."

"We need the address of where you are supposed to send the photos."

The speaker of the group rattled off an address which was copied down.

"How did you find us?"

"We were told that you were in either Berlin or Frankfurt, so we started calling hotels. After a day or two, we found one that said you were a guest and gave us your room numbers when they connected us. It was easy." John and Marty exchanged looks.

"Who told you that Misters Haman and Cabot were in Germany?"

"We still have contacts within the Committee of State Security. They have a source in the Bundespolizei office that collects the names and numbers of passports when they are reported by hotels when you register."

Lev looked at the man thinking, if the Bulgarians know, then probably the Stasi does as well. He hadn't thought of that, nor had anyone else on the team. They were all using their own passports. New ones were needed.

Josh walked from where he was sitting to just in front of the three men. "Who was the shooter?"

"I was." The man on the far right answered.

"How many rounds did you fire?"

"Four."

"You're not very good."

"It was windy."

"That is no excuse." Josh started to walk away as he tried to contain the simmering emotions, but then he thought of how close this man had come to making Rebekah a widow, and rage boiled over. Pivoting on one foot, he spun and hit the man in the cheek and nose, knocking him to the floor. He shook his hand and flexed his fingers. "You fucking son-of-a-bitch. I hope your friends cut your balls off with a dull knife before they shoot you." Blood was streaming from the man's nose and beneath his eye when Marty pulled him upright.

"We are cooperating! There was no need to do that!" The man at the end spoke up, trying to change the subject and maybe prevent his friend from being beaten up. He directed his question at Lev. "What is going to happen to us?"

"We're going to put you on ice for a few days while we figure out what to do next. We're not sure whether we will turn you over to the West Germans or put the word out that you rolled over on your employer. We'll decide based on how truthful you have been with us."

Chapter 20
Dueling Controls

Monday, December 27th, 1976, 1000 local time, RNAS Yeovilton
Over the weekend, Josh and Lev had volunteered for staff duty, to allow their team mates a much needed break. John spend the time with his family, enjoying a traditional British Christmas and Boxing Day, while the others relaxed and celebrated locally. On Saturday, Rebekah had visited Josh, bringing both children and a picnic for their Sabbath. Now, however, work resumed.

Alerted by a phone call from the Armed Forces Courier Service office at Mindenhall, the 66th Joint Operations Group knew to expect the uniformed courier, arriving from Andrews Air Force Base in Maryland. The courier, who was carrying a .45 caliber Model 1911 pistol, had no idea what was in the briefcase handcuffed to his wrist. Once the contents were signed for, he left, carrying a double-sealed envelope that had a formal report of their activities that the team had prepared for the admiral.

Josh addressed his team leader. "Marty, John, Lev, and I would like to talk to you in the back office."

"Sure, what's up?" Marty asked, more photos of Zelendorf in hand.

"I'll tell you when we're there."

All four carried their cups of favorite morning drinks into the small, cramped office.

Josh separated from the group. "O.K., Lev and I want to suggest a recon. We're ninety percent sure we found the compound that it is Red Hand's bomb factory and maybe its headquarters." With that, Josh plopped down a folder on the desk and pulled out a picture of a rectangular compound that had several wrecked cars inside the concrete walls, as well as a flatbed truck parked just inside the gate.

Josh looked at his friend and fellow warrior. "Marty, here's how we'll do this: Lev and I fly to Sweden, rent a car, take the ferry to Rostock and drive to Berlin. On the way, we take a slight detour just south of Laage to Zehlendorf. The Zehlendorf exit is between two of the autobahn checkpoints."

"How are you going to get into East Germany with an American passport?"

"He's not." Lev answered the question. "He'll have an Israeli one. I've already checked with my embassy, and they'll provide ones with the necessary visas and permits that allow us to travel into East Germany. They can get it done in a few days."

"Josh, what's the cover story?"

"For the record, the status of forces agreement with both Germanies, which the Russians signed, allows Americans to travel through East Germany. But it takes forever to get permission from both sides, and lots of questions would be asked, and we would have Stasi tailing us everywhere, including the bathroom. So, our plan is that we are two Israeli businessmen traveling between Sweden and Berlin. I'm the trainee and Lev is the senior guy."

Josh looked at Lev, who was half sitting on the table with his palms resting on the edge, and nodded slightly.

"So far, so good. Go on," Marty commanded.

"Lev's family is in the medical equipment business in Israel, so we can get brochures and other material. He knows enough to get through any interrogation, and both of us will study up. And, if they check by making a call, we'll be 'employees.' On the travel permits, the purpose of the trip is to visit the site of the Ravensbruck concentration camp outside Malchow where we both lost relatives."

"What if they ask either one of you what you did in the Israeli military?"

"Simple. Lev can say he was in the infantry, and I can say I was a helicopter pilot. With a bit of reading, I think I can convince anyone that I've flown an H-53. Both of us are now reservists but inactive, since we spend so much time outside Israel. We're scruffy enough to look like we're civilians."

"Josh, how do you explain you don't speak Hebrew?"

"Easy, I am an American who emigrated to Israel, so I am still learning to speak Hebrew. Plus, the reason the company hired me was because I speak German, French, and some Spanish, so I can sell in the U.S. and Europe."

"Josh, how long have you two been plotting this?"

"Since I found out the bomb factory was in Zehlendorf. Once I saw the pictures, the rest was easy. It is a short detour off the road and we can say we're looking for a place to eat. We won't be off the highway long."

"You realize that this area may be crawling with East German Army and Air Force people. It is just south of the Rostock Air Base. And if Red Hand is sanctioned by Stasi, however unofficially, the base may be under observation, even protected."

"Yeah, we know." Josh paused for a second. "I don't think it will be a problem because we're not going to go anywhere near the air base other than pass by it on the autobahn."

"How long do you think this little trip will take?"

"Three days, max." Josh tapped the table. "Day one, we take a commercial flight, or John flies us to Gothenburg, Sweden. We picked Gothenburg because a lot of folks fly there to pick up their Volvos and it is an industrial center with lots of business people going in and out. Then, we drive to either Helsingborg or Trelleborg where we pick up the midnight ferry that gets to Rostock at 0700 the next day. Day two, we drive to Berlin, and on the way make our little detour. We turn in the rental car in Berlin either that night or on the morning of day three, which is the day John can pick us up at Templehof, or we can take a commercial flight back to London."

"What do you think we'll get that we can't see on a satellite photo?" Marty demanded.

"We'll get photos of the compound from a different angle. If nothing else, we'll get a feel for the area around it. We may get lucky and see someone we recognize."

"You're doing a recon for a raid." Marty was making a statement rather than asking a question.

Josh decided to plead guilty. "I learned from the master. So, yes, someone is going to have to put them out of business. We can't keep letting Red Hand kill people."

"That's not for you to decide." Marty felt the reminder needed to be said.

Josh suspected that, in his heart, his friend wanted a plan, but felt constrained as the officer in charge to obey orders. So he reconciled the plan with the orders. "Right now, we have a mission, and it is to find the perpetrators of the bombings. And, my good friend, that's what we are doing. It is the first step to executing our orders, which I remind you are to *find, neutralize, and render harmless enemies of the United States.* This falls under the category of finding." Josh pressed both hands flat on the table and leaned forward. "Last time I checked, Red Hand qualifies as the enemy that we have been so directed by Admiral Hastings to *find*."

"I'm not disagreeing with you, but other things come into play." Marty knew Josh was going to be relentless, but at least for the time being, he wanted to exercise caution. "This puts both Lev and you at risk deep in Indian country without any easy way to get you out. We have no evidence that Red Hand is making car bombs in Zehlendorf. All we have is our suspicions. Don't forget we need to get approval for this little foray."

"True, but the evidence is mounting. The photos show several VWs in various stages of disassembly in that compound. This sneak and peak is one way to find out more." Josh was adamant.

"We also have the transcript of the interrogation of Mohammed Alouf," Lev interrupted. "What if we see one or more of the Libyan Six there? If we do, it will confirm that it is one of their bases, if not their factory. This trip is very low risk and has the potential for a big payoff."

"Both of you are nuts." Marty ignored the question. "What if I said no?"

"If you order me not to go, you know I'll make you miserable until you change your mind."

"Josh, good buddy, that's what I was afraid you'd say." Marty thought for a second. "Do you have the SEAL recon mission planning checklist? If you don't have a copy, get it from Senior Chief Jenkins and use it to create a viable plan. Then we'll talk some more. Then I want to brief Admiral Hastings."

"Already done. This folder has all the details in accordance with the checklist. We just haven't made all the slides yet, which will take Lev and me about an hour." Josh slid the folder across the desk. "When do you want the formal briefing?"

"Let's do it right after lunch, and everyone will grill you. There's a lot of experience on this team, so let's take advantage of it."

Thursday, December 28th, 1976, 0746 local time, East Berlin
Colonel Grünewald had been in the office for about an hour and the first thing he did, after unlocking the large black safe in

the corner of his office, was to pull out a red folder that contained a top sheet with signatures authorizing Stasi's support of Red Hand. Under his signature, were two more: the head of the Main Administration and Reconnaissance Department, and Markus Wolf, the head of the Stasi.

Under the cover sheet, there were eight other pages in the folder labeled "Red Hand Options." The first of four bold faced lines on the first page read *Option A—Terminate Red Hand Members*. In that section was the outline on the steps he would ask Stasi to take, detailed on two pages.

The single page for *Option B—Confine Stiglitz to East Germany Indefinitely*—was followed by three pages for *Option C—Transfer Red Hand Members to a Friendly Country*. The two sheets for *Option D—Turn Over Red Hand to West Germans* were the ones he pulled out of the folder. The option's premise was that the DDR would gain favorable publicity by handing Stiglitz and company over to the West Germans as a good will gesture without having to answer the question of whether or not it had provided support. Even if Dieter tried to implicate Stasi, the East German position would be to deny any official involvement and put the blame of criminals. It even had a phone number for the Bundespolizei liaison officer that he could call. But once he made that phone call there was no going back, and before he did, he would need approval from his director who would have to get it from Honecker himself.

There were two major negatives noted. Despite the possibility of favorable publicity, the investigation could lead to questions that the DDR may not want to answer. And, as he had noted when he wrote the document, this option would send a very negative message to other radical groups opposed to the West. That the DDR could not be relied on as a sanctuary.

Nevertheless, the more he thought about it, the more attractive Option D seemed to Grünewald. Stiglitz had gone too far; he had chosen the wrong targets. Red Hand had tweaked the tail of the American dragon, which awakened with unpredictable results, as Yamamoto had discovered 34 years ago. He put the folder back in the safe, realizing that suggesting Option D to his boss or Direktor Wolf would also have unpredictable results on his career.

Monday, January 3rd, 1977, 0817 local time, Frankfurt
Josh flipped the keys to John as they headed toward their car. The traffic on the Alte Brücke or "Old Bridge" over the Rhein River

wasn't heavy as they headed south to pick up Route 3, which would take them to the autobahn and the exit for the Egelsbach airport. The plan was to take a quick trip in the Navajo back to Yeovilton, look at the material that was to be delivered by courier, study it and then come back to Frankfurt.

John glanced at the mirror as he changed lanes. He frowned slightly, then slowed and changed lanes again. "Josh, I think we're being followed."

"You sure?"

"I'll make a few more turns down some of these streets and see if they are still tailing us."

"Good, meanwhile, I'll try to call Marty on the radio and tell him where we are, and they can send the cavalry. I hope it is not the Bulgarians again."

After a few more directional shifts Josh spoke up. "Are they still behind us?"

"Looks like."

"OK. I know this area; there are some soccer fields behind a group of apartment buildings where I played a few games as a kid. It is not a nice neighborhood. In a few blocks, you'll see drab, ugly apartments on the right. Turn right after the first building. The street dead ends in a small, roundabout. Go around the circle and stop so you are facing toward the street at an angle."

"Got it." John made the first turn. "Won't that have us boxed in?"

"Yes, but it will force them to follow us, which will blow their tail, so they either have to confront us or move on. When Calhoun and Goodson arrive, we'll have them in a sandwich."

"Josh, remember, we have to be careful not to create an incident and call attention ourselves."

"Whatever we do, we'll do it quickly and leave."

"This is a public area! Someone may get our license plate numbers."

"True. But my gut says find out who is tailing us. If it is the West Germans, then we have to level with them. If it is someone else, we need to know who and put a stop to it."

"O.K., but I don't like it."

"Me neither, but I'd rather have to justify my actions than be dead." Josh opened the glove box and pulled out a nine millimeter Browning Hi-Power and slid the thirteen-round magazine into place with an audible click. He racked the slide to make sure a round was in the chamber and leaned forward to settle the weapon in the small of his back. Two of the five spare clips went into his front pocket. Before loading the second Hi-Power, he screwed a long noise suppressor on the threaded extension of the barrel. "We'll sit in the car to see what they do. If they get out, I'll go meet whoever comes toward us. My guess is that they are not police, so as I get out, you do the same and cover me with the suppressed pistol that you can steady on the hood of the car. That will send a message that we are not to be fucked with. And, if anyone turns us in, the plates are fake so it will be difficult to trace us."

"Are you expecting a firefight?"

"No, but I want to be prepared. If they draw weapons, then use your own judgment, but I don't want you to stand next to Rebekah at my funeral or vice versa."

"Got it. This is why the colour sergeant has been such a dick about us practicing on the SAS range and kill house every week, not just punching holes in paper."

"Yup. Show time—they're out of the car." Josh got out of the car, scanning his surroundings and planning. The broad shouldered man coming towards him was a good twenty to thirty pounds heavier, albeit several inches shorter.

A West German policeman would show identification; the man didn't. With about five yards between them, Josh took the initiative.

"Why were you following us?" His German was rapid, but spoken as if he were speaking to a friend, not a potential adversary.

Instead of answering, the man charged. Josh braced himself but still wasn't prepared for the power of the two hands that slammed into his chest. He staggered back, and the man to came at him again. This time, Josh stepped to the side and grabbed the man's right forearm with both hands. He used the man's momentum to his advantage as he twisted and rotated the man's arm up and behind his assailant's back. Now, with total control of his adversary, he shoved him face first into the door of the nearby Mercedes.

"Who are you?" Josh pushed the man's wrist toward the base of his neck with his left hand and put the thumb and forefingers of his right on the back of the man's head just behind the ears and squeezed. "Answer me, or your face will be smeared all over this Mercedes."

Looking over his shoulder, Josh saw the long, menacing end of the suppressed Browning Hi-Power pointed at the other man, who was standing in the middle of the street with his hands out to his side, palms showing. Smart move. *At this range, John could put three rounds into your chest less than an inch apart and you'd be dead or dying before you hit the ground.*

"Answer me!" Josh hissed.

No sound came out of the man's mouth, so Josh shoved his left hand up as hard as he could and felt the shoulder muscles and tendons tear as his arm popped out of its socket at the same time, he again slammed the man's face into the metal. The man screamed in pain as he went limp. Then Josh let the man go and spun him around to let him slide down to a sitting position against the front wheel of the Mercedes. Blood seeping from his nose and mouth covered the lower half of the stranger's face and his left arm hung limp. There was no resistance as Josh held the man's head with his right hand and fished through his coat with his left. In a shoulder holder, he found a Makarov pistol which he shoved into his belt. He banged the back of the man's head against the fender as he shoved him on his side and pulled a wallet out of the man's back pocket.

Josh flipped through the wallet and found an identification card that had the crest of the East German government. "Stasi? Undercover?"

The man nodded.

"Are you protecting or following a member of Red Hand?"

No answer. The man's eyes were defiant.

"Don't make me hurt you any more than I have already." Josh grabbed the man's hair. "Protecting or following?"

His opponent spoke one word, "Both."

"What's his name?"

"Dieter Stiglitz."

Tuesday, January 4ᵗʰ, 1977, 1323 local time, East Berlin

Grünewald was reading an editorial in the *Frankfurter Allgemeine Zeitung* on the government's inability to put Red Hand out of business when his intercom buzzed. It was Captain Hans Hueber reporting in. The Colonel listened with mounting alarm to Hueber's report. Not only had the two men outmaneuvered and overpowered Hans and Oskar, they'd seen their Stasi ID. It was imperative to find out with absolute certainty who they were.

"Describe them."

Grünewald listened carefully to the description, then yanked out a file from the drawer behind him and dumped the pictures on his desk. *Haman! It has to be Haman. If not him, Cabot! Shit, shit, shit! They know Stasi is involved. That is a very, very ugly dot.* "Hueber, when you and Schultheiss get back, I want you to look at some pictures."

Wednesday, January 5ᵗʰ, 1029 local time, Wiesbaden

Grenfel had just put the phone down in his office when there was a knock on the door. "Come in."

An officer in the forest green of the Bundespolizei came to attention at the front of his desk and handed him a padded envelope. "Sir, this arrived a few minutes ago. As per your standing orders, we checked it for finger prints and x-rayed it to make sure it does not contain a bomb. We found no prints. The envelope, also as per your instructions, has not been opened."

Grenfel glanced at the man's uniform to read his name tag. "Officer Kappel. Thank you. You may go."

The young officer performed a military about face and left without a word.

Grenfel used a razor blade to cut about two millimeters off the end of the envelope and dumped onto his desk two sets of identification—Stasi and West German identification cards, East German passports and driver's licenses. The last thing that fluttered onto his desk was a typewritten note:

January 5ᵗʰ, 1977

Herr Grenfel,

You might want to ask why Captains Oskar Schultheiss and Hans Hueber, both members of Stasi, are following and protecting a West German citizen by the name of Dieter Stiglitz, a.k.a. Wilhelm Gestner, who I think is a member of Red Hand. I do not know if the addresses on their papers are real or are fakes. While we were collecting these documents, Oskar Schultheiss managed to wrench his arm so that it came out of his shoulder socket and to lose a few teeth. I suspect Captains Schultheiss and Hueber will try to get back to the DDR in the near future.

Their presence here in the Bundesrepublik suggests to me that the Stasi is involved in Red Hand up to its Communist red ears. What does it tell you?

Your friendly source

Tuesday, January 11th, 1336 local time, East Berlin

Grünewald's assistant handed him a thick, sealed folder as he unlocked his office door after lunch. At first, he just tossed the daily update on foreigners entering the DDR into his "out" basket, knowing that it contained routine material that was, on most days, not worth wasting his time studying. However, something in the summary list on this particular folder made his brain itch.

Copies of the travel logs sent in by the Volkspolizei checkpoints that were on the DDR's autobahns and other main roads were clipped together in a sequence that let the reader follow each foreigner's trip through the DDR and compare it to the times and dates logged on the travel permit. The logs were turned in when the foreigners left the DDR and sent to Stasi for filing. Whenever possible, pictures were taken of the foreigners at each check point and sent to a lab in the Stasi headquarters for processing. Each foreigner's complete file—pictures, vehicle license plate number, travel permit, visa application, and checkpoint logs—were indexed and filed in a massive underground archive in the basement of Stasi headquarters.

From these, a summary report was prepared and distributed to selected recipients. Grünewald was on the list because, among other responsibilities, he was interested in foreigners traveling in the DDR. Some could be recruited, others could be compromised and later blackmailed, and still others could be threats.

If a foreigner didn't keep to his schedule, Stasi and the Volkspolizei would initiate a manhunt. In most cases, the reason for the deviation was an impulsive side trip. In others, the travelers were questioned, and in some cases, arrests were made.

There were three lines on the list that caught his eye, which was unusual. For the first two, he called his assistants and asked them to research both individuals and verify that they traveled from Rostock to Leipzig and then exited at The notes on the third reported that two Israelis stated the reason for their trip through the D.D.R was to visit the site of the Ravensbruck concentration camp on the way to Berlin. Anyone who had done any research would know that the camp was razed after the war and there was nothing left except a few stone tablets marking its location. Still, as

Jews, there was a possibility that they had relatives who were gassed or tortured at the camp.

Grünewald picked up the phone and dialed a number and waited for the person to answer. "Colonel Grünewald here. I am calling in reference to foreigner's trip log number 77-000001479. I want a full copy of their travel log and copies of any pictures that were taken of Herr Mogen and Herr Gutman. And I want them as soon as possible."

On the other side of the wall, just a few blocks from where Grünewald was sitting, Josh was walking through the Berlin army barracks looking for the sign for the 502nd Infantry Regiment's officer of the day. Finding it, he pulled out his ID card and handed it to the soldier sitting at the desk.

"Good afternoon Sergeant, I need to make a secure phone call. Where can I do that?"

The sergeant examined the green identification card and looked at Josh. "I'm sorry Lieutenant Haman, but we can't let just anyone walk in here and ask to use a secure phone. You need authorization from the commanding officer."

"Where is he?

"He's not available."

Sure, why would a colonel want to talk to a lowly Navy lieutenant? "How about the command duty officer?"

"Sir, he's too is not available."

Josh looked at the man's name tag. "Sergeant Weathers, please read what this card says." He handed him the laminated one with the presidential seal.

The sergeant hesitated, eyed the strange officer before him, glanced at the card, and felt his eyes begin to bulge. He picked up the phone, and in less than a minute Josh was standing in front of a lieutenant colonel whose black armband bore the letters CDO in white. He did not look impressed or amused. He looked annoyed and interrupted.

"Lieutenant Haman, what is so urgent?"

"Colonel Stone, sir, I need a secure line to make a ten minute telephone call."

"On whose authority?"

"Sir, the president of the United States, the chairman of the joint chief of staff, the chief of staff of operations on the joint staff. Take your pick." Josh tried not to sound flippant or sarcastic but his patience was growing thin as he showed the lieutenant colonel the plastic card with the seal of the president on one side and the words and a phone number on the other.

"You have ***got*** to be kidding me! This is not some chapter in a dime store spy novel, Lieutenant. This is the headquarters of the Five Hundred and Second Infantry Regiment of the United States Army. Anyone could have one of these made. You're bullshitting me."

"No sir, I am not and I can assure you that the card is not a fake. Sir, where is a secure phone I can use?"

"If you think this card will let you barge in here and make demands, then you are mistaken, lieutenant."

"Sir, that card ends any discussion in my favor. I need to make a phone call right now that is a matter of national security. Now, if you don't believe me, I suggest that you call the number on the card. Then if it doesn't check out, arrest me. In the meantime, please allow me to make the call. Or, if you want to retire tomorrow, I will walk out of the Kaserne, make a collect call on an unsecure phone to this number, and by the time I get back here to use a secure phone, I will be meeting with your replacement."

The colonel considered. The impertinent junior officer had spoken in an even, confident tone of voice that was not threatening, just matter of fact; he did not look or sound drunk. Colonel Stone palmed the card.

"Sir, please give me the card back. You can write down the number so you can call it, but you can't keep the card. It has my name on it."

"Let me see some other forms of ID. You don't look very much like the man in uniform in this picture."

It was true. Between the civilian garb and the beard, Josh did not at all resemble the image on his military card. He fished out his passport and presented it to the colonel, who took it, scrutinized it, then sighed with exasperation. "How long do you need the phone for?"

"Ten minutes, fifteen at most, sir." Josh stopped before adding, "And a room with no one else in it and no one in your command listening to the call."

The lieutenant colonel wrote the number down. "Lieutenant Haman, I'll take you to the room, but if this doesn't check out, I *will* have you arrested, given a haircut and put into solitary confinement until I figure out what charges are appropriate. Armed guards will be outside the room."

"Colonel, sir, that's a deal. Now please show me the phone."

Josh heard the door latch behind him in the special compartmented intelligence facility that was several stories below the main floor of the barracks. The phone rang once.

"Center." It was the word they had decided to use in case the West Germans had tapped the line.

"John?"

"Good day, mate. Are you calling from Stasi headquarters or are you in West Berlin?"

"I'm in Berlin and don't have much time. Tell Marty that we got great pictures and followed a Volkswagen driven by Reinhard Dorf out of the compound into Berlin. He's probably here for the night. We managed to tail it to the Hotel Cheimsee at 41 LützowStrasse in the Tiergarten district. Lev is in the lobby watching the hotel's front entrance. We're checked into the same hotel, under our real names."

"What do you need?"

"Help to follow Dorf. I'm at the 502nd Infantry Regiment's headquarters. Here's the hotel phone number: 49 30 15 64 71. Got it?"

"Yes I do. Good show. I'll fire up the Navajo and bring four of us. We'll be there in less than three hours."

"Be careful, the weather is supposed to get ugly."

When he tried the door handle, Josh was expecting it to be locked and was surprised when the door opened. Standing a few feet from the door was a full colonel as well as a surprised Lieutenant Colonel Stone. There was not another soldier within twenty feet.

"Lieutenant Haman, this is Colonel Saxton, the commander of the regiment. How can we be of service?" The change in attitude and pleasant demeanor were very noticeable.

"Gentleman, do you have four pairs of the latest portable radios that I can have? I don't know what model to ask for, but something like a PRC-90 would be great. It is important that they are all on the same frequency. Whatever you give me has to be small and have a range of two miles or more, and as many spare batteries as you have. You can charge to the account on this card and I'll sign for them."

"How soon do you need them?"

"ASAP, as in now."

The colonels looked at each other and then Saxton turned and called out. "Sergeant Halifax! Take Lieutenant Haman to the communications shop and give him everything he needs. Make a list of what you give him by serial number and he'll sign it. He needs this done in less than ten minutes. The send out another requisition for whatever you give him, because something tells me we won't get this stuff back. Charge it to the code on the card."

The Same Day, 1848 local time, West Berlin

Marty raised his glass toward Josh and Lev. "First, I'm glad you made it out of the DDR. What did you find?"

Five members of the team, Marty, John, Josh, Lev, and Colour Sergeant Calhoun were sipping drinks in a corner of the hotel's bar. Sergeant Goodson was sitting in the reception area, as the look-out.

Lev nodded to Josh, who started talking. "The trip was uneventful. The Grenzetruppen glanced at our documents and were delighted we spoke passable German. When we were about two hundred feet from the compound this morning, the gates opened enough to let out a battered Volkswagen. A guy runs back inside and comes back to the car with a small duffel bag. We got several good photos of the driver and the car. The gate was still open as we passed, so Lev took a bunch more photos of what was inside. Lev and I are sure the driver is Reinhard Dorf."

Josh held up a handful of rolls of film. "So, we followed him at a discrete distance. There's not a lot of traffic in the DDR, so we just followed him the two hundred or so kilometers to East Berlin. We stopped when he stopped and sort of leap-frogged him at the check points. When we got to East Berlin, we got lucky."

"How so?" Marty was curious, because both of them believed luck was the result of smart, thorough planning that considered all the options.

Josh continued. "He drove to Checkpoint Charlie, which is the only place where we could cross. When we got there, we were motioned into a line for foreigners which went much faster. They looked at our log, our passports, asked us to open the trunk, opened one bag, took a look at the brochures and sent us on our way. We got through before Dorf, so we waited for him on the West German side and tailed him here."

Josh then went on to describe making the call from the military base.

"Why didn't you just call us from the hotel?" John asked.

"I didn't want to risk someone listening in on the switchboard," Josh replied. "Where's the plane?"

"One of my dad's pilots came with us and flew it back to Yeovilton," John responded. "I figured we wouldn't need it, and I didn't want it sitting around Berlin. The forecast now says this part of Germany will get six to ten inches of snow. Now, our guess is that Dorf is headed for West Germany. I figure we need three teams to track him, and I want the plane where we can get to it in a hurry."

"Did you get any radios?" Marty knew communications would be the key to any surveillance.

"Yup. I used the card, and it is a real attitude changer!"

Marty laughed. "Pity the person who calls the number. So where are the radios?"

"In the car. But Marty, what do we do about Dorf's car? It's evidence."

It is, and I want to see where he takes it. We're not going to touch it."

"You know if we lose him, we lose the evidence, and more people are going to be killed."

"None of us are explosive ordinance disposal experts. I don't want to open the door and have everyone in a two hundred foot circle blown all to hell."

"Marty, we can call the police. They arrest him and take possession of the car."

"All Dorf has to say is,'It's not mine' and he's home free. And how do we explain our role? No. I want to see if he will lead us to other Red Hand members, and I think it is worth the risk."

Josh was disturbed, but he knew it was Marty's call to make.

Wednesday, January 12th, 1976, 1532 local time, Weitze

The driving snowstorm turned a two hundred and fifty kilometer trip that on a dry day took two hours into a six hour slog. Josh radioed the car behind when Reinhard Dorf steered his Volkswagen into the rest stop just north of Weitze on the Hannover-Hamburg section of the autobahn. Calhoun raced ahead and parked in front of the building that had a cafeteria along with a small shop and a gas station, then radioed Josh and Lev to join him.

The VW's tracks in the nearly empty parking lot compacted the freshly fallen snow. Dorf got out, fiddled with the fan belt, then dropped the engine cover in frustration. After pulling a suitcase and a small bag out of the back seat, he slammed the door shut before locking it and headed into the restaurant.

"What do we know?" Marty asked. The six of them were sitting around a table about thirty feet away from Dorf, who was by himself reading a book and drinking a beer.

"He called someone named Hans and asked him to come get him. There was not much else to the conversation, other than he said the car had some kind of problem."

"Before we got out, we could hear him turning it over, and it didn't start," Josh explained. He'd parked their rental Opel close to Dorf's VW.

"What do we do about the car?" Marty wanted suggestions.

"Someone has to watch it." Josh was thinking out loud. "The windows are all frosted up so we can't see inside. What we don't know is what he was doing while he sat there for a few minutes. He could have been setting the timer or wiping his prints off the wheel."

"That means that whoever watches it must keep a safe distance."

"Lev and I will watch it." Josh tapped the table. "For sure he is not going to have the mechanics in the garage look at it."

"Why you two?"

"Because we've been following him and we don't want him to notice the same Opel is dogging his every move. When he leaves, you guys tail him and we stay here."

Marty looked his good friend in the eyes. "Don't do anything stupid that I would have to explain to Rebekah without you standing next to me."

"Trust me, we won't."

"O.K., the rest of us follow Dorf. If you get out of radio range, call Senior Chief Jenkins and he'll coordinate."

An older man came into the rest stop and looked around before heading toward Dorf, who was engrossed in his book. The two men had a short conversation, and Dorf downed what remained of his beer and followed the elderly man out the door.

"Show time." With that, Marty and Sergeant Bentley departed. About two minutes later, John and Sergeant Goodson followed.

Josh looked at his watch and noted it was 1845, almost ninety minutes since Dorf had locked the car.

"I don't think he set the fuse," Josh said.

"Why?"

"Because this place doesn't fit any Red Hand target profile. There's no statement to be made here. My guess is that the hunk of junk genuinely broke down. He'll call Stiglitz to come get the car and fix it. The question is, when? How long do we have to babysit the car?"

"I'm going to make a call." Lev got up. "Why don't you check out what we can have for dinner?"

"Who are you calling?"

"The Bundespolizei inspector leading the investigation. This way, we will know where the car will be." Lev smiled as he headed for the phone and dialed a number from memory.

When the phone started ringing, Grenfel had been thinking about heading home. In fact, he had been getting up to go. Instead, he lifted the handset to his ear. "Grenfel."

"Good evening Herr Grenfel. You don't know me, but I am the man who sent you the packages of photos."

"Who are you? How did you get this number?" Grenfel sat up in his chair and pushed the papers on his desk aside so he could make some notes. The man on the phone spoke German with an odd accent.

"It doesn't matter. I want to help you stop Red Hand," Lev said quietly into the receiver. "I am going to tell you where a car which may be one of Red Hand's car bombs is parked and waiting for you to come pick it up. How long it will be here, I don't know."

"I'm listening." Grenfel decided to get the information first; questions could come after.

Lev rattled off a description, finishing with the numbers and letters on the license plate. "Got that?"

"Yes, yes, thank you. I will send a team out there to get it. Who are you? How do you know this?"

"How I know this is not important," Lev said emphatically. "What is important is that you get here as fast as possible to pick up the car before someone else does. And be careful how you handle it. We are not sure if it is in fact a car bomb, or, if it is, whether the fuse has been set. We do know that one of Red Hand's members, a Reinhard Dorf, just drove it from East Germany to

Berlin and then into the Bundesrepublik." Lev hung up, not wanting to give Grenfel time to trace the call.

"I need to tell you something." Josh waited until Lev sat down and was facing him. "Back in Frankfurt when I beat up that Stasi officer, a fury came over me that I had never experienced. I've been in fights and shot at, and it makes me angry, but I've never felt rage like this before. I could have bashed that man's head in and not regretted it for a second."

"So you are feeling guilty because you were angry enough to kill him?"

"I guess so."

"Why? He came at you and you defended yourself."

"I keep wondering if anger got the better of me and clouded my judgment. Maybe my subconscious equated Stasi with the KGB."

"I think the fact we're having this conversation and you are having guilty feelings is healthy. It tells me that you are normal, which for someone in our business is good. Look, for the first time in your life, you are living the nightmare that our parents and grandparents faced during the pogroms in Eastern Europe and the Soviet Union, where harassing and killing Jews was a favorite government-sponsored activity. You're angry that, in 1976, Jews are being killed again."

Lev stirred his tea. "In Israel, we are surrounded by people trying to kill us every day, and you never get used to it. So when you get a chance to defend yourself and your country, you do it with a purpose and fury that gives your enemies something to remember, and you hope they will not attack you again. Israelis *cannot* fail when we are forced to defend ourselves. That is what gives us an edge. You are the same way. When you go into an operation, you have plan A, B, and C. If needed, you improvise to make sure you do not fail. It is a very different mindset from the usual, and it is why you are very good at this business. Does that make sense?"

Josh hesitated while his brain processed what it had just heard. "Yes. Yes, it does. Thanks."

Lev looked at his watch. "I give it ten to fifteen minutes until that VW is surrounded by policemen. I suggest you move our car so that when they arrive, we can disappear."

"How'd you get Grenfel's number? Why did you call him?"

"How is not important. Why is..." Lev paused. "I called him because it is in our best interest that the Germans solve this case.

We'll take the bastards out if we have to, but right now the Germans need a break, and this will help them."

"So *you* have been sending them the pictures we have read about in the reports."

"Yes, I sent them by courier. There is no way they can be traced back to me or us, or even my government."

"What if Red Hand gets here first?"

"My guess is that this is the first time a breakdown has happened. Dorf left the car, betting that no one will pay attention until the snow melts or someone comes to fix it. I think he wiped it clean so there are no prints. I am also willing to bet that the car has no registration or other identifying documents. Or, if it does, they are fakes."

Josh nodded his head.

"So, my friend, let's finish our dinner and call in to see if we know where Herr Dorf is headed. At least, we'll be able to spend the night in the hotel rather than at this rest stop assuming the police come collect the car." Lev waited a few seconds and answered the obvious question. "I'll talk to Marty so you don't take the heat."

The Same Day, 1745 local time, East Berlin

While Josh and Lev were contemplating the menu at the rest stop south of Hannover, Colonel Grünewald was swearing at the pictures sitting on his desk.

The driver at a checkpoint outside Malchow was the same man in the folder given to him by Colonel Krasnovsky. It was also the same man that Oskar Schultheiss identified. *The Americans have a team led by Haman searching for Stiglitz, and the West Germans don't know it. Or at least, my sources in East Germany don't know it.*

He started scribbling questions:

1. Why would a U.S. Navy Lieutenant use an Israeli passport?
2. What did he want to see at Ravensbruck?
3. Who is the other man? American? British? Israeli? Other?
4. Did he deviate from the approved route? If so, where did he go? Do the Americans and West Germans know about Zehlendorf?

5. If they went to Zehlendorf, what did they see and learn?
6. Did Stiglitz and company know he was there?

None of the possibilities were good!

Outside, the snow was coming down at two centimeters an hour, and the grayness outside made the mood in his office darker. After he completed his detailed comparison of the logs and a roadmap, he concluded it was time to push Krasnovsky's hot button.

"Colonel, we need to meet soon; and before we do, you need to talk to Moscow." Grünewald made sure his tone conveyed the urgency of his request over the secure phone. That his conversation was, at least on the Stasi side, being recorded was in his mind a positive thing: he could defend his request because he was seeking help from a sister agency that had more resources and greater reach than the Stasi.

"Why?"

"The Americans have a team in Germany searching for Stiglitz who are not part of the official Bundeskriminalamt liaison team." Grünewald stated this with conviction so that Krasnovsky would know that he considered it a fact, not a hypothesis.

"Are you sure?"

"Yes. I am sure. Two of my men had an encounter with Lieutenant Haman and he asked my man if he was *protecting* or *watching* Red Hand. I do not think the official American team helping the West Germans knows about this group; at least, they have not been asking any such questions."

"Fascinating. I will call Moscow and get back to you."

Thursday, January 13th, 1024 local time, Meckenheim

Despite his heavy woolen overcoat, the cold damp wind off the North Sea made Grenfel shiver in the minus fifteen Celsius air. The hills west of the West German capital had gotten at least twenty centimeters of snow, which he thought would stay around awhile. He was peering through fifteen centimeters of bullet-proof glass in a concrete wall that let him see the Volkswagen more than a football field's length away. Snow, shoveled out to clear the area, was piled up to his thighs. He turned to the man beside him. "So this is our prize?"

"Yes, sir." Metzger was the head of the agency's bomb squad. "We are taking our time. It is out in the middle of the bomb range so if it blows up, it will not damage any buildings. After you leave, we plan to put a tent around it with some heaters to make it more comfortable to work on, and hopefully defrost it so we can see inside."

"Doesn't look much different than any other battered Volkswagen, does it, Herr Metzger?" Grenfel was peering through the glass again.

"No sir, there are hundreds of thousands of these in Germany. Whoever put it back together knew what he was doing. From what we can tell, the mechanic did just enough to make it roadworthy."

"Any chance I can take a closer look?"

The explosive ordinance disposal expert thought for a few seconds, then spoke into a telephone handset that he pulled out from a recess in the concrete wall, which was at least half a meter thick. Two men appeared from behind the VW, waved, and moved off to the side. "Herr Grenfel, I told them to stop work while we walk around."

"Understood." Grenfel followed the stocky man out from behind the wall and down the well-trodden path in the snow to the VW.

"So far," Metzger picked up his narrative as they covered the hundred and fifty meters to the car, "we have inspected and photographed the exterior. The car is in gear and the parking brake is on, so when we move it, we do so via crane. As a precaution, we weighed the flatbed truck before we sent it out, then weighed the truck with the VW on it. But to make sure, we weighed the VW again, and it is about twenty-five kilos heavier than, according to Volkswagen, what it should be, assuming it was full of fuel."

"So, we are assuming that the difference is the explosives and ball bearings?"

"Yes, Polizeioberrat Grenfel, that is our theory. The weight difference, based on our analysis of the other bombs, consists of five to ten kilos of Semtex and the rest in worn ball bearings." The head of the Bundeskriminalamt's explosive ordnance disposal group lead Grenfel around the snow covered car. "After we examined the suspension for wires or contact points, we put the car on jacks so we could look underneath. Then we started to disassemble it by taking off one piece at a time, inspecting what we could see, and then moving on to the next part. Before we unbolted the engine and rear axle assembly and removed it, we made sure that no connections to the battery were broken, nor were there any sensors in the motor mounts. Next step, after you leave, we plan to take off the front wheels and axle, and then the front fenders."

"Then what?"

"Then it gets very dangerous, because we have to figure out how to disconnect the battery and get inside the car. We do not know what electrical connections there may be to the fuse or a timer, so we are not cutting any wires or opening the doors or the trunk lid or the hood until we are sure we won't set the thing off."

"Herr Metzger, when do you think you will be done?"

"I don't know, Herr Polizeioberrat Grenfel. My guess would be Sunday morning at our current pace."

"Call me when you have it disarmed." Grenfel stopped for a second. "Good luck."

Friday, January 14th, 1977, 1207 local time, East Berlin

On the walk over to the restaurant Grünewald noted the snow had turned a dirty gray, partly from the dirt from the streets, but also from the soot from coal stoves that still heated so many buildings. Grey-black snow piled against buildings and narrowed the sidewalks, and ice filled in where salt and cinders had temporarily melted it. The cold, along with the snow, was not going to leave them soon.

It was a relief to step inside and be greeted politely, and to smell aromas of sausages, cabbage, and good beer. Krasnovsky had already arrived was seated at their table; Grünewald followed the silent waiter to the private room. Soon drinks had been brought, and the two of them were comparing what they knew. Krasnovsky had more intelligence on the annoying Lieutenant Haman.

Grünewald tried to be angry, but he knew the limitations Krasnovsky operated under. Information was power, and was only doled out in small increments to create debts that could be collected later to the political or career advancement of the holder. Still, he felt safe enough in their relationship to express his annoyance without worrying that he was putting his career at risk.

"Whoever sent the information you gave me may have withheld important data that could have prevented two spies from entering the DDR. Someone in Moscow decided not to send everything, without knowing what was needed." Grünewald tapped the folder on the table that had the pictures of Haman inside the DDR.

Krasnovsky let his friend vent, knowing he had a point. Both knew that he had no control of what the KGB would share about Lieutenant Haman. When he had raised hell with his boss in Moscow, a second package with pictures of Haman in Vietnam and in dress uniform, along with several recent press clippings, had arrived by courier the next day. Included was an explanation of his ribbons based on the KGB's analysis of their significance.

Krasnovsky had quickly forwarded the information to his German counterpart.

"This guy is a fucking hero, and the bastard drove from Rostock to Berlin and we didn't know who he was or that he was in the DDR!"

Krasnovsky sat motionless and opened his hands with his palms upward. "What can I say? I would like to think, after the shit storm I raised, that what you have is what we have, but there is no way of knowing for sure, unless I went to Moscow and looked at the file."

"I shouldn't be pointing my finger at the KGB. Stasi operates much the same way. So, while it made me angry, I am not surprised. In this case, we missed connecting the dots!"

Krasnovsky shifted on the hard wooden bench to let time pass before changing the subject. "So, how does this affect Herr Stiglitz?"

"Good question." Grünewald took a deep breath and shoved the folder away. "The number of bombings has declined and he won't risk driving car bombs across the border. He is setting up a shop in West Germany."

"Who is helping him find safe houses and equip a workshop?"

"He's got another partner besides Fatah."

"Who?" The Russian stirred his tea.

Grünewald knew that how he answered could suggest whether or not he was still in control of the operation. "The New German Party has a direct action group, and we deduce a link through his father."

"How do you know that the New German Party has a direct action group?"

Grünewald sat back in his chair, tossed and caught an unused spoon he'd been toying with on the table. "We know that several opponents of their candidates died just before the election where the New German Party candidate won. I don't think it is a coincidence. So far all the police have are several unsolved crimes on their books, or they ruled the event as an accident. Call me very suspicious."

"We are paid to be suspicious, my friend." It was the nature of their jobs.

Grünewald smiled at the allusion to their governments' suspicious view of their citizens. "I know some of the men supporting the New German Party, and for them, giving Stiglitz explosives and weapons won't be a problem. Money won't be either." Krasnovsky sampled his tea so see if it was cool enough to drink. "So what is your theory about Haman?"

"Someone in the American military outside NATO authorized a hunt for Red Hand. Who better to lead it than someone our North Vietnamese comrades called the ghost? Somehow, they found Stiglitz and wanted to verify whether he had a bomb factory. Assuming they know Stiglitz is the bomber they have several choices. They can turn over what they know to the Bundeskriminalamt; if they do, we'll know the next day when the West Germans officially ask us to hand him over. Or, they wait for Stiglitz to enter West Germany, and capture or kill the members of Red Hand one at a time until they are convinced they put them out of business."

"There is a third option, isn't there?" Krasnovsky sensed Grünewald's hesitation.

"Yes, there is. The Americans could wait until the members of Red Hand are all in Zehlendorf and then raid their compound. That way, they'd get them all. Reading Haman's file, raids are his specialty, so we can't rule it out."

"I see." Krasnovsky seemed to condense, and his eyes were hooded. "You know, a raid is an act of war."

"Sure it is, but so is supporting a terrorist organization!"

"That's never stopped either one of our governments before." Krasnovsky blurted out the words, and both colonels laughed.

Saturday, January 15th, 1977, 2002 local time, Kassel
The front desk clerk was delighted to rent six rooms to men who presented American Express cards. Their arrival at the small, thirty-six room, three star hotel meant that the occupancy rate for the night went from sixty-six to eighty-three percent. The new

owner, who checked the occupancy rate on a daily basis, would be pleased. The six were seated together in the hotel's small restaurant enjoying dinner. The clerk approached and spoke politely. "Herr Haman, excuse me?"

"Jawohl?" Josh looked up. The only English he'd spoken since arriving at the hotel was with the other members the team.

"Herr Haman, you have a call from a Herr Goodson. If you wish, I can transfer it to the phone in the lobby."

Josh nodded and followed the German, whose limp that suggested he had an artificial leg. The balding man nodded to a phone on a small table in an alcove, under a large mirror.

Josh picked it up. "Haman."

"Sir, Goodson here. Our friend has company. Need four of you to come out here. Suggest you leave the Colour Sergeant in his room so we can communicate with him. Don't know what it is, but something is brewing."

Thirty minutes later they were standing in a darkened area across the street from one of the apartment buildings. Goodson wasted no time on greetings.

"You won't believe this, but since we called, Kimmel, Gestner, Von Berg, and others we didn't recognize arrived. There must be at least ten people in the apartment, and I don't think it is a party."

"I think it is time for me to call Herr Grenfel again." Lev was shivering in the cold, clear night air. It was already down to -10 celsius and dropping.

"It is Saturday night, he won't be in his office," Marty pointed out.

"My bet is that his private line is forwarded. If not, I will call the main number. The operator will track him down when I tell the reason I need to speak to him."

"OK, here's the plan." Marty spoke in a husky whisper, his breath frosting the ends of his moustache. "Go back to the hotel in pairs, check out, and come back here. Each of you will follow one of the known Red Hand members if they leave before the police get here. I'll have the assignments when you get back. If they don't leave before the police arrive, then as soon as the cops show up, we go back to the last hotel we stayed at in Frankfurt."

The pooled their change so Lev could make the call to Grenfel's office from the pay phone that Marty had used to call them.

The phone rang once.

"Grenfel."

"If want to arrest some members of Red Hand, they are in an apartment in Kassel."

"Who is this?"

"The same friend who called you about the VW at the rest stop in Wietze."

"That car blew up at nine last night. It killed four members of our bomb squad and injured several others."

"I'm so sorry." Lev didn't want to ask for details, because it would keep him on the line too long.

"It is not your fault." Grenfel wanted to be angry at the voice but he couldn't. It wasn't the caller's fault, and a harangue might cause the man to hang up. And if here was a chance to catch the men who made the bombs, he wanted to make that happen. "Who's there?"

"Stiglitz, also known as Gestner, von Berg, Dorf, Kammer, and others."

"How do you know their names?"

"I've done a lot of research. Those may or may not be their real names. If you get here in time to arrest them, ask why they spend a lot of time in Zehlendorf in the DDR."

"How do you know this?"

"Not important. Do you want the address?"

"Yes." Grenfel knew he was not going to get any information about the caller. He was convinced, however, that he was not a native German. Something about the voice was off.

"18 Wilder Strasse, Kassel. Apartment 6B. It is on the front side of the building on the left side of the stairway."

"How do you know the apartment number?"

"I was in the building."

"Where are you?"

"In Kassel watching the apartment. Don't look for me because I will be gone before the police arrive. Hurry, or you will lose them."

Grenfel was left with a dial tone. He quickly make the first of two calls. By the time he hung up, he was sure the helicopter was waiting on the pad for the very short flight to Kassel.

Lev was walking toward the apartment when Josh drove up in the rented Fiat they now shared.

"Some of them are leaving," he said. "Get in. We've got Kammer. Marty and Goodson are already following Gestner and von Berg, and John is waiting for Calhoun to come with his car. They're going to sit on Dorf."

Josh was uneasy as he followed Kammer's increasingly fast moving four-door Mercedes Benz 220 on the autobahn headed north. At one hundred and ten kilometers per hour, the Fiat's tires squirmed and the car swerved on the cinder-covered autobahn. He was easing the car into the left lane when the radio crackled.

"We just passed the split off to Bremen," Marty's voice came over the speaker. "They're headed north to Hamburg." That meant they were within two miles of Marty. The thought ran through Josh's mind that their quarry were running. But where? Would they converge or go separate ways?

About thirty kilometers south of Hamburg, the olive drab PRC-68 crackled again. "We're at a rest stop. The bastard took a piss and made a phone call. Von Berg is in the ladies' room right now."

"We're entering the rest area now. Our target car is a white Mercedes 220 with Kammer driving and a passenger, but we don't know who."

Marty rogered the radio call. They kept to their separate cars, but at least four of them were together.

The Same Day, 2156 local time, Kassel

When he walked after the uniformed policemen stormed into the apartment, the first thing that Grenfel thought when he saw Dorf and three others handcuffed and sitting on separate chairs was that he will be able to tell Starkeholz he made an arrest. It was a good thought. Just last Friday afternoon, as he was giving the Hauptpolizeidirektor a summary of the week's activities, Starkeholz had speculated that on Monday he would be asked to resign. Now maybe he won't have to.

Dorf looked just like the man in the photos he'd been sent. Grenfel nodded to the armed polizei behind him and pointed to the others. "Keep them separated. I want to talk to this man first." Grenfel waited until the others were led out. "Reinhard Dorf."

The young man in the chair looked defiant and pathetic at the same time. Grenfel pulled up a chair and spun it around before straddling the back of the chair. "Is Reinhard Dorf your real name?"

No answer.

"Look, we can do this the easy way, or the hard way. The easy way is that I ask you questions and you provide truthful answers. The hard way is less pleasant, and the Minister of Justice authorized aggressive interrogations for members of Red Hand. The definition is a bit fuzzy, so I am not sure where the line is between aggressive and torture. So, I suggest you talk to me and save yourself a lot of pain. Either way, I will get the information I want from you."

Another police officer who was searching the apartment handed him several passports. Grenfel made a ceremony of looking at one, then the other, several times. "Hmmmm, look at this one. It says your name is Reinhard Dorf and it shows you visited the DDR a few days ago. Oh, this West German one in the name of Hermann Berger shows you were in Libya and Morroco last fall." Grenfel tossed the passports on the table behind him. Then he lifted Dorf's chin so their eyes met. "Look at me when I talk to you."

Dorf eyes shone with anger and hatred. Grenfel had seen that look many times before and knew he had a cornered and frightened animal.

"So, we have our first crime. Not a big one, but enough to hold you until we figure out who you are and which passport is genuine. This makes you a flight risk because we don't know how many passports you may have, so there won't be any bail."

"Herr Polizeioberrat." The words had a commanding tone as if to say, *please pay attention.*

"Yes?" Grenfel did not turn his head.

"Come with me for a minute. I want to show you something."

Grenfel followed the plainclothes policeman into the larger of the two bedrooms. Laid out on the bed were two AK-47s, twelve loaded magazines, ten empty magazines, and a sealed tin of ammunition that, according to the Russian label, contained five hundred rounds.

"Where'd you find this?"

"One rifle was in the closet and the other was taped to the back of the bed. We photographed them as we found them. Both were loaded, but we pulled the magazines out. The spare loaded magazines were in the night stand and the empty ones and the ammo can was under some boxes in the closet."

"Excellent."

"Yes sir, and if you look over here, we found this."

Grenfel was shown a hole in the floor which had been covered by a loose tile under the nightstand. Visible were several bundles of cash and two more German passports.

"How much money?"

"We haven't counted it yet, but my guess is about fifty thousand marks."

"I think the time to be polite is over. Take all of them to the nearest police station, do not let them talk with each other, and put all of them in solitary confinement."

"One more thing, sir."

"Yes?"

"The other three men we captured have Turkish passports, but I don't think they are Turkish."

"Why?"

"Because one of my best friend's parents are Turkish *gastarbeiter* and they speak German with a distinct accent. These guys don't sound like Turks."

Chapter 21
Lost But Presumed Found

**Sunday, January 16th, 1977, 0029 local time,
Helsingborg, Sweden**

Smoke curled up from the tail pipes of Josh and Marty's cars as they sat idling nose to tail just outside the entrance to the ferry pier in Helsingborg, Sweden. The harsh yellow light from the arc lamps made both cars, despite their difference in colors, look a dull shade of dark gray. Four men stood shivering in the cold, watching the last ferry depart from Helsingborg to Rostock. On it were Gestner/Stiglitz, von Berg, and Kammer, along with another woman they didn't recognize but guessed was Anna Schlemmer.

The PRC-68 on the seat of Josh's car crackled. "Where are you?" With the volume turned up and the window rolled down, it was audible and Josh recognized John's accent.

"We're freezing our asses off right outside of the entrance to the ferry terminal. Where are you?"

"Just getting off the last ferry from Copenhagen."

"Meet us at the Marina Hotel by the pier. We'll be there in five minutes." Josh heard the two clicks that acknowledged his radio transmission.

The hotel on the pier next to the ferry terminal was happy to rent rooms that would have gone empty that night. After dumping their bags, six weary men gathered in the empty bar just in time to get a round in before it closed at one a.m.

"So, what do we know?" Marty asked. He was simultaneously too tired and too wired for small talk.

Josh tasted his beer before answering. "Our four drove their cars onto the ferry to Rostock. It docks at seven tomorrow morning and they should be in Zehlendorf, assuming that's where they are going, by nine."

"We saw Dorf led out of the apartment along with three others," John reported. "That's when we left and headed north."

"So we can assume that Dorf is being interrogated by the Bundeskriminalamt, and they will see if they can get him to roll over on the others."

"I agree. What else do we have?"

"Not much. I suggest we get a good night's sleep. We'll go back to the U.K. in the morning and figure out what we do next." Josh hoped he didn't look as tired as he felt. "There's not much we can do here other than go into the DDR after them, which, without a good plan, isn't a bright idea."

"There is one thing we can do in the meantime," Lev offered. "I call my good friend Herr Polizeioberrat Grenfel and tell him who escaped. My guess is he will be grateful."

"Make the call."

"I'll bet I don't wake him up!!!" Lev drained his beer and headed off to his room.

Monday, January 17th, 1028 local time, East Berlin

Grünewald leaned back in his chair with his hands tented under his chin as he thought about the call he'd just completed. He often mused that he measured success in terms of the number of dots he collected during the day and his ability to connect them. The first dot of the day came from a Stasi source within the Bundeskriminalamt who reported Polizeioberrat Grenfel commandeered a helicopter in the middle of the night, followed by a lot of activity and arrests, but no details on who or where.

The second call came through the switchboard not five minutes after he hung up with the agent. It was the researcher, who wanted to tell him that a company in which Gruppenführer and Lieutenant-General of the Waffen SS Bruno Glockner was a shareholder, had just bought a building well outside the city limits of Marburg. This was, in the woman's opinion, the type of transaction that might become the shop Stiglitz wanted. She mentioned that SS records showed that Glockner had at one time been Helmut Stiglitz's brigade commander, and said the full report on the New German Party would be delivered to him at the end of the day.

That made two more dots that connected. *Glockner had a reputation of being a hard-nosed Nazi bastard*. He was pulling out his file of senior officers in the SS who were still alive when his personal line rang.

"Allo."

"Colonel Grünewald." It sounded more like a statement than a question.

"Yes."

"Stiglitz here."

"Dieter, it is good to hear from you. Are you in our fair country?"

"Yes, I am in Zehlendorf."

"What can I do for you?" Grünewald wondered how much of what had happened Stigliz knew, or would admit to.

"Nothing. Just wanted to let you know we're going to be here for a few weeks, maybe longer, and will need new papers to get back into West Germany or go to Libya."

"Who's we, and why?"

"Maria Holz, Gustav Dortmann, Giselle Bischoff and me." Dieter paused for a second. "Things were getting very hot so we left."

"Has anyone been arrested?" Grünewald probed. The young man did not bluff very well.

"We're not sure. Dorf and Finchafen are still in West Germany."

"What about your Arab friends?" It was time to show he knew about the Fatah connection.

At his end, Dieter bit his lip. When he'd called that last time, the person picked up on the wrong ring, and then his German accent was not similar to Mohammed's classical German. Dieter had hung up without speaking, and he suspected the worst. "We have four here, but you know about those. I don't know if the other four have been arrested. Dorf was planning to come here today."

Grünewald knew by the higher pitch of Stiglitz's voice and rapid speech that he was more than a little scared. Fear, he knew from experience, is a great motivator. "I will make some inquiries and find out. Do you have enough supplies?"

"Yes, Herr Colonel. We have enough for a few days."

"Gut. Stay there and don't leave the compound without telling me first."

"O.K."

Grünewald planned to keep them confined to the compound while he figured out what to do next. If he was told to make them disappear, he wanted them in one place. And while it would be relatively easy, he was not going to put them on a flight to Libya any time soon. "Did anyone follow you into the DDR?"

"Not once we got on the ferry."

My, young Stiglitz is more forthcoming than usual. "What about before you got on the ferry?"

"Yes, I'm pretty sure we were followed."

"By whom? Police?"

"No, I don't think they were police. Here is the weird thing. I believe I've seen at least one or two of them before, but I don't know where."

Grünewald dropped his pencil. "Would you recognize them if I showed you some pictures?" he said carefully.

"Maybe. At first I thought it was my imagination, but then I was pretty sure it was the same two men. I never got a good look at them."

"Are there any more bombs set to go off?"

"Yes." Dieter began to rethink his answer. "Well, I am not sure. Max Finchafen has control of two. I also left two with long term timers. They should go off sometime tomorrow."

"Where are the two you left behind?

"Frankfurt and Stuttgart."

"Who else knows where they are?"

"No one but me."

"Finchafen's?"

"I don't know where they are."

"Are there any more being built in West Germany?"

Dieter hesitated. "Yes. I told you I had a new place in West Germany outside Marburg." He didn't think he needed to mention that two cars were already torn apart in the shop that the New German Party had acquired for him and were waiting to be packed with plastic explosive that was supposed to be delivered today.

"Is there anyone else involved that I should know about?"

Dieter wondered where *that* question came from. "Other than some people I was trying to recruit and those from the New German Party, no."

"Who is your contact from the New German Party?"

"I don't know his name and I never have met him. I just call a number and the person who answers gives me another number. When I get to the right person, I tell them what I need. I never see the people making the deliveries."

"Do they know you are Red Hand?"

"No. They think I am a liaison. One of the conditions we agreed upon is that they never come into the shop and it is not being watched."

The answer astonished Grünewald. *Dieter, you are so naïve! By now, the New German Party knows everything it can about everyone who enters that shop.* Here was another dot that had to be connected. "I'll be up there tomorrow to show you some pictures. In the meantime, stay put."

Stiglitz hung up the phone and walked back into the bedroom with two bottles of mineral water.

"You're scared aren't you?" Giselle had overheard his half of the conversation.

"Worried, yes. Scared, I am not sure." Dieter popped off the top of one bottle and handed it to his lover.

"Do you think the Bundeskriminalamt is on to us?"

"I am sure they are getting closer, but we are safe here in the DDR."

"Do you trust the Communists and Stasi?"

"As long as they see us as valuable, they will protect us."

"You know we could wind up in prison for a very long time, or even be killed." Giselle caressed his cheek with her fingers.

"Yes." Dieter nodded. "But, we can turn our trial into a circus to get out our message, and many people will agree with us. They can criticize our methods, but not our message."

Tuesday, January 18th, 1435 local time, Wiesbaden

Grenfel was head down making notes along the margin of the latest transcript from the interrogation of Reinhard Dorf. The half inch thick, double spaced document was next to a lined pad on which he was writing questions that either he or other investigators would ask. On the other side of the cleared space on his desk, cluttered with files, were three notebooks stacked in a neat pile. They were filled with annotated photographs of the evidence that his team had compiled.

"Good afternoon, Herr Polizeioberrat."

Starkeholz's voice startled and surprised him. It was rare that the Hauptpolizeidirektor came down to his office, much less used his title.

"Good afternoon, sir." Grenfel started to stand.

"Please, sit." Starkeholz plopped down into one of the forest green plastic chairs in front of Grenfel's desk. Once settled, he reached behind and closed the door. "I want to pass on the minister's congratulations on breaking this case. He is very pleased."

"Please tell him thank you for me."

"I won't have to. You are going to meet with him this afternoon at four."

"I have a lot of work to do. This case is far from closed."

"I am aware of that. Be grateful, the arrest is good for your career."

"But not as good as solving this case with enough evidence so that Dorf and his comrades never see the outside of a prison. I have to prepare more questions."

"I am sure you do." Starkeholz paused. "How long are you planning to hold him in solitary confinement and not meet with a lawyer?"

"You told me that I had seventy-two hours."

"I did. The minister wants to know when will you be ready to file formal charges. It has to be soon, or the government will have a hard time in court. Before he is charged, Dorf will need access to a lawyer, which means the fact that we have young Herr Dorf will become public. What do you think Red Hand will do?"

"I don't know what they will do. If they have not already, they may flee to someplace where we cannot get to them. Or they could try to free him, or kill more of our fellow citizens and demand his release, or some combination of these. The bombings won't stop until we get them all."

"The minister will want your opinion."

"Sir, the truth is, I don't have an answer. Two more bombs went off over the weekend. Another thirty Germans are dead and fifty or so are injured by a bomb that went off near another synagogue. Many of the dead and injured are *children*." Grenfel straightened out the file in front of him. "I am ready to have this discussion with the minister. I just don't know if he will accept my answer. I am assuming you will be there as well."

"Of course." The time had come to ask the question that had been bothering him for days. "The minister will want to know about your source."

"I don't have a name and that will disappoint the minister, but it is the truth. All I know is that he has my direct line and every time he has called the information has been accurate and helped us make progress. He provided photographs, let us know about the car parked at Weitze, the address of Dorf's apartment, and today a call saying that four other Red Hand members went into the DDR Sunday morning."

"Can't you trace the calls?"

"They are all made from a public pay phone and he is on the line for less than a minute. So the answer is no."

"Informants are a vital source of information. It is still an excellent piece of police work." Starkeholz let the compliment stand before continuing. "Please meet me in my office at 1530 and we can go over together."

Wednesday, January 19th, 1452 local time, Frankfurt

Starkeholz parked his car right outside the international arrivals area of Rhein Main and put the police placard on the dash so no one would bother it. Even a casual observer would note that the black Opel with government license plates was not an ordinary model. The antennas, the larger tires, and the radio telephone between the seats confirmed that it was a government vehicle. He took off his gloves and shoved them into his pocket before he unbuttoned his loden overcoat and found a position near the doors from which he could study the comings and goings of passengers.

He was thinking, as he watched the stream of passengers, mentally processing them as potential terrorists or criminals, that old habits die hard, when he saw Von Ritter emerge from Customs and Immigration.

"Good afternoon Herr von Ritter, I trust you enjoyed your extended vacation. Your bag will be picked up by one of my men and brought to my office."

"Thank you, Herr Hauptpolizeidirektor." Von Ritter thought it proper to respond formally. The two men fell in step and began the walk back to Starkeholz's car. "It was good to get away. Eilat in southern Israel is a wonderful place to spend a month or so this time of year. I enjoyed touring battlefields from modern wars as well as those in the bible. I drove around Sinai and it still is littered with destroyed tanks. The Israelis have cleaned up their side of the Golan Heights, but the Syrians haven't."

"I'll tell you more when we get back to the office, but we are waiting for the minister to approve our recommended actions and prepare the arrest warrants."

"What do I have to do?"

"We have some material for you to examine and questions that came out of our investigation that we hope you can answer, or at least point us in the right direction. Then, if any of these go to trial, you may have to testify, so we'll have to prepare for that eventuality, if it gets that far."

"What do you have on von Theissen, Glockner, Horst, Brunner, and the rest of them besides what I gave you?"

"A lot. We are hoping to save the taxpayers the cost of a trial. If it does go to court, it will be messy."

Von Ritter looked at Starkeholz, thinking of several ways to interpret his comment, when he heard a shot, at the same time he staggered from the impact of a bullet just to the right of his left armpit. "Shit!" was all he could say as he fell backwards, which was when the second round ripped through his upper left thigh.

Two more rounds shattered the glass of the car Starkeholz dragged him behind. Pinned down, Starkeholz knew his .380 caliber Walther PPK pistol was useless against sniper fire from hundreds of meters away.

Von Ritter propped himself up against the wheel and busied himself turning his belt into a tourniquet with one hand to stop the flow from his thigh. Looking down, he was glad to see the bullet hadn't torn his femoral artery; so while he was bleeding from two wounds, he wasn't in immediate danger of dying.

Sirens wailed in the background as three more bullets announced their presence with metallic pangs and the smell of oil and coolant dripping onto the ground. A fourth sent a shower of concrete chips past them. Two police officers with the patches of the airport security on their uniforms came running in their direction, carrying Heckler & Koch G-3 7.62mm rifles with large scopes. Quickly they took up positions at each end of the car and scanned for the source of the bullets.

Von Ritter saw more police officers with rifles taking up positions around the exit area of the international terminal while Starkeholz helped apply pressure to the shoulder wound.

"We'll get you to a secure hospital and then to a safe house," Starkeholz was saying. "I didn't like being shot at during the war and I don't like it any better now! I've had enough of this shit."

A drab olive four wheel armored car stopped between von Ritter and the line of fire, and two medics helped him onto a stretcher before sliding it inside the vehicle, using its armored doors for cover. Once inside, they stuck a needle in his arm, started an IV and took his vital signs. Satisfied he wasn't going to expire right then, the medic yelled at the driver to go as they latched the armored rear hatch.

"Sir, short of an anti-tank missile, we're safe in here." The Stabsunteroffizer wearing the camouflage uniform of the Bundeswehr bent down. "This is the ambulance version of the Thyssen Henschel 416. We'll have a police escort and a reconnaissance version with a full squad from the parachute regiment all the way to the American hospital at Landstuhl. We were just entering the airport for an exercise when we heard there was a shooting."

"Good timing. I shall schedule all my most sensitive meetings during such exercises in future." Starkeholz looked around the pale green interior of the armored car. "Do you have a secure radio?"

"Yes sir." The vehicle commander, now standing up in the turret swiveling what Starkeholz could see was a modern version of the MG-42 light machine gun used by the Wehrmacht in World War II, held out his hand with a headset and mike, and pointed to a control box next to the seat on which he was standing. "I am on channel two to talk to the other vehicle, and that frequency is monitored by our command center. If you want the command duty officer, use channel four. All the channels are secure. Our call sign is Reaction Four. Just so you know, we're from the parachute regiment of the air mobile division."

Starkeholz nodded and put on the headset. He sat back on the small padded seat thinking that this was a much nicer armored car than the last one he rode in back in 1944. Only the confidence of the young soldiers in the vehicle hadn't changed.

After a short radio exchange, Starkeholz deftly spun the radio selector switch to the 'intercom only' position. "Stabunteroffizer, you should know that your wounded passenger is Oberst Klaus von Ritter, who was with the First Parachute Regiment during the war and the commander of your regiment when he retired."

"Tell the Oberst that I thought I recognized him from the pictures on the wall in our barracks. I am glad you let the command center know he is on board. If they are needed, we will have many volunteers who will help ensure his safety."

Thursday, January 20th, 1977, 0945 local time, RNAS Yeovilton

The brightness of the sun made it feel warmer than it was. Just seeing the sun for the first time in a week cheered everyone up, and the light streaming through the window made the overhead fluorescent lights redundant. This was the first meeting since they'd gotten back from Sweden and, on Marty's orders, taken a couple of days off.

"Everyone gather round." Marty stood in the center of their ops room. "Our photo interpreter, Petty Officer Second Class Edmund Wilson, just got a new batch of satellite photos in this morning's courier package."

"We need to figure out how to get into the DDR and take care of the bastards." Josh got right to what he'd been going over in his mind since their return.

"Are you thinking about a body snatch, or a raid to kill them?" Marty was prepared for this discussion because he too was thinking about a raid. "You are assuming they are still in Zehlendorf."

"I am, and these photos tell us they are. But we need more. I don't want another Son Tay." Josh was referring to an attempt to free POWs held in North Vietnam. The rescuers had gone in only to find that the Americans had been moved months earlier.

Josh continued. "And if you go back to our orders, our mission is to find, neutralize, and render harmless Red Hand. I can make an argument that by being in the DDR, they are found and neutralized, for the time being, but they are not rendered harmless. Therefore, our mission has not been completed. To neutralize them they have to be either in jail or dead. To forever render them harmless, they have to be dead. I prefer dead because then we don't have to bring them out. But to prove that we have ended the threat, we need to interrogate them. So, I am torn between a body snatch and a raid to take them out."

"You are, of course, assuming that either in death or in jail, they do not become martyrs. Our mission does not include invading another country and engaging in a firefight," Marty shot back, with a look over at Lev, who nodded reluctantly, even though the Israelis routinely conducted raids in neighboring countries.

"And authorizing a raid of any type is well above the pay grade of anyone in this room."

"Nobody said to conduct a raid without authorization, but my thought is we ought to have a plan in case someone asks us. I believe General Cruz and Admiral Hastings are thinking along these same lines, or else they wouldn't have created this little unit." Josh stood his ground. "We all know that if Red Hand is allowed sanctuary in the DDR, they will come back."

"OK. What's the task—kill or capture them?" Marty continued the jousting while the others watched the two friends spar. By now, it was not new to any of them.

"I prefer killing them and letting the East Germans deal with the bodies, but that doesn't give us the proof we want. So I think a body snatch is the best way to go. This way they get put on trial, and if they have any, their ties to former Nazis can be exposed. Then they go to jail until they die or they are hung. Getting in and capturing them is the easier task, getting them out is the challenge."

"I agree. Extraction is the tougher problem." Marty knew how difficult it was to maintain control of uncooperative prisoners.

Josh thought for a second. "What I want to do is to take them someplace so we can interrogate the hell out of them before we turn them over to the West Germans. Or, better yet, take them back to the States so we can execute them for murdering Americans."

"Suppose you were given the go-ahead, how do you plan to get a team into the DDR?" Marty continued testing.

"I can answer that." Colour Sergeant Calhoun stood up. "The East Germans like to think that their coast is impenetrable, but in reality, for a small team, it is porous as hell. We've gone in and out several times."

"Define small?" Marty was assessing rather than being argumentative.

"We could get four to eight men in, under the right conditions, this time of year. Wouldn't want to swim in from the three mile limit, but if we got close enough to shore, let's say within a mile or less, we could swim in without any trouble. We've got the equipment to survive in cold water. Hell, we do it all the time in Norway."

"Four more could come in by car," Josh added. "We can take the ferry from Sweden to Sassnitz, and then there is a coast road that heads toward Rostock. We could pick the swimmers up on the way. We can pick a route that bypasses the checkpoints." He went over to the large map of both East and West Germany that was tacked to one of the walls. "Here, let me show you."

"OK, how do you get the swim team into position? It would be tough to get a submarine through the Kattegat. And a Royal Navy ship would set off all kinds of alarm bells."

"By a yacht," John spoke up. "We can charter a boat through my father's company and carry a rubber boat that has enough fuel to take the swimmers to their launch point from outside the three mile limit, and if needed, return to pick up the team on the way out. Remember, these waters are Danish as well East German, so we can stay in Danish waters most of the time. As long as the yacht is three miles out, we don't have to worry about violating the D.D.R's territorial waters. The rubber boat won't be picked up on their radar."

"Getting out by boat means we have to get the prisoners into wet suits for the swim out. That'll be hard if they don't want to cooperate, and we risk drowning them. Or, we bring the rubber boat to the beach so we can get everyone out. That means four trips by boat, two in and two out, which doubles or quadruples the chances we'll be discovered." Marty paused. "What about driving them out? There's a crossing near Selmsdorf that is about an hour's drive away from Zehlendorf."

"That won't work unless we have the necessary paperwork. It is only for Germans," Lev weighed in. "One way we could do that is to have the passports ready with false names, then take their pictures after we capture them and paste them in the documents. But a word or a gesture or scream out of any one of them and we're screwed. Way too many things that could go wrong. Plus, we would also have to account for the extra bodies at each of the check points on the transit logs. The internal travel permits specify the number of passengers, and I don't want to take the risk of trying to hide someone in the trunk.

"For the guys who drive in," Lev continued, "I think Berlin would be a better destination because it gives the guys in the car more time for a plausible delay, even though they will be in the DDR longer. Carrying additional people in the cars is way too risky unless we are prepared to shoot our way out, which means some of us and our prisoners will get hit. Extraction by boat would be a good option, but with uncooperative and untrained people, the risk is too great."

"There is another, much better way." At the sound of Josh's voice, Marty's eyes rolled back into his head. He addressed the room.

"Josh, before you say anything, everyone needs to realize that at this point Lieutenant Haman here is about to toss out an outlandish idea. It will sound completely ridiculous until you start looking at how he has thought through the details, at which time you will realize there is a sixty to seventy per cent probability that it could work. The operational concept, of course, will be based on his extensive training and experience in special operations." Marty stopped speaking until everyone in the room, including Josh, stopped laughing. "Now, in all seriousness, continue." With that, Marty bowed at the waist and waved to his friend.

"We fly everyone out except those who drove the cars. If we get our timing down, the guys in the cars won't be at risk. We can come up with some sort of excuse, like a flat tire, that explains a delay."

"So you want to fly a plane into the DDR and then out again?" Lev was being sarcastic.

Before Josh could answer, a phone began ringing and he picked it up. Just a few people had these numbers. "Haman."

"Josh, it's Rebekah. The BBC just announced they were going to switch to a press conference being held by the West German Minister of Justice. The tease said they had made an arrest in the Red Hand case!"

"Did they say when the press conference was going to going to start?"

"Yes, 1030. About thirty minutes from now."

"We'll be right over."

"I was afraid you would say that. The house is a mess."

"We'll help you clean up." Josh turned around as he hung up the phone. "Rebekah has invited us over to watch the news conference with the caveat that we have to help her clean up the house."

"That's fine," Jenkins said, as he hung up the other phone. "I just got off the secure horn with Admiral Hastings' administrative assistant. He's going to be at the U.S. Naval Forces European headquarters with the chairman on February 1st. He wants the four of you," the senior chief pointed at the officers, "to brief the chairman on what we know and possible options."

The Same Day, 1526 local time, Schloss Theissen

The five meter long cord allowed von Theissen to pace the floor of his third floor office when he spoke on the phone. Out the window, the gray sky reflected his mood. "I saw on the news there was a shooting at the airport. Did you kill him?"

"We are not sure. My spotter said I hit him in the chest and lower torso. We were about four hundred meters away."

"Is he dead?"

"I don't know. Someone dragged the target behind a car before I could hit him again. Then an armored car showed up and they loaded him into it and drove off."

"Shit. You wounded four bystanders. How many rounds did you fire?"

"That could not be helped. We fired ten rounds and the injured were hit by ricochets." It was a lie and the shooter knew it. He'd emptied a whole twenty round magazine in frustration.

"Anyone see you?"

"No, we got away clean. The Bundeswehr guys appeared out of nowhere with machine guns and a half dozen armored cars. There was no way I was going to continue shooting."

You are supposed to be an expert sniper, Von Theissen thought, *yet you failed to kill von Ritter at four hundred meters. That means you are not very good or you hurried your shot. I should have hired a Russian woman.* "Do you know where they took him?"

"Yeah, the U.S. Army hospital at Landstuhl. We followed the convoy. Who is this guy?"

"A former paratrooper."

"No wonder. The airmobile brigade has surrounded the hospital and neither they nor the Americans are letting anyone in or out who doesn't work there. Even the Americans are armed, and visitors are being searched and escorted. There's no way we can get in there to finish the job."

"You need to finish the job to get the rest of your money." Von Theissen wanted to get the man focused on finishing their assignment so he appealed to greed.

"There is nothing we can do until they move him."

"And then?"

"Unless they move him in an ambulance, we need something that will destroy an armored car."

"Like what?" Von Theissen knew he was not going to like the rest of this conversation.

"Anti-tank rockets. More than one because we may have to take out the whole convoy."

"What kind and how many do you want?"

"Six American M72 LAWs."

"Done." *Holy shit*, von Theissen thought, *this is going to get expensive*. He was pretty sure he could get them. *Cost is not an issue; the new Fourth Reich will be worth it*. "I'll arrange for delivery in forty-eight hours. That should be soon enough." Von Thiessen was thinking that they would not want to move von Ritter for a few more days.

"Yeah, well I am not finished with my list."

"What else do you need?"

"The route. We need it in advance so we can set up an ambush."

Von Theissen thought that with their contacts within the police and Bundeswehr, that would be doable. "Understood. I'll work on it. What else?"

"More money. To blow up one of those vehicles, my associate and I will have to be a lot closer, i.e. within a hundred meters, which means more risk. More risk means more money."

"How much more?"

"I want a million marks for each of us."

"You're out of your fucking mind." But von Theissen knew he would have to give in; he had no choice unless he wanted to start all over and find another team. *From that perspective, these guys are cheap at twice what they are asking.*

"Not if you want this ex-paratrooper killed."

"Half when I deliver the missiles, half when you finish the job," Von Theissen countered.

"No, we want half of it now and the balance with the missiles."

"This extra risk would not be necessary if you had not *bungled* the job the first time, when it was easy. Half with the missiles, the rest when you have succeeded, *if* you succed. Call me in eight hours to make arrangements."

Von Theissen's hand was shaking when he put the phone down. He spilled some of the thirty year old Highland Park single malt scotch as he poured four fingers' worth of the expensive amber liquid into a glass and then finished it in two gulps. Back in his chair, he had trouble dialing the number for a call he did not want to make, thinking *This is more dangerous than flying fighters on the Western Front.*

Friday, January 21st, 1977, 1249 local time, East Berlin

Krasnovsky waited until late in the lunch before getting to the real topic of the meeting. Throughout the meal, Grünewald had the look of a man who had valuable news but was prepared to hold onto it until asked. *Interesting.* "So how was your visit with young Herr Stiglitz?"

"I think the best word to describe it would be fatherly." Grünewald thought his Soviet counterpart would appreciate what followed.

"How so?"

"Well, first, young Stiglitz and his friends have learned that generating political change in a democracy by using violence is a lot harder in practice than in theory. One's fellow citizens get very mad when you start setting off bombs." Grünewald savored his beer. "So lesson one is, you need much more than radical ideas and kilos of Semtex."

Krasnovsky twirled spaghetti onto a fork capped with a spoon, waiting for lesson two.

"I think for the first time in his life, he is afraid of getting caught and maybe dying. Stiglitz built and set off bombs and didn't think about much else, other than fantasizing about how he is going to change Germany. He is now dealing with how it has changed his life. He knows that he has crossed a bridge that no longer exists and he cannot go back. That's lesson two.

"Lesson three," Grünewald took a bite of his ravioli before continuing, "is that he now realizes that his actions have real consequences that may not be what he dreamed. Before Red Hand, spending the rest of his life by himself in a two meter by four meter cell was an abstraction. Now it is a real possibility. So, he's dealing with that as well."

"Sounds like Dieter Stiglitz just got a dose of reality."

"Very true. Then there is lesson four. He knows he is no longer free to go anywhere he wants. In fact, his options are very limited, and home to mother is not one of them. He now understands that he is a prisoner of his own actions and his jail is the DDR. I don't think he likes the idea of spending the rest of his life in our socialist paradise. He doesn't have the money to buy his long term safety, so his choice is to become a fugitive on the run or a guest in a country where the dictator may decide to sell him out to the highest bidder. It is not a rosy future."

"So what are you planning to do?"

"At the moment, nothing. The propaganda ministry will have a field day when Dorf is brought to trial. My orders are to keep an eye on Herr Stiglitz and don't let him get captured or killed."

"How do you plan to do that?"

"We've added security in the area to keep him there. And we've told him to stay put and report to my office twice a day."

"Do you think the Americans or the Israelis would try to capture him, à la what they did in Argentina with Eichmann?"

"That is a very good question. But Argentinean society is more open and they are a democracy of sorts. The DDR is not. However, that is why I am very interested in this Haman fellow. If Haman and his friends are in Europe, I have to believe the Americans may try. My director doesn't agree with me, and the generals laughed when I asked them if the Americans could sneak in a small raiding party. They said it was impossible. But I am also paid to evaluate possibilities, which I made known through the proper channels, so they are on the record. So now I am, as they said after the last war, just following orders."

Krasnovsky laughed at the former SS officer's reference to the excuse many of his peers used to justify their war crimes. "Well, good luck." Krasnovsky reached into his coat and pulled out a sealed envelope and slid it across the table. "This will keep you awake at night."

"Why?"

"It took some work, but I got a copy of the complete KGB folder on a Navy SEAL by the name of Cabot. Lieutenant Colonel Loi told you that Cabot worked with Haman in the past. Now he is assigned to a secret unit called SEAL Team Six which focuses on hostage rescue and hunting terrorists. Connect those two dots and I agree with you that the chances the Americans will try something go way up."

Monday, January 31st, 1047 local time, West of Bonn

Twelve kilometers from Bonn, the pilot of a forest green and white Messerschmitt-Bölkow-Blohm Bo 105, bearing police markings in large green letters and the shield of the state of Hessen, kept his speed at around one hundred and twenty knots until he was over the lawn and gardens of an isolated estate. He then gently flared and set the skids on the center of a helipad, a large slab of concrete beside the gray stone building that the government uses for foreign guests.

Starkeholz was the first to step out. He bent over to keep his head well below the rotor blades and tried to make himself useful by holding an extra blanket as a male nurse assisted von Ritter into a wheel chair. He was following the nurse on the walkway when one of the guards ran up to him.

"Sir, there is an urgent phone call for you. I'll hold the helicopter; the caller said you would be getting back on it."

Struggling to control his breathing after sprinting to the house, Starkeholz gave his name and listened for about two minutes before speaking into the phone. "Keep the area clean and don't let anyone touch anything. Get a hazardous materials team on the way, and make sure the policemen stop traffic so the helicopter can land on the highway. I'll be there in less than thirty minutes."

The whine from the Bo-105's engines got more noticeable as Starkeholz stepped outside. He met von Ritter as he was about to be wheeled into the house. "There's been an interesting development," he murmured, in answer to the look of inquiry on the injured man's face. "I'll be back as soon as I can and will tell you more when I know more. Enjoy the hospitality. They'll take good care of you here."

Forty minutes later, Starkeholz was looking at two bodies in Bundeswehr camouflage uniforms, sprawled alongside six olive drab boxes set in a neat row in a small clearing off the road near the U.S. Army hospital in Landstuhl. The scene stank from a mixture of fresh vomit, urine, and human excrement. Next to each body was a U.S. M72 Light Anti-Tank Weapon, and with the tubes pulled out to extend the trigger mechanisms and sight, they were ready to fire.

"Has anyone touched anything?" Starkeholz demanded of the Landespoleizei sergeant, the senior policeman on the scene.

"Other than to determine they were dead, Herr Hauptpolizeidirektor, no. That's when they called it in and were told to call you. The officers stayed about five meters from the bodies as instructed."

"Good." Starkeholz turned to the head of the hazardous material team. "There is a high probability that these men were killed by sarin on the missiles or the cases. You need to test for that poison and others as soon as possible, and tell me what you find. Then we need to search for their vehicle and check it as well. It can't be far from here. Understood?"

The men in the yellow suits were holding their helmets and hoods in their hands. The team leader stood one step in front of the others. "Jahwohl, Herr Hauptpolizeidirektor."

Starkeholz looked around and pointed to a large tree with his hand held radio. "I will wait over there."

Fifteen minutes later, the leader of the hazardous materials team approached, pulling off his hood and then his oxygen mask. Despite the below freezing temperature, he was sweating.

"Sir, here are the car keys we found along with the wallets. They are not contaminated. Someone sprayed the sarin on the rocket tube that is pulled out to cock the weapons. When I was in the Bundeswehr, they taught us to pull the tubes out, cock, and shoot in one quick motion. My guess is whoever sprayed them was counting that they would follow that procedure, and by the time the missile was on the way, the shooters would be dying. I think they got a missile out and cocked it to get it ready then died before they could shoot. My question is, who or what target was valuable enough to use anti-tank missiles on, and then poison gas to silence these guys?"

"Thank you. Let's just leave it that the target was someone who is helping us preserve our government from an internal enemy. What are you going to do with the missiles?"

"Take them back to our lab and examine them further before we destroy them. We'll also test the area around the bodies to make sure there is no sarin residue and put the bodies in the bags. We'll follow the medical examiner to his lab where we can help him decontaminate the bodies and clothing."

"Excellent." He turned to two members of his team, who had arrived on the scene and were standing off to the side listening. "See if you can find a car near here that matches these Mercedes keys."

"Sir, we saw a gray Mercedes 190 sedan parked over in the trees a few hundred meters away. It is just off a road and close enough to make it easy for men to carry the missiles here."

"Let's go." Starkeholz turned to the hazardous material team leader. "I need one of your team members to go with us and test the car before we touch it."

"I'll go." The man turned to his team and issued a series of orders, and one brought him a small, bright yellow tool box.

Ten minutes later, they were standing around a gray blue Mercedes pulled off the side of the road and positioned so that a driver could get in, start the car, and drive off. After testing for sarin and looking for possible explosives, one of the technicians opened the car and stepped back, motioning for Starkeholz to come over.

Inside, Starkeholz could see a Heckler & Koch G3 rifle with a scope along with another rifle. Next to the rifles was an olive drab ammunition can. "Check this out for chemicals and let's get a crime scene team here as well." The Hauptpolizeidirektor watched as the two rifles and ammo can containing twenty loaded magazines, along with two P-38 pistols with eight magazines, were placed on the ground.

"Sir, the registration on this car matches the identification from one of the bodies. It is an address in Frankfurt." The inspector was rummaging through the glove box.

"Good. I'll call to get a warrant and another crime scene team to meet us there, along with additional officers. We'll do the driver's place first, then the other address."

"Thirty minutes later, Starkeholz was standing outside an apartment door with his PPK drawn and held down, pointed at the floor. Stacked up on either side of the door were four members of the Hessian Landespolizei, each man armed with his nine millimeter Heckler and Koch P7 semi-automatic pistol. Starkeholz inserted the key in the lock.

When he felt the tumbler fall into place, he slowly rotated the handle and opened the door a couple of millimeters and then froze. A member of the bomb squad inspected the door jamb. With a tweezer, he pulled out a small piece of paper and showed it to Starkeholz.

"If this was on the floor, the residents would know someone had been in here."

The member of the bomb squad nodded and stepped to the side. "*Alles gut, geh.*"

Eight men poured in and spread out through the one bedroom apartment. Sixty seconds later, Starkeholz was standing in the center of the living room facing the police sergeant. "Nothing, Herr Hauptpolizeidirektor. Nothing."

"Have four of your men stay here. Call in to get more people to cordon off the building. Touch nothing and wait until the forensic team arrives, then help the inspectors talk to their neighbors. The rest of you come with me."

Starkeholz headed down the stairs trailed by by five men. It took about ten minutes to get to the second building and two families were startled to see five armed men climb the stairs to a fourth floor apartment. The four police officers took up positions on either side of the door while the man from the bomb squad inspected the door jamb. When he was finished, Starkeholz slid the key into the lock, felt it release and took a deep breath as he cracked open the door. Again, a small piece of paper fluttered to the tile.

The seconds that it took the man from the bomb squad to make sure there were no triggers attached to the door seemed like an hour, but as soon as he nodded, Starkeholz shoved the door open so violently, it banged off the stop as he charged was inside. Two steps into the room, he yelled "Everyone stop at once."

On the floor in front of him were two identical suitcases and duffle bags. "Make sure that no one is in here and then get into the hallway while I call the hazardous material team. Do not touch anything."

Starkeholz stepped back out onto the unheated landing and realized that he was sweating heavily. The first thought that went through his mind was that he was too old to be making forced entries.

Monday, February 1ˢᵗ, 0815 Local time, West of Bonn

Starkeholz was directed to where von Ritter was eating breakfast at a table that overlooked the snow-covered grounds. Von Ritter was in a wheelchair, his left leg stretched out on a board. "Good morning Herr von Ritter, I trust you had a restful night."

"I did. I knew better than to wait up for you. What was so urgent?"

"We are pretty sure we found the bodies of the men who shot you. They were killed by sarin, and when we searched their apartment, we found money sealed in plastic that was also sprayed with sarin."

"That is very good news. Where did you find them?"

"Along the route of your evacuation. They had six portable American anti-tank missiles at an ambush site. The route for the ambulance was a decoy; I had no intention of allowing you to travel by road. The team who planned the evacuation didn't know that, so we know where to start looking for a leak."

"I bet it will lead back to von Theissen and his friends." Von Ritter smeared apricot preserves on top of the melting butter on a hot mun brötchen before taking a bite.

"We think alike." Starkeholz pulled two Polaroid pictures out of his pocket of his sport coat. The name Sigfried Blucher was written on the white area at the bottom of one, and Gerd Werz on the other. "Do you know these guys?"

Von Ritter studied them for a few seconds. "No."

"I didn't think you would." Starkeholz waited until the sugar melted in his coffee. It gave him a chance to put a couple of rolls on his plate. "These guys weren't very sophisticated. We found several phone numbers on a piece of paper on their desk by the phone. One is Baron von Theissen's and another is for Godfried Himmel, who was a member of Otto Skorzeny's commando unit. He still follows Skorzeny around and we suspect he does dirty work for high ranking Nazis and SS officers. His specialty is torturing witnesses who can tie a person to a specific war crime into revealing what they know before he kills them and destroys any evidence they may have. We've not been able to pin anything on him, but when we do, he will go to jail for a very long time."

Starkeholz took a sip and sat back in his chair. "Himmel is tied to another guy by the name of Horst. He uses his jewelry stores as distribution points to ship and receive packages. Horst mailed you the information on your targets."

"I remember a man named Himmel. He was in the parachute regiment before he joined Skorzeny. Do you have a recent picture of Horst? I might recognize him. He used to look like a weasel."

Starkeholz laughed. "We have many pictures of Horst and Himmel, and I'll have a selection sent up."

"What's next?"

"I am going to be busy for a few days, but you stay here and heal. I have something in mind for you in a week or so."

The Same Day, 1440 local time, London

"Attention on deck," Josh called out as Admiral Hastings entered the secure briefing room at the headquarters, U.S. Naval Forces Europe. All four officers came to the position of attention, which was the same despite being members of the armed forces from four different countries: heels together, legs straight, shoulders back and thumbs along the seams of their trousers.

"At ease, gentlemen." Admiral Hastings looked at Josh and John. "The chairman was very impressed and pleased. Well done. I wasn't surprised at how good the plan is, but he was."

"Thank you, sir. That's good to know." As the unit's commanding officer, Marty spoke for all four.

"Haman, Osborne, are your wives here in London with you?"

"Yes, sir. They are at Grosvenor House just down the street."

"Gentlemen, please invite them to have drinks with us, if you don't mind. Jeanie has another shopping list."

"Yes sir, what time?"

"Five thirty."

The quiet hotel bar featured overstuffed chairs set in small groups that facilitated private conversations. Just a few of the tables were occupied.

As Josh and Rebekah approached, Josh could see the Admiral's aide gather up several stacks of messages into four colored folders and stuff them in his briefcase. Then he disappeared into a distant corner of the bar. Close enough to be on call, but not close enough to participate in the conversation.

By the time Rebekah sat down, John and Gwen Osborne arrived. Gwen was, as usual, dressed in fashionable, conservative clothes which didn't always show off that she could have been a model, even after having a baby.

Rebekah was jealous because she had to work like hell to loose the weight she gained during pregnancy.

After the drinks arrived, Admiral Hastings went through his notes on his wife's hand-written shopping list before handing it to Rebekah and turning to Josh and John, "Would you give your wives and me about five minutes?"

Surprised, the two young officers knew an order when they heard one. Josh picked up his beer. "Yes, sir. We'll be at the bar."

"Thanks." Admiral Hastings waited until the two officers were out of earshot and turned to the two surprised women sitting across the small marble-topped table.

"Please humor me and keep what I am about to tell you to yourself, for it is very sensitive information. I want you to know how much both our countries appreciate the outstanding work that your husbands and the others on the team have done during the past few months. I know they cannot tell you much, but you should know that this team has managed to find several members Red Hand and facilitate the capture of one of their members. That is in itself a remarkable accomplishment and a testament to them. Their involvement is not known to the German government at this time, and we want to keep it that way. We will tell the Germans, but how and when is above even my pay grade.

"According the press, we're at peace. Yet a nasty mix of ex-Nazis and Arab terrorists supported by Fatah, Stasi, and their KGB friends are killing people. This is a new kind of war that is waged without armies and navies going into battle. In many ways, the 66th Joint Observation Group is an experiment that, so far, has been very successful."

Admiral Hastings took a long sip of his Glennfiddich that emptied his glass. He was delighted when the waiter approached as if on cue and asked if he wanted another glass of either the twelve or twenty-five year old single malt. He chose the older and beamed. When the waiter retired from delivering his drink, he returned his attention to the ladies.

"One last point, which I am sure you already know but needs repeating, is that you cannot talk about the unit, period. Public conversations about the unit cannot happen. The members of the unit will get recognized, but there will be no publicity."

Gwen nodded her head. "I understand. My family has been involved in secret operations since my cousin, Lord Louis Mountbatten, helped form the Royal Marine Commandos and what we now call the SAS. My extended family has also paid a terrible price for its actions. I married John knowing that he was a Fleet Air Arm pilot and might be involved in this type of work. So, I am not surprised. Fate has brought him together with a good lot, for which I am very grateful. He's told me on numerous occasions that the worst part of working with Josh and Marty and the others is knowing that someday it will end."

"Admiral, when I married Josh, I knew what I was getting into," Rebekah said. She paused for a second. "I just didn't know how often."

"Well, my hat is off to both of you. I think you have the tougher job, because you don't know what your husband is doing, so all you can do is worry."

Both women nodded and Rebekah spoke. "Sir, thank you for taking the time to talk to us. Jeanie has taken me under her wing and on the last trip the three of us talked a lot. Gwen and I both know what is at stake."

"You are welcome, and I will pass your thanks on to Jeanie." Admiral Hastings waved to the two officers, who had just turned around to look at the threesome. "And I will save some marital strife and late night discussions by saying that this little conversation was *my* idea. Your husbands have not, repeat *not*, asked me to talk to you."

Wednesday, tFebruary 2nd, 1024 local time, Wiesbaden

Starkeholz finished reading the latest transcript from Dorf's interrogation and the list of evidence. He reached for the phone, thinking that what they needed was a link between the guns, the explosives, and the car to make sure that the courts would send Dorf away for life. He dialed a number and a familiar voice.

"Herr Grenfel, the next time your source calls you, can you ask him a question?"

"It depends. He doesn't stay on the line very long. What do you want me to ask?"

"Will he testify? It would help our case."

Grenfel had thought the same thing. "I will ask, but don't get your hopes up."

"If he cares enough to warn us, perhaps he cares enough to see this through. My guess is that he is with Mossad."

"Herr Hauptpolizeidirektor, are you suggesting that my source is an Israeli?"

"I am."

"Your hypothesis is logical based on who has been killed," Grenfel said reluctantly, after a long pause. "The Israelis have agents all over the Arab world."

Grenfel, knowing that his boss was former SS, was very careful when he brought up anything that had to do with Jews. He hadn't known that his own mother's family disappeared into one of the concentration camps until she mentioned it, after he told her he was picked to lead this investigation. Until then, he'd had no idea that any of his relatives were Jews. All she'd said when he was growing up was that her parents lived outside Nuremberg and died during the war.

"That is what I was thinking as well. Good day, Herr Grenfel."

Chapter 22
Round Up

Sunday, February 6th, 1977, 1537 local time,
Schloss Theissen

From the passenger seat in a helicopter approaching the large courtyard, the turn-of-the-century building looked impressive. This approach afforded von Ritter an unimpeded view of the three story gray stone mansion, its gardens in the back, and the long garage that housed the car collection.

The green and white Gazelle helicopter settled on its skids. Starkeholz got out first, along with the two members of GSG 9, West Germany's elite counter-terrorist and special operations unit. The two soldiers knelt in the gravel about five meters outside the rotor blades, and Starkeholz helped von Ritter and the other passenger out of the helicopter. As they exited, a small army truck parked at the edge of the forest that surrounded the house disgorged a dozen soldiers in full battle gear who deployed in pairs to pre-planned stations around the house.

Von Ritter used a crutch under his right arm; the other man leaned on a cane. Starkeholz supported each man with a hand on their elbows as they limped up the light gray granite steps toward the front door.

Sturmer, dressed in his clean, bright, white-starched coat with silver buttons and black trousers, stood in the open door surveying the unfamiliar scene and uninvited but recognized visitors. He addressed himself to Starkeholz.

"Excuse me, gentlemen, but we were not expecting either Herr Oberst von Ritter or Herr General Werfel. I'm sorry, sir, I do not know you. Who may I tell Herr Baron is here with these other gentlemen?" His tone was neither haughty nor rude, just firm and demanding. Their uninvited appearance, along with the soldiers, told him that *alles var nicht in ordnung*.

"I am Hauptpolizeidirektor Friedrich Starkeholz of the Bundeskriminalamt and I would like to speak with Herr von Theissen. You already know the distinguished gentlemen on either side of me."

Sturmer didn't have a chance to answer before von Theissen came out the door. Seeing the three men, he stumbled slightly and his tanned, handsome face paled. Von Theissen then gathered himself and came to a more formal position with his hands clasped behind his back in a position of superiority and power. But Starkeholz took the initiative and spoke first.

"Herr Baron, I believe you know Brigadier General Werfel and Oberst von Ritter. I am Hauptpolizeidirektor Friedrich Starkeholz of the Bundeskriminalamt. In another time, I was a SS Standartenführer in the Das Reich division." As much as he hated referring to his SS rank, he hoped his Nazi credentials made his appearance more credible.

"What is your business here? I don't remember inviting you. This is private property." Anger and defiance flashed in von Theissen's eyes.

"Herr Baron, it is my sad duty to tell you that I am here to arrest you—"

"For what!" Von Theissen cut him off.

"Herr Baron, at the top of the list is conspiracy to commit murder of at least a dozen of your fellow citizens. Two of the citizens, to be precise, General Werfel and Oberst von Ritter, both of whom I am happy to say are standing next to me, will testify at your trial. You are also charged with sedition. The charges will note you were a leader of a group of former Nazi government officials and members of the SS who were planning a coup. A word, Herr Baron, that you would understand which equates to sedition is *putsch*. I prefer the word treason, but our prosecutors have assured me there is a legal distinction." Starkeholz reached into the pocket of his suit coat and pulled out a sheath with a thick blue cover sheet bearing the Justice Ministry logo. "This is the warrant for your arrest and a list of all the charges which is, I am afraid, quite long."

Von Theissen grabbed the papers from Starkeholz's outstretched hand. He scanned the sheets, then slapped his thigh three times with the refolded papers in an attempt to dismiss their implication.

"So what happens now?"

"You come with me to Bundeskriminalamt headquarters, where we will formally arrest and charge you. There is a lot of paperwork that has to be completed in an arrest of a man of your stature, Baron von Theissen." Starkeholz wanted to play to von Theissen's ego. "At that time, you will have a chance to call your attorney, who will ask for bail at a court hearing, which will not be granted because the Bundesrepublik will justify its claim that you are flight risk. And then you will be taken to a jail cell, where you will stay except for court appearances and to meet your attorney in a secure room. Oh, once the arrest has been completed, the justice minister will hold a press conference announcing your arrest, as well as several others. He will be quite explicit on the charges, the type of evidence we collected, and the sentences the government will ask for if you are convicted. I am confident that if you elect to go to trial, you will be convicted and sent to jail for the rest of your life. Or, if the government and its allies decide to try you under the Nuremberg statues and you are convicted, you will be hung."

"And who are my fellow conspirators?" Von Theissen's sarcasm was obvious.

"Vicktor Horst and Alois Brunner have already been arrested. From Brunner's safe, we took several ledgers and bank records that are of interest to us. We found a treasure trove of information, as well as jewelry and gold bars, which we believe came from the concentration camps, in Horst's safe. The justice minister has already decided that he will have Horst tried for crimes against humanity under the Nuremberg statues. There are others on our list. Bruno Glockner, for example, fled the country, but we know where he is. Others, who were less involved in the murders, will be interviewed by the Bundeskriminalamt and the justice ministry."

"I see." It was all von Theissen could say. From his position on the top step, the leafless trees and the forest seemed starker and colder than ever before.

Starkeholz kept his hands clasped in front of him. "Oh, based on the evidence, I have no doubt you will be convicted, at which time the government will seize most, if not all, of your assets as a fine."

"What if I don't want a trial?"

"You could accept a life sentence without any chance for parole, so you will be in jail until you die. The fine will be less punitive, but large nonetheless."

"Not very pleasant choices, are they?"

"No. They are not meant to be. I am not sure which is worse, the murders or the planned *putsch*."

"Do I have any other choice?"

"Yes, one." Starkeholz reached into his overcoat and pulled out a Walther PPK and held it out. The black pistol was not much larger than his hand.

"I understand." Von Theissen did not move.

"Herr Baron, what is going on?" Sturmer took a step forward from his station beside the open door. Concern colored his voice.

"It appears that I am about to be arrested and charged with some very serious crimes; and, to use Herr Standartenführer Starkeholz's words, when I am convicted, I will spend the rest of my life in jail. Or, I can take matters into my own hands and end the process with what, I presume, will be honor. Am I correct, Herr Standartenführer?"

"My correct title is Hauptpolizeidirektor." Starkeholz kept his voice even so as not to betray his annoyance with von Theissen's use of his SS title. "I am no longer a Standartenführer. That role ended in May, 1945. However, Herr Baron, the justice minister has authorized me to tell you that if you take this third option, you will be buried with full military honors befitting your wartime rank and no mention of the charges will be made. There will be a small fine that will be taken from your estate. The legal matters will be handled discretely without any publicity."

"Herr Baron, I don't understand. Please explain." Sturmer took another step towards his employer and leaned forward.

"Sturmer, I am being given the choice of rotting in jail for the rest of my life or dying for wanting to create a Fourth Reich. Do not worry; I have set up a trust fund that has enough money so you will be comfortable and not have to work for the rest of your life. You will also get the Mercedes 220SE that you love to drive. After I am gone, it will be up to my heirs to decide what your role will be in this household, but whatever happens, you will have plenty of money that no one can touch as a reward for your loyal service for all these years. That is also true for the rest of the household staff."

"But, Herr Baron, you are not dead."

"Unfortunately, that will change today, as I will be soon be in another world." Von Theissen's voice had the softness used when talking to a loved one or child. He turned to face the three men facing him.

"Herman, I gather you do not want a stronger Germany, independent and in control of its destiny?"

"Albert," Werfel replied, "I like where Germany is today and where it is headed. It is painful for me to stand, plus it is cold out here, and we're not going to have that discussion again. Suffice it to say that every day I wake up, I thank God that the Third Reich is dead and gone."

Werfel looked around before he continued. "The trouble with you, Albert, is that you don't realize how much better you have it today than you did under Hitler. You had one of your supporters who will now go to jail for a long time put a bomb in a jet and make sure that airplane was assigned to me. That act disgusts me and shows how far you have fallen from the very capable fighter pilot I once knew."

"Von Ritter," Von Theissen pointed to the former paratrooper. "You are a hard man to kill. Do you not want a strong Germany?"

"Von Theissen, I agree with General Werfel. I didn't trust you for a minute, which is why I kept detailed records of everything that went on. What little respect I had for you as a fellow warrior went out the window when we found sarin on the bills that were our last payment. To you and your kind, the four of us were items to expunge when we became loose ends. I vowed I would get even. I am not proud of what I did for you, in fact, it bothers me every day. I will have to live with that for the rest of my life and that is my burden. But I am proud of the fact that I found my moral compass and turned you in so you can rot in hell."

Von Theissen looked up and admired the clouds and blue in the cold sky; he took the pistol out of Starkeholz's hand along with the magazine. "It is a lovely day to fly and a good day to die." After inspecting the magazine with its single bullet, he slammed it into the pistol, pulled the slide back, and let it go to make sure the single round was seated in the chamber.

Von Theissen clicked his heels together and stuck out his arm in a Nazi salute. "Heil Hitler. May god grant Germany the Fourth Reich." Then, he put the pistol under his jaw and pulled the trigger.

Chapter 23
Icing on the Cake

Monday, February 7th, 1977 1225 local time, Trelleborg, Sweden

Josh kept looking at the pitch black sky that made the gray-black water of the Skaggerat even darker. White foam from waves made by the bow quickly faded as he and John stood along the railing on the upper deck of the Trellborg to Sassnitz ferry. "The storm is coming in fast. If the weather guessers are right, there should be several inches of snow on the ground when we get to Sassnitz. That should keep Stiglitz and his friends holed up in Zehlendorf."

John checked to make sure his charcoal gray ski parka was zipped all the way up to the fold of his heavy, dark gray wool turtleneck. Flakes of blowing snow were collecting on his beard. "Yes, the worse the weather, the better for us."

"Maybe it will make the East Germans less vigilant."

"If it does, that will be a first. You know, you are taking a considerable risk entering the DDR a second time. I just hope you are right that by the time they recognize you, we'll be long gone."

"Me too. My other choice was to swim in, and that's something I've not been trained to do. This is just one of those compromises. I hope my scruffy beard and long hair will make it harder for them to recognize me."

"I guess I would have made the same choice. You realize, once we get off this ferry, there is no turning back."

"Yup, we're committed."

John pointed at the pier illuminated by yellow-orange lamps about half a mile away. "Show's on. Let's get in the car."

Render Harmless

After seven hours at sea, the Koenig IV, a fifty-three foot Hatteras Sport Fisher, was plowing through the gentle swells of the Kattegat where the waters of the Baltic are tamed by the shelter of the Danish island of Lolland. Lev was down in the cabin with Colour Sergeant Calhoun, while twenty-five year old Charles Wilson, the Navy intelligence specialist from the DIA, was on the raised bridge of the thirty ton boat.

A subdued background hum from the twin six hundred and fifty horsepower Detroit 8V71T1 diesels could be heard in the cabin. On the bridge, only a slight vibration indicated they were running. When they'd picked up the boat, Lev had acted as an interpreter for Wilson, but it had been clear that the young man was familiar with the controls, which he said were identical to those on his father's fishing boats, just a whole lot newer.

Wilson kept the Hatteras at a comfortable twelve knots on a southeasterly heading until Lev, who was using the boat's radar to fix its position, climbed up on the bridge. "Head one-eight-zero for one hour and keep it at twelve knots over the bottom."

Then Lev went below. "Ron, about fifteen minutes to drop off."

"Right. We'll finish getting dressed."

On the fantail, Van der Jagt helped Bentley, Goodson and Thorne lay out the equipment bundles that they would take ashore.

Before the four SAS troopers inflated the rubber boat, Wilson slowed the Hatteras until it was just making steerageway to make it easy to slip the boat over the side and manhandle the outboard motor onto its mount. After a couple of pulls, the one hundred and fifty horsepower outboard engine started. Van der Jagt let it idle for three minutes to make sure it was ready, as all four swimmers and the colour sergeant got into the boat. From the deck of the Koenig IV, the muffled outboard motor couldn't be heard, even with the two diesels at idle. Van der Jagt slipped the Evinrude motor into gear and the boat pulled away.

As they approached shore, he leaned forward. "Calhoun, are you sure the beaches are not mined?"

"Trust me, they're not. If they were, the East Germans couldn't go there on vacation. The beaches are patrolled and there's wire and mines offshore that we can get through, but in this weather it'll be a piece of cake, because the guards will be staying inside as much as possible. Even if they were out, we'd have to almost run over them before they saw us. I'm more worried about leaving footsteps in the snow that they can follow than I am about being seen! See you in a couple of hours. Don't be late!"

The Colour Sergeant motioned to his men and, one by one, they slipped into the thirty-four degree water, each pulling a buoyant equipment pack containing weapons and ammunition, winter clothing, and equipment for two men.

Van der Jagt waited until their bobbing heads disappeared into the blackness before heading back to the Koenig IV on the reciprocal heading of his run in. He knew enough about radar not to worry about the East Germans seeing the small radar reflector on top of the motor. Twenty minutes later, he peered into the driving snow, thinking he was lost in the blackness and had underestimated the drift caused by the current. Then, off about twenty degrees from his port bow, he saw a blinking light; and ten minutes later, he was being helped over the side of the Koenig IV.

The Same Day, 1935 local time, Sassnitz

The driving snow made it very hard to see as Josh drove the black Volvo wagon off the ferry, and he was glad both cars had new all-season tires. There was about two inches of snow already on the ground, and in the headlights, the large white flakes looked like millions of white blobs floating in front of a curtain of darkness.

The glum customs official, who was unhappy because he had to work in the small shed that a small kerosene heater couldn't keep warm, stamped the South African passports Josh and John presented and their route card without saying a word or looking at them. He was more interested in moving the line along so he could go back inside than monitoring who was coming into the DDR. Josh noted that the time stamp was 1935.

Once out of the glare of the lights at the ferry terminal, John slid the PRC-68 radio out from its hiding place under the dash and answered the call "Rolling" with two clicks. Little was said as they drove through the driving snow deeper into the DDR.

Josh kept his eyes on the road as they passed through the western edge of Straslund, two towns west of Sassnitz. "Keep a sharp look out, or we'll drive right past Grünhufer Bogen Strasse." In the darkened town, the glow from the few street lights was dimmed by the heaviness of the falling snow. "There it is." The white type on the blue street sign on the building was half hidden by the snow that had collected on the top of the sign.

The Royal Navy lieutenant nodded. "Turning one." The radio call told the second Volvo they had turned on Grünhufer Bogen Strasse.

About a minute later, "Turning one" meant that Marty in the second dark blue Volvo wagon had also found the street.

Three minutes later, Josh slowed and turned left. John radioed, "Turning two."

From Barthter Strasse Josh turned right for the short jog on Stralunder Strassse to Prohner Strasse when the radio crackled again. "We're here, waiting." Two clicks acknowledged, and Josh slowed to a crawl as both men started to look for a flashing light on Gross Mohrdorf Strasse. Here the snow was already three inches deep.

"There." John saw two long followed by two short flashes of light.

Josh stopped the Volvo and two men came out of the darkness. One opened the rear hatch and tossed two heavy bundles into the Volvo. Twenty seconds later, the two men were in the Volvo and Josh was moving again. About a minute later, the AN/PRC-68 crackled again. "Three and four aboard."

Josh turned to Sergeant Bentley. "How was the swim?"

"Cold." Bentley was pulling off the top of his rubber suit and stuffing it into a canvas bag. "We made it right through the gap between the Grosser and Kleine Werder and then to the beach. Van der Jagt got us about a half mile from the gap, and in this muck no one saw us. Then it was a quick scamper to the pick-up point. Piece of cake."

By the time they reached the outskirts of Rostock on Route 105, Sergeants Bentley and Goodson had swapped their rubber suits for jeans and dark gray turtleneck sweaters. The guards at the checkpoint south of Rostock didn't come out of their little shelter. Instead, they motioned for Josh to come in and get his travel permit stamped.

Once clear, Sergeant Goodson handed John a map, along with satellite photos with distances to each check point on the route to Zehlendorf marked. It was about twenty kilometers to Laage and then another twelve to the turnoff to Zehlendorf. The speedometer said they were making about sixty kilometers per hour, which was faster than Josh first thought they could go on the sloppy, slushy roads. The two drivers alternated speeds and varied the distances between so as not to appear to be in a convoy.

By the time they passed Laage in light but steady traffic on the unplowed autobahn, they were driving through four inches on the ground. The forecast said by the time the storm moved off to the east, it would leave almost a foot along the coast and six to eight inches inland around Zehlendorf.

"Turning nine." This was the turn off toward Zehlendorf. Each turn along the route was numbered, making it easy to follow as well as keeping radio calls short and hard to intercept.

"Three hundred meters behind you."

Josh could make out the dim view of lights, but as soon as he turned east, he slowed. Three vehicles passed and then one turned to follow.

"The satellite photo says there should be a BTR-60 about a click and a half down this road," John said, looking at the map and the photo that showed the eight wheeled armored personnel carrier parked off to the side of the road. Josh turned off the lights and kept going at about twenty kilometers per hour in the darkness.

"My guess is it is about two to three hundred meters in front of us." Josh let the car slow to a stop. "I don't think they can see us in the snow."

"Be right back." Both Goodson and Bentley got out, pulled up their snow suits over their civilian clothes and trotted off, each carrying their Skorpion machine pistols in one hand and an olive drab canister in the other.

Josh let the car idle and the wipers on to keep the snow from obscuring their view. While they were waiting, he looked at the satellite photo. "The turn off to the compound is just past the BTR. When they get back, we'll park about three hundred meters past the turn off and go do our thing."

Goodson and Bentley appeared out of nowhere ten minutes later, slipping on the frozen slush beneath the snow.

"They'll be asleep for a while." Sergeant Goodson wasn't even panting. "The BZ Agent 15 knockout gas worked like a charm. They had the hatch propped open for ventilation so I lit one spray can off and fed it into the passenger compartment's intake, and then once that one had been going for about thirty seconds, we tossed the other into the cabin. I took a deep breath as I opened the side hatch and they were already out cold. We unloaded their weapons and dropped them into the snow about halfway back here. They'll wake up with a nasty hangover, but other than that, they'll be fine."

Five minutes later, all eight men got out of the two Volvos parked two hundred meters north of the compound. Josh pocketed the PRC-68 along with a spare battery as he slung the .32 caliber Skorpion vz.61 over his shoulder and buckled a harness over his white snow suit that held eight 20 round magazines, two anti-personnel grenades, a holster with a CO_2 powered gun and six tranquilizer darts. Two extra CO_2 cartridges went into his pants pocket. He figured the Skorpion was about five pounds with the magazine and suppressor; all told, he was carrying about twenty-five pounds of essential equipment.

He turned to Marty, "We'll need an hour. Call me if you need to talk." He stuffed the ear piece to the PRC-68 into his ear. "John, let's go. We got a schedule to keep."

John had four anti-personnel grenades on his harness but no dart gun. "You're sure about this?" This walk through the woods was a lot more than bird and deer hunting around his family estates. They were deep in what Josh referred to as Indian country.

"You bet. Walk in the park." Josh paused and smiled. "Plus, we have a great back-up plan, and a back-up plan to the back-up plan."

"That's what Marty said you would say!"

Both, as they had practiced, counted one hundred steps and paused. They looked through the falling snow, which was ell above their ankles and gettingt deeper, and listened. The stops let John's compass settle so they could maintain the proper heading. Based on the imagery, their destination was just under fifteen hundred meters from where they'd started.

Forty minutes after they started out, both men were on one knee, crouching behind a tall pine tree, while John pointed out the direction of their next move. "It should be less than a hundred meters."

Josh gave him a thumbs-up, slid the safety off the Skorpion, and made sure he selected the semi-automatic instead of full automatic mode so he could conserve ammunition. Satisfied, he slid a tranquilizer dart into the breach of the CO_2 gun and cocked it before making sure the safety was engaged. Then he headed toward his destination with his senses tuned to his surroundings.

After a quick reconnaissance of the outside of the compound, Marty signaled for the three remaining fire teams to deploy. Marty and the senior chief went to the back, while the soldiers went over the wall. After making sure no one was in the workshop, Colour Sergeant Calhoun and Sergeant Thorne crouched on either side of the front door of the stone and concrete building as they each pulled the pin out of a G60 stun, also known as a flash bang grenade. Sergeants Bentley and Stockton were by the one window that overlooked the compound.

In the back, Marty and Senior Chief Jenkins stood next to two large windows that looked out over the snow covered fields. After detaching a G60 flash bang grenade from his web gear, Marty held up three fingers and Senior Chief Jenkins acknowledged by pulling the pin on his grenade and squeezing the handle to keep it from arming until he tossed it.

"Teams 2 and 3 in position and ready." The words came from Calhoun via the headset and short range radios.

"On my mark. Three, two, one. Go." On the last word, the men smashed the windows with their elbows and tossed the G60s inside.

The one hundred and sixty decibel noise from each grenade deafened everyone inside, and the three hundred thousand candlepower of light flashing through the house simultaneously woke and stunned the occupants. Inside, Marty and the chief found two couples sitting up in their beds, wondering what just happened. In another larger room, the muffled staccato sound of suppressed Skorpions being fired was interrupted by three rounds fired from an AK-47.

Chapter 24
Stick Time

The Same Day, 2223 local time, Zehlendorf

"What the fuck!" Josh muttered the words loud enough for John to hear. Josh peered into the cockpits as he darted from one Mi-2 to another. "These are hangar queens that have become parts bins. Their parts situation must be worse than ours!"

"I don't think this is an operational base. These are derelicts and there is no supporting equipment for the helicopters around here." After peering into a third helicopter, John turned to his friend. "And, as you know, the Russians are famous for decoys."

"That's true, but we've seen enough imagery from different days to suggest that they operate helicopters out of this facility. I *saw* one take off when we were here last month. We just have to find them."

"I agree, but we don't have much time to look around."

"True." Josh spun around in the shadow of one of the Mi-2s that had flat tires. "Let's look over there by those trees."

The two men were moving behind the row of scavenged helicopters when Josh raised a balled fist, signaling John to stop. He held up one finger and pointed. The glow of a cigarette held by a solitary, hunched over figure pinpointed his target. Josh mouthed the word "sentry."

It took Josh another five minutes to creep within fifteen feet of the lone East German soldier bundled up against the cold. *Where there are sentries, there is something to protect!* Behind the sentry were other helicopters and very little snow on the ground. Josh looked up and understood why the man was standing where he was. He was under some kind of netting. As Josh and John moved back into the trees, they counted four Mi-2s in the nearest row.

From his new position, Josh could see a second sentry moving toward him, also head down and hunched up against the cold, his AK-47 slung over his shoulder. Josh pushed John back so they could retreat farther into the woods.

"You ready? We're on our way." The PRC-68 crackled in his ear.

Josh turned his head to muffle his voice and pressed the mike switch. "Not yet, but we'll be ready when you get here." Two clicks acknowledged his call. Josh felt the fleeting doubt that he may not be right flash through his mind. "I'm going to take them out one at a time with the dart gun and then go look to see if these are workable helos."

"Let's not shoot anyone unless we have to. I'll cover you."

"Agreed. Let's move in amongst the helos. My bet is that they'll not expect anyone coming from that direction and it will enable me get closer. We'll pick a helo after we put them down."

Just as the two pilots were getting ready to come out from the woods and under the shelter, the guard called out to his compatriot. John looked quizzical, and Josh translated. "He just wanted to see if his companion was awake."

John nodded.

"I'll take him out. If he goes down without a sound, we sneak up on the other one and do the same. If he makes noise, be ready to shoot."

John nodded again and watched as Josh moving from helicopter to helicopter as he closed on the East German. He unfolded the stock of his Skorpion.

Josh said "Allo" as he stepped out from behind the fuselage of a Mi-2. The startled East German soldier froze when he saw the white snow suit, which gave Josh time to aim and fire a dart. The East German grabbed his neck and staggered three steps; Josh closed the distance separating them and lowered the unconscious soldier to the ground without a sound. He slung the man's AK-47 over his shoulder and stuffed the disarmed soldier's two spare magazines into one of his pockets.

It took another minute to get close to the second sentry. Josh, with the reloaded pistol hidden behind his back stepped out from behind the last Mi-2 in the row.

"Do you have a cigarette?"

While the East German soldier struggled to get his AK-47 into position to shoot, Josh fired the tranquilizer gun. The dart was visible in the man's cheek as he crumpled to the ground. Josh dragged him under the second helicopter in the line of four. Josh tossed the AK-47 into the trees and added the three magazines to his collection.

Next Josh opened the cockpit door on the Mi-2 at the end of the line and flipped a few switches, expecting to hear the familiar noises of a helicopter coming to life. "Shit, no battery. God dammit!"

John came around the front. "It's got fuel and fluids. What's wrong?"

"No battery."

John opened a hatch and stuck his head around the nose, "It's been removed."

Looking around, Josh pointed. "There, in that shed, the one with the thick cable. They may be on chargers in there."

John kicked the lock, which flew off the door. "Batteries." They lugged two of the heavy lead acid units over to the helicopter and slid one into position. As soon as the leads were connected, Josh flipped the battery switch to the 'on' position and the cockpit lit up.

"We have a taxi." Josh spoke into the handheld radio. "We're about two hundred meters to the north from where we thought the helos would be, where are you?"

"Five hundred meters east from where you are."

"When you come to the pad in the open, move to your right and follow it around and you'll come out under a camouflage net. You'll know you are there because the concrete doesn't have any snow on it. We're in the first Mi-2 on the left as you are looking forward."

Two clicks acknowledged his transmission.

"Josh, I hope you remember how to start this bastard."

"Piece of cake."

"And how many times have you started a Mi-2, much less flown one?"

"You already know the answer: never, but there is always a first time. And your point is?"

Josh didn't look up; he was busy familiarizing himself with the instruments and controls.

"And you're not worried about flying it?"

"Don't have time to worry. Look, it has a cyclic and a collective. How hard can it be?" Josh tossed John a loose-leaf binder with a set of laminated cards that had rested on the glare shield over the instruments. "These are just like ours. Here are the East German Air Force checklists."

John flipped through them before tossing them into the cabin, then pulled out the notebook of laminated checklists that had been brought ashore with the weapons. "Might I remind you that most of these helicopters were made in Poland based on a Soviet design? That means the first checklists were written in Russian. Then they were translated into Polish before translated into Arabic, then to Hebrew, and finally into English. I suspect that there are some variances between the original version and the one I am looking at."

"Minor detail. If you spoke German, then we wouldn't have that problem!" Josh grinned before keying the mike on the PRC-68. "How many? How long?"

"Six as planned. We see the open door of the helo."

Josh then turned to John. "We've got juice. See if you can make sure all the switches are in the right position so we can start while our passengers are getting on board. I'll help you with the German if you need it." With that, he pulled off his gloves and shoved earplugs into each ear.

Sergeant Goodson emerged from the clearing, towing a string of two men and two women with their hands tied. One of his arms was in a sling and his white insulated snow suit had a dark splotch on the front. Colour Sergeant Calhoun was towing a small sled made from a VW fender. On it, Josh knew from the plan, were the insulated wet suits, all their weapons, plus anything they'd captured.

As soon as the four roped individuals were hauled aboard, the Colour Sergeant tapped Josh on the shoulder, "Sir, would you mind getting this windmill started so we can get the fuck out of here? Goodson took a ricochet in the shoulder. I've got the bleeding more or less stopped. He should be fine."

Josh nodded and engaged the starter motor for the first engine.

"One more thing, sir." Calhoun's was grinning ear to ear as he spoke. "I don't want to put any more pressure on you than there already is, but Lieutenant Cabot said that you never failed to get him out of Indian country, no matter how difficult the situation. I do hope that this will not be the first time."

Josh stuck his middle finger up in the air and shouted, "Ye of little faith!" as the rotors began to turn and the second engine spun up.

"Sir, how much flight time do you have in the Mi-2?"

"Calhoun, I'll tell you when we get to Denmark."

"We've got company!" John pointed to a half a dozen figures running across the ramp.

Josh could see the lights in a building on the far side of the ramp coming on in a sequence. "Colour Sergeant, use the AK first and shoot only if you think they are going to try to prevent us taking off." He glanced down at the gauges and wasn't sure if they were ready, but he didn't have time to study them. The Mi-2 was vibrating and shaking like a helicopter, so it was time to find out if it flew like one.

Josh raised the collective and pushed the cyclic forward, and the Mi-2 began to roll on its wheels. John stuck his head out of the co-pilot's window and yelled, "The tail rotor is clear of the camouflage netting. Let's get the hell out of here."

With that encouragement, Josh pulled up on the collective and felt the helicopter wallow as it rose into the falling snow. As he pushed more on the cyclic and raised the collective a bit, he was delighted and surprised to feel the helicopter accelerate and rise, but it yawed ten degrees to the left. *Dummy, you forgot the rotor turns in the opposite direction from U.S. helicopters, so you have to add right rudder when you add power instead of left.* A touch of right rudder brought the nose back around to the direction they wanted to fly. More collective, and Josh noticed the gauge that he thought was the airspeed indicator was increasing and the one for rotor rpm wasn't going down. Both were good signs.

Josh glanced to his left and saw several East German soldiers waving at him as others aimed their AK-47s in their direction. Josh saw the muzzle flashes and sensed that the helicopter was taking hits but nothing on the instrument panel flashed in either red or yellow suggesting damage to a vital system. Unless something crazy happened, Josh could now concentrate on keeping the Mi-2 in the air.

More collective and another gauge, which might be the altimeter, began to increase. That was when a row of holes appeared in the side window and exited the front, showering both pilots with shards of broken Plexiglas. One came through the floor board and hit the rudder pedal, forcing the helicopter to yaw to the left. Another went past his face, close enough for him to feel the air it displaced and smell the powder that sent it in his direction.

The staccato of an AK and a Skorpion being fired at full automatic stopped and started. "They punched a bunch of holes in the floor and the back of the helicopter!" Calhoun was shouting. "There are at least six we can count and I know there are more in the tail. If you want, I can take a look!"

"OK. Please do. Let me know if there are any fluids in the cabin or dripping on the outside." Josh didn't know what else to say. By now the helicopter was well clear of the pad, passing one hundred meters in altitude and making what Josh thought was about one hundred and fifty kilometers per hour.

"Sir," Colour Sergeant Calhoun touched Josh's shoulder. "I ripped off the canvas cover to the tail pylon and can't see any visible damage with my flashlight. Looks like the bullets went in one side of the tail cone and out the other. There's no oil dripping from the overhead or on the outside of the helicopter. But then again, I'm no expert."

Josh turned and shouted back, "Thanks!"

"We're all O.K. back here, but Sergeant Goodson has a new hole in his body!" Colour Sergeant Calhoun yelled. "It's not serious; he'll survive and have one more scar to show his grandchildren. I'll get him bandaged up and he'll be ready to go in no time."

Then the helicopter entered the clouds, so Josh lowered the collective until the helicopter descended and they could see the ground through the streaming snow. Somehow, they had to fly through this muck and land in Denmark. Worrying about Sergeant Goodson's wounds was way down on his list of priorities.

"Turn left to three-three-five," John yelled in his ear. He had the map and the strip of satellite photos that Wilson had taped together that showed what was on the ground along their planned track. John pointed to a gauge in front of Josh that he had figured was the directional gyro. "That heading should take us the coast west of Rostock."

"Steady up on three-three-five." Josh was repeating the heading he was given to make sure he had it correct. "At this altitude, it'll be hard for them to track or, with this snow, even see us. The helo seems stable and easy to control at one hundred and fifty clicks per hour, so I'll keep it there. That's about ninety knots."

"There are no power lines or towers or major towns along the route. In this weather, I don't think they'll launch any of the fighters from the Rostock airbase."

"Me neither. Nobody in their right mind ought to be flying tonight!" Josh wondered for a second why he was trying to fly a stolen East German Mi-2 with an unknown amount of damage from AK-47 rounds in the middle of a snowstorm. The sum total of his instruction in the Mi-2 was a two hour conversation with an Israeli who'd flown a captured Egyptian Mi-2, plus several hours of studying pictures of the instrument panel and flight manuals. The Israeli's final words, "We captured several Russian and Polish built Mi-2s, and no two of them were the same," kept running through his mind.

Holding two hundred meters, Josh yelled, "See if you can figure out how much fuel we have. It was full when we took off. The data we got said that with full tanks, we can go about two hundred miles or about three hundred and fifty kilometers, which should be plenty to get to Denmark."

"Will do." John looked down at the chart. "Head three-three-zero now. Next landmark is the town of Schwaan."

"Got it. Turning to three-three-zero." Josh slowed the helicopter to one hundred and twenty kilometers per hour. His altitude, depending on the bottom of the cloud deck, was running between one hundred and fifty and two hundred meters. As they got closer to the Baltic, the clouds were forcing him to fly lower and lower.

John tapped Josh on the shoulder. "I'm pretty sure we're leaking fuel from one of the tanks. The manuals we have say there is one central tank that feeds both engines, but it also has a divider, so that below a certain level you won't lose all the fuel. The engines pull fuel from both sides. I don't read Russian or German, but this is the fuel gauge and it shows the left side has less gas than the right."

Josh studied the instrument panel for a few seconds and then pointed to a few switches. "I think that one is for fuel transfer. Let's see if we can pump fuel from the left side to the right. If our brief is right, we can keep both engines running from the right side."

"When we started, both fuel gauges were pegged at the top, so we should have had just over one hundred and sixty-five gallons or one thousand pounds when we took-off, which is good for about an hour and a half. At least that's what we were told. " John was shouting over the engine whine. "I don't know what this pig burns, but my guess is we are down to forty minutes or less of gas. We can fly ninety nautical miles at most, and it is eighty to eighty-five miles to the beach at Lolland. It is going to be close."

"Where will we be in twenty to twenty-five minutes?"

"My best guess is two to three miles, maybe more, off the coast. We don't have much of a headwind component."

"Ouch! We'll break radio silence ahead of schedule!" Josh was shouting over the whine of the engines. "Let's go as direct as possible. East Germans won't be able to shoot us down unless we run over somebody with a gun or missile. As soon as we get our feet wet and halfway to Lolland, start calling Lev."

John gave him a thumbs-up as Josh handed him the radio and waited as his co-pilot pulled the mike and earpiece cord out via his collar. "Meanwhile, I'll try to keep us from hitting something hard."

"Follow the road north for about seven minutes and then let's jog a bit to the east on a heading of three-four-zero to make sure we don't fly right over Bad Doberan. It won't cost us much fuel."

"Got it." Josh nodded and looked at his watch. By now he'd been able to identify all the instruments and was more comfortable flying the helicopter. While the presentations on the gauges were different than in the U.S. and British helicopters he'd flown, small movements of the collective and cyclic enabled him to watch the various needles move. It wasn't intuitive yet, but he was getting more and more confident.

"Searchlights!" John pointed to several strong beams of light off to their right that disappeared into the clouds. "I just want you to know that, no matter how this comes out, this is a much better alternative than stealing the BTR and crashing through the barricades at Selmsdorf or trying to get everybody into a rubber boat and then going out to the Hatteras. That looked very dicey to me. Now I can tell my grand children that I helped steal an East German Mi-2, got it shot up, and still flew it to Denmark!"

"You are assuming that we make it to Denmark and land in a controlled manner, as opposed to crashing on Danish soil or dying of exposure as we drown in the icy Baltic."

"I'm an optimist. Anyway, we should be coming up on a strip of water just east of Neinhagen in about three minutes." John held up the map, his finger pointing to the spot where they were, and lit the map with his flashlight with the red lens "Once we pass it, turn right to three-five-five, which should take us to this little strip of beach that sticks out from Lolland and the Danish town of Gedser. If we can make the thirty miles or so, it'll be a good place to put down, and Lev can pluck us off the beach."

"Turning to three-five-five." Josh kept looking straight ahead but shifting his scan from side to side to compare what the altimeter was saying with his own visual picture, all the while trying to limit his control inputs to minimize fuel consumption. They were down to around a hundred meters, and the heavy snowfall at times obscured the ground. He knew this was not the time to learn how to fly a strange helicopter on instruments. Once they were "feet wet" over the Baltic, he knew he could fly as low as ten meters over the water if he had too.

"Twenty minutes to flame out. That's based on the assumption we had thirty minutes of gas when we decided to transfer fuel. It should be enough. The right tank gauge isn't dropping and the left one is almost down to zero."

"John, I'm hoping that with this load, we can fly on one engine. Tell the guys in the back that we may lose an engine and may have to ditch. Don't open the doors. Then, remind me about our fuel state every five minutes. Who knows, the Russian fuel gauges may be accurate or they could be as unreliable as ours when the tanks near empty."

"Always the pessimist."

What little ambient light from Neihagen that was reflected by the clouds disappeared a few seconds after they went feet wet. The water was a gray black that looked as cold as death, and both knew survival in the Baltic would be measured in one or two minutes. It was only a question of what would kill them first—drowning as their water-logged clothes dragged them under, or the cold water stopping bodily functions. The snow kept spilling from the black sky as if it were trying to drive them into the water, and the lack of ambient light made the clouds fade into the inky blackness that surrounded the Mi-2. The water below was his only visual reference.

Josh wished he knew the true fuel consumption of the two Isotov GD-350 engines. The few notes that the Israelis provided about the Mi-2s had estimates which varied by country of manufacture. Averages were used in planning their escape, but both pilots knew they were just ballpark numbers, not something you could use for an accurate fuel plan. The good news was that even with eight people on board, the helicopter didn't feel as if it was overloaded.

The snow ended as if they'd gone through a door, and suddenly there was light from the stars and a half moon. Josh took a few seconds to get a good look at the water. "I don't know if this is a sucker hole or not, but I am going to climb to give the radio better range. Bad news is, the wind now looks to be about fifteen knots from our ten o'clock, reducing our ground speed by somewhere between eight and ten knots."

Josh noticed a subtle change in the engine noise, and then he could hear and feel the left engine unwinding. He compensated for the yaw brought about by the loss of power with the rudder pedals and lowered the collective to stop the climb. The Mi-2 slowed and Josh watched the rotor rpm decay a few percent as he added collective to compensate. So far, the helicopter was happy to fly on one engine and stay about three hundred meters off the water at a comfortable one-hundred and twenty kilometers per hour.

"So, we're now single engine. I'm not going to touch anything because I don't know what will happen. So far so good; the right engine seems to be humming along and I think we'll be able to maintain this altitude."

Escape to Denmark

John nodded in acknowledgement and held up the radio. "Lion, this is Butterfly. Do you copy?" John repeated the call and then shouted, "It may be too soon. On the ground this thing has at best a three to five mile range. At three hundred meters we will be lucky to get six, maybe eight."

"Assuming we're on course and he's where he is supposed to be, we should pass within range in a few."

John waited two minutes then keyed the mike again. "Lion, this is Butterfly, over."

"Give me the spare battery."

Josh pointed to the zipper pocket on his parker and lifted his right elbow so John could fish it out. The process took about a minute.

"Josh, fifteen minutes to flame out. If we're lucky, we may see the light from the house that is at the tip of the spit of land before we have to ditch. It is a few kilometers north of where we want to go, but it'll help us fix our position." John held up the map to show Josh about where they were over the Baltic. Both men knew it was a crap shoot now as to whether or not they would have to ditch in the thirty-four degree water.

John waited a full three minutes before making another call that was greeted with stony silence. He looked in the back at the four prisoners; they were slumped over on the middle of the floor, numb from the cold, vibration, and the shock of capture.

In the back corner of the cabin, Sergeant Goodson sat on one of the bench seats with his Skorpion on his lap; Major Calhoun was sitting with his back against the fuselage frame just behind Josh's seat. He too had his own Skorpion ready, and had laid John's and Josh's between his hip and the cabin wall as far from the prisoners as possible.

Josh flipped a few switches on the overhead on and off until he was satisfied that the external rotating beacon was on, as well as what he hoped were the position lights.

"Ten minutes to flame out."

"I'm going to hold three hundred meters until five minutes and then drop to ten meters, so when the right engine dies, all I have to do is flare and plop it in the water."

John nodded, and another radio call was answered with silence.

"Butterfly, this is Lion. Do you copy?" Lev's radio call perked John up.

"Lion, this is Butterfly, say your position?"

"Butterfly, this is Lion, do you copy?"

John returned the call but got no answer. He looked at his watch. "Seven minutes. They're calling us, but I can't reach them."

Josh nodded. "I'll hold at three hundred meters here for an extra minute or two."

"Butterfly, this is Lion, we see your lights. Looks like you are at about two hundred meters heading north and a mile from us. Say intentions. Over."

"Lion, we're headed for that small spit of land on the southern tip of Lolland, about five miles south of the town of Nyland. We're low on fuel and may have to ditch. Over."

"Roger. It is about two miles in front of you. We have you in sight and will follow and close the beach. Over."

"Two miles, and by my watch four minutes of gas."

"We're going to get as close to the beach as possible or land on it!" Josh shouted, and again reminded himself to make as few control movements as possible to conserve precious fuel.

"Beach, twelve o'clock, about half a mile."

"Got it. John, tell everyone to brace for a hard impact."

Josh heard John yell and the cabin got a lot colder as the doors were slammed open. As soon as he was sure that they were over the surf, he lowered the collective to let the helicopter descend, hoping for enough fuel to find a flat place to land when he heard the right engine unwind.

"Autorotating!!!" Josh yelled as he bottomed the collective and eased forward on the cyclic to keep the helicopter at about one hundred and twenty kilometers and hour. A glance at the vertical speed indicator told him they were descending at about three thousand feet per minute.

"We'll make it. Just try not to bend it too badly!"

The g forces from the flare caused the rotor blades to speed up and, for few seconds, compensate for the loss of engine power. Josh, with his stomach churning, allowed the nose to drop and the Mi-2 to settle. When he thought they were about ten feet above the sand, he pulled up on the collective and used the cyclic to make sure the helicopter was under five knots forward airspeed and level as he fed in just enough rudder to keep the nose pointed in their general direction of flight.

As the rotors started to slow, out of energy, The Mi-2 hit the sand with a sickening thump, followed by the screeching sound of tearing metal as it slid along the sand before coming to rest tilted down and to the right. As the rotor slowed to a stop, Josh sat, afraid to move. He was telling himself over and over again they'd made it when the Colour Sergeant opened the cockpit door, unbuckled his seat belt and shoulder straps, and pulled him out. Josh needed the soldier's support because his knees and legs were shaking so bad he was afraid they would buckle.

By the time they walked the hundred feet to where Sergeant Goodson was standing guard over the four prisoners in a small depression in the sand, Josh felt his heart slow down and his breathing return to normal. He realized Calhoun was speaking to him. "Sir, Van der Jagt is in the rubber boat on his way in from the

Koenig IV, which is about a hundred yards off shore. It'll take two trips, but we should all be on the yacht and on our way in less than fifteen minutes."

Josh nodded, still trying to convince himself that they'd made it. He looked back at the Mi-2, now sitting silent on a sand dune in Denmark, with its engines crackling as they cooled down. He wondered if either he or John had remembered to turn off the battery. It didn't matter now. Tomorrow, when the Danes found the bullet-damaged helicopter abandoned and out of fuel, this would be the lead story in the news. Then the search for defectors would begin.

For some reason, he looked at his watch; it glowed 2358.

"Colour Sergeant."

"Yes sir?"

"The answer to your question about my experience in the Mi-2 is, I now have a total of fifty-eight minutes of flight time and one take-off and landing."

About the time Josh crash landed the Mi-2, Marty was on the A-19 Autobahn approaching the city of Malchow, ninety kilometers south of Zehlendorf. The snow had lessened to flurries, and in the light traffic he was cruising at an easy one hundred kilometers an hour on a bumpy wet highway that had seen little in the way of repairs since the end of World War II. It was now a matter of driving the rest of the way to West Berlin, which he calculated in his head, for the umpteenth time, would take at his current speed just over an hour, more if he had to spend a lot of time at the checkpoint in Neurippin and exiting East Berlin. Forever, if their documents and cover story din't hold up.

He'd heard over the radio that the team had made off in the helicopter, so now his primary worry was whether or not the East Germans had figured that Zehlendorf had been raided and closed the borders.

"A penny for your thoughts?" Senior Chief Jenkins asked as they accelerated out of the Neurippin checkpoint, less than fifty kilometers from the outskirts of Berlin and eighty from the freedom of West Berlin.

"I was just reviewing the ex-filtration plan in my mind."

"Boss, it is a little late for that. We've executed two thirds of it already, and we're almost home safe and sound."

"I'm still worried about our Australian documents. So far, the Volkspolizei haven't paid much attention to us."

"That's because we don't look like we're military. Neither one of us have had had a haircut in three months, and you've got a two month beard. I couldn't grow a beard if my life depended on it. Our Aussie documents are good, and we sound like Aussies. G'day mate!" Jenkins tried to add some levity to the conversation with his proper lilting use of the traditional Australian greeting.

"O.K., but we don't know about Stockton and Thorne. We didn't see them at the last control point, and we don't have radios so we have no idea where they are."

"Sir, they're good men. Stockton spent two years as an advisor to the South African Special Forces Brigade and knows his way around both Cape Town and Durban. He was confident he could bluff his way through any questioning. He got Thorne up to speed on South Africa. Lev got the Israelis to make them emigration papers from the U.K. to South Africa as well as their passports. They they should be covered."

"I don't like leaving men behind. We came in as a team, we should leave as one." Marty kept his eyes focused on the road ahead.

"Sir, I don't want leave men behind, but we came in pairs and that's how we're leaving. So what are you worrying about?"

"That the photos on their travel documents are not the same as the ones that entered the country."

"Sir, the East Germans are not supermen, and they don't have the capability of comparing the photos on the original documents to the ones we have in real time. The originals are ashes in Zehlendorf that no one could piece together. So what else are you worrying about?"

"We know the helo took off and that's it. Josh knew he didn't have a good plan B or C. Stealing the helo was the only viable option. I don't like not knowing if they made it or not. "

Marty glanced down and realized that he'd accelerated to one hundred and forty kilometers per hour, which was above the speed limit. He lifted his foot to blend in with a few other cars.

"Boss, we had a very good plan, great support, and everyone knew the risks. We evaluated them one by one and we all agreed every element in the plan was feasible. It even got by the guys back in San Diego, who gave us an unqualified thumbs-up. We executed the body snatch without a hitch. The helos were where they were supposed to be and they took off. If anyone can fly a strange helicopter, Mr. Haman and Mr. Osborne can."

"That is exactly what worries me. So far, the plan is going as advertised. I'm waiting for Murphy to take charge."

"We've had setbacks. We're behind schedule for one, but we're managing and adapting. Goodson was wounded. The weather was worse than expected. Don't underestimate Lieutenant Haman's and your abilities. I've been on way too many missions with both of you, and you two are the best there is at this kind of op. The very thorough planning we went through is the surest way to keep Murphy out of the operation. If anyone could come up with, and execute a good, almost fool-proof plan, it is the two of you, which is why I am sitting next to you in this car."

"Chief, thank you for your support. But I don't like the word fool-proof, because only fools think their plans are fool-proof. So, are we the fools?"

"Sir, I've said my piece." Jenkins, who was never very talkative, changed the subject. "The sign just said we're ten clicks from Berlin."

"You didn't answer the question."

"Sir, Mr. Haman is not into one way missions, and neither are you, me, or the rest of the unit. The SAS guys would have raised the bullshit flag long ago if they didn't think we could pull it off."

"I hope you're right." Marty stopped the Volvo under the harsh yellow lights of the East German side of Checkpoint Charlie, the one checkpoint that non-Germans can use to drive in and out of East Berlin. The nose of their car was less than a foot from the red and white bar. Seeing the East German border policeman coming toward the car, he rolled down the window.

The Grenztruppen Oberfeldwebel, looked at the Swedish plates and walked around the Volvo before stopping at the driver's side window. After adjusting the AK-47's sling, he leaned forward. "Passport." Stale tobacco breath assailed both American's nostrils as he emphasized the second syllable.

Marty handed him the two passports with the visas, along with their travel log. The sergeant first class looked at Marty, then leaned down to get a look at Senior Chief Jenkins, then compared their passport pictures to the faces. He held up the palm of his hand. "Moment." The border policeman emphasized the second syllable, and the Americans, who had not said a word, took it to mean *wait*.

The East German nodded and disappeared inside the small building by the side of the road. Neither American spoke; they were worried that the East Germans might have someone with binoculars who could read lips. Three minutes later, the sergeant emerged, following a man with the gray Grenztruppen officer shoulder boards. As the two men got closer, Marty could see the four gold diamonds of a captain.

Two more guards came out and stood at opposite ends of the Volvo, and when the officer spoke, he said, "Bitte, please get out of the car."

Marty opened the door and stood up; Senior Chief Jenkins levered himself up and rested his crossed forearms on the top of the door.

"Here." The captain pointed to a spot that was about two feet in front of him. Both Americans complied and stood as if they never heard the words attention or parade rest. He held up each passport photo next to each man's face. "Australia?"

"Yeah, mate." Marty spoke.

"Business?"

"In Berlin."

"Why route?"

"Shortest distance from Stockholm to Berlin."

The East German looked at the trip log. "Long trip?"

"Yeah, mate." Marty was controlling his heart rate as if he was getting ready for a sniper shot. "Too much bloody snow. Took too long."

"Snow bad. Fast car?"

"No. Rental car. Not fast."

The East German smiled. "Moment." The East German reached into his coat and pulled out a piece of paper. As he unfolded it, Marty could see it had four photos. He tried to be casual as the officer held it up next to his face. When he held it next to Senior Chief Jenkins, the wind flapped the thin paper and he could see one of the pictures. He hoped the East German didn't see his reaction.

"Wait here." The East German officer pointed to the ground in front of them and spit out instructions in German. The three soldiers responded with "*Jawohl, Herr Hauptman.*"

Marty turned around in time to see the three soldiers open the doors and begin looking through their car. One man raised the hatch and looked through their two bags and rifled through the papers in the two briefcases. Satisfied, he shone his flashlight around the cargo compartment and then the area under the front seat. One of the men then picked up a pole with a mirror and looked up and down under the car before they raised the hood and looked over the engine compartment.

The sergeant approached the officer in charge of the checkpoint. *"Alles gut, Herr Hauptman. In ordnung."*

The captain handed Marty back their passports and visas. "Go. All is O.K."

"G'day, mate."

Neither man spoke until the soldier waved them through the checkpoint and they were into the traffic of West Berlin. "Boss, I didn't dare turn my head to see those pictures. Did you get a look?"

"Yes I did. They were pictures of Josh and me. All I could think of was that we were so near, yet so far from the border, and what were our chances if we made a run for it."

Chapter 25
WTFO A.K.A. "What the F___? Over"

Lev Mogen found the solitary pay phone at the end of one of the long, snow covered piers of the marina on the bay that emptied into the Baltic. The office was locked, and he suspected that the employees weren't expecting a boat to come in at this dull, dark hour of the morning. By now, the steady snow had been replaced by clouds that were becoming lighter gray with the approach of dawn. Sunrise was still hours away. The temperature gauge on the Hatteras said it was +2C.

The phone rang just twice after he fed his last one Deutschmark coin into the phone. "Herr Grenfel."

"Yes. Who's this?"

"Your source."

"Good to hear from you."

"I don't have much time, but I want to give you a present. In my possession, I have Schlemmer, von Berg, Gestner, and Kammer. I believe Gestner is the founder and commander of Red Hand, and his real name is Stiglitz. They are a little cold, but other than that, they are untouched and unharmed. I also have lots of documents that support my claim that they are the core of Red Hand."

"Where are you?" Grenfel grabbed for a pen.

"I will tell you that after we make a deal."

"What do you mean?"

"We need to agree to the terms under which we will hand them over to you."

"Which are?"

"You will not ask our identity, nor will you interfere with our departure from the turnover point or from Germany in any way. We'll give you all the evidence we captured with Red Hand. Then we will leave, and no one follows us, asks who we are, or how we captured them. I am sure your prisoners will be able to tell you how we got them and brought them out. Also, no pictures. The highest levels of the German government will be briefed later in the day as to who we are. At that time, we will make arrangements to give your government the intelligence we used to find these terrorists. Do you understand, and do you agree to these terms?"

"Yes, I do, and I understand."

"And, Herr Grenfel, let me make this clear, if you violate these terms, your government will be embarrassed, because how we found and captured them will be made public. Do you understand?"

"Yes, I do. There will be no slip-ups."

"Good, then I will meet you at the Prinz Marina in Helligshafen at 0600 tomorrow morning at the very end of the pier. The prisoners will be with me. You won't need an army, just a van to carry them away. We just want to hand them over and be gone."

"I understand."

"Good, see you tomorrow morning at six."

The Same Day, 0715 local time, East Berlin

His administrative assistant came running up and popped to attention as he was keying the numbers to the cipher lock on his door. "Colonel Grünewald, sir. There is an urgent request from General Geyer that you attend a meeting in his conference room at once."

"Did he say what the meeting was about?" The colonel had not even shaken the snow off his coat when he handed it to his assistant.

"No Herr Colonel, other than it was very urgent."

"Please tell him I am on my way."

Grünewald was surprised to find the Minister of State Security in the room along with the Volksarmee general who commanded the troops in the northern part of the country, his boss—General Geyer—and the Director of Main Coordinating Administration for the Ministry for State Security, which worked with other intelligence agencies like the KGB

"Colonel, I am very glad you could join us, please sit down." The minister closed the door to the conference room and continued speaking. "Last night, there were some developments that should get the attention of everyone in this room. One of our Mi-2 helicopters took off on an unauthorized flight from an air force base near Laage. Then we found out that an entire squad was knocked unconscious by drugs. In the same report, we learned that Dieter Stiglitz and three other members of Red Hand are missing. We found tracks between the Red Hand compound and the helicopter base, along with evidence that British flash bang grenades and Czech Skorpion pistols were used." The minister looked down at his note pad to avoid the stares he was getting from the men around the table. "There is more."

He used his forefinger to tap the table. "This is the most disturbing part of this episode. On their seven o'clock news report this morning, the Danish TV-Avisen told its viewers that a helicopter with DDR Air Force markings and numerous bullet holes crash landed on the island of Lolland. The press report made no mention of defectors, and there were no witnesses. This has the look and feel of a military operation carried out by of men who had excellent intelligence..."

The minister looked around the table and saw nothing but faces with blank expressions in front of minds thinking, *How can I avoid blame for this fiasco?* "So, Colonel Grünewald, since Stiglitz and Red Hand are your operation, let's start with you. What can you tell us?"

"That fucking Haman!" Grünewald laughed for a few seconds after he said the words. The others around the room looked at him as if he were a Martian.

"I'm sorry, Colonel, but the rest of us don't see the humor in the events of last night. Please explain who or what this fucking Haman is." The minister, who was anticipating an unpleasant session with President Honecker, glowered at Grünewald.

"My apologies, Herr Minister, but let me explain. I thought something like this might happen. In fact, I even asked our comrades in Moscow to provide me with background information on two American naval officers, one of whom was a Lieutenant Haman. We had nothing on the men, but the KGB had an extensive file." Grünewald nodded to the balding, overweight director in charge of their relationship with the KGB who, he was sure, had seen his request. He guessed it was probably stuck in a file, because the man was always looking for ways to hang someone, not connect dots.

"My analysis is the reason why I asked the Volksarmee's Landstreitkräfte to provide protection for Stiglitz, and why I sent pictures of two American officers, Lieutenant Haman and Lieutenant Cabot, to the Grenztruppen and the Volkspolizei to distribute at all the border crossings and internal checkpoints." Grünewald paused to consider how much he should reveal. "Last month, I was eighty percent sure that Haman entered the DDR using an Israeli passport with another man on a reconnaissance mission of some sort. At the time, I wasn't sure of the target."

"Why do you suspect this American?" The question came out of the jowly face of the Director for Main Coordination for Reconnaissance for the Minister of State Security.

"One part paranoia and one part tidbits of information that lead me to a hypothesis." He wanted to say that if the director ever read and analyzed the information he collected, he would have seen the same picture. But he dared not; the man was very well connected. "The conclusion I came to was that the Americans were planning an operation to either capture members of Red Hand or kill them."

"Again, why?" The man's beady eyes looked at Grünewald with a look that was meant to be penetrating, but the Stasi colonel took it as frustration. "Our friends in Moscow assured me that neither the Americans nor the British were about to try something."

"I saw those reports as well. However, it seemed to me that compartmentalization in either the British or American governments could result in such information being... less accessible than out friends in Moscow realized," Grünewald responded in an even, professional, non-threatening tone. He was skating perilously close to a critique of Stasi.

"So, what else do you know?"

The man wouldn't give up, so Grünewald would give him another two tidbits. "Stiglitz was pretty sure he was being followed when he came to the DDR the last time, and he recognized Haman and another man from photos we had."

Grünewald looked around the table, and it didn't bother him that all eyes were focused on his face. In a strange way, he was enjoying this, knowing that they would pay the consequences for the raid, not he. "From the KGB, I learned that Haman and a British Fleet Air Arm Lieutenant by the name of Osborne, and someone else who I think was an Israeli, visited the Simon

Wiesenthal Documentation Center in Vienna last fall looking for information on SS and Wehrmacht officers living in West Germany. The question I asked was, why?" Grünewald paused to let that sink in; every person at the table had at one time sworn allegiance to Adolf Hitler.

"My thought was that Haman and Osborne guessed that Red Hand had the backing of former Nazis." Another pause for emphasis. "About that time, two other events occurred. Haman and others were at the Vienna train station to meet some Soviet Jews. Later, I find out that two KGB officers disappeared and are believed to have defected."

The overweight general with the beady eyes and the responsibility for their relationship with the KGB wiped his sweaty brow and glowered at him. "The KGB told you all this?"

"Yes, sir, my liaison Colonel Krasnovsky gave me this information and has been very helpful. I am sure that he made sure that your office has copies."

The minister of the interior stopped taking notes and took over the questioning. "Very thorough. You think this American by the name of Haman led the kidnapping of the Red Hand terrorists, but you do not have any proof."

"Yes, Herr Minister, that is correct." He didn't want to say he would bet his life on it; anything said in a meeting like this could and would be twisted and held against you.

"Did you stress the danger to Stiglitz in your memo that requested protection?"

"I did. My memo was very explicit in outlining the danger to Dieter Stiglitz and the others in Zehlendorf." Grünewald looked around the table. "I didn't know when the kidnapping would occur, so I said the danger existed for the next sixty days, which would give me time to find more information. Sir, if you'd like, I can have my assistant bring my file of the memo, my notes and the report here."

"That won't be necessary," the Minister of State Security stated heavily. "Gentlemen, I have decided on what we will do. I want all photographs of foreigners taken at checkpoints from the past two days on roads that lead to Zehlendorf sent to Colonel Grünewald. He seems to be the one person who has an idea of what happened. He will be given all the logs turned in during the past two days from cars that have driven on roads near Zehlendorf. Colonel Grünewald will be responsible for the process of determining if or when the American Haman and any of his comrades entered the country, the route they took, and if any of our citizens were involved. I want to know who conducted this operation and will provide the manpower to find out. If Colonel Grünewald asks you for anything, you are to assume that request is coming from me."

Grünewald realized with chagrin that finding Haman had just been dumped into his lap.

"To my knowledge, no DDR citizen was injured. Embarrassed, yes, drugged, yes. Harmed or injured, no. The DDR will deny any relationship with Red Hand and will refuse to cooperate with the West Germans because West German criminals, not law abiding East German citizens, were kidnapped. Yes, they were living in our country, but we, as a nation, are innocent. Colonel Grünewald already has a theory that is plausible. Let's find out if he is right."

The Same Day, 0800 local time, West Berlin

About the time Grünewald was getting his instructions, on the other side of the Berlin Wall Marty was paying his hotel bill when Sergeant Bentley yelled across the lobby.

"Sir, you have to see this!" On the screen was a picture of an Mi-2 sitting on a sand dune near the water in Denmark. The smiling SAS trooper waited until the commentator switched subjects. "Sir, I don't speak much German, but I think they said was the Danes found this helicopter sitting on the beach on the island of Lolland. It has DDR Air Force markings and several bullet holes. They are assuming that it was flown there by defectors. The investigation has begun into how the helicopter got there and where the occupants went."

Marty felt relief course through his body. "They made it!!! Out-fucking-standing." Then he came back to reality. "That calls for a major celebration when we get back."

Wednesday, February 9th, 1977, 1400 local time, Bonn

Flanked by Starkeholz, who was grinning like a proud papa, and Grenfel, the two-hundred-and-twenty centimeters tall Minister of Justice, Reinherd Jurgend strode to a cluster of microphones in the entrance hall of the ministry. Behind them, it was a smiling who's who of the Bundeskriminalamt. Grenfel winced and squinted as the strobe lights flashed.

The minister, used to this type of scene, paused to let the photographers take their pictures. "I would like to announce that we have arrested four more members of Red Hand, including the man we believe was the leader of the organization. The arrests were made earlier this morning. Until we notify their families, we will not reveal their names. Their capture may lead to the arrests of those who helped them, and this should put an end to the bombings that have killed and injured so many Germans and our American and British friends."

The minister paused to let the reporters scribble their notes. "I hope that there will not be copy-cats. If they conduct attacks such as we have suffered for the past ten months, they too will be hunted down and brought to justice."

He placed "Herr Grenfel, working his hands on the shoulders of the men beside him. for Hauptpolizeidirektor Starkeholz, led this investigation from the beginning, and he will answer what questions he can about what is still an open investigation. Herr Grenfel..."

Chapter 26
Blowback

**Thursday, February 10th, 1977, 1048 Local time,
Sinai Peninsula**

The small convoy had been on the asphalt road between Bur Said, Egypt, and Gaza for over an hour. The plan was to have the four trucks parked in one of Fatah's secure garages in Gaza by sunset. So far, traffic on the well-travelled and often patched highway was moving at eighty to one hundred kilometers per hour, with gaps between clusters of trucks, busses, and cars.

In the passenger's side of the back seat of the Mercedes 220SE that was leading the convoy, the bearded Ahmed ibn Khaldun was deep in thought as he watched the desert slide by. Next to him, a clean shaven man dressed in an expensive three piece suit was using his briefcase as a desk as he flipped back and forth through several printed documents, making notes with a Mont Blanc fountain pen.

Up front, Khaldun's driver and bodyguard were relaxed as they maintained a speed that was ten kilometers per hour slower than the top speed of the following trucks, which were loaded to their maximum weight of three and a half tons. Every so often, Khaldun would turn around and see the vertical grills of the first of four GAZ V-8 powered trucks keeping a safe distance behind the Mercedes.

At regular intervals, his bodyguard would speak into the old, Korean War vintage U.S. made PRC-6 handheld radio to communicate with the truck drivers. According to their plan, the trucks were maintaining one hundred meter intervals so that they could allow faster vehicles to dart in and out as the heavily loaded vehicles were passed.

"Ahmed," the man in the suit finished his review of papers, "the next shipment will have two hundred rocketpropelled grenade launchers, each with a crate of six missiles, as well as two dozen 12.7mm DShK heavy machine guns with ten thousand rounds of ammunition, of which two thousand are armor piercing. In addition, it will also have a thousand mortar shells, one hundred kilos of Semtex, and ninety thousand of rounds of rifle and ten thousand of pistol ammunition."

"Excellent. You have already made the arrangements?"

"Yes. As soon as I get to Gaza, I will authorize the transfer of the final payment."

"Very good." Ahmed leaned forward. "Where are we?"

"About sixty kilometers from Bir Abid. At this pace, it will take us forty minutes to get there." The driver spoke without taking his eyes off the road. "We can stop at a restaurant to take a break if you'd like."

"That is a possibility. Let me know when we are about ten minutes from the town and I will decide."

When he bought the car, Khaldun was told that the ballistic glass and steel plates in the car's body would stop a rifle round unless it was fired at point blank range, and would allow them to fight from the car as they escaped. Behind a sliding panel, each door had a small firing port.

Under the back seat, two AK-47s and a dozen thirty round magazines were stored, and between the front seats was another Kalishnikov with six clips, in addition to the American .45 caliber Colt his bodyguard favored. Ahmed preferred to carry a Makarov semi-automatic pistol with three spare magazines because it was much easier to conceal, although it didn't have the stopping power of the big American made pistol.

After his battered Opel Commodore passed the four trucks, a dark-skinned man with a thick beard looked at the Mercedes as it accelerated past. The bodyguard watched the dust-covered car go by and then disregarded the man; he didn't appear to be a threat.

As soon as the Opel passed the next car, the man in the passenger seat picked up a small hand radio. "Target will be in your area in less than five minutes." Two clicks acknowledged the message.

On a sand dune about eight hundred meters south of the road, two men of Sayeret Maktal leaned on their elbows as they studied the coast road with their binoculars while one scanned the desert on both sides and behind.

"I see the convoy. Standby."

With that, the senior man flipped the switch on a small sand-colored box, and was satisfied to see a green light above each of the four buttons.

"Counting. Five, four, three, two, one."

At the word *one*, the team leader pushed each button as fast as he could. The first explosion detonated before he released his finger from the fourth button.

Under the Mercedes, a kilogram of C4 backed by a steel plate that had been installed a week before when the car was in a Cairo repair shop, sent a pressure wave of more than six thousand pounds per square inch into the passenger compartment, crushing the internal organs of the occupants before the four thousand degree Fahrenheit fireball incinerated all four men. AK-47 and .45 ammunition in the car lanced out in every direction as the fireball, fed by the car's gas tank, sent a black plume skyward.

Behind the ball of fire that once was the Mercedes, four kilogram bombs impregnated with flakes of magnesium, set in place when the trucks were waiting on the pier by Israeli agents disguised as Egyptian Customs inspectors, detonated under the four trucks. The explosions ignited the Semtex packed into each of the first three trucks. Hidden between the fuel tank and the truck's frame, the burning magnesium ignited the diesel fuel, creating three large pillars of dirty black smoke from the fires that cooked off thousands of rounds of 7.62 millimeter ammunition like lethal firecrackers.

Instead of ammunition, the bed in the last truck had a security squad of twenty Fatah soldiers. Those that survived the initial blast found their flesh burning from the incendiary mixture kneaded into the C4, and the burning diesel fuel sucked the air out of their lungs as they were incinerated.

Satisfied by the five fire balls, the four Sayeret MAKTAL commandos dismantled their hide and drove off in their special desert vehicles at a slow speed that didn't kick up a dust plume. Long before the fires subsided and the ammunition stopped exploding, the four men passed back into Israel near the border town of Ezuz in the Negev.

2032 local time, the Same Day, Moscow

Colonel Khozurov, the KGB's Higher School's head of security, nodded to Brigadier Vuong, the senior military attaché from the Vietnamese embassy in Moscow, and used his arm and extended palm to point to the door of room 312. The front desk had confirmed that Lieutenant Colonel Loi had returned to his room after dinner. Before knocking on the door, Vuong waited for the two members of the KGB's school security detail to take up positions out of sight on each side of the door. Each cradled a loaded AK-47.

"Who is it?"

"Brigadier Vuong."

"Yes, sir, please come in." Loi opened the door as he was buttoning his uniform blouse. As the general entered, he came to attention even though he was not finished dressing.

The general did not close the door. "Please finish."

Loi nodded, and within seconds he was dressed and standing at attention in the dark brown uniform of a lieutenant colonel in the Vietnamese People's Army, complete with the ribbons that showed his courage and competence under fire. Since Vuong hadn't said anything, Loi waited for the general to speak.

Although Vuong was about the same height as Loi, he was much heavier. He faced the junior man and spoke in their native tongue, also from a position of attention. "Lieutenant Colonel Chinh Loi, I have the sad duty to place you under arrest for embezzlement of state funds and conducting an unauthorized assassination operation in a foreign country."

With those words, Colonel Khozurov stepped into the room and handcuffed the surprised Vietnamese officer while the two armed soldiers watched. "Loi, we will speak later after you arrive at the embassy." The brigadier refused to use the man's rank now that he was under arrest.

Vuong rode in a staff car that followed the KGB van carrying Loi, whose handcuffs were chained to a bar that ran along the ceiling of the van. When he arrived at their embassy, Loi was led to a cold, damp empty cement room with a small hole in the floor for a drain which, just minutes before he arrived, had been hosed out and still reeked of disinfectant. Vuong let him sit there for three hours without food or water before a guard opened the door and put a chair up against one wall.

"Stand at attention."

Loi's wrinkled uniform was stained by the dampness of the cell. . Still the proud officer, Loi tugged at the bottom of his tunic in an unsuccessful attempt to make it more presentable.

Vuong didn't look at the dossier he was holding, containing the formal arrest documents when he spoke. "Citizen Loi, you authorized a transfer of funds to our Bulgarian embassy in the Vietnamese Dong equivalent of ten thousand U.S. dollars. While you were in Sofia, you collected the money, of which we have recovered half. That is the first charge."

The general didn't wait for Loi to speak. "The second charge is that you hired three Bulgarians to kill two American Naval Officers named Haman and Cabot. This was an unauthorized mission. The decision to assassinate citizens of another country is made by the Politburo, not by lieutenant colonels." Vuong eyed the man before him coldly.

"Citizen Loi, you have broken the trust that your superiors had in you based on your excellent combat record. Your actions have caused them to lose much face. I am embarrassed that I had to arrest you." For the first time Vuong moved his hands, more in disappointment than anger. "If you are convicted, you can be sentenced to death. Do you understand the charges?"

"Yes, sir, I do."

"Loi, what do you have to say for yourself?" As far as Vuong was concerned, Loi was a criminal and no longer qualified to be an officer in the People's Army.

"Are the two Americans dead?"

"No, they are not. The Bulgarians are now in a West German jail awaiting trial."

"Then, sir, I have failed."

"What?"

"I have failed twice." Loi's disappointment hung in the pungent, chemical air of the cell.

"How so?"

"I have failed to avenge the death of Colonel Nguyen Thai. He was the finest combat leader I have ever had the privilege to serve with, and I served under many. These two Americans killed him and I failed to protect him."

"That war is over. I too lost many friends and comrades, but we are focused on unifying and rebuilding our country, not on killing former enemies."

"For you that may be the case, for me, sir the war is not over." Loi took a deep breath. "Sir, may I have your pistol?"

The general unbuckled the flap and waived off the guard as he handed his Makarov pistol, butt first, to Loi, who chambered a round before saluting Vuong. "Long live Vietnam." With that, he put the gun to his temple and pulled the trigger.

Friday, February 11th, 1330 local time, RNAS Yeovilton

Sandwiches had been delivered by the officer's mess but had sat uneaten for almost an hour while the admiral conducted the debrief.

"So, let me make sure I understand," Admiral Hastings summed up what he had heard. "Sergeant Goodson was hit by a ricochet in the shoulder and another round in the thigh. He is in the hospital and will make a full recovery. Four members of Red Hand were turned over to the German authorities, including the guy you think is the leader. At the moment, we don't know how many people were arrested in Berger's apartment, but we think four, maybe six. Four Palestinians were killed in Zehlendorf. And last, Lev, you're pretty sure that Grenfel doesn't know who you are, and that none of the rest of you were identified by the West Germans."

The nine men around the table nodded in affirmative.

"And we have the four rolls of regular and two of infrared film on what you saw in Zehlendorf, of which I will make sure the Israeli and German government gets copies. The rented yacht was returned undamaged." The admiral paused. "So what's the bad news?"

"Sir, none per se, but two things remain to be done," Marty replied. "Our president has to tell the German government what happened, and do it soon. If not, we think there will be a shit storm of the first magnitude. Better they find out from our president, who can say mea culpa, than from the Red Hand defense attorneys, who will try to claim their capture and arrest was an illegal kidnapping."

Hastings nodded, and Marty continued. "Next, we owe John's dad's company our gratitude and thanks, as well as a lot of money. We haven't totaled it up yet, but it is close to four hundred thousand dollars, for use of the Navajo, office space, and cars."

Hastings nodded again. "The president already knows what happened. The chairman briefed him as soon as I talked to you. He will, if he hasn't already, talk to the West German president. I'll take care of making sure that Mr. Osborne is paid in full. Just make sure my assistant gets the receipts and bills, along with a description of the expense if it is not obvious. I will make sure that both governments send him a note of thanks. Her Majesty's Special Forces and in particular the SAS already know about his contribution, and I am sure they will convey their appreciation of his support."

"My father will love that. It'll be better received than money!" John spoke up.

"Great, gents, then let's eat." Admiral Hastings started toward the food laid out on one of the desks. "After you finish your formal report and pack up this stuff, both governments have authorized everyone in this unit sixty days of gratuitous leave. Lieutenant Cabot, make sure that I give you the signed paperwork before I leave. All you have to do is fill in the start dates and send it back via mail to me. Lev, John, and the gentlemen from the SAS, you send yours to the appropriate people."

Monday, February 14th, 2133 local time, Damascus

Bruno Glockner leaned back in his sofa, enjoying the music of Mozart, while he waved his hands conducting an imaginary orchestra. By his side, in his 10th floor, three bedroom, six hundred square meter apartment in the wealthy Damascus suburb of Mezze, was a glass of his favorite apple flavored schnapps. On the coffee table was a red, three inch thick loose leaf notebook with the words *Plans to Create the Fourth Reich* in Gothic Fraktur German type under the black swastika.

"Obersturmbahnführer Glockner."

It wasn't the use of his title, but the authority of the unfamiliar tone that made Glockner's head swivel toward the voice.

"How did you get in here?" he demanded.

The man wearing black pants, a black wool sweater kept his suppressed Browning Hi-Power in front of him as he pulled off his baklava. "Easy. We arrived as plumbers earlier in the day and then stayed in the elevator equipment room."

"What do you want?"

"Everything. We want all your plans about the Fourth Reich, along with your address book and bank accounts. If you don't give them to us, we'll get them on our own."

"Impossible." Glockner began to slide his hands along the edge of the sofa.

"Are you looking for this?" The stocky man, who was about five foot ten, held out a Walther PPK. It had a Nazi eagle on one side and the SS logo on the other side of the slide.

Deflated, Glockner sat back. "I don't have what you want."

"That's a lie. We already found the safe and know what is in it. My partner is opening it." The man with the Browning pointed at the coffee table. "And, we'll take this notebook."

"Who are you?"

"Your worst nightmare." Behind Glockner, the man's partner held up a briefcase and a backpack and used a thumbs-up to signal that he had what was wanted.

"Are you a goddamned, worthless Jew?"

"Worse. I am an Israeli and the son of German Jew who died at Dachau. I am going to save the German government the cost of a trial because I am going to kill you." The impact of the one hundred and fifteen grain hollow point slug snapped Glockner's head back as the bullet came apart in his skull, and the shock wave blew the back of head off and his brains all over the white leather couch.

Chapter 27
Conversion

Tuesday, February 15th, 0730 local time, Wiesbaden

Grenfel was late arriving at his office because he had been on the phone most of the night awaiting the results from a tip about two car bombs. The bomb squad had followed the precise directions given by the caller and defused the bombs. He was just hoping that, by the time he reached his office, fingerprints, if any, would have been found, when he saw Friedrich Starkeholz waiting outside his office door. "Herr Hauptpolizeidirektor, to what do I owe this honor?"

"I'd like a private word with you."

Grenfel nodded and put his leather briefcase down as he unlocked the door to his office. "Do you want to get some coffee before we talk?" Grenfel wanted some social time to gauge his superior's mood.

"No. This will take just a few minutes."

Grenfel went behind his desk and motioned the Hauptpolizeidirektor to sit in the chair. When the older man sat, Grenfel did the same.

"I want to share something with you that is known to just a few people within the Ministry of Justice. Since your very, very successful investigation touched on the subject, the minister wanted me to tell you, so you don't keep pushing on something that has already been resolved."

Alarm bells went off in Grenfel's mind. His orders, often restated, were not to ignore any avenue in his investigation and pursuit of Red Hand. The prosecutors were convinced they had enough evidence to put every member of Red Hand in jail for the rest of their lives. *Was Starkeholz about the cross the line?*

"Another investigation into the activities of many former members of the SS and the Nazi regime was reporting to me. I was, to some extent, using my relationship with my former comrades as a cover. What we found was that the New German Party is a modern version of Hitler's National Socialist Party. Different name, but they have similar goals. There were a group of ex-SS officers and former party officials who wanted to create the Fourth Reich, and this new political party was their vehicle. They helped their candidates with the same tactics they used in the twenties—assassinations and intimidation. We found out they were planning a *putsch* after they had won more seats. This turned my stomach and focused the attention of the ministry on their activities."

Starkeholz held up his hand as if to say, *Wait, there is a lot more.* "Over the past few weeks, prosecutors from the Ministry of Justice have had private meetings with the senior leadership of the New German Party who were affiliated with Hitler's regime. They are being told in very blunt terms to resign and cease participation in the New German Party at once, or they will face prosecution. One, a former obersturmbahnführer, left Germany, and we tracked him to Syria and let Mossad know."

Grenfel observed that the Hauptpolizeidirektor was more relaxed than he had been in months. "With each citizen, we outlined the evidence we would present at their trials. Before they were allowed to call a lawyer, each was given three choices. One: agree to a sentence without a trial that would put them in jail for the rest their life without parole and a healthy fine. Two, if they wanted a trial, the government would oblige, and, if they were convicted, seize all their assets as a fine and they would be sentenced to life in jail, again without any chance of parole. The third choice was a pistol and a single bullet, burial with military honors appropriate to their government or military rank, no publicity, and a modest fine. If you want, I can give you more details on who these people are."

"Sir, that would be most helpful." Grenfel relaxed in his chair. "I would like to see the list because we may have evidence that can help."

"I think that is a very good idea. Tomorrow morning, I will set up a meeting with the lead investigator from this team."

"I will make sure we have our information ready." Grenfel thought for a second. "Were you involved in any of those meetings with the New German Party leaders?"

"Just one. The minister thought it best if my name was kept out of the limelight. These bastards already consider me a traitor and may try to do something stupid like try to kill me."

"Thank you for telling me."

"I owe it to you; furthermore, I knew that when you started seeing links between the New German Party and Red Hand, you would have started asking questions about my objectivity, or worse, my involvement."

"To be honest, Herr Hauptolizeidirektor, the thought crossed my mind, but there was no evidence linking you to the New German Party. All we found was that you made a trip to Argentina, and every month or so, you went out to dinner with several members of your unit who survived the war."

"Just so you know, we are friends and meet to honor those who did not come home." Starkeholz stopped to let the pang pass. "The men I meet with, while former members of an SS division, are honest, hardworking Germans who did their duty with, under the circumstances, honor. They would oppose any government that was related to Hitler or his way of thinking."

"I did not know that the two teams crossed paths." Grenfel was very surprised by the revelation.

"I know." Starkeholz paused. "I needed to tell you. The minister wanted to keep the two investigations separate until we had evidence that Red Hand and the supporters of the New German Party were working together. That was looking more and more like a real possibility when Red Hand was shut down."

"Thank you for telling me that. I am most grateful."

"You are welcome." Starkeholz got up to leave. "Oh, one more thing."

Grenfel kept his mouth shut.

"We will be, in the very near future, peers. I may be a bit more senior because I have had my rank longer, but we will be peers nonetheless. Herr Jurgend signed the papers yesterday." The older man didn't wait for an answer and strode out the door leaving Grenfel in a stunned, smiling silence.

Friday, February 18th, 1977, 1145 local time, East Berlin

Krasnovsky had a beer waiting when Grünewald sat down. On the table, there was a half consumed bowl of small pretzels, which suggested that the Russian had been there for awhile. "I wanted to have lunch with you to offer my hearty congratulations." The KGB officer was smiling as he spoke. "I hear you have been promoted and have a new job. Well done."

"I have not assumed my new duties yet. I still have to finish my investigation, and the director has to approve my promotion, but yes, I have been told that I am going to be the head of Main Administration for Struggle Against Suspicious Persons. This is the group that monitors the movement of any foreigners in the DDR. It was something my predecessor didn't do well." Grünewald popped a small pretzel into his mouth and smiled. "My guess is that the person holding the position at the present time was encouraged to retire, which meant there was a vacancy."

"As you are fond of saying, he failed to connect the dots." Both men enjoyed a chuckle and held up their beers and tipped them to each other as a salute.

"I understand you will become a major general as well."

"That is also true, assuming the minister gets approval to promote me."

"So," Krasnovsky continued, "What have you learned?"

"Are you asking about Haman and Cabot?"

"Yes, and anything else that would be of interest."

"You can ask for my report through official channels, you know," Grünewald said, smiling.

Krasnovsky laughed. "I was hoping to not have to wait for the officially censored version."

"I found photos from the ship's surveillance cameras that were taken in Sweden, before the ferry left for Sassnitz. The heavy snow and poor light made for a very bad picture, but I would wager a lot of money that Haman and Cabot were aboard. What is clear is they knew where the cameras were located and did their best to avoid them. My report, however, says it there is a sixty per cent chance that it was them."

"So you could be wrong or you could be right."

"Oh, I think I am right, because it gets better." Grünewald sipped his beer. "They did not use their own names and had valid Australian and South African passports, visas and travel permits approved by the DDR. No surprise. But when you compare the photographs on the ferry with the photos of the four men in the two Volvos that exited in Berlin, Haman was not one of them. We are pretty sure Cabot was there in another Volvo with another man, but the man with the South African passport that had

Haman's picture on entering the DDR was not the same man who left."

"So how many men entered the DDR?"

"We are ninety percent sure there were eight. Four, two in each car, drove to Berlin." Grünewald took a bite of his roasted potatoes that surrounded his bratwurst. "When we looked at the snow around Stiglitz's compound, our investigators believe that eight men conducted the kidnapping. Four left in the helicopter, probably flown by Haman with the hostages. So, I ask you, how did the other four get into the DDR? Both cars were searched while on the ferry."

Krasnovsky picked away at some stuffed cabbage. "Do you have any ideas?"

"No. The best way to come in is by boat or by parachute, but that snowstorm would have made either method unlikely. Swimming in from a submarine in water that is one degree Celsius is very difficult, even for your Spetznaz. They would have been well over three miles out and that is a very long swim in very cold water. There two other options. One is that they entered the DDR earlier and were waiting to participate in the raid, or if it was called off, go home. The other is that DDR citizens were involved. We think that this is unlikely because it would have made maintaining operational security very, very difficult. Neither option explains the fact that the raiding party used Czech made Skorpion machine pistols and ammunition. How did they get the guns into the country? Smuggling them in via car is very, very risky. They are not available in this country."

"So you don't know how the others got in?"

"No, not yet. It will take awhile, but one day, we will find the answer."

Krasnovsky raised his beer in salute, then changed the subject. "You know I am being posted back to Moscow."

"You told me earlier that you were expecting this."

"Yes, my three year tour of duty is up this spring."

"Do you know what you will be doing?"

"Not yet. I have been told there will be several choices, but it could be anything from, 'Thank you, colonel, you have had a good career and good bye,' to something either dull or dangerous. If I am lucky, it might be interesting."

"Well, whatever they ask you to do," Grünewald poked his finger in the direction of his Russian friend, "Don't forget to connect the dots."

Thursday, February 24th, 1100 local time, Frankfurt

Grenfel stopped to look at the scarred concrete surrounding the frame of the new oak door, stained a dark brick red. He had been told that the bloodstains on the concrete hadn't and wouldn't be cleaned. The brass plaque next to the door had two large dents caused by ball bearings hammering into it at a very high speed. It too was not going to be replaced.

He swallowed hard as his eyes watered and looked back at the person sitting in his Volkswagen. After a few seconds, he opened the unlocked door, noticing that his palms were sweaty. The interior exuded a quiet peace that contrasted the carnage that been inflicted four decades before, and again less than year ago. Again Grenfel paused, adjusting to the stillness, then headed in the direction of voices muted by walls and distance.

Inside a large book-lined office, he saw a man in his forties, sitting in his shirt sleeves behind a large desk covered by stacks of paper. The messiness offended his policeman's need for order and organization. Sensing someone in his doorway, the man looked up. Seeing Grenfel, he rose. "Can I help you?" He tried to pull up his tie, then gave up when it wouldn't get into the proper position.

"My name is Heinrich Grenfel. If you are the rabbi, I would like to talk to you. Do you have a few minutes?"

"I do. Please sit down." The man gestured to a couch, which had papers and books piled on one end. "Why do you look so familiar?"

"Oh, I am sorry. I am Polizeioberrat Grenfel from the Bundeskriminalamt. You may have seen me on TV a couple of times in the past few months."

"Yes, yes.... You are the man who led the investigation into Red Hand." The man paused for a second, enjoying the fact that he had put together a name with a face. "Well done. It was an excellent piece of police work, and we all should be proud of you." The comment was a statement made without rancor. "I am Rabbi David Eisenmann. What I can tell you that I have not already told your investigators?"

"Thank you for your kind words, Herr Rabbi Eisnemann." Grenfel swallowed hard. "The investigation is not why I came here."

"Please, please sit down." The rabbi cleared some of the books off the couch so the two men could face each other. Fifteen years as a rabbi meant he wasn't surprised by what came out of the mouths of people sitting on his couch. Counseling was included in his job description. "May I get you something to drink?"

"No, no thank you." Grenfel sat on the front edge of the black leather cushion.

"Well, Herr Grenfel, what brings you here?"

Grenfel cleared his throat. He had been rehearsing, or at least trying to rehearse, the speech in his mind all the way from Vienna. Yet he didn't know where to begin. "Two days ago, I was at the Simon Wiesenthal Documentation Center, because I wanted to know where my mother's parents died. The center's records show they were gassed at Dachau."

"I am sorry to hear that."

"Until a few months ago, my mother never told me about her parents. When it became clear that Red Hand was targeting Jews and Jewish owned businesses, my mother asked me to lunch. After we ate, she told me how her parents forced her to marry my father, who was also a policeman. He was paid a lot of money, which would have been seized if the Nazis ever found out, and he would probably have been either killed or sent to the camps. In the thirties, as part of the agreement, he made sure that any records about her birth parents and religion were, shall we say, changed. It cost large amount of money, which my mother's parents provided. This is why she was never taken to the camps. I was born two years later, and was ten when the war ended."

The man on the couch said nothing, but there was sympathy in his eyes. Without Grenfel noticing it, which was unusual because his training conditioned him to observe everything and ask questions, not to answer them, someone had closed the door to the office.

"During the lunch, she gave me these." Grenfel undid the brass buckles on his battered, dark brown leather briefcase r and pulled out a book and a small box. "My mother said her real maiden name was Rosenberg, and her family tree is documented in the book. The family's geneology ends in 1936."

The rabbi took the worn book and opened it, taking care not to tear or damage any one of its pages. "This is a prayer book from a small synagogue that used to be in Cologne. I see it was printed in 1868. It was a common practice for families to record the marriages, births and deaths of each generation in a prayer book. From it, you could create a family tree."

"That's what she said. My mother now lives in Frankfurt. She said that before 1933, Cologne had a sizeable Jewish population." Again, emotion took charge of his voice.

The rabbi sat in silence, respecting Grenfel's pain.

"Then she handed me these." Grenfel opened the box and pulled out two gold chains with Stars of David hanging from their ends. "She said this one was hers and given to her by her mother when she was sixteen." He held out a twenty-two carat gold star, about three centimeters in diameter, that had silver inlays and diamonds set into the tips of the star. "This one," he held up a plain, but very elegant, smaller star, designed for a man to wear, "was my grandfather's. He was an artillery officer and wore it during the Great War. She told me that he often pressed it to his chest and prayed when they were bombarded by British artillery. He thought his prayers saved his life."

Tears flowed down Grenfel's cheeks as he struggled to talk. His voice was choked with emotion. "She kept these hidden from the Nazis, and from her husband, all these years. When she gave them to me, she said she had just showed them to him. My father wanted me to have the one my grandfather wore. All these years, my mother was afraid to talk to anyone, including her husband, about her heritage and her family."

Rabbi Eisenmann took both Stars of David in his hands and let them dangle while he admired the craftsmanship and their simple elegance. "They are beautiful, and thank God she hid them from the Nazis." He laid them gently on Grenfel's thigh. "Tell me more about your mother."

"My mother was in tears as she told me about her childhood and her arrangement with my father about religion. Other than my father, no one knows the truth about her early life." Grenfel sniffled and the rabbi handed him a kleenex. "Now I know why my mother never participated in any church services. She would go just for ceremonial events and always stayed at home while my father went to church. For Christmas, we had a tree with a star and some decorations, but nothing about Jesus. Now my mother is relieved and happy that it is out in the open."

"Good. It is very difficult to keep those kinds of secrets locked up inside for an entire life. It must have been terrible for her. The emotional struggle and pain your mother endured is difficult to imagine. Now that it is out, it will be a relief, and maybe even give her a sense of freedom. It won't, however, make it easier for her to deal with the sorrow, or the guilt of being her family's sole survivor of the Holocaust."

"I wish she would have told me sooner."

"You are not alone. It is a story I have heard before, and sometimes talking helps. Herr Grenfel, I am honored that you came here. What can I do for you besides listening?"

"Two things." Grenfel's knees were shaking so bad he was afraid that his nerves were showing. "First, my mother is outside sitting in my car. She has not been in a synagogue since the Nuremberg Laws were passed in 1933 and is still afraid to come in one." Grenfel took a deep breath. "Second, she wants to begin practicing Judaism again, and I want to become a Jew. We want to do it together, if we can."

"Well, then, let's go bring her inside. You never told me, but what is her name?"

"Karen."

"That is a traditional Hebrew name, which translates to ray of sunlight. Appropriate, no?" Rabbi Eisenmann smiled. "My suggestion is that we let her sit in the sanctuary for awhile, with the two of us for support because it will be a very emotional experience for her. Most—men and women—start to cry, and that is often a good thing. They are often grieving for a life and a religion they have lost. Then, we can talk there or in my office. The synagogue has a program for those who were traumatized by the Nazi regime and want to come back to Judiasm. And, we have a program for people who want to become Jews."

The rabbi got up and pointed to the door. "Our program is run by a gentleman by the name of Louis Ferman. He was in his mid-teens when he was sent to Buchenwald with his family. After the war, he went to university and became a psychiatrist, and he is with a group of doctors that specialize in helping camp survivors. He is also our cantor."

"What is a cantor?"

"He helps with leading prayers. As you will find out, music is a big part of our services, and the cantor is responsible for selecting the music as well as leading us in song. Louis has a wonderful, haunting voice and could have been a professional singer, but what the Nazis did to him changed that. We are very, very lucky to have him."

Render Harmless

Sunday, February 27th, 1977, 1043 local time,
Eastern Mediterranean

M.V. Beaufighter II rolled gently in the quartering Mediterranean swells northeast of Valencia, Spain, its twin three thousand horsepower turbocharged diesel engines moving the two hundred fifty foot custom built luxury yacht along at twelve knots. It was a pleasant seventy-five degrees Fahrenheit, and the passengers were sitting in the salon after spending a couple of hours by the pool located on the main deck. All eight of them—the two couples, three children and a nanny—had arrived in Valencia, Spain the evening before in the Osborne Shipping Limited's Hawker business jet. *Beaufighter II* had put to sea as soon as they passengers were on board.

A steward, dressed in white pants with a white and dark blue striped shirt, placed a plate of cheese, crackers and fruit, along with pitchers of fruit juices, on the coffee table.

"This is way beyond nice, it is spectacular." Rebekah waved her hand, trying not to gush after finishing a tour of the boat, which included a dining/conference room that could accommodate 30 people, a wet bar, and a helicopter deck.

"It is." John agreed. "My dad uses this boat for corporate meetings, lends it to customers and also charters it to wealthy individuals. There's one owner's suite and ten guest staterooms. He says the charters pay for its upkeep, and for him, *Beaufighter II* is a great getaway. This is the first time Gwen and I have been on it since our honeymoon, four years ago."

"Wow, the ultimate command at sea!" Josh poured from the pitcher of fresh squeezed, pulp-filled orange juice he'd taken from the tray. "O.K., what kind of helo can you land over there?"

"I knew you'd ask, because that was my first question when Dad told me he was adding the deck. It is big enough for a Jet Ranger, or an Aerospatiale Gazelle, or the new Augusta 109. This way, people who want to charter the boat can use their own jet."

"Mr. Osborne, the captain just gave me this to pass on to you." The senior steward handed John a small sheet of paper.

"Thank you, Randolph." John looked at it for a few moments,.

"And this is?" Josh was holding Sasha, but passed him to Rebekah to take the paper John held out. Suddenly he surged forward with a look of alarm on his face. "Holy shit, this stuff is supposed to be classified!"

"What is supposed to be classified?" Rebekah and Gwen asked the same question almost at the same time.

"Ship schedules!" Josh waved sheet of yellow teletype paper. "This has the dates of all the planned port calls for the next three months for all the U.S. and Royal Navy ships in the Mediterranean!"

"Classified? That's ridiculous," Rebekah laughed. "Just ask the wives. They are told when the ships are going to pull into port so they can meet their husbands, and if they don't know, the hookers do!!! Gwen and I had the Mediterranean cruise schedule for the *Fearless* back in August!"

"The truth is, the information comes from the husbanding agents," John pointed out. "The ships need fresh food, and the agents buy it for them and have it on the pier waiting. So they have to know the dates."

"Oh. I never thought about it that way." Josh sat back, deflated.

"The reason that I asked for it was to discuss where we are going." John poured some coffee from an insulated pitcher on the table. "It is late February, so if we want to do a bit of skiing, I suggest we head up to either the French Rivera or Genoa. Or, if you want to go where it is warm, we can head to Majorca and then the Greek Islands. Or, we can do all of the above. We have almost two months to enjoy!"

"Ladies?" Josh turned to the two women.

"Skiing." Gwen knew Rebekah loved to ski. And she wanted to go as well.

"Skiing, for a week or two, then on to a beach," Rebekah said as she nodded in agreement.

"Excellent." John took a sip of the coffee. "I will tell the captain, and he will make the arrangements in Sestriere in Italy for the first week. The skiing is wonderful, and the food will be spectacular. Then we can go someplace like Verbier or Val d'Isere."

"We have Grace to watch over the kids while we ski." Gwen looked over towards their nanny, who was sitting by the hot tub, smiling as she kept an eye on both babies in the double perambulator.

Sasha completed his umpteenth trip to the railing, came over and snuggled into his mother's lap. He leaned back to feel the warmth of his mother's body and Rebekah wrapped her legs over his shorter ones and pulled him close.

"Gwen, John, we can't thank you enough for all this." Rebekah couldn't believe their good fortune. "There is no way we can ever repay you."

"Rebekah, don't worry about it. It is my father's, my family's, and most importantly, Gwen's and my pleasure. Believe me, if he didn't want us to spend a couple of months on this tub, he wouldn't have offered. This is my father's way of saying, thank-you for fighting the good fight, because each generation has to answer the call. And yes, you can pay us back." John held up his glass, which was touched by three others. "It is called friendship for life."

THE END

Postscript

I didn't start out to write RENDER HARMLESS as a story with major characters who were members of the SS and Nazi party members. The original plot was supposed to be about a Naval Aviator and a SEAL hunting terrorists supported by the Stasi and the KGB But, as I wrote the story, my mind kept going back to living in Wiesbaden, West Germany as a teenager in the 1960s.

Back then, everywhere I went there were subtle and not-so-subtle reminders of the war. Most visible were unrepaired bullet and shrapnel holes in brick and concrete walls. By the sixties, the rusted tanks in the fields were all gone, but every month, I'd read a news story about a wrecked airplane found in a forest or unexploded artillery shells or bombs that were dug up in a farmer's field or in a foundations of a building being rebuilt.

Psychological memories were stirred by news stories about well-known members of the Nazi regime. Some were about Nazis being released from prison, i.e. Albert Speer and Karl Doenitz. Adolph Eichman's capture and execution in 1962 generated another round of articles detailing the continuing search for Klaus Barbie, Joseph Mengele, and others who were high on the Allies' war crimes list.

Survivors of the war were still grappling with the aftermath which cost Germany a generation and a half of its men, millions of women and children, along with much of its wealth and historic buildings. I remember grudgingly polite Dutch, Danish, and Norwegian businessmen taking the German tourists' money, while still considering them pariahs.

In those countries, if one couldn't communicate in English, before the conversation went any further, my family always showed our U.S. passports or said, *Ich bin eine Amerikaner* (I am an American) to make sure they knew we were not Germans.

The Germans I knew were trying to forget, but even as a teenager, I could sense a nagging ache plaguing the national psyche. It was more than guilt. There were times you could see it, often you could sense it, and some times, once you got to know someone who lived under Hitler, he or she would even talk about it.

One of our family jokes was that we never could find anyone who supported Hitler or who fought the Allies on the Western Front. Listening to our German friends, one would think that Germany battled just the Russians to keep the hated communists at bay east of the pre-war German border. But there were still many people who believed what Hitler had told them, and the formal act of surrender didn't change those beliefs. Looking back, it is clear that the passing of the generation that supported Hitler would not soothe the national guilt, nor would Germans totally de-Nazify their country.

No matter how some attempt to rewrite history, the travesty of what the Nazis forced on Europe sixty-nine years before this book is published must be remembered. Every day, the survivors of the camps and the war leave us. Soon all that will remain is what they have shared with us in books, movies, videos, and tape recordings.

In the everyday pace of life, it is easy to let the horrors of what Hitler and his Gestapo party and SS minions did fade from our collective memories. *We must not forget.*

Many, including me, grew up knowing concentration camp survivors. The numbered tattoos on their forearms was only a visable reminder of the horrors perpetrated on those sent to the concentration camps. Their experience in those places is difficult to imagine. No, they are beyond comprehension.

This novel is my one small contribution to reminding the world that the Nazis murdered more than six million Jews, and millions of gypsies and others they deemed unworthy. RENDER HARMLESS is about the ultimate nightmares for the post World War II Bundesrepublik, which is that Germans were once again killing Jews.

For those who never read it, the National Socialist Party Platform was first promulgated in 1920. Hitler later gave us his plan to transform Germany in his book *Mein Kampf,* which many translate as *My Struggle* or *My Story,* which is incorrect. Kampf is the German verb for "battle" or as a noun it translates to "military conflict." The book was written while Hitler was in jail for his role in a failed coup in 1923 known as the Beer Hall Putsche.

This early National Socialist Party platform is worth reading again and again until you understand the implication of every ugly sentence, because what came later should not have been a surprise to anyone. It is too bad that many leaders in Western Europe didn't take Hitler and his Nazi minions seriously and the rest, as they say, is history.

The Nazis taught the world a lesson that leaders in the west should remember today as they listen to members of radical Islam express their desire to create a new Caliphate (there were four of them that controlled the Mediterranean litoral and they preceded the Ottoman Empire) and implement Sharia law. It is very clear, if you are an infidel, what their intentions are. The parallels to Hitler and his followers are chilling.

We—the United Kingdom, France, and other European countries, and the United States—failed to understand who Hitler was and what he stood for despite the fact it was literally in black and white in the party platform and in *Mein Kampf.*

The lack of understanding and the naïve assumption that we could negotiate with Hitler and he would abide by his agreements, coupled with the unwillingness to stand up to a bully, led to a world war. Appeasement and negotiations cost the lives of more than twenty-three million soldiers and forty million civilians.

It will only take you a few minutes to read the entire Nazi manifesto as it was delivered to the German public ninety-two years ago on February 24th, 1920. The document follows this postscript in its entirety. It is much easier than wading through *Mein Kampf,* and its chilling concepts leap off the page as a reminder of what can happen again. We didn't take Hitler seriously in the 1930s. Eighty plus years later, have we learned our lesson?

Marc Liebman
March, 2014

The Nazi Party Platform , 1920
The Program of the National Socialist (Nazi) German Workers Party

The Program of the German Workers' Party is a program for our time. The leadership rejects the establishment of new aims after those set out in the Program have been achieved, for the sole purpose of making it possible for the Party to continue to exist as the result of the artificially stimulated dissatisfaction of the masses.

1. We demand the uniting of all Germans within one Greater Germany, on the basis of the right to self-determination of nations.

2. We demand equal rights for the German people (Volk) with respect to other nations, and the annulment of the Peace Treaty of Versailles and St. Germain.

3. We demand land and soil (Colonies) to feed our People and settle our excess population.

4. Only Nationals (Volksgenossen) can be Citizens of the State. Only persons of German blood can be Nationals, regardless of religious affiliation. No Jew can therefore be a German National.

5. Any person who is not a Citizen will be able to live in Germany only as a guest and must be subject to legislation for Aliens.

6. Only a Citizen is entitled to decide the leadership and laws of the State. We therefore demand that only Citizens may hold public office, regardless of whether it is a national, state, or local office.

7. We demand that the State make it its duty to provide opportunities of employment first of all for its own Citizens. If it is not possible to maintain the entire population of the State, then foreign nationals (non-Citizens) are to be expelled from the Reich.

8. Any further immigration of non-Germans is to be prevented. We demand that all non-Germans who entered Germany after August 2, 1914, be forced to leave the Reich without delay.

9. All German Citizens must have equal rights and duties.

10. It must be the first duty of every Citizen to carry out intellectual or physical work. Individual activity must not be harmful to the public interest and must be pursued within the framework of the community and for the general good.

We therefore demand:
11. The abolition of all income obtained without labor or effort.

Breaking the Servitude of Interest
12. In view of the tremendous sacrifices in property and blood demanded of the Nation by every war, personal gain from the war must be termed a crime against the Nation. We therefore demand the total confiscation of all war profits.

13. We demand the nationalization of all enterprises (already) converted into corporations (trusts).

14. We demand profit-sharing in large enterprises.

15. We demand the large-scale development of old-age pension schemes.

16. We demand the creation and maintenance of a sound middle class; the immediate communalization of the large department stores, which are to be leased at low rates to small tradesmen. We demand the most careful consideration for the owners of small businesses in orders placed by national, state, or community authorities.

17. We demand land reform in accordance with our national needs and a law for expropriation without compensation of land for public purposes. Abolition of ground rent and prevention of all speculation in land.

18. We demand ruthless battle against those who harm the common good by their activities. Persons committing base crimes against the People, usurers, profiteers, etc., are to be punished by death without regard of religion or race.

19. We demand the replacement of Roman Law, which serves a materialistic World Order, by German Law.

20. In order to make higher education—and thereby entry into leading positions—available to every able and industrious German, the State must provide a thorough restructuring of our entire public educational system. The courses of study at all educational institutions are to be adjusted to meet the requirements of practical life. Understanding of the concept of the State must be achieved through the schools (teaching of civics) at the earliest age

at which it can be grasped. We demand the education at the public expense of specially gifted children of poor parents, without regard to the latter's position or occupation.

21. The State must raise the level of national health by means of mother-and-child care, the banning of juvenile labor, achievement of physical fitness through legislation for compulsory gymnastics and sports, and maximum support for all organizations providing physical training for young people.

22. We demand the abolition of hireling troops and the creation of a national army.

23. We demand laws to fight against deliberate political lies and their dissemination by the press. In order to make it possible to create a German press, we demand:

a) all editors and editorial employees of newspapers appearing in the German language must be German by race;

b) non-German newspapers require express permission from the State for their publication. They may not be printed in the German language;

c) any financial participation in a German newspaper or influence on such a paper is to be forbidden by law to non-Germans and the penalty for any breech of this law will be the closing of the newspaper in question, as well as the immediate expulsion from the Reich of the non-Germans involved. Newspapers which violate the public interest are to be banned. We demand laws against trends in art and literature which have a destructive effect on our national life, and the suppression of performances that offend against the above requirements.

24. We demand freedom for all religious denominations, provided that they do not endanger the existence of the State or offend the concepts of decency and morality of the Germanic race. The Party as such stands for positive Christianity, without associating itself with any particular denomination. It fights against the Jewish-materialistic spirit within and around us, and is convinced that a permanent revival of our Nation can be achieved only from within, on the basis of:

Public Interest before Private Interest.

25. To carry out all the above we demand: the creation of a strong central authority in the Reich. Unquestioned authority by the political central Parliament over the entire Reich and over its

organizations in general. The establishment of trade and professional organizations to enforce the Reich basic laws in the individual states. The Party leadership promises to take an uncompromising stand, at the cost of their own lives if need be, on the enforcement of the above points.

Munich, February 24, 1920.

ABOUT THE AUTHOR

MARC LIEBMAN

Marc Liebman is an experienced writer as well as a Naval Aviator combat veteran of both Vietnam and Desert Shield/ Desert Storm. He retired as a Captain after twenty-four years in the Navy and a career that took him all over the world. He has just under 6,000 hours of pilot-in-command/co-pilot flight time in a variety of tactical military, civilian-fixed and rotary-wing aircraft. In the business world, he has been the CEO of an aerospace and defense manufacturing firm, an associate editor of a national magazine and a copywriter for an advertising agency. Marc lives in North Texas with his wife of 48+ years, Betty, and two dogs. He spends a lot of time visiting his four grandchildren.

Big Mother 40

By

Marc Liebman

Big Mother 40 is a story well told and one in which aviation and special warfare veterans of the Vietnam conflict will identify, and about which they will tell their friends. Younger readers will enjoy the book simply as a great adventure.
— Michael Field, Captain USN (retired) Wings of Gold, Winter 2012 issue

Liebman skips macho combat images to plunk us into the deeper connections of war, from fear and courage to the truer realms of human relationships. His detail is authentic, and he lends even greater validity to the operations he describes with valuable author notes at the back of the book including a historic analysis of the time, military glossary and roster of characters. Despite the book's intensity and detail, the story is fast-paced. For a book you won't forget, you have to read BIG MOTHER 40.

PENMORE PRESS
www.penmorepress.com

INNER LOOK

BY

MARC LIEBMAN

International Espionage, NKV Russian Intelligence , US Intelligence, CIA, Argentina spy story, Peril at Sea , Helicopter stories , Sea stories,

After John Walker and Jerry Whitworth are arrested for passing top-secret information to the Soviet Union, the project Inner Look is initiated to determine if there are any other spies operating within the government intelligence agencies. Navy SEAL Marty Cabot and naval aviator Josh Haman are assigned to the project in the hopes that their unconventional approach and out-of-the-box thinking will yield more answers.

Cabot and Haman discover that the security leaks go higher up than anyone imagined. Furthermore, the leaks have compromised many of their missions.   For Josh and Marty, it's not just about national security, it's personal.

Their pursuit turns international, taking them into dangerous waters. Nothing but their skills will keep them alive when the KBG sends assassins to silence the traitor and neutralize the threat they pose.

PENMORE PRESS
www.penmorepress.com

When the Jungle Is Silent

by

James Boschert

Set in Borneo during a little known war known as "the Confrontation," this story tells of the British soldiers who fought in one of the densest jungles in the world.

Jason, a young soldier of the Light Infantry who is good with guns, is stationed in Penang, an idyllic island off the coast of Malaysia. He is living aimlessly in paradise until he meets Megan, a bright and intelligent young American from the Peace Corps. Megan challenges his complacent existence and a romance develops, but then the regiment is sent off to Borneo.

After a dismal shipping upriver, the regiment arrives in Kuching, the capital of Sarawak. Jason is moved up to Padawan, close to local populations of Ibans and Dyak headhunters, and right in the path of the Indonesian offensive. Fighting erupts along the border of Sarawak and a small fort is turned into a muddy hell from which Jason is an unlikely survivor.

An SAS Sergeant and his trackers have been drawn to the vicinity by the battle, but who will find Jason first: rescuers or hostiles? Jason is forced to wake up to the cruel harshness of real soldiering while he endeavors stay one step ahead of the Indonesians who are combing the Jungle. And the jungle itself, although neutral, is deadly enough.

PENMORE PRESS
www.penmorepress.com

SHIPS AND SEALING WAX AND MANY THINGS

BY

ROGER PAINE

Roger Paine, retired Navy commander and former secretary to the trustees of the National Maritime Museum, Greenwich, has authored a collection of true stories about fascinating people and places. If you have an interest in the sea, you can learn about how the cells in one of Scotland's biggest prisons were emptied to provide crews for merchant ships in World War II, or how the father of a young musician playing in the palm court of the *Titanic* was sent a bill for 75p for new buttons on his uniform jacket two weeks after he drowned.

In his landlubberly tales, Paine gives a guided tour around more than twenty ancient village churches in southern England. Wonder at how a gruesome collection of human skulls provides an attraction to visitors in a parish church, and discover how a young girl waited in vain for her lover from the vicarage next door and eventually died of a broken heart. Spend springtime with Robert Browning, summer with William Morris, autumn with John Keats, and Christmas with Kenneth Grahame—and find out what inspired these poets to write as memorably as they did.

This delightful treasure trove of stories will keep you amused, astounded, and warmed in equal measure.

PENMORE PRESS
www.penmorepress.com

www.ingramcontent.com/pod-product-compliance
Lightning Source LLC
Chambersburg PA
CBHW050604170726
48283CB00001B/96